A former au pair, bo___ ___ seafront trader, **Jessica** ___ ___ vironmental charity in ___ ___ daughter, one fluffy do___ ___ spends her time avoidi__ ___ ___ found with her nose in a book. Jessica writes emotional romance with a hint of humour, a splash of sunshine and a great deal of delicious food—and equally delicious heroes!

Melissa Senate has written many novels for Mills & Boon and other publishers, including her debut, *See Jane Date*, which was made into a TV movie. She also wrote seven books for Mills & Boon under the pen name Meg Maxwell. Her novels have been published in over twenty-five countries. Melissa lives on the coast of Maine with her teenage son; their rescue shepherd mix, Flash; and a lap cat named Cleo. For more information, please visit her website, melissasenate.com

BOUND BY THE PRINCE'S BABY

JESSICA GILMORE

A FAMILY FOR A WEEK

MELISSA SENATE

MILLS & BOON

First Published in Great Britain 2020
by Mills & Boon, an imprint of HarperCollinsPublishers,
1 London Bridge Street, London, SE1 9GF

Bound by the Prince's Baby © 2020 Jessica Gilmore
A Family for a Week © 2020 Melissa Senate

ISBN: 978-0-263-27887-3

0720

MIX
Paper from
responsible sources
FSC® C007454

This book is produced from independently certified FSC™
paper to ensure responsible forest management.

For more information visit: www.harpercollins.co.uk/green

Printed and bound in Spain
by CPI, Barcelona

BOUND BY THE PRINCE'S BABY

JESSICA GILMORE

For Dan and Abby, always.

PROLOGUE

Eight years ago

THE CAR PURRED to a stop and the driver got out, walking as stiffly as if he were on parade to the rear passenger side and opening the door. Amber Kireyev pulled her hated kilt down to her knees before she grabbed her rucksack and shimmied out of the car under his always watchful gaze.

'Thank you, Boris,' she said with a smile, but as usual there was no glimmer of a return smile, just a curt nod.

'Princess Vasilisa.'

'Amber,' she said, as she always did. 'Call me Amber.'

But Boris didn't acknowledge her words as he stood tall and imposing, waiting for her to walk through the entranceway; he wouldn't move until he had seen her go into the building and the doors close behind her.

Amber suppressed a sigh. She knew that most people would consider selling their soul to occupy an apartment in this grand Art Deco building overlooking Central Park, especially a penthouse in one of the two iconic towers, but to her the apartment was more prison than home. Hefting her backpack onto her shoulder, she walked, chin held high, up to the doors and pressed the button for admittance. The doors swung silently and ominously open and, without a backward glance at the sun-filled afternoon, she walked inside.

The opulent high-ceilinged marble and tile foyer was so familiar to her she barely noticed its glossy splendour, but she did notice the smiling man behind the concierge desk, dapper in his gilt and navy uniform.

'Miss Amber, Happy Birthday to you.'

'Thank you, Hector.'

'Do you have something nice planned to celebrate?'

Amber tried not to pull a frustrated face. Her fellow pupils at the exclusive girls' school she attended had all thrown extravagant parties for their eighteenth birthdays, renting out hotel ballrooms or heading off to their Hampton Beach homes for the weekend. Even if they had invited her Amber wouldn't have been allowed to attend, but they'd stopped asking her years ago. 'Grandmama said that we might go out for dinner, after my lessons, of course.' Not even on her eighteenth birthday could Amber skip her dancing or deportment or etiquette lessons.

'I have something for you,' Hector whispered conspiratorially and, after looking around, he pulled out a large brown envelope from under his desk and held it out to her.

Amber's heart began to beat faster as she took in the familiar postmark. 'Thank you for letting me have it sent to your house.' Her future lay in that envelope. A future far away from here, far away from her grandmother.

'London?' Hector asked and she nodded.

'The university prospectus. London is where my parents met and worked, although we lived just outside, in a little village. I always promised myself I would go back as soon as I was old enough. Applying to university is just the first step.' She slipped the envelope into her backpack. 'Thank you again.'

'I also have this for you.' With a flourish he produced a large cupcake, extravagantly iced in silver and white. 'There's no candle. The fire alarms, you know. But Maya told me to tell you to make a wish anyway.'

'Oh, Hector.' Amber hated crying but she could feel hot, heavy tears gathering in her eyes. 'This is so kind of you and Maya. Give her my love.'

'Come see us again soon; she has a new recipe she wants to teach you.' Hector cast an anxious look up at the huge clock which dominated the vestibule. 'Your grandmother will be calling down soon; you'd better go. And Amber? Happy Birthday.'

The lift—Amber refused to say elevator, clinging onto her English accent and vocabulary as stubbornly as she could—was waiting and she tapped in the code which would take her up to the penthouse, nibbling her cake as the doors slid shut and the lift started its journey.

The doors opened straight into the penthouse hallway. Usually Amber could barely put a toe onto the parquet floor before her grandmother querulously summoned her to quiz her about her day and criticise her appearance, her posture, her attitude, her ingratitude. Amber steeled herself, ready for the interrogation, the brown envelope, safely stored in her bag, a shield against every poisonous word. But today there was no summons and Amber, half a cake still clutched in her hand, managed to make it to her bedroom undisturbed, slipping her backpack onto the floor, taking out the envelope and concealing it, still unopened, at the back of her wardrobe. She'd look at it later tonight, when her grandmother was asleep.

Sitting back on her heels, Amber checked to make sure there was no hint of the envelope visible through her clothes and then clambered up, her feet sinking into the deep pile pink carpet. Her whole room was sumptuously decorated in bright pinks and cream which clashed horribly with her auburn hair and made her pale skin look even paler. But she had as little choice in the decor as she did about her schooling, wardrobe and pastimes.

Wriggling out of the hated blazer and kilt, she slipped on a simple blue dress, brushing out her plaits and tucking her mass of hair into a loose bundle before heading out to find her grandmother. The silence was so unusual that she couldn't help feeling a little apprehensive. For one moment she wondered if her grandmother had planned a birthday surprise, before pushing the ludicrous idea away. Her grandmother didn't do either birthdays or surprises.

Padding along the hallway, she peeped into the small sitting room her grandmother preferred, her curiosity piqued as she heard the low rumble of voices coming from the larger, formal sitting room her grandmother only used for entertaining. The room was light thanks to floor-to-ceiling windows with stunning views over Central Park but stuffed so full of the furniture that had been saved from Belravia during the revolution that it was impossible to find a spot not cluttered with ornate chairs or spindly tables, the walls filled with heavy portraits of scowling ancestors.

Amber hovered, torn. She hadn't been officially summoned, but surely her grandmother would expect her to come and greet whichever guest she was entertaining.

Just a few more months, she told herself. She'd graduate in a couple of months, and by the autumn she'd be in London. She just needed to apply to university and figure out how to pay for it first. She'd saved a couple of thousand dollars from her allowance but that wasn't going to cover much more than the plane ticket.

Okay. She would worry about all that later. Time to go in, say hello and act the Princess for as long as she needed to. It was so much easier with escape within smelling distance. And of course, now she was an actual adult, her grandmother's control over her had come to an end. At last.

Inhaling, Amber took another step forward, only to halt as her gaze fell on a masculine profile through the part-opened door. A profile she knew all too well: dark hair brushed smoothly back from a high forehead, a distinctly Roman nose flanked by sharp cheekbones hollowing into a firm chin, mouth unsmiling. Amber swallowed. She had spent too many nights dreaming of that mouth. Her heart thumped painfully, her hands damp with remembered embarrassment. What was Tristano Ragrazzi doing here, on her birthday of all days?

Tristano—or, as he was more commonly known, His Most Excellent Royal Highness Crown Prince Tristano of Elsornia—was Amber's first crush. Or, if she was being strictly honest, only crush, despite the four-year age gap and the not insignificant fact that on the few occasions they'd met he'd barely deigned to notice that she was alive. This small detail hadn't stopped a younger Amber weaving an elaborate tale around how he would one day fall in love with her and rescue her from the tower: a tale she had stopped weaving the day she had tripped over one of her grandmother's many embroidered footstools and spilt a tray of drinks and olives over him—perfect hair, exquisite suit, handsome face and all. Hard as she tried, she had never forgotten his incredulous look of horror, the scathing, contemptuous glance he'd shot her way. She hadn't seen him since—and that was more than fine with her.

Amber started to tiptoe backwards—far better to face her grandmother's wrath than His Highness—when Tristano spoke and, at the sound of her name, she froze again.

'Princess Vasilisa is still very young.'

'Yes,' her grandmother agreed in her usual icy, cut-glass tones. 'Which is in your favour. I've ensured she's been kept close; she can be moulded. And of course she has had no opportunity to meet any males. A virgin princess with no scandal attached to her name, excellent academic qualifications, educated in statesmanship and diplomacy is a rare prize and that's before we consider her dowry. She's unique and you know it, Tristano. So let's not play games.'

It was all Amber could do not to gasp. For her grandmother to be discussing her virginity with anyone was mortifying enough but with his Royal Hotness? Her cheeks felt as if they might burst into flame any moment, and not just with embarrassment, with indignation. She was *not* some prize sow to be discussed in terms of breeding! She was surprised her grandmother hadn't mentioned her excellent teeth—unless her dental records had already been discussed!

'Of course, the Belravian fortune,' a male voice she didn't recognise cut in. He had a similar accent to Tristano, only far more noticeable: a little Italian, a little Germanic. 'Is it really worth as much as it was when the country fell?'

'More, thanks to some wise investments as we waited for a Kireyev to sit on the throne once more. But empires have risen and fallen and it's clear that our country is no more, and with it our throne. So we look to another throne, another country in which to invest our money and our blood. Your throne, your country, Tristano.'

Silence fell. Was Tristano tempted, disgusted—or indignant that she was being bartered as if she were part of the fortune, not a living, breathing human? Hope for the latter filled her, only to be dashed when he finally spoke.

'But the fact remains, the Princess is still very young.'

'Let's not be hasty,' the unknown man said. 'The Princess may be too young to marry, but there's no reason not to enter into a formal betrothal. And that's what we are here to discuss. The papers are right here.'

The *what*? She had to be dreaming, surely. Amber barely breathed as she listened.

'I'm her legal guardian,' her grandmother said. 'I can sign right here, with the Duke as my witness. All you need to do is sign as well, Tristano, and then I suggest you take Vasilisa back to Elsornia with you. She can spend the next three years finishing her education to your liking and then, when she comes of Belravian age at twenty-one, she will make you a perfect bride. The perfect Queen.'

A perfect bride indeed! If Amber hadn't been so horrified she would have laughed out loud. She hadn't even been kissed yet; there was no way she was marrying a prince until she had tried a lot of frogs. Besides, she had her own plans for the next three years and they didn't include being finished off in a castle in the middle of Europe. No, she was going to live like a normal girl. She was going to laugh and learn and flirt and find those frogs and enjoy every moment.

Amber's first instinct was to burst in and tell them all in no uncertain terms that the only person who could sign that agreement was her and she did *not* consent. To remind them that now she was eighteen her grandmother was no longer her guardian—and that even if she was she had no right under US or UK law to marry her granddaughter off, that any betrothal they plotted wasn't worth the paper it was written on. But caution quickly replaced the anger. She had no doubt that her grandmother was capable of taking her forcibly to Elsornia if she chose to. No, better to be careful.

Amber backed away as silently as she could, resolution filling her. She was more than the heir to a long gone throne; she was also English on her mother's side, and it was long past time that she went home. The last sound she heard was a pen scratching over thick paper as she inched back towards her bedroom. Passport, money and she would be gone. And she wouldn't be looking back.

CHAPTER ONE

'ALEX? WHO IS THAT? Standing next to Laurent?' Amber did her best to hiss her question discreetly, aware that television cameras were pointing directly at her and her two fellow bridesmaids. A royal wedding was always An Event, even when the royal in question ruled a tiny Mediterranean kingdom. The kind of event that Amber had avoided over the last eight years—and now here she was, centre stage. But what could she do when one of the three people she loved best in the world was getting married to a Crown Prince?

'That's the best man.' Alex gave her a curious glance. 'Tristano, I think Emilia said he was called. Why the interest? He doesn't look like your type, but he is pretty gorgeous.'

'I'm not *interested* interested,' Amber protested, still in a hiss through as rigid a mouth as she could manage, the last thing she wanted was for someone to read her lips and broadcast the conversation across social media. 'I was just surprised. I thought Laurent's cousin was best man.'

'He was called into surgery.' Laurent's cousin was Head of Surgery at the local hospital and dedicated to his job. Rumour said he was openly praying for a royal heir to push him down the succession within the year. 'Tristano was on standby—he and Laurent have known each other for years apparently.'

'How convenient.' *Not.*

Amber bit her lip as she considered her options. Feigning illness would make her even more conspicuous than she already was—and, she had to face it, bridesmaid at a royal wedding televised for a global audience of millions was already a pretty conspicuous position to be in. She had thought long and hard about trying to wiggle out of the job, knowing that if she was ever going to be recognised, a room full of European royals was the time and place. But in the end she had reasoned that there were only a handful of people who had known her back then.

It was just her luck that one of those people was standing unsmilingly next to the groom, clad in a gilt-covered dress uniform that on anyone less austerely handsome would look gaudy.

She'd changed beyond all recognition, she consoled herself. Like her favourite fictional redhead, her hair had darkened from carrot to auburn and she was no longer a thin, gawky teenager. She'd grown, literally and metaphorically, during her first year of freedom, and was several inches taller and two dress sizes curvier than she had been in New York. Last time Tristano had seen her she'd been wearing a kilt and blouse, her hair in plaits, make-up free, and she'd tipped a tray of olives over him. There was no way he'd recognise that awkward teenager in the buffed and polished designer-clad bridesmaid. She was completely safe.

Besides, what was the worst that could happen if Tristano did recognise her? It wasn't as if they had ever actually *been* engaged; he had probably forgotten about that particular debacle years ago, nor could she be compelled to return to the life of a royal. It was just that she loved the anonymity of her life; not even her three close friends and business partners knew of her discarded title or those long lonely years in New York. She'd put life as an exiled royal behind her the day she'd left her grandmother's apartment and had no intention of ever reclaiming it.

The sound of the organ recalled her to her surroundings and Amber lifted her chin and squared her shoulders as the two flower girls began their sedate walk down the aisle, scattering white rose petals as they went. Alex went next, as tall and elegant as ever in the ice-blue and silver dress all three bridesmaids wore, the silk falling in perfect folds to the ancient stone floor. The choir's voices swelled, filling the medieval cathedral as Harriet, with a wink at Amber, followed Alex. Amber quickly looked back at Emilia, ethereal in white lace, her face obscured by her veil, her hand tucked in her father's arm. 'Love you,' Amber mouthed. And then it was her turn.

For the first time she could remember she was grateful for the hours and hours of deportment lessons she'd suffered in her teens as she slowly followed Harriet down the aisle, managing to block out the curious, appraising stares. Amber didn't look to the left or the right as she progressed, not until she finally reached the very front when she couldn't stop her gaze sliding right. Laurent was staring behind her, his face lit up with joy and reverence. Amber swallowed quickly, a lump forming in her throat at the sheer raw emotion the usually reserved Archduke showed so openly, only for her heart to lurch in her chest as she looked past him and met the clear grey-eyed gaze of the Crown Prince of Elsornia. A gaze directed at her, heat flickering in its depths. Had he recognised her after all?

But it wasn't recognition she saw dancing there.

It was desire.

Tris wasn't a huge fan of weddings, and he had never been attracted to redheads, so why couldn't he stop staring at the flame-haired bridesmaid as she processed with poise and ease down the aisle? Like the two bridesmaids who'd preceded her, she wore blue silk shot through with silver, the blue so faint it was like the reflection of ice, but the colour looked warmer on her creamy skin, set off by a mass of glorious hair set with crystals. She looked like the thaw, warm and welcoming and ever so slightly dangerous. Not that there was anything welcoming in her expression as she met his gaze squarely before turning away. But Tris could see the rosy glow spreading over her neck and shoulders and knew that she wasn't quite as impervious to his interest as she made out. Intriguing.

Or not. He didn't have the time or freedom to dally with bridesmaids, however enticing they were. What he needed was a wife and an heir within the next five years or he'd forfeit the throne, thanks to the crazy old-fashioned laws that still prevailed in his crazy old-fashioned country. With his reckless cousin next in line after him, failure was not an option.

The music swelled to a crescendo and as it ended Tris turned his mind back to the matter at hand. He didn't have to do much, apart from making a speech suitable for broadcasting; after all, the first rule of royal friendships was that you never spoke about royal friendships. Laurent's secrets, tame as they were, were safe with him.

The Armarian Archbishop stepped forward and the wedding ceremony began, following time-hallowed tradition with its well-worn words, repeated by millions of voices yet made unique with each new utterance. Tris couldn't help but get caught up in the spell-like moment as Laurent and Emilia made their vows, promising each other fidelity and honour, love and respect and he was aware of a momentary but sharp envy. Laurent was marrying for love. How many men or women in their position were so lucky? How many got to choose this one part of their destiny?

Not Tris. He had betrothed himself to a girl he barely knew, not for the famed Belravian fortune but because she had been available, suitable and bred for the role. No wonder she had run away at the very idea. Sometimes he envied her; other times he wondered how she could forsake her duty while he was bound to his. Princes and princesses weren't supposed to follow their hearts—although Laurent was following his right now and he had never looked happier, or more at peace.

The wedding progressed with all due pomp, tempered by the sincerity and love blazing out of the happy couple's faces as they repeated their vows. One lengthy sermon, several solemn choral songs and a demure yet smouldering kiss later, the bells rang out as the couple headed back down the aisle hand in hand, to the claps and cheers of the congregation. Tris courteously gave his arm to Laurent's mother, regal in dark blue and diamonds, but as he escorted her back up the aisle his gaze was drawn to the undulating step of the red-headed bridesmaid, the way the ice-blue silk displayed the curve of her hips, the straight line of her back.

'Her name is Amber,' Laurent's mother informed him drily. 'She works with Emilia, as do the other two bridesmaids.' She paused, eyebrows slightly arched. 'I believe she is currently single.'

'The best man and the bridesmaid?' Tris smiled. 'A bit of a cliché, is it not?'

'A cliché isn't always a bad thing; sometimes it's just that things are meant to be.'

'I didn't have you down as a matchmaker, Your Majesty.'

'I'm not planning on making a habit of it. But you're thirty, Tristano. Thirty and single. Noticing a pretty girl at a wedding is allowed, even for a Crown Prince.'

'But I'm not single. Technically, I am betrothed.'

'Technically is the right word; after all, you're be-trothed to a woman you haven't seen for eight years. It's time you gave up on Princess Vasilisa. You deserve a bride who wants to be by your side.'

'We can't all be as lucky as Laurent.' Tristano slowed as they reached the end of the aisle. Photographers awaited them outside the cathedral and he automatically straightened even more, ensuring his expression was cool and bland. 'This situation is of my own mak-ing. I shouldn't have agreed to my uncle's suggestion of a betrothal, nor should I have accepted the Belravian Dowager Queen's assurances that she knew where her granddaughter was and that the marriage would go ahead as planned. I wasted too many years thinking Vasilisa was completing her education abroad, and by the time her grandmother confessed the truth the trail was cold. By Elsornian law I am engaged and cannot marry anyone else, and by that same law I must be married with an heir by thirty-five. If my cousin was a different man then it wouldn't matter so very much.'

Laurent's mother nodded. 'And, of course, Nikolai is both married and the father of a son. I do find it ridiculous in this day and age that an Elsornian Crown Prince cannot become King until he is thirty-five and must have fathered an heir to do so.'

'Agreed. The requirement that he must have led troops into battle and sacked a border town have become ceremonial only, thank goodness. I don't see my neighbouring countries taking kindly to a sacking. This law is the last remnant of our medieval customs. I plan to overturn it, and to overturn the primogeniture rule as well. But I can only do it with the agreement of my heir, and Nikolai will never agree.'

'What about Parliament? Can they not help?'

'They are reluctant to take the lead. I have lawyers trying to find a way to encourage them, but so far nothing. But this is not the occasion to discuss my troubles; it's a happy day.'

'It is. And so forget matters of state and missing brides and enjoy yourself, Tristano. Flirt with the pretty redhead, enjoy your youth, for one day at least.'

Tristano escorted the Dowager Queen out of the cathedral, posing momentarily for the horde of photographers thronging the square outside the magnificent Gothic building before handing Laurent's mother into a waiting horse-drawn carriage. She would travel alone in the ceremonial procession through the streets, Tristano was to join the three bridesmaids and two flower girls in a larger carriage. An hour with nothing to do but wave to the excited crowds and make small talk with Emilia's friends. Maybe the Dowager Queen was right, maybe today he should forget his cares and responsibilities and enjoy himself. And if enjoying himself meant exploring this unexpected attraction further then what harm would it do? A little bit of flirting hurt nobody.

Luck was with him as he approached the larger carriage. The tallest bridesmaid, Alex, sat on one side with the flower girls, the other two bridesmaids on the bench opposite, Tris's seat between them. The coach driver shook the reins as Tris sat down and the carriage jolted into movement, taking its place in the procession.

'This is so cool,' the littlest flower girl breathed as the carriage rolled out of the square. People were crowded onto both sides of the street, waving flags and holding pictures of Laurent and Emilia, cheering loudly as the carriages passed slowly.

'Wave back,' Amber encouraged them and, at first shyly but then with increasing confidence, the girls did so.

The noise of the crowds and the echo of the horses' hooves made small talk difficult and the occupants of the carriage were busy responding to the enthusiastic crowd, but Tris was preternaturally aware of every shift Amber made. She sat tall and straight, rigid, her face averted from him as if she didn't want to be seen by him, to engage with him. Tris was aware of a ridiculously oversized sense of disappointment. He didn't know this woman, had no idea of her likes or dislikes, her views, whether she had a sense of humour or not, preferred dogs or cats, savoury or sweet. Her studied indifference to him should be meaningless. And yet he had felt a sense of connection the moment he had first seen her, as if at some deep level he did know her. Clearly that sense was one-sided.

By the end of the hour even the flower girls, Saffron and Scarlett, were exhausted. 'My cheeks ache from smiling and I don't think I can wave any more,' the older one said as the carriage came to a stop. 'And I didn't know carriages were so bumpy!'

'You did really well,' Tris told her and was rewarded with a beaming smile.

The carriages pulled up back outside the cathedral, where cars waited to whisk them away to the palace just a few kilometres outside Armaria's quaint medieval capital city. Here a formal banquet awaited the five hundred wedding guests, to be followed by a much more informal and intimate party for close friends and family only. Tris exited the carriage first, aware that hundreds of cameras were trained directly on him. Now Laurent was married, Tristano was one of the few unmarried European royals left, and the only male in his early thirties. Come Monday he'd be on the front page of every gossip magazine and tabloid, a bull's-eye stamped on his face. Up to now he'd been so busy in Elsornia he'd managed to stay out of the papers, magazines and gossip sites. Being Laurent's best man meant he would be thrust straight into the spotlight, whether he liked it or not.

Ignoring the photographers' call for him to look at them, Tris handed each bridesmaid down in turn, swinging Saffron and Scarlett onto the floor before extending his hand to first Alex, then Harriet and finally Amber. She paused before taking it, her eyes averted before, with a visible breath, she tilted her head, looked him straight in the eyes and took his hand with a cool, firm grip.

Tris was unprepared for the zing that shot up his arm as she touched him, unprepared for the way his breath caught in his throat, his pulse speeded up. As soon as Amber was on steady ground, he let go of her hand. By the flush creeping up her face, he knew she had felt the connection between them too.

But it didn't matter. Laurent's mother could give him all the advice she liked but it changed nothing. He was not free to react to any woman, no matter who she was. He couldn't walk away from who he was, not even for an evening, his duty so ingrained in him that he bled Elsornia.

Tris watched Amber join her friends and head towards the nearest car and made no move to join them. It was safest alone. It always had been. He'd just never *felt* so alone before.

CHAPTER TWO

'HE HASN'T TAKEN his eyes off you all night.' Harriet nudged Amber and not too subtly nodded towards where Tristano sat, his long fingers toying with the stem of his glass in a way which made Amber's stomach clench in spite of herself. She had no idea whether the involuntary reaction was from fear that he somehow had recognised her or because of a desire she barely recognised, one that had ignited the second Tristano had taken her hand to help her from the carriage. Which was ridiculous. It was a light touch, a cursory helping hand, one that had been extended to all of them.

But Harriet was right. Amber had been aware of Tristano's hooded gaze fixed on her all afternoon and into the evening. It was like a caress, dark and dangerous, a wisp of velvet awareness across her bare skin.

'I think he just has a naturally intense, brooding thing going on,' she said with an attempt at a laugh. 'All he needs is a pair of breeches and he would be a dead ringer for Darcy at his most snooty stage.'

'And does that make you Elizabeth Bennet?' Harriet asked with a sly smile and Amber shook her head.

'I have no intention of civilising any man. I want the finished article, thank you.'

'Oh, I don't know, the civilising can be fun.' Harriet looked over at her fiancé, Deangelo, as he leaned against a wall, deep in conversation with Finn, Alex's boyfriend, and Amber groaned.

'I don't want the lurid details, thank you.'

At that moment they were interrupted by a spotlight shining on the dancefloor and an announcement that the bride and groom were about to take to the floor for their first dance. The band struck up a tune, and Laurent led Emilia out onto the floor. She'd changed into a simple long cream dress, her hair loose and Amber thought, with a lump in her throat, that she'd never looked so beautiful. More beautiful or more distant. This was it. Emilia was married, Harriet would be following her down the aisle in the summer and Alex was spending more time at Finn's country estate than she was at the Chelsea home they had all shared until this week. Her life had seemed so settled and perfect, and now it was all changing. Her friends were moving on and she just wasn't ready.

Taking a sip of the tart refreshing champagne, Amber propped her chin on her hand as she watched the pair waltz to a soft romantic tune, no showy choreography or carefully rehearsed moves, just two people holding each other, lost in each other. Slowly her wistfulness faded, replaced with happiness for her friend and she applauded enthusiastically as the dance ended and the band struck up a much jauntier tune. Other couples began to spill onto the dancefloor and Deangelo stalked over and extended a hand to Harriet, enfolding her in his arms as he led her onto the dancefloor, while Finn whirled Alex out to join them. Taking another sip of her champagne, Amber tried not to look like she minded being the bridesmaid wallflower.

'Would you like to dance?'

Amber jumped at the sound of the deep, faintly accented tones. She knew what—who—she'd see before she looked up. She took another gulp of the champagne before turning her head. Tristano stood beside her, one hand outstretched in invitation—or command.

'You don't have to ask me, you know. It's not a real rule that the best man has to dance with the bridesmaid.'

'I'm not asking you because it's my duty. I'm asking you because you are the most beautiful woman in the room and I really, really want to dance with you.'

'Oh…' Amber swallowed 'I…' She should say no. It was too dangerous to spend any time with Tristano. Besides, she had no interest in dancing with the Crown Prince of Elsornia. Even if she wasn't afraid of being recognised, she didn't actually *like* him. Sometimes she still heard his voice in her nightmares, sentencing her to a marriage she hadn't consented to, a life in a castle she didn't want to live in.

Only tonight he didn't look pompous or arrogant. He'd changed out of his glossy dress uniform into a perfectly cut dark grey suit, stubble coating his cheeks, his hair no longer neatly combed back but falling over his eyes. But it wasn't his slightly more relaxed appearance that made her pause; it was the heat in his eyes. Want. Desire. For her. Just as she had once dreamed.

'No one has ever called me beautiful before,' she

said a little shyly as she took his hand and allowed him to pull her out of her chair.

'I find that hard to believe.'

Amber tilted her chin, reminding herself that she was no longer a schoolgirl, desperate to be noticed. 'It's true. Of course, sometimes I get called hot. Often fit. Nice sometimes. Occasionally gorgeous. But never beautiful.'

Tristano's mouth curled disdainfully. 'Englishmen.'

She laughed. 'I get worse online, but that's always a useful guide—instant block. There're far too many ginger fetishists out there. One comment on my hair and that's a warning light I always heed.'

His hand tightened on hers. 'What on earth are you doing meeting men online?'

'I'm a twenty-something living in London; there's no other way to date.' She tried to sound worldly and nonchalant, not letting on how soul-destroying the apps and websites were. 'I always promised myself I'd kiss a lot of frogs before I met Mr Right. I just underestimated how un-kissable most frogs actually are.'

'Do you believe in Mr Right?' The music slowed as they reached the middle of the dancefloor and Amber tried not to tense as Tris took her into a practised hold. This was just a dance, a polite social custom, nothing more, but she could feel every imprint of his fingers burning through the silk of her dress, the places where his body touched hers igniting with a sweet, low heat.

'I believe in soulmates. My parents found each other despite leading very different lives and they were perfect together. So yes, somewhere out there is the right man for me. I just need to find him.'

Warmth flooded her cheeks as she spoke. The champagne and the candlelit ballroom must have loosened her tongue. 'What about you?' she asked, curiosity getting the better of her. 'Do you believe there's someone out there for you?'

Tristano didn't answer for a long time and when he did he sounded resigned. 'I don't believe in true love, no, although seeing Laurent so happy could make a man change his mind, tonight at least.' There was something meaningful in the way he said the last words and Amber's whole body flamed to match her cheeks, her stomach tumbling with heady excitement. She swallowed, moistening her lips with the tip of her tongue, aware of his gaze fastened on her mouth before he continued. 'But Laurent is lucky. Not every prince can follow his heart. It's easier to accept that if you never try.'

'Never try what?'

'Love. The most a man like me can hope for is mutual liking and respect.'

Mutual liking and respect. That was the fate she had been intended for, and yes, she wanted both of those in any future partner, but as part of a much larger whole, a whole that included love and desire.

'Why?' she asked, emboldened by the almost reverential yet possessive way he held her and the intensity in his eyes. 'Why settle?'

'It's complicated.' He smiled then and Amber's breath caught in her throat. The smile wiped away his rather austere, remote expression, making his good looks more boy next door rather than unobtainable gorgeous. 'I'm sorry, that's even more clichéd than the best man dancing with the bridesmaid, but it's true. To explain it I would need to bore you with one thousand years of Elsornian constitution and laws. To be honest, I'd really like to forget about it all for one evening. To just be me, Tris, lucky enough to be dancing with a beautiful woman at a beautiful occasion. You must think I'm a little mad.' His smile turned rueful and it tugged at Amber's heart.

'Not at all. I know something about expectation and tradition and wanting to just be yourself,' she confessed. For one moment, struck by the relief—and the loneliness—in his dark grey eyes, she thought about going further, thought about telling him who she was, how she maybe understood how he felt more than anyone else in the world, but the sense of self-preservation that had kept her happy and safe for the last eight years kicked in. 'So how about for tonight you forget about it? Be whoever you want to be. Who would you be if you were just Tris and not Crown Prince Tristano?'

'No one has ever asked me that before.' He looked so adorably confused for a moment that she had a crazy impulse to touch his cheek, to trace the sharp line of it round to his solemn, finely cut mouth. 'I'm a qualified lawyer...'

'By choice?'

'Not exactly; it made sense to study law as it helps me do my job. But, to be honest, constitutional and business law can be a little dry.'

'So not a lawyer, something not office based, I guess? Gardener, chef, pirate, actor, survivalist, athlete?'

'They all sound more fun than Privy Council meetings. I like looking at the stars. Maybe I'd be an astronomer?'

'Or an astronaut, living on the space station?'

'I'll imagine I'm there when the Privy Council meetings get too much. How about you? Are you living your dreams?'

Amber couldn't believe how easy it was to talk to Tris; and not just small talk either, but intimate and honest conversation. If only her teen self could hear them confiding in each other, just as she'd dreamed they would, all those years ago. 'In a way. I always wanted to go to university—my dad was an academic and he instilled this huge love of history and learning in me—but, for various reasons, I went straight to work.' Reasons that included not finishing high school, mostly because of the man holding her close and listening to every word as if she was the most interesting person he had ever met.

It was strange to think that in another universe they might be attending this wedding as husband and wife. How would her life have turned out if she had gone along with her grandmother's plans, if the betrothal had been real and followed through? Would they have danced and talked or sat in silence, with nothing to say? It was easy, nestled in his arms, desire thrumming through her in time with the music, to imagine the former, but common sense told her that the latter would have been the more likely outcome. She had been too young, too unformed to marry anyone, even if she had been in love and loved, not harbouring a one-sided crush. A crush that had never quite gone away judging by the butterflies dancing away inside her, and the way her breath caught with every one of his rare, sweet smiles. 'I would still like to take my degree one day.

But I love my job. It's different every day, always a new adventure, new things to learn, new people to meet.'

'You are very lucky,' he said softly, but Amber shook her head.

'I made my own luck,' she told him.

'Then you are beautiful and brave.' Sincerity rang in his voice, smouldered in his eyes and as the music played on and his grip tightened it was too easy for Amber to believe him, for tonight at least.

She had told herself that one dance couldn't hurt, had promised herself that she wouldn't have any more champagne, not when it loosened her tongue and made her forget who she was and who she was with. But somehow one dance turned into two and then two more, and at some point, warm from the exertion, and from Tristano's proximity, she agreed when he suggested that he collect an iced bottle of champagne and two glasses and escort her out onto the terrace. It was a crisp, cold February night, the snow still heavy on the distant mountains, the sea air sharp even on the south Mediterranean coast, and Tristano slid out of his jacket to drape it around her shoulders. Amber smiled her thanks. 'How gallant.'

'Not at all, but if you're too cold we can go in,' he said.

'Oh, no. Not when the stars are so beautiful.' What was she doing spending time in a secluded corner with Tris? Playing with fire, that was absolutely certain, because she hadn't misunderstood the heat in his gaze, the way he touched her, held her, as if they were the only people in the entire castle.

It was like all her teenage daydreams come to life, the way he had finally noticed her, seen her, wanted her… To the lonely teenager still inside her, his attention was more intoxicating than the moonlight and champagne combined. Only the reality was better than her daydreams. This older, more mature Tris had a sense of humour she had never suspected, a humanity that drew her to him.

Tris guided her to a corner of the terrace and set the bottle onto a nearby table, opening it and filling a glass before handing it to her. Amber sipped the tart fizzy liquid more quickly than she intended, suddenly shy at being alone with him, even though she could hear the music playing and the babble of voices in the ballroom just a few steps away. 'I've never seen so many stars all at once,' she said, taking another sip and realising her glass was almost empty. She held it out and, after an enquiring raised brow, Tris refilled it. 'I live in London so obviously with all the pollution the sky is never so clear, the stars are faint, but even in the countryside it never looks like this. It's like the sky is filled with crystals, each more beautiful than the last.'

Tristano was so close to her she could feel his breath. 'There's Orion.' He pointed upwards. 'Can you see his belt, and there's his bow, just there. No telescope needed on a night like tonight.'

'Yes…' She barely breathed the word, the heat of him burning into her, despite his thin shirt in the winter air and the thickness of the jacket she wore. 'I see.'

'And there…' he took her hand and moved it, so it pointed to a different spot '…those are the Pleiades, the Seven Sisters, daughters of Atlas.'

'Atlas? He holds the earth on his shoulders, right? Do you think he looks up at his daughters at night?'

'Probably.' She could feel his smile in the way he shifted, in the tenor of his voice.

'Who else can we see?'

'The twins, Castor and Pollux, just there. Twin sons of Leda and brothers of Helen, the most beautiful woman in the world, or so they said. There are some who say she was a redhead.'

She turned to face him, hand on hip mock indignantly. 'I thought I warned you about redhead comments.'

'Ah, but I didn't realise that I was susceptible until tonight.'

As soon as he said the words, Tris wanted to retract them, but how could he when he was standing so close to Amber he could feel every shift and movement, could smell the rich scent of her perfume, when his vision was transfixed by the rich red of her hair?

'Very smooth,' she said, but she was smiling as she spoke.

'Thank you. Like I said, I'm a little unpractised at this.'

'This?'

'Talking to beautiful women. Flirting.'

'Flirting? Is that what we are doing?'

'I hope so.' Tris wasn't sure what had got into him. He never forgot who he was, what he represented, his responsibilities and ties. Never allowed himself as much as a moment off, because if he did then how could he carry on shouldering the duty and the burden, the traditions and all that came with them? No, better to stay on the path he had been put on before he was even born and never look to the left or right.

Only tonight he had allowed himself to glance to the side. Tris didn't know what had caused his uncharacteristic sidestep. Was it seeing Laurent follow his heart, somehow balancing his own royal commitments with marriage to the woman he chose? Showing Tris how his life and the traditions that bound it were as archaic and pointless as he had always secretly thought they were, though so deep down he had never articulated it to himself.

But right now he actually had a choice, even if it was a temporary one-night deal. He could let the moonlight and the champagne, and the undeniable attraction lead him wherever Amber was willing to go. Or he could keep his life simple and turn back to the straight, unyielding path he trod, pick up his burden and march on, letting the last couple of hours fade away, putting them down to a temporary enchantment.

Did he always have to do the right thing? Wasn't even the Crown Prince allowed a night off? Just once?

For one long second he wavered, and then he was overwhelmed by the moment. By the cold air whistling through his thin shirt, the slender-stemmed glass in his hand, the tart champagne lingering on every taste bud, the tang at the back of his throat, the scent of winter flowers mingling with the rich scent of the woman standing before him. By her hair, long and thick, falling in waves, a deep auburn, set off by the silvery blue of her dress and the cream of her skin. By the softness of her breath and the music in her voice, the tilt of her smile and her long, long lashes, lashes half lowered as she looked up at him.

And then he could think no more. Instinct took over, the man pushing the Prince aside for the first time he could remember as he curled his hand lightly around Amber's waist and tilted her pointed chin up so that he could look her full in the face, looking for agreement, for consent, for desire.

Her mouth curved in invitation, her eyelids fluttered and she took an unmistakable step closer until their bodies were touching.

'What do you think? Have I got it wrong, or are we flirting?' He barely managed the words, the light touch of her body flaming through him.

'I think that I hope so too,' she said and with those soft words he was lost. There was no tentativeness in the kiss, no hesitancy as he pulled her to him and nothing but enthusiasm as Amber kissed him back, one of her hands sliding to fist the material at the small of his back, the other to his nape as she rose to meet him. The kiss went from nought to sixty in record time, the first touch igniting a fire and desire almost completely foreign to Tris, who had kept any previous romances as businesslike and emotion-free as he could without making the encounter an actual business transaction. Feelings were too messy for a man who wasn't free to feel. But tonight he was all feeling, every nerve alight with want, consumed by the feel, by the taste of her.

Some dim part of him was still aware of where they were, that anyone could round the corner and see them, and there was enough of the Prince in him still—and enough of the possessive lover even after such a short time—to rebel at the thought of something so intimate being witnessed. 'Come with me?' he whispered against her mouth. 'Inside.'

She pulled back to look up at him. 'Back to the reception?' He couldn't tell if she was affronted or relieved by the idea.

'If you'd like. Or we could go to the suite I am staying in.'

Something he couldn't identify flickered briefly in her eyes, so swiftly he might have imagined it, before she took his hand.

'I vote for the suite,' she said. 'Let's go.'

CHAPTER THREE

'I KNOW ALEX thinks they're worth pursuing, but seriously, is any account worth this much hassle? Amber, are you even listening to me?'

Amber blinked and tried to concentrate as Harriet paced up and down in front of her desk, but waves of tiredness rolled over her and her head was pounding. Straightening, she stretched, closing her eyes as she did so. What was wrong with her? She'd been feeling exhausted for days. At first she had put it down to the shock of seeing Tris again, but several weeks later she still felt weak, shaky and ridiculously tearful.

'Amber, are you all right?' Harriet looked at her friend with some concern. 'You are awfully pale.'

'I've been feeling a little peaky,' confessed Amber. 'I think I've picked up some kind of virus, and I just can't seem to shake it.'

Harriet perched on the edge of Amber's desk and lightly touched her forehead, her hand cool and soothing. Amber leaned against it gratefully. 'It's been a while now, hasn't it?'

Amber nodded. 'Maybe I should go and see a doctor.'

'That's not a bad idea,' said Harriet. 'How long exactly have you been feeling like this?'

Amber didn't have to think too hard; she knew exactly when she'd begun to feel ill, as soon as the guilt had hit. 'Since the wedding, I think.'

'The wedding?' Harriet raised her eyebrows. 'Since you and the luscious Prince disappeared off for the evening, you mean?'

Amber's cheeks heated. She had said very little to her friends about that night and they hadn't pressed for any details. The unwritten rule of their friendship was that they never ever pried. All four of them had come into this friendship and business partnership with secrets. Over the last year many of those secrets had been excavated, but Amber's were still intact, including her tryst with Tris. Her friends were all so happy, so in love with men who adored them, she had been ashamed to admit she'd been swept off her feet by the best man at a wedding, only to wake up with nothing more than a note, no matter how beautifully composed. She didn't want to be the single cliché in their group.

'Want to talk about it?' Harriet asked, then frowned. 'No, it's not a question; you haven't been yourself for weeks. I am going to make us both a cup of tea and then I am going to listen, just like you have listened to me and to Alex and Emilia when we needed you.'

'I didn't mind,' Amber protested. 'And really, there's nothing *to* discuss.'

Harriet crossed her arms and did her best to look fierce. 'No arguing. Leave that report and come through to the kitchen.'

Amber opened her mouth, then closed it again. Harriet was usually the easy-going one out of the four of them, but once she was set on something there was no swaying her. She pushed back her chair, closed her laptop lid and followed Harriet into the back of the Chelsea townhouse which was both their head office and their home.

Alex had inherited the Georgian terrace house a couple of years before and with her legacy came the opportunity to make the business they had planned a reality. Their skills in PR, events and administration were the perfect combination for an agency offering both temps and consultancy to private and corporate clients and a year after opening their business was booming.

There were times when Amber still couldn't believe this gorgeous space was theirs. They had decided to use most of the ground floor as both office and reception; wooden floorboards shone with a warm golden glow and the original tiled fireplaces had been renovated to shining glory. Two comfortable-looking sofas sat opposite each other at the front of the room, inviting spaces for potential clients or employees to relax in, the receptionist's desk on the wall behind. Their own desks, an eclectic mixture of vintage and modern classic, faced the reception area in two rows, paperwork neatly filed in the shelves built into the alcoves by the back fireplace. Flowers and plants softened the space, a warm floral print on the blinds and curtains, the same theme picked up in the pictures hanging on the walls.

The door at the back led to a narrow kitchen and a sunny conservatory extension they used as a sitting-cum-dining room and they each had a bedroom on the first or second floor, two to a floor, sharing a bathroom. Only Emilia now lived in Armaria, Alex spent most of her time in the country at Finn's and Harriet would move out when she and Deangelo married later in the year. Their time together had been all too brief.

Harriet directed Amber to sit on the sofa while she made tea and peered into a cupboard. 'No biscuits or cakes?' She glanced over at Amber, her forehead crinkled. 'You haven't baked this week?'

'I haven't felt like it.'

'That's it. Something is definitely up. For you not to bake? That's like, well, there's no metaphor serious enough. Amber, what's wrong? Is it to do with the wedding? With the Prince?'

Amber took the cup of tea gratefully, her eyes hot and heavy, chest tight with unexpected pain. 'Oh, Hatty, I messed up.'

Harriet curled up in the opposite corner of the huge sofa and sipped her tea. 'You don't have to tell me, but it might help. Did you and Tristano spend the night together?'

Amber stared down at her cup. 'Yes.'

'And how did you leave it?'

'We didn't. By the time I woke up he was gone.'

'And he hasn't contacted you?'

'No. But I didn't expect him to. You see, he left a note.'

'A *note*?' Harriet's tone made it very clear what she thought of that and Amber rushed to explain.

'No, no, it's fine. It was actually really lovely.' She still had it, in her bedside drawer. It was a beautifully composed note: an apology, a love letter and a farewell, all in one. He thanked her for giving him an evening where he didn't have to pretend to be someone he wasn't. He thanked her for her kindness. He apologised for leaving her with nothing but a note, but explained that he had no choice, that he couldn't offer her any more than the one night and he asked for her understanding. The part where he told her that she was the most beautiful woman he had ever met, that the memory of that night would stay with him for many, many years to come, were harder to read. For, whether she had meant to or not, Amber knew that she had deceived him...

'Hatty, do you know anything about his situation?'

Harriet frowned. 'Laurent's mother did say something. Doesn't he have to marry and have a son by the time he's thirty-five or the throne goes to his cousin? Have you ever heard anything more absurd?'

'Yes. I didn't know about it during the wedding but Laurent's mother mentioned it the next day. Apparently the cousin is a bit of a playboy and would be a disastrous king.'

'So that's why Tris snuck off, leaving you with a note? Because he needs a queen? That's even worse, no wonder you're upset. You would make a wonderful queen!'

'Harriet, I can't think of anything worse. I would hate to be a queen. But no, that's not why. There's more.' She took a deep breath. 'Eight years ago he entered into a formal betrothal with someone, but she ran away and he hasn't seen her since. But apparently the betrothal is binding in his country and he can't marry anyone else, unless she formally breaks it.'

Harriet's eyes widened. 'That's absolutely crazy! His country—Elsornia, isn't it?—sounds positively medieval. So that's why he hasn't been in touch, because he's engaged to a missing woman.'

'That's about it.' Amber could hear the blood roaring in her ears, every part of her aching with worry. How had this happened? She'd had no idea that Tris would consider the betrothal binding, that eight years after she'd left his whole life would have come to a halt because of her actions. It simply hadn't occurred to her when she had left her grandmother's house, that the freedom she had claimed came with a price. A price that Tris had to pay. Was paying.

She had to tell Tristano who she really was, now she knew the impact her actions had had on him. She could still summon up the memory of her righteous anger at his arrogance for betrothing himself to a girl who wasn't even in the same room, let alone consenting, but the bitter dislike that had fuelled that anger had dissolved, replaced with a reluctant admiration, and an even more reluctant liking. Every day she started to write to him to tell him who she was and to tell him that he was free. Every day the letter remained unwritten. Amber knew that as soon as Tris realised who she really was, his desire and admiration for her would be replaced by anger. Her friends loved her, but she was also so alone in this world that to have been seen as someone worthy of desire, to have been wanted was so intoxicating it was hard to let go. But let go she must.

'Harriet…' But she couldn't quite bring herself to say the next words. To admit that she was the missing Princess and for her world to change. She took a deep breath but before she could speak Harriet put her tea down and took Amber's hand.

'Amber,' Harriet said slowly. 'Do you think that maybe there's a reason you've been feeling so ill? I mean, you were careful, weren't you?'

'Careful?'

Harriet flushed, her cheeks staining a deep, dark red. 'Could you possibly be pregnant?'

'Of course not!' Amber's cheeks were on fire. 'That is…technically, I guess, it's possible.'

Most groups of girls in their twenties who were as close as Amber, Emilia, Alex and Harriet probably spoke about their love lives in great detail. But that kind of gossip had never been part of their friendship. Partly because of the unspoken rule not to pry, but mostly because none of them, Amber aside, had really dated before meeting their partners and as a result contraception was not something they often discussed. Especially in the practical rather than the theoretical sense.

'Possible, but really unlikely. I'm not an idiot; we used protection, obviously we did.'

'Protection?' Harriet looked steadily at her friend.

'Yes, protection.' Amber really wanted this conversation to go away now.

'Condoms?'

'Harriet! I can't believe you're asking me this. Yes, condoms. Happy?'

'You do know that those things aren't one hundred per cent, don't you? It's easy for mistakes to be made in the heat of the moment.'

Amber swallowed. 'I know that but I'm pretty sure…' She *was* pretty sure they had been careful. No, she knew they had. But they had also been a little intoxicated. Not just on the champagne, but on the night itself. With each other. And it hadn't been just once…

'Amber…' Harriet put a careful hand on her shoulder. 'Before we book that doctor's appointment, maybe we should take a pregnancy test.'

Amber managed a smile at that supportive *we*. 'I appreciate your help, but I think this is something I will definitely have to do alone.'

But Harriet was shaking her head. 'No, you are never alone. Remember that, whatever that test does or doesn't say, you are not alone.'

Amber squeezed her friend's hand gratefully, fear tumbling around inside her. Were Harriet's suspicions correct? They made perfect sense. The lethargy, the melancholy, the strangeness in her body. She'd put it down to guilt and something less definable. Not heartbreak exactly—how could she be heartbroken about a man she didn't know? More sadness for a life that wasn't hers, for the wish that she could be simply Amber Blakeley, meeting a man she liked, seeing where that liking might take her, without centuries of tradition and expectation and lies lying between them.

But if Harriet was right then Amber knew that she would be alone. Her friends couldn't support her in this. If she was pregnant with Tris's baby, then she couldn't avoid telling him who she was any longer, and not with a letter setting him free but in person. And all her work to build a life free of Belravia and her grandmother's plans would be for nothing.

But she had no choice. Honour demanded it, and she had this much honour left at least.

CHAPTER FOUR

NORMALLY AMBER WOULD be thrilled to visit Paris. The city had been her first stopping point after she had left her grandmother's apartment, when she had spent a couple of months as a chambermaid in the beautiful French capital before interrailing her way around the continent, finally ending up in London. Her initial plans to go to university had been derailed by her lack of funds and formal qualifications, but instead she had used her hotel experience to get a job as first a receptionist and then a concierge in a London hotel before Deangelo had headhunted her.

She had always meant to return to Paris; the city held such warm and happy memories—memories of freedom, of finding out who she was and what she wanted, memories of evening walks and calorie-filled dinners, of not having to watch what she ate, how she walked, what she wore, what she said and who she spoke to. She would always love the city for those precious few weeks of happiness.

But today she was sitting in the waiting room of the kind of discreet, expensive lawyers who served the royal houses of Europe, knowing that in ten minutes' time she would see Tris again. Amber pressed her hands tightly together and allowed herself a moment of weakness, a moment of wishing she had taken up her friends' offers of companionship and support. Finn, Laurent and Deangelo had all been more than willing to appoint themselves her knight in shining armour, but she had turned down both their money and attempts to accompany her here today. This was something she had to do by herself. This was an appointment only the Princess of Belravia could attend.

'Mademoiselle Blakeley?' The perfectly chic receptionist looked up unsmilingly. 'Please go in.'

Stepping through the open door, Amber looked around nervously. The lawyer's office felt more like a sumptuous library than a place of business. The glossy wooden desk was clearly antique, and the shelves were laden with leather-bound books of all types, not just dry texts. Huge windows let the sunlight bounce in, bathing the room with golden light. It reminded her of her grandmother's study, and for a moment she felt like the sullen schoolgirl she had once been, trying to wrestle her outer self into compliance, even as she raged with rebellion inside.

'Please, *mademoiselle*, sit.'

The receptionist gestured towards a brocade-covered chair by the coffee table at the far end of the room and Amber gratefully sank into it, her legs shaking with nerves and memories. This polite, ruthless, moneyed world was no longer hers, not any more. But she needed the best to guide her through the next few minutes, hours and days and, from all she had heard, Monsieur Clément was the best of the best.

'So, Mademoiselle Blakeley,' Monsieur Clément said in perfect if heavily accented English, 'it is good to finally meet you in person.' If he was at all curious about Amber and the case he was presenting on her behalf, he hid it well. She supposed that was what she was paying for. The lawyer had been suggested by Laurent, who had also offered to pay for him, but Amber had her pride; right now it seemed that was all she had.

She managed a smile. 'Will the Prince be much longer?' She hoped she hadn't betrayed her nervousness through the quiver of her voice.

'He should be here on the hour,' Monsieur Clément said reassuringly. 'I thought it best if we met first, to give you the advantage of the home ground.'

'Of course.' She stilled her trembling legs and tilted her chin. She did have an advantage here; she was the only person in the room who knew the full story. All that Tris knew was that his missing fiancée had shown up at last. He was coming here to verify her identity, and to nullify their betrothal.

And then she'd be free. If she didn't tell him, she would be free.

But how could she keep her pregnancy a secret? They had close friends in common—and she didn't doubt that his people would keep a close eye on her for some months to come. Even if telling him the truth wasn't the right thing to do, it was the only thing to do. If she was going to keep the baby...

Despite herself, her hand slipped to her stomach. As if there was really any doubt. How could a girl who had spent her life longing for someone of her own to love not jump at the opportunity of that, no matter what strings—or chains—came along with it?

She looked up at the silent clock on the wall—only five minutes until the hour. Each second lasted an eternity and yet no time at all had passed when she heard the sound of the outer door opening and the rumble of voices in the reception area. For one dizzying moment she wished she had taken up her friends' offers to accompany her, wished she had the moral support she so desperately needed. But she squared her shoulders and sat back in her chair, every single one of her grandmother's lessons echoing through her head. She was, whether she liked it or not, the Princess of Belravia. And she held all the bargaining chips. 'If you'd like to come this way, Your Royal Highness.'

This was it. There was no going back. Amber clutched the sides of her chair, her knuckles white, and waited.

She didn't recognise the first man who stalked into the room. She guessed he was in his late fifties, greying hair slicked back, dark eyes cold and keen. But the moment he greeted the lawyer she knew his voice, a chill shivering through her. This was the unknown man who had been in her grandmother's study eight years ago. The man who had bargained with her grandmother for her virginity, her hand in marriage and her substantial dowry. Her eyes narrowed even as her breath quickened. This man could be no friend of hers; she was as sure of it as she was her own name. What kind of hold or influence did he have over Tris? But the stranger was forgotten as Tris followed him into the office.

Amber had a couple of seconds to notice the shadows under his grey eyes, the faint stubble coating his sharply cut cheeks and the slight disarray of his usually meticulously combed hair. He looked as if he had barely slept for days, if not weeks. She knew the feeling. She pressed her lips together, not knowing what to say, but knowing that whatever she did say would be the wrong thing.

Tris looked around, his gaze alighting on Amber, surprise and confusion warring on his granite-like face. 'Amber?'

'Hi, Tris.' She winced. *Hi?* It was completely the most inane thing she could have said, but she had no other words.

'What are you doing here?'

'I—'

But the lawyer interjected, 'Please, Your Highness and Your Grace, be seated.'

Nothing more was said for several torturous moments as Tris and the strange man her lawyer had addressed as 'Your Grace' sat in chairs opposite Amber. The unsmiling receptionist carried in a tray stacked with cups, a jug of rich-smelling coffee that made Amber's stomach recoil in horror and tiny little dry biscuits. She set the tray on the coffee table before them and busied herself pouring drinks and handing around biscuits as if they were at a tea party. All the time Tris stared at Amber as if he could not quite believe that she was here.

It wasn't until the receptionist had left the room that Monsieur Clément spoke again. 'Your Highness, Your Grace—Her Royal Highness Princess Vasilisa of Belravia has asked me to speak on her behalf.'

But Tris was on his feet interrupting the lawyer. 'I

don't understand,' he said, looking intently at Amber. 'Amber, what are you doing here? Do you know the Princess? Why didn't you say so at the wedding?'

Amber swallowed. She couldn't hide behind a lawyer, no matter how experienced he was, not when Tris was looking at her with such confusion. 'Tris, I'm not Amber... At least I was christened Amber and it's a name I've always gone by.' She shook her head impatiently. Why was she making such a mess of this? 'But my grandmother called me a different name, ignored the name my parents gave me and the surname my father took when he became a British citizen. She could never accept that he had given up any claim to the long-gone throne of a country that no longer existed, that he wanted nothing to do with her dreams of Belravia.'

The confusion in Tris's eyes had disappeared as if it had never been, replaced with a clear, bright anger that hurt her to look at it. 'I am really, really sorry,' she said, aware of how futile the words were. 'I didn't mean for any of this to happen. I just wanted to be free.'

She just wanted to be free. *Free?* Tris could have laughed—if he wasn't quite so angry, that was. Angry with himself for his shock and the stab of hurt that pierced him as her words sunk in and he realised just who she was. Angry with her for knowing all this time and never saying a word, even as he had bared as much of his soul to her as he had ever bared to any other person. Angry at the whole universe for this quirk of fate, a joke played squarely on him.

'Free?' he repeated, voice chilly with numbness. Who did this woman think she was? No matter what she called herself, no matter who she thought she was, she was a princess born and bred, and with that title came responsibilities not freedom. He had accepted that long ago; it was time she did too. 'So to achieve that freedom you did what? You ran away?' Scorn replaced the numbness, biting through the sunlit air.

Amber had been sitting stock-still, eyes fixed on him, a plea in them he had no intention of heeding, but at his words, his tone, her green eyes flashed. Good. She was angry too; anger he could cope with. Anger he understood. Matched.

'I'm not here to go over what happened that day. All I will say is that I don't accept any betrothal entered into on my behalf without my consent and without my knowledge was, or is, valid.'

During their brief conversation, Tris had been aware of his uncle statue-like beside him, frozen with disbelief. But as Amber finished speaking, her last hurt syllable fading away, his uncle's reserve broke at last and he jumped to his feet. 'Your grandmother had every right…'

Amber held up one slender, pale hand. 'I don't think we've been introduced.' Her voice matched his uncle's in disdain. 'Just as we had not been introduced on the occasion of my eighteenth birthday when you sat discussing my dowry, my future, my body, without *once* considering my wishes.'

Laying a calming hand on his uncle's arm, Tris pressed him back into his seat. 'This is my uncle, the Duke of Eleste. And you're right, Amber. We were wrong that day to enter into negotiations without you. I assumed your grandmother had discussed the proposal with you; I should have ensured that she had before signing anything. But I think we both know I have been punished for that presumption over the last eight years.'

Amber inclined her head, her cheeks still pale, just a spot of colour burning in the centre of them, the warm blush accentuating the cut of her fine bones, the tilt of her chin. 'Thank you.'

'But,' Tris continued; this was not a one-way blame game, no matter what she told herself, 'you were also wrong to just run away. That was the act of a naughty schoolgirl, not a princess.'

Only a faint quiver showed that his words had struck home. 'If you had ever bothered to get to know me...' Her eyes were still fixed on his, as if there was no one else in the room. Her lawyer had stopped remonstrating, his uncle silenced by Tris's gesture. 'If you had ever tried, then you would have known that I was still very much a schoolgirl at heart, even if my grandmother didn't present me as anything but the Princess-in-waiting. If you had bothered to get to know me then you would have known that my hopes and dreams didn't lie in the direction of a throne and a handsome prince.' Her voice was scathing now. 'All I wanted, just like my father before me, was a normal life. That's all I still want. What I have worked for every second since I left.'

'It's been two months.' Tris didn't have the capacity to properly consider her bitter words right now. There was too much truth in them for any quick resolution. He knew that back then uncertainty and the need to find his place in a world where his destiny was so set had made him come across as arrogant. No, not just come across as arrogant; he *had* been arrogant. Arrogant, single-minded and resolute. The last few years, with his destiny suddenly so uncertain, had chipped away at the arrogance, if not the reserve. The only time he had really lost his reserve had been at Laurent's wedding. How unspeakably ironic that it was with this woman. 'Two months since you and I spent time together. I told you I wasn't free; I thought you were aware why. I will absolve you of any deliberate malice towards me before that date. But I'm struggling to understand why, knowing what you know, it's taken you two months to come forward.'

'I was going to write. That's why I engaged a lawyer. I was hoping that you would never have to know who I really was.' Amber's gaze finally broke from his and she looked over at the window, her eyes focusing on the street outside. 'When we… I knew who you were. Of course I did. And I admit I was intrigued. How could I not be? With so much history linking us. But that's what I thought it was, I swear to you. History. I have never once considered myself engaged to you, Tris. And it didn't once occur to me that a betrothal entered into eight years ago, without my consent, thousands of miles away, was still considered valid. I didn't know the entire truth until the next day, when Laurent's mother told me everything.'

Tris briefly closed his eyes. What a mess and, unlike Amber, he knew it was a mess all of his own making.

'I take it—' the Duke finally spoke '—that you are here to revoke the betrothal agreement. That you have decided to do so in person.' Tris could see the machinations behind the smooth expressionless face. His uncle knew as well as he did that they had five years.

Five years for Tris to find a wife and father a son. No doubt his uncle had already prepared a list of suitable candidates who would be ready to wed him within the month. He should be relieved. *Was* relieved. His life could move forward at last. He wasn't going to dwell on why he suddenly felt so bereft.

For the first time, Amber faltered. Tris watched her throat move as she swallowed, reaching blindly out for the water in front of her, her gaze still fastened on the window, maybe dreaming once more of escape. 'Tris, I need to speak to you alone.'

'I don't think that's a good idea…'

'Tris, leave the details to me.'

His uncle and the lawyer spoke in unison. But their words were just background noise; all Tris was aware of was Amber. She sat fully erect, her hands folded in front of her, mouth set firm. She was every inch the Princess she was so desperate not to be.

'So be it.' He turned to his uncle. 'Thank you for accompanying me here today, but I need to do this by myself. Actually, Amber and I need to do this by ourselves. If this betrothal had started that way, maybe we wouldn't be ending it here today.'

After a quick, sharp glance at him, his uncle nodded, standing up and moving towards the door. 'I will wait for you outside.'

Amber nodded at her lawyer who, with a slightly anguished backward glance at his client, followed the Duke out of the office. The door closed firmly behind them.

Finally, they were alone. The silence echoed around them until Tris could hear every beat of his pulse, the thunder of his heartbeat as he waited for Amber to say the words severing the link between them. But after one quick glance in his direction she stayed still and silent.

Despite everything, Tris was conscious of an urge to hold her, to take her tightly folded hands in his, to touch her expressionless face and coax a smile from her bloodless lips. He still couldn't believe it, couldn't reconcile the laughing, flirtatious, fiery bridesmaid with this marble statue.

Nor could he believe he hadn't recognised her at the wedding. True, he hadn't seen her for many years, but her photograph had been on his desk for all that time—an attempt to familiarise himself with the woman who was supposed to have been sharing his life. Not that the gawky teen in the photo bore any resemblance to the woman who sat before him.

'We are alone,' he said, absurdly aware of how redundant the phrase was. 'Whatever you need to say to me, say it. We both know why we're here. Set yourself free.'

In one fluid movement Amber stood, turning to face him, her face so pale she was almost translucent. 'It's true that once I realised that you still considered yourself betrothed to me, once I realised what that meant for you, I planned to end the betrothal.'

'Planned?' Tris tried to dampen down the unwanted hope rising inside him.

'I don't want to be a princess or queen or live anywhere but London. But we don't always get what we want, do we, Tris?'

Nothing she was saying made any sense. This was the woman who had run away with barely anything but the clothes she stood in, in order not to marry him. But, of course, this was also the woman who had shared one of the most passionate nights—if he was being honest, *the* most passionate night—of his life with him.

'No, we don't. But Amber, you always had a choice. Nobody was ever going to drag you to the altar. You could have said no at any time.'

She flushed. 'I appreciate that now but, as I said before, I was very young. My grandmother is very formidable when she wants something. All she ever wanted was to see me on a throne, any throne. Saying no sounds so much easier than actually doing it.'

'Your grandmother is not here now. Say no, Amber. End it.'

'It's not that easy, Tris. You see, I'm pregnant.'

CHAPTER FIVE

AMBER SANK INTO the nearest chair, relieved that she was finally alone, and began to take in her surroundings. She'd spent her teens living in lavish if uncomfortable opulence, but she'd never seen anything like this before. Whoever had designed the suite she'd been allotted in the royal castle of Elsornia had taken luxury and mixed it with style and comfort to create something truly stunning. From the antique four-poster bed, hung with silk, to the brocade-covered walls, her allotted bedroom was perfect.

Almost perfect.

Oh, sure, it had a huge bathroom, too big to be a mere en suite, and the kind of walk-in wardrobe guaranteed to induce envy in all her friends, stairs leading down to an equally beautiful sitting room and study. Windows looked out onto views of rolling hills and green fields with snow-capped mountains rising beyond and the whole suite was tastefully and newly decorated in delicate silvery grey, blue and aqua, priceless antiques juxtaposed with expensive, handmade designer modern furniture. If she was to design an apartment for herself, money no object, then she would probably have designed something very similar to the rooms she now surveyed. But not here. Not in Elsornia, not in a castle and definitely not in rooms located in a tower.

No doubt Tris—or more likely his housekeeper— had thought it was every girl's dream to have a fairy-tale suite of rooms set on two floors in the turret of a medieval castle. But, having spent six long years staring out of the tower windows at Central Park at a world she was not allowed to be part of, Amber knew there was nothing lonelier than a tower.

'That's it!' Amber jumped up and headed to the curved staircase in the corner of her bedroom, which she had been told led up to the large terrace topping the turret. Sure enough, she emerged out onto a spectacular circular paved terrace. A glass roof covered half of the space, chairs and a sofa arranged enticingly beneath, a cosy blanket draped on the back of the sofa. She stepped out onto the exposed stone floor and inhaled the bracing spring air, the breeze refreshing on her skin.

Another deep breath of the clean air helped clear her head and she winced at the thought of how close she had come to a good bout of self-pitying tears. 'No more feeling sorry for yourself, Amber Blakeley. You are no longer a child and you're not a prisoner. You can sulk and feel sorry for yourself and spend the next few weeks feeling unhappy and resentful or you can make the best of it. After all, Tris is right. Like it or not, you were raised to cope with all this. You had eight years of freedom; now it's time to grow up.'

She wandered over to the carved stone balustrade and leaned on it, looking out over the formal palace gardens to the countryside beyond. Shivering, Amber pulled her cashmere cardigan closer around her, eyes blurring with cold as she stared out at the mountains with their promise of escape. It was insane how quickly her life had changed. Less than a week had passed since the meeting in the lawyer's office in France and, instead of interviewing new nannies for the agency as her work calendar said she should be doing, she had flown on a private jet to spend a month in a country she had sworn never to set foot in. Her friends and their partners now all knew her identity and the circumstances that had led to her leaving New York, and they all knew of her pregnancy and what that might mean for Tris and his country.

But throughout the revelations and the confessions and the arrangements she had clung onto one resolution: she wasn't here to rush into a marriage; she was here for a trial before making a decision that would irrevocably bind her life to Tris's and all that came with him. Her hand slipped down to splay over her still flat stomach. Who was she kidding? Their lives were already irrevocably bound. But that didn't have to mean marriage, didn't have to mean spending her life here. There were just too many unknowns.

At least she had ensured the betrothal agreement was nullified *before* she set foot on Elsornian soil. Any future agreement between her and Tris would be their decision to make and theirs only. She had also received a promise that her stay would be both low-key and anonymous; if she didn't marry Tris then there was no reason for anyone outside their immediate circles to know who she was.

One priority was finding out what he wanted to do

JESSICA GILMORE   61

if the baby was a girl. Would he expect her to provide him with a son within the next five years? Her hands tightened on the balustrade. One child, a baby already on the way, was one thing, but planning a second...? Giving him a son would mean a full marriage in every way. And what if the hypothetical second child wasn't a boy either? She might need to give him a third, or even a fourth...

Giggling a little hysterically, she tried to ignore the heat stealing through her body at the thought. '*Making* the babies isn't the issue, is it?' she asked herself aloud, her words falling into the stillness. 'After all, if you weren't attracted to Tris then you wouldn't be in this situation, would you? Although there's a world of difference between having one baby and signing up to be a baby-making machine.'

She giggled again at the image, her smile quickly fading as the reality of what marriage to Tris would mean sank in. Attraction wasn't the problem. She'd felt its exquisite ache in Paris, despite her embarrassment and the awkwardness of the situation. But from the moment Tris had learned her identity he had been all urbane, polished politeness. Gone was the darkly desirable best man who had turned her head and in his place was the perfect Prince. But perfect princes were not the happy-ever-after she had dreamt of.

A chime rang out through the terrace, breaking into her thoughts and, turning, Amber saw a light on an intercom by the terrace door. Amber walked over, hands shaking as she pressed the button. Was it Tris? She wasn't ready for a tête-à-tête. Not yet.

'Hello?' To her relief her voice sounded steady, showing a confidence she certainly didn't feel.

'Hi, Amber. It's Elisabetta—Tristano's sister. Is now a good time? Tell me if not. I promise not to be offended!' Amber sagged against the wall, thankful that not only was her unexpected guest not Tris but by the friendliness in Elisabetta's voice.

'Now is fine. Hold on while I figure out how to buzz you in.' She pressed a green button and heard the unmistakable sound of a door unlocking and, after giving Elisabetta a good few seconds to push the door open, released the button and made her way back down the curving stairs to meet the Elsornian Princess in the sitting room two floors below.

Tris's sister was standing by the window when Amber arrived, but she rushed over to greet Amber with a continental double kiss followed by a hug. An exceptionally pretty girl of around Amber's own age, the Princess had Tris's colouring, her dark hair worn long and loose, grey eyes sparking with a life and mischief her brother rarely displayed as far as Amber could see. Chicly and expensively dressed in a short woollen dress teamed with knee-length leather boots and a scarf knotted with elegant nonchalance, Elisabetta's smile was warm and seemed genuinely friendly and Amber returned it; it was so good to see a friendly face.

'Here you are at last! I've been dying to meet you for ever, although I quite understand why you went MIA. I am fully aware how high-handed Tris and our esteemed uncle were. Betrothal agreements indeed, the idiots. But I am very happy that you have decided to give Tris a second chance—he's not so stuffy when you get to know him. But I guess you know that, or you wouldn't be here.'

Amber had no idea how to respond. She didn't know how much Tris had told his sister about her visit here, if anyone apart from the two of them—and her friends—knew about their pregnancy.

'Hi.' It seemed an inadequate response to the voluble, friendly greeting she had received, but Elisabetta didn't seem to notice.

'So, Tris has asked me to give you a hand until you know your way around a bit more. You have your own assistant, of course—you've met Maria? Good. Maria is fantastic and will be able to help you with anything you need. She grew up here; there's nothing she doesn't know. If you need anything at any time, just ring the bell here.' Elisabetta indicated a rope pull hanging in the corner.

Amber couldn't help raising her eyebrows at the sight. 'An actual bell?'

'Oh, yes, the walls are so thick that even though Tris has tried to modernise the whole castle, it's easier to stick with the old ways. The Wi-Fi is always cutting out unless you are on the ground floor or up on the roof.'

'Maria showed me to my room; she seems very nice and her English is flawless.'

'Her mother is English and she went to London for a couple of years after school so she is pretty much a native speaker. Her grandmother was a lady-in-waiting to *my* grandmother, but in those days the poor girls were expected to be in traditional dress with hair neatly plaited at all times of the day and night. At least there's a night staff nowadays. Some of Tris's reforms are more successful than the Wi-Fi has been.'

Maria's appointment as her assistant might be a coincidence, but Amber couldn't help wondering if Tris had purposely picked a fluent English speaker to help her settle in. 'I hear that Elsornian is a mixture of French, Italian and a sprinkling of German; is that correct?'

Elisabetta nodded. 'You could say that, but it's a little bit more complicated. We have many words unknown in any other dialect or language. But don't worry, most people speak English and really appreciate anyone trying just a few words of Elsornian.'

'Hopefully, I'll pick some up. Luckily, I speak tourist-level French, Italian and German...' actually diplomatic-level, thanks to her grandmother '...and I've picked up a little Armarian over the last year, but I'm no natural linguist. Every word has been learned by repetition and more repetition.'

'Any help you need, just ask either me or Maria,' Elisabetta said. 'And when my sisters are home, I know they'll say the same. The palace can seem a little stuffy, so you'll need as many guides as possible to explain the crazy etiquette, who everyone is and, more importantly, all the secret ways we pretend don't exist. Our ancestors were robber barons, you know, so this place is a smugglers' paradise, even if the contraband is only teenagers breaking curfew nowadays!'

'Thank you.' Amber meant it wholeheartedly; it had been hard enough to wrench herself away from the life she had built for herself, but to leave her friends behind, not knowing if she would return, to consider a move to a new country had been almost more than she could bear. Elisabetta's frank, open friendliness was a balm to her soul. 'In that case, there is something you could help me with. I really want to explore the gardens, but I'm not ready to face anyone yet.' Amber was uncomfortably aware that by anyone she meant Tris. 'Do you think you could introduce me to one of those secret ways you just mentioned?'

Elisabetta's eyes lit up with glee. 'I knew I'd like you! Come on, you won't need a ball of wool when you're with me, but don't try this alone until you're a lot more confident—they say there are miles of hidden tunnels beneath the castle and it's easy to take a wrong turn, believe me. Which way do you want to go first? Wine cellars or stables? You choose. And as we walk you can tell me all about what you've been up to and how Tris persuaded you to give him a try. I promised my sisters I would ferret out all the details and I always keep my word!'

CHAPTER SIX

TRIS EXITED THE courtyard and took a moment to enjoy the late afternoon spring sunshine warming his face. He loved this time of year, when the spring flowers began to bloom in earnest and, despite the April rain and the chill that still came with the night, lighter nights and warmer days banished winter. But his moment of enjoyment was fleeting. He had given Amber several hours to settle in before offering to show her around the castle. However, when he had rapped on her door there had been no answer. A few questions had elicited the information that his sister had gone to introduce herself to his fiancée. Which meant the two women could be anywhere, inside or outside the castle.

Elisabetta knew the castle as well as he did, including every secret way out into the gardens and into the land beyond. After all, they had explored the secret passages and grounds together, along with his other sisters, their cousin Nikolai and the other palace children, before his mother and his sisters had left the castle and Tris had had to start growing up. He had never allowed himself to envy his siblings and other companions for the years of childhood they'd still enjoyed whilst he was learning about tradition, etiquette and what being King really entailed. Never allowed himself to mourn the distance that had naturally grown up between them. His father had told him that a king was always alone. It hadn't taken Tris very long to realise how true those words were. The only time he hadn't felt alone in the twenty years since his mother and sisters had left was the night he'd spent with Amber.

But that night had been a lie. Which meant that while he planned for them to marry within the next few months, live together to raise their child and do their best for the country he had been born to rule, he would still be alone, no matter that his pulse speeded up at the very sight of her, that he wanted to wipe away the forlorn look on her face and promise her that everything would be okay.

It wasn't a promise he was qualified to make; all he could do was his best. Do his best not to make Amber as lonely and unhappy as his mother had been, his best to let their child be a child and not a mini monarch in waiting.

His child. Tris stopped. What kind of father would he be? He had no concept of what a good father looked like. He set his jaw and sent out a silent promise to his unborn child; he didn't know how to let go, how to have fun, how to be anyone but the decisive and responsible King, but his child would be more. Would have a childhood full of love and laughter and fun.

The castle gardens were vast, a perfectly designed jigsaw of formal gardens, careful wildernesses, follies, lakes, mazes and woodlands. A man could wander in them for hours and not find the person he was looking for but there was one place everyone visited: the famed fountains that cascaded down the terrace leading to the lake. It was one of the most famous sites in Elsornia, pictured in a thousand books and millions of social media posts. Sure enough, as he reached the first terrace and looked down towards the lake, Amber was sitting on a bench below, the sun glinting off her red hair.

She looked up as if sensing his presence, gazing directly at him, her expression distant, as if she were only half there. Slowly but purposefully, Tris made his way down the stone steps bordering the fountains to join her.

'So, this is where you slipped off to.'

'I know it's a really obvious place to come,' she said, her welcoming smile mechanical rather than genuine. 'But I've seen this view so many times in pictures and paintings, I simply had to see it myself. It's breathtaking.'

'Which way did Betta bring you?' Tris asked. 'Through the wine cellars, or the tunnels that run behind the stables?'

Amber's smile widened, this time reaching her eyes, and Tris couldn't help responding in kind. 'So you know about those?'

'I know all the tunnels,' he said. 'I spent most of my childhood exploring them.'

Her smile dimmed. 'It's hard to imagine you as a small boy, exploring and getting dirty. I'm glad to know you did though, I'm glad to know it's possible. My grandmother always made it sound as if growing up in a place like this was all responsibility and no fun. I don't want that for my child, no matter what the future holds for him or her.'

'Nor do I, Amber.' Tris shifted round to look her

straight in the eyes, tilting her chin until her green-eyed gaze met his. 'I promise you, I promise the baby, that his or her childhood will be as full of play, magic and mayhem as any child could wish for.'

'Thank you.' Amber reached up and touched his cheek, the light caress burning through him; he could feel her touch long after her hand fell away. 'Your sister was called away, but I wanted to explore a little more. Would you like to join me?'

'Of course.' Tris stood up and extended a hand to Amber and, after a second's hesitation, she took it and allowed him to help her to her feet. 'Where would you like to go?'

'I don't mind. No, actually, I do have a request. I would like you to take me to somewhere that means something to you. Would that be possible?'

'Somewhere that means something?' Had he heard her correctly? He'd been expecting her to suggest the ornamental lake, the maze or the woodland path, or any of the other places on the tourist map.

'Yes.' She took a step away and looked back at him. 'This is where you were born, where you were brought up; I would really like to see somewhere special to you. Would that be okay?'

Tris didn't answer for a long moment. Somewhere special? The request implied an attempt at intimacy, that Amber was trying to get to know him better. Tris didn't even know where to start. His life wasn't about individual special moments or places; it was about duty.

Only, maybe there was one place…

'Are you warm enough? It's about a twenty-minute walk.'

Amber nodded and they set off. Neither spoke for the next few minutes as Tris led them down the stone steps until they reached the large pond at the bottom of the fountains. Amber turned to look at the water cascading down, a riot of froth and foam and sparkling drops, and Tris watched her, enjoying her evident awe at the famous sight, giving her plenty of time to enjoy the spectacle before resuming their walk. A small stream snaked away from the pond carrying the water towards the lake and Tris followed it, Amber by his side.

'How did you find my sister and Maria?' Tris asked at last as the silence threatened to become oppressive.

'They're both really lovely,' Amber said. 'Thank you so much for suggesting that Maria help me; it was really thoughtful to assign me someone who is both Elsornian and English. And your sister has been very kind. I think I'm going to like her a lot.'

'Betta is one of a kind; her heart is very much in the right place. Just don't believe everything she tells you; she is an incorrigible chatterbox. And I'm glad you like Maria. I hope she'll convince you that Elsornia isn't too bad a place to live.'

Tris knew a little about the life Amber had led after leaving New York, the months travelling through Europe before settling in London and painstakingly building her life there. The busy, noisy city had no parallels in his small mountainous country. If it was urban culture and living she craved, she was going to find it hard living here. His mother had struggled, had never really adjusted. He didn't want his own wife to resent his country the way his mother had.

'Oh, I'm sure she will. Even from the very little I've

seen it's clear Elsornia is extraordinarily beautiful. I love London, but I love the countryside too. But Tris, there's something I really need to make clear to you.' She paused, clearly uncomfortable.

Foreboding stole over him. Whatever Amber wanted to say, he had a feeling she didn't think he was going to like it. 'What's that?' He did his best to sound reassuring. 'It's okay, Amber. I really want you to feel that you can speak to me, however difficult it might seem. If we're going to be married we have to be able to communicate.'

'But that's it. I realised after I agreed to come here that you thought that meant I was also agreeing to marry you. But I'm not, at least not yet.'

A curious numbness crept over Tris. Of course it couldn't be this easy. Of course the girl who had looked at him with desire and light and laughter didn't want him when all the baggage that came with him was included. Of course the answer to the dilemmas he had been wrestling with for the last eight years couldn't finally be within his grasp.

'I don't understand,' he said as evenly as possible. 'In Paris, when you told me you were pregnant, you also said you knew this meant you couldn't end the betrothal. I know you are here for a month so we can get to know each other better, but I thought we would announce our engagement at the end of that month.'

'Tris, I *am* here to get to know you better—and I'm here so you can get to know me. And I am absolutely considering marriage—now I understand your situation, I know that's your preference. But Tris, if you didn't have to marry, would it even be an option for you? Honestly? Marrying someone you've met just a handful of times? Having a baby together doesn't mean we have to spend our lives together, not any more. We can easily co-parent, raise this child together; we don't have to be married to do it well. We don't have to be in a relationship at all.'

Amber's words hung in the air. Would marriage to her be his choice without the ticking clock hanging over him? He pushed the thought away—what was the point in hypotheticals?

'How exactly do you see this civilised co-parenting working? You back in London, me here, unless you're planning to settle in Elsornia?'

She shook her head. 'I don't know.'

'I thought not. So are you planning on granting me the odd weekend and a few weeks in the summer? Is that the plan?' Tris struggled to keep his voice conversational, to hide the biting anger chilling through him.

But, judging by the wary look Amber threw him, he wasn't succeeding. 'There is no plan...how can there be? This is all so new and so unexpected. There's no manual, no guidebook.'

'But there is a law and there is a deadline and I've wasted enough time, thanks to you...'

'That agreement had nothing to do with me.' Her green eyes flashed and his own blood stirred in response to her passion. 'I did you the courtesy of nullifying it, but my lawyer agreed the only court it would ever stand up in was here in Elsornia—and even then there were no guarantees.'

'Maybe. But the fact remains you are carrying my child.'

'And you think that means I have to marry you? Like some medieval maiden, compromised and helpless?'

'Amber, you came to my bed willingly. You came to my bed willingly and in full knowledge of who I was and what our relationship was. Knowledge you didn't share with me. If anyone was compromised by the events of that night, it was me.'

'You? You've got exactly what you wanted. An heir on the way and if I marry you a substantial dowry, along with the Princess your family chose for you. It's all worked out for you, hasn't it?'

Tris bit back an angry retort. He knew how she felt, the lack of control, the realisation that life would never be the same—it was the feeling that had forced her to flee eight years ago. He couldn't let her leave again, but he had to allow her to feel she had a say. More, he had to actually give her a say—and ensure, however difficult, that her answer was the one he needed.

'What exactly are you proposing?'

Amber turned to him, eyes bright with hope. 'I'm proposing that you convince me that Elsornia is right for me and, more importantly, right for this child. If we don't marry, he or she can still grow up with two loving parents, can grow up wanted and cherished and happy, free from all the obligations that you and I know come with a royal title. That's all my father wanted for me; of course I want the same for my child. But it's your baby too. So I need you to show me that if I marry you Elsornia is worth all the sacrifices we both know this baby will make. That it's worth the sacrifices I'll make. That I can be happy here and with you. Are you willing to show me that, Tris?'

Tris had been so intent on the conversation that he hadn't noticed how far they had walked and, with a jolt of surprise, realised they had entered the woods and were close to their destination: the large hollow tree where he had played countless games pretending to be one of the fearless folk heroes he had idolised as a child stood right next to them. And as he put a hand onto the rough bark, realisation hit him hard. He wanted his child to play in this tree, in these woods, to grow up with Elsornia in his or her veins and blood, just as it was in his. All he had to do was convince Amber that it was the right place for her, the right place for their child. Convince her to marry him. How hard could it be?

'How long do I have?'

'I agreed to a month and I'll keep my word,' Amber said. 'At the end of the month I'll be fourteen weeks along, and I'll have had the first scan so hopefully we'll know the baby is healthy. You have until then. Show me your Elsornia, show me why you love it and if you can convince me then we'll talk next steps. I know how important marriage is to you, and why. But you have to understand that I always wanted a very different kind of marriage, a very different life. I am willing to put that aside if you convince me that staying here and marrying you is the right thing for me, for the baby and for you. Fair?'

Was it fair? Tris had less than five years to marry and father an heir. The solution to all his problems was tantalisingly in reach and yet frustratingly far away. But he couldn't deny that Amber had a point. She had to come to this marriage willingly. And if he couldn't convince her, what kind of king was he anyway?

He extended a hand and she took it cautiously. 'Okay. You have a deal.'

He wasn't usually a gambling man, certainly not with stakes this high, but he had no choice. He had to win.

CHAPTER SEVEN

'YOU'RE A REAL natural with children,' Tris said. He sat beside Amber in the car as tall, straight-backed and formal as ever, expression neutral and eyes unreadable. But he was trying; she had to give him credit for that. True to his word, Tris was showing her Elsornia. Over the last week Amber had accompanied Tris and Elisabetta on a tour of a chocolate factory and stood unobtrusively in the background on visits to a hospital and schools. They'd taken her to a production at the Theatre Royale, an impressive baroque building in the capital city, and to several fancy restaurants as well as a trip to a glacier.

But she still hadn't seen beneath the tourist-friendly sites and gloss. She hadn't visited small neighbourhood restaurants or strolled along cobbled streets or shopped in little local stores. The only people she spoke to for more than five minutes were Tris, Maria and Elisabetta, who weren't exactly representative of the normal population. She had yet to use public transport, to order her own drink, to ask directions or sit with a coffee and watch the world go by. How could she decide if this was a place where she could live when she was sheltered from the real world?

It had been an entertaining week, but it felt more as if she was on a whirlwind tour—*The Highlights of Elsornia*—rather than beginning to know and understand Tris more. At no point in the last week had she seen any sign of the man who had made her head spin, for whom she had thrown caution to the wind. They were rarely alone, barely even made eye contact and never touched. She'd asked for time and space and she'd got it, but instead of it helping her resolve her feelings she just felt more and more confused with every busy and courteous day.

'I'm really fond of children; I've worked with a lot, especially since working for Deangelo and starting the agency.' Amber looked out of the window at the gorgeous mountain scenery, so different to the Chelsea streets she usually trod, and her chest ached with homesickness—for the city, for her friends, for her work. For the life she had worked so hard for.

She made herself carry on, cringing at the artificial brightness in her voice. 'It's strange to think that we've only really been open for a year. Things have changed so much, not just our personal lives, but for the agency too. When we started I was busy with small concierge jobs, sourcing babysitters, doing a bit of nannying and arranging domestic chores. Alex was pleased to be doing the PR for a couple of local restaurants and Emilia's first event was the opening of the café down the road. Opening a new agency was tough without contacts and a reputation. That's why Harriet went back to work for Deangelo for what was supposed to be a short contract.' She smiled a little wistfully. 'Looking back, I think we all knew that she was in love with him but hadn't admitted it to ourselves. They're so perfect for each other.'

Amber stopped, painfully aware that yet again she was babbling to fill a silence Tris seemed far more comfortable with than she was. At least talking about her friends was a small step up from this morning's small talk attempt, which had incorporated everything from the cuteness of the local Alpine cattle to the excellence of the palace food to that old staple, the weather. It was a lot easier on the days when Elisabetta accompanied them—or when Tris had to work and the two girls went out alone.

They'd decided to tell people that Amber was a friend of Elisabetta, which meant that she would attract minimal attention, although her presence at Laurent and Emilia's wedding alongside Tris had started some low-level speculation. Luckily, any rumours were still confined to Elsornia and hadn't yet reached the royal-gossip-hungry European magazines. Amber hoped it would stay that way; if she and Tris decided against marriage she didn't want anyone to know who she was or guess at the parentage of her child. Tris's involvement meant secrecy wouldn't be easy but, luckily, she was an old hand at staying under the radar.

Another silence fell and Amber resumed her study of the landscape, searching for a new topic of conversation, one that actually would help her understand Tris better. 'The nursery school was so cute; I loved the song they did. Do you spend a lot of time on visits like this?' Amber hadn't imagined him being quite so visible day to day. Her grandmother's preparation for Amber's future royal life, hopefully on the miraculously restored

Belravian throne, had concentrated more on entertaining diplomats and neighbouring royals and less on visiting schools.

'Not a lot, no.' Tris looked regretful. 'Which is a shame because I actually quite enjoy them now. When I was younger I found it a chore to have to try and connect with every single person I met, to shake all those hands and keep smiling so people didn't think I was standoffish. To find things to say that didn't seem stuffy or dull.'

Amber blinked in astonishment. This was probably the most insightful thing Tris had said to her since she had arrived in Elsornia. 'My grandmother insisted I learn how to make small talk; she said it was one of the most invaluable tools in a royal's arsenal. Although, as she spent most of her time interrogating people rather than talking to them, I'm not sure how she knew.'

'My father was more of an interrogator too, which is probably why I found small talk so excruciating. But now my time is so taken up with diplomatic business, politics and negotiation that a day out actually talking to people is a relief. Sometimes visits and openings seem like an indulgence, especially with three sisters who are so popular with the people and who all find it a lot easier than I do, but it's really important that I remember why I do what I do. When I'm in a school, a hospital or retirement home or at a village fair, I can see exactly why it's so important that we have the right deals in place, why I have to spend hours in meetings that seem to have no point. I don't do it for me but for the children who need a solid economy to pay for their schools.'

'I'd never thought about it like that,' Amber confessed. 'My grandmother never really made me see the point of being a princess; it felt like unnecessary rules and restrictions, etiquette for etiquette's sake.'

'There's an element of that, and for a long time I would have put public appearances and visits in that category. Like I said, it was a chore. Something I had to do because, rightly or wrongly, it makes people feel special when someone from my family visits their place of work or their home town or village. Also, it brings attention. If any of my sisters are photographed at a museum, gallery or a nature reserve then the footfall for that place instantly doubles. We know that our attention has an economic benefit. We can't ignore that, just because we might want to stay home and relax.'

'What? You never get to chill out? In that case I'm definitely not staying.'

'Never officially.' For the first time Tris's smile looked both easy and genuine and Amber's heart gave a small traitorous leap. She mentally scolded it and kept her attention on the conversation at hand.

'Okay. It's time to confess—what do you do when you relax? What's your comfort watch of choice? It's been a long day, it's raining outside, you've put on…' Amber had been about to say PJs but thought better of it; this conversation might be flowing easier than usual and she and Tris might have managed to achieve a truce over the last week, but she wasn't ready to talk nightwear with him yet, especially when even the word PJs made her remember in such vivid detail the night when he hadn't bothered with any nightwear at all '…casual clothing,' she managed lamely. 'You're curled up on the sofa, phone set to silent, the remote in your hand. What do you watch? And what do you eat while watching it?'

'I…' Tris looked genuinely discomfited. 'My phone is switched off?'

'On silent,' she corrected him. 'My imagination isn't strong enough to imagine you without a phone or two.' Tris seemed to carry at least three phones at all times, all switched on, all checked regularly and all needing constant attention.

'Usually one of my sisters would choose,' he prevaricated, and Amber shook her head mock sternly.

'That's cheating and you know it. Go on, are you a sci-fi movie franchise man? Must-see dramas? Or do you prefer an epic fantasy series, complete with battles for the throne and dragons? Or is it a little bit too close to home?'

'Honestly? No drama or fantasy series has anything on my ancestors,' he said. 'Remind me to take you to the portrait gallery soon; there's more betrayal, treason, adultery and murder in one room than all of Shakespeare's plays.'

'From what I can tell, my ancestors were pretty bloodthirsty too,' she confessed. 'I don't think my many times great-grandfather got to be King because of his diplomatic skills; I think he hacked his way to the throne. Not that I know much; my grandmother wasn't interested in any of the really fascinating history. She was more concerned with the wrongs done to us during the revolution. But, to be honest, I don't think I blame the populace for getting rid of us. Sounds to me like we were a fairly shady lot, looting half the country's wealth as we left, for instance.'

'Your dowry?'

'My dowry.' She sighed. 'You know, when I left New York I felt completely free for the first time in so many years. I didn't feel guilty about not letting my grandmother know where I was because I never felt like she ever cared for me, just what I represented. I was always flawed, a disappointment. I still don't feel guilty. But I've never felt comfortable about that money. It doesn't really belong to us, does it? I'd like to give it back, only my grandmother still has it and will have until I marry, I guess.' She managed to refrain from adding *If I marry*, but the words hung there.

'You're of age now; it belongs to you and you can do anything you like with it, including giving it back. The only problem is, Belravia doesn't exist any more. It's been carved up and absorbed into at least three countries.'

It belonged to her? It had never occurred to Amber that once she'd turned twenty-one she would legally have charge of the famed Belravian fortune. 'So I just keep it? I couldn't—it doesn't seem right.'

'I'm not saying keep it, but how you'd go about restoring it when Belravia no longer exists I'm not sure. If you'd like, I can do some investigating. There might be some charities or hospitals in the old Belravian towns and cities where the money could be distributed. Or you could set up a charitable foundation; a lot of your people dispersed during the revolution and people continue to be dispersed from their countries today and need a lot of financial aid; that might be a fitting use for it.' He paused then turned to look at her, sincerity in his face and voice. 'Amber, it's important that you know that your dowry was never part of my motivation back then. Although I am sure my uncle thought differently.'

Amber stared at Tris in some confusion, her thoughts in tumult. She'd been so used to thinking of her dowry and the betrothal as one, it was odd to have to disentangle them—and to absolve Tris of being only interested in her money. Plus the insight he showed in thinking of ways she could use her fortune was illuminating, his insightful solutions for a problem that occasionally kept her awake at night. Whether she married him or not, she knew it was finally time to face her grandmother, reclaim the money and do something good with it.

'Thank you. I'd really appreciate your help and advice. It's too important a job to get wrong and I don't really know where to start.'

'You're not even slightly tempted to keep it, to keep any of it?'

Amber shook her head. She might be confused about many things at the moment, but she'd always known that the fabled fortune wasn't hers morally, even if the law said differently. 'No, I know my dad always intended to return it somehow, but his father was still alive then—he didn't die until a few months after my parents' accident—and so he hadn't figured out what to do with it yet.' She stopped, remembering the austere, autocratic old man who'd barely spoken to her in those long, lonely first few months in New York. Maybe he'd been grieving his son; she'd never know. She did know that neither he nor his wife had treated her own grief with any consideration or empathy.

She pushed the memories away and tried to lighten the mood. 'However, I am tempted to see what it's like when you relax. You still haven't answered my question. Is it shameful? You don't have to worry. I'm not going to judge you.'

'Okay then.' Tris's expression was as unreadable as ever. 'Why don't you come over tonight to my rooms for dinner and a movie?'

Go over to his rooms? Amber hadn't been invited into Tris's quarters since she'd been at the castle, nor had she attempted to go there. The invitation was a definite step in the right direction. Nerves fluttered in her stomach. Every small step brought her closer to a decision, closer to deciding the course her life would take.

'Okay, then.' Amber tried her best to look as inscrutable as Tris. 'You choose the movie and I'll bring popcorn.'

She sat back and stared out of the windows again. This was her chance to find out something real about Tris. To discover who he was when he wasn't the perfect prince, the consummate host or the seductive dance partner. It was a lot to ask of dinner and a movie, but right now she would take whatever insight into Tris she could get. Time was ticking away and she was as far from a decision as she had been the day she arrived. Something had to change and maybe, just maybe, tonight was the night.

CHAPTER EIGHT

'THIS SHIRT? OR this one?' Tris held up first a blue and then a grey shirt and looked hopefully at his sister.

'I thought this was supposed to be a relaxing evening.' Elisabetta raised a knowing eyebrow. 'Box sets and chill? We all know what *that* means. About time, big brother, about time.'

'I barely know her,' Tris protested, trying not to think about how in some ways he knew Amber very well indeed. He knew how silky her skin was beneath his fingertips, he knew the taste of her, the way she gasped, the way her eyes fluttered half shut and she lost herself in sensation. He knew all that and yet in many ways he didn't know her at all.

'Those shirts make you look a little...' Elisabetta put her head to one side and studied him '... stuffy.'

'Stuffy?' Tris regarded the shirts in consternation. They were handmade linen shirts. 'What on earth is wrong with them?'

'You're supposed to be sitting on the sofa, sharing pizza and watching a film. Don't you think you should be in something a little more casual?'

'More casual?' These were casual. They were open-necked and short-sleeved; he'd never wear them in public. 'Like silk pyjamas and some kind of smoking jacket?'

'I was thinking about jeans and a T-shirt,' Elisabetta said. 'But if you want to scare the girl off then go with silk pyjamas.' She studied him, eyes narrowed. 'This means a lot to you, doesn't it? Do you like her?'

Tris refused to meet her gaze. 'She's very pleasant.'

'It's okay; you're allowed to like her, you know. Don't take our parents' marriage as a template; most people *want* to be with the person they marry.' She wandered over to the window and said with studied nonchalance, 'I was talking to Mama earlier; she sends her love. I didn't mention Amber, but I know how relieved she would be to know she was here and that you might be marrying soon. Why don't you take Amber to visit her? Mama would like that.'

'If she wants to know anything about me then she is always welcome here,' he said gruffly. His mother hadn't set foot in Elsornia since the day after his father's funeral and Tris had neither time nor inclination to assuage her conscience by visiting her. He knew the distance between them upset his sisters, but it wasn't of his making, His mother's rooms were always ready if she should change her mind.

Elisabetta didn't answer but he could feel her disappointment as she sighed and looked out of the window.

'What film shall I choose?' The question was a way of changing the subject and it worked as she turned immediately, rolling her eyes in exasperation.

'How can you be so bad at this?'

'Because I've been engaged for eight years with no actual fiancée to spend time with?'

'And because, between Father and our uncle, you've been brought up to be a cross between a monk and a robot? But I know you dated before the betrothal and I know you've had a few *friendships* in the last four years. It's not as if you've never spent time alone with a woman before.'

Tris compressed his mouth grimly. There were many things he and his sisters never discussed—their parents' separation and their mother's decision to leave Tris with his father; the countdown to Tris's thirty-fifth birthday; their father's autocratic ways—and they certainly never discussed the few relationships Tris had had after they'd learned that Amber wasn't studying but had disappeared without a trace.

His partners had been carefully chosen for their discretion: an old friend hopelessly in love with another man, a widow who had no intention of remarrying, a friend of Elisabetta's who was training to be a doctor and had no time for a serious relationship. Trustworthy women who didn't want a long-term love affair, didn't mind secrecy and who would never go to the press. Each affair had lasted for just a few months, ending by mutual agreement when the secrecy became too oppressive. Tris wasn't proud of these relationships, but neither was he ashamed. They'd been necessary, brief interludes of humanity in his duty filled life. If at some level he'd felt that something was missing, he'd pushed that feeling away. He knew that in his world it was all too rare to find true understanding in friendship or relationships. Far better to keep expectations simple than hope for too much and be disappointed.

'I'm sorry,' Elisabetta said, walking over to give him a hug. 'I know being yourself isn't easy for you. But that's all you need to do. I promise, just let Amber get to know you, Tris, let her see the man we see.'

Tris hugged her back, but it was already too late. He had shown Amber his true self and it had made him vulnerable. He had no intention of being vulnerable in front of her again. He needed her and she knew it. He wanted marriage and to be a father to their child all the time, not just on weekends and the occasional holiday. But that was it; he didn't need her to understand him or to see inside his soul.

It was far safer if she didn't.

An hour and two changes of clothes later, Tris was beginning to wish he'd never *heard* the word relax. He'd ordered two pizzas and a salad from the palace kitchen and they sat in a small kitchenette he barely used, ready to be heated up. Elderflower *pressé* cooled in the fridge alongside non-alcoholic beer and sparkling water.

'Get hold of yourself, Tris,' he told himself aloud, pacing over to the open French windows that led out onto his terrace. 'It's just dinner and a film—how hard can it be?'

He turned at the sound of a gentle rap at his door. Opening it, he saw Amber standing there, wearing light blue trousers in some kind of silky material teamed with a creamy-coloured T-shirt and a large white cardigan which she held wrapped about her as if it was armour.

'Hi,' she said.

'Come in.'

She stepped inside, her posture wary, and looked around. 'This is lovely,' she said but her voice sounded carefully neutral. Tris looked at his rooms and tried to see the familiar furniture and decor through her eyes.

His suite of rooms were on the first floor, looking out over the front of the castle, and the large sitting room doubled as an informal receiving room. White walls topped with intricate gilt coving and lined with valuable landscapes of the Elsornian countryside were matched by a polished wooden floor and a selection of antique furniture. Everything in the room was made in Elsornia, the only personal touch a photo of his three sisters on one of the bookshelves. His study was furnished in a similar fashion; his bedroom likewise. His sisters were always trying to persuade him to redecorate, but Tris didn't see the point. He was the Crown Prince, and no amount of wallpaper, photos or cushions would change that.

'Make yourself comfortable,' he said and, with a slightly doubtful look, Amber perched on the nearest brocade sofa.

'This is very…erm…firm.' She wriggled as if trying to get comfortable. True, the sofa wasn't very comfortable. None of the furniture was, but Tris had got used to it. It wasn't as if he spent much time relaxing anyway. In fact, he spent very little time in his rooms, apart from his study, at all.

'Would you like a drink?'

'Thank you, that would be lovely.'

Tris busied himself with getting them both drinks and checked that Amber was happy with the pizzas he had selected before giving her a quick guided tour of his rooms. She seemed interested and asked several questions, but her gaze was a little puzzled and she glanced at Tris several times as if considering saying something. It wasn't until he showed her out to the terrace that ran the full length of his rooms that her smile seemed to become more genuine. She walked from one end to the other, pausing to admire the plants and potted trees that turned the austere stone space into a green paradise, stopping by the telescope set up at the far corner. Reaching out one hand, she touched the telescope lightly and Tris wondered if she, like him, was thinking about the evening he'd shown her the stars. 'So, this is where you spend most of your time when you're alone?'

'I suppose it is.' Tris had never really thought about it before, but she was right. 'How can you tell?'

She shrugged. 'It just seems a little bit more like you, I suppose. Your rooms are lovely, but they're a little impersonal. I could be walking through any show room in any stately home. But out here? This doesn't look like it's been put together out of the Palaces-R-Us catalogue. It looks like someone has curated it with love and care.'

For a moment Tris was so taken aback he didn't know how to respond, and Amber covered her mouth, eyes huge with embarrassment. 'I am so sorry...' she began but Tris interrupted her.

'I moved into these rooms when I was sixteen,' he said. 'My uncle arranged for them to be prepared for me in what he deemed to be the most appropriate style, and I've never got around to changing them; there doesn't seem to be much point. I don't spend much time here anyway. But the terrace is different, I designed it myself and this is where I come when I need to think, to remind myself that the world is bigger than this castle and my responsibilities.' He stopped, a little embarrassed by how much he'd given away.

Amber nodded. 'That makes sense. I couldn't quite believe it when I stepped in…the difference between your rooms and the ones I've been given…mine are so beautiful and so individual.'

'You can thank Elisabetta for that. I asked her to make them as welcoming as she could. I tried to tell her a little bit about you so that you felt at home; I hope I got it right.'

'They're perfect,' she said softly. Amber looked up at him, confusion, doubt and something that looked a little like hope mingling in her eyes. Tris wanted to reach out and touch, to run his finger down her cheek, to bend his head to hers to taste her once again. He wanted to pull her into his arms, to run his hands through her glorious mass of hair, to slide his hands down to her waist, to touch her silky skin, as he had dreamt of every night over the last few weeks. If he did, he was almost sure that she wouldn't push him away; he could almost taste the anticipation in the air.

For all the awkward silences, for all the ways they danced around each other, trying to work out just how much they would need to give and take in any future relationship, for all they avoided any conversation about the night they'd spent together, barely even mentioning her pregnancy even though it was the reason she was here, attraction still hummed in the air between them. Almost visible, tangible, audible it surrounded him every time she was near. And by the way she was so careful not to touch him, the way she sometimes slid a glance his way, Tris knew she felt it, saw it, heard it too.

Kissing Amber, reminding her of that physical attraction, reminding her of how good they were together in one way at least, would give him a shortcut to the marriage he needed. But he'd never been a man for shortcuts; he needed Amber to agree to stay because she wanted to, not because she had to. That ill-judged betrothal needed to be wiped out of history. Seducing her into a decision would be almost as bad as coercing her through a legal document she had had no say in. It almost physically hurt to step back, to keep his polite mask in place, but Tris was used to doing things the hard way.

'I don't know about you,' he said as smoothly and unemotionally as possible, doing his best to pretend the moment that had flared up between them had never happened, 'but I'm hungry. Let's go in and I'll heat up the pizzas. There is a selection of films lined up; you choose.' Tris didn't know if the disappointed glance she sent his way was because Amber had thought he had been about to kiss her or because he was ducking out of their agreement by giving her the choice of film but, either way, this choice was right, safe. And Tris always did the right thing, no matter the personal cost.

CHAPTER NINE

FEELING SLIGHTLY RIDICULOUS, Amber tiptoed along the corridor, unable to stop herself glancing over her shoulder—although whether she was checking for flesh and blood or ghostly watchers, she wasn't sure. What she was sure of was that there was nothing quite as eerie as a seemingly deserted castle at night.

The dimly lit, thickly carpeted corridor which led from her turret into the main part of the castle eventually gave straight onto the grand main staircase which descended majestically into the huge receiving hall at the front of the castle. But somewhere before there was a discreet door which opened into the passages and stairs the servants used to move around the castle relatively unseen. She had had a full tour the day after she'd arrived but there were so many twists, turns, rooms leading into each other, hidden doors and staircases that she wasn't entirely sure which piece of panelling was the door she needed, and which was a secret way into a bedroom or receiving room; the castle was riddled with secret connecting doors and passages, most of them used either for smugglers or affairs. Tris was right; his ancestors were a scandalous lot.

Pausing beside an engraved panel, Amber could see the tell-tale break in the carving that indicated a door. But was it the right door? More by luck than judgement she selected the right door first time and found herself descending the back stairs leading to the kitchen areas. She'd only had a whistle-stop tour of the palace kitchens, which were ruled over by the kind of temperamental French chef she'd thought only existed in films and who even confident, vivacious Elisabetta regarded with wary respect.

Once down in the airy basement that housed the service apartments and rooms, Amber found she remembered the way to the kitchen easily. Pushing the heavy door a little nervously, she peeped into the simply lit room, her heart jolting with relief when she saw it was both empty and tidied up and cleaned ready for the next day. She stepped in, closing the door softly behind her, and looked around the huge room, with its stainless steel worktops, saucepans hanging from racks and range ovens. It was almost impossible to believe that next door there was an even bigger kitchen used for state occasions and this gleaming, gadget-filled professional room was used just for day-to-day catering.

Tiptoeing over to the light switches, Amber put on the spotlights which illuminated the side benches, holding her breath in case she triggered some kind of alarm, but the only sound was that of her own wildly beating heart roaring in her ears. The night staff had an office at the other end of the basement with another small kitchen for late night orders. She should be able to use this kitchen completely undisturbed.

Fifteen minutes later Amber had filled the worktop

in front of her with a selection of eggs, flour, sugar, flavourings and a whole host of bowls, baking tins and wooden spoons. The terrifyingly technical oven nearest her was finally switched on after several false starts, and she had started to mix ingredients together for a simple sponge cake, propping her tablet in front of her and logging into her video chat, hoping that one of her friends might also be finding it hard to sleep.

Amber preferred to cream the butter and sugar by hand, the repetitive exercise giving her the brain space she needed. As she started to turn two separate substances into one she recapped the evening she'd just spent with Tris in excruciating detail. There was so much to unpick she didn't quite know where to start. The shock of his impersonal rooms followed by the relief when she'd stepped onto the terrace and seen the beautiful outside space he'd created. The moment by the telescope when he'd looked at her in exactly the same way he'd looked at her at the wedding, all heat and want. With that one look turning her bones molten, her body limp with need. Only for him to turn away as if it had never happened.

She mixed harder, mind ruthlessly marching on to the disappointment flooding her when he'd left it to her to select the film as if he couldn't share even his cultural taste with her. Choosing a three-hour Jane Austen adaptation was maybe cheap revenge, but he deserved it.

Was it too soon to give up? He was trying, she knew that, probably as much as he was able, but she could not live the rest of her life in bland companionship, no matter how luxurious the surroundings. Her unhappiest years had been spent in the lap of luxury.

The sugar and butter were creamed at last, so smooth a paste it was almost impossible to imagine that just ten minutes ago they had been separate substances. Picking up the first egg, Amber amused herself by cracking it on the side of the bowl and letting the contents slide into the bowl one-handed. She picked up the second egg and at that moment an alert from her tablet showed her Harriet was trying to call. For one moment she considered not answering, despite her earlier need to speak to her friends, unsure what to say and how much to give away. But her need for companionship was greater than her desire for secrecy and she accepted the call.

'Harriet! How lovely to hear from you.' Amber hoped her cheery smile and tone would be enough to fool her friend that all was fine. She should have known better. Harriet narrowed her eyes.

'You're baking?' Harriet said it in the same way that she might have said *You're drinking* or *You're weeping on a sofa watching a sad film*. 'What time is it there?'

'Not yet midnight,' Amber said airily, mixing in the eggs as if making a cake in a castle kitchen at midnight was a completely normal thing to do. 'Why, what time is it where you are? Actually, where are you?' Since Harriet had got engaged to Deangelo she spent a lot of time travelling around the world with him.

'I'm in New York,' Harriet said. 'I've been catching up with the company Alex worked with at Christmas and my report will be with you all at the end of the week, but right now I'm sitting in a hotel room waiting for my fiancé to finish *his* business and to take me out for dinner. Amber, what's going on? You only midnight bake when you're stressed.'

'I'm not stressed,' protested Amber, sieving in the flour and folding it a little more vigorously than usual. Harriet didn't reply, her silence all too effective, and Amber rolled her eyes in the direction of the tablet. 'Okay, okay, maybe I'm a little stressed. Did I tell you that Tris put me in a freaking tower? Like I'm some helpless princess and now he's impregnated me he's ready to save me.'

'To be fair, it's not as if he knew you were a princess when he impregnated you,' Harriet said, a smile twitching her mouth. 'None of us did.'

'I was talking about a metaphorical princess,' Amber said with as much dignity as she could as the flour flew into the air under her less than tender care and coated her nose and top. 'Dammit, look at the mess I'm making. Besides, I'm not here because I'm a princess, and I'm definitely not here to be saved. I'm here because I'm pregnant and I promised myself to give Tris a chance to show me I could be happy here. Happy with him.'

'And how is that going for you? Or does the large amount of flour currently decorating your face tell me everything I need to know?'

'The pregnancy? I feel surprisingly well, not so tired and I haven't been sick once. It's easy to forget I'm pregnant at all and then I wonder what on earth I'm doing here. I guess that will change next week; I'm flying home for the first scan. Harriet, will you be around? I really don't want to go on my own. Part of me wonders if I'm going to get there and the doctor is going to tell me I'm crazy and there's no baby; I'd like someone else to prove it's real.'

Amber paused. Despite all the problems the pregnancy was causing her, the question marks over her future, she couldn't help but be thrilled at the thought of a baby. Her baby. Her own family for the first time in more years than she cared to remember. No, she reminded herself as she looked at Harriet. She did have a family, one born of love and respect and friendship. Their marriages would inevitably change that, especially as they would no longer live together, but they wouldn't change those bonds. No matter what happened, the baby had three readymade aunts and godmothers ready to love him or her.

'Of course I'll be there if you want me. But Amber, shouldn't Tris be with you?'

Shaking her head, Amber dislodged flour, sending even more to the floor. 'We're still keeping the pregnancy and, more importantly, Tris's involvement, a secret for now. To be honest, if we don't get married, I'd really like to keep it a secret for as long as possible, until the baby is an adult at least. Growing up with that kind of interest and publicity is not ideal, to put it mildly. Nor is growing up with a meaningless title healthy either. I should know; I crossed an ocean to escape mine.'

'I thought it was your grandmother you wanted to leave behind, not the title. After all, if you know it's meaningless, then what does it matter?'

'It matters because I'm here. Do you think if I was just some random bridesmaid Tris had got pregnant I'd be living in the castle being prepped for Queen? No way—they'd be paying me off quicker than you could say *royal emergency.*'

'Do you really think that?' Harriet shook her head, her eyes warm with understanding. 'I think you're there because Tris wants you there, because he wants to be part of the baby's life and part of your life.'

'Harriet, he barely speaks to me. There is no trace of the man I met at the wedding, at least barely any trace. I can't see beneath the surface; he won't let me in.'

'Why is that, do you think?'

Amber huffed a little as she started to prepare the ingredients for shortbread biscuits. She couldn't just stand here and chat while her cakes cooked; she had to stay busy. Maybe pastry after this, puff or filo—something tricky which needed a lot of physical work. 'He thinks I lied to him that night.'

'And did you?'

'No! I mean, he didn't ask me, did he? At no point did he say, *Excuse me, are you the long-lost Belravian Princess who I managed to get engaged to without once asking her if it was what she wanted?*' Amber could hear the bitterness in her voice and concentrated on beating the butter as hard as she could.

'Be careful with that butter, Amber, or it will have you up for assault. Okay, he didn't ask you and he didn't recognise you, so why does he think you lied?'

'He thinks I lied by omission.' Amber put the bowl down and faced the screen—and her friend. 'In some ways, I guess I did. Obviously, I knew who he was, but I had no idea he still considered himself betrothed to me. If I had, I wouldn't have danced with him, I wouldn't have slept with him. I wouldn't have complicated things so badly.'

Harriet's nod was full of understanding. After all, she and Deangelo had had to find their way from desire towards love. 'Amber, tell me to mind my own business, but *why* did you sleep with him? Knowing who he was, knowing he is the reason you left your grandmother's house before graduating. I'm not judging,' she added hastily as Amber picked the bowl back up.

The heat in Amber's face had nothing to do with the vigorous beating of butter and the newly added sugar and everything to do with embarrassment. Harriet had just said what they were all thinking, herself too, no doubt Tris as well. What *had* she been thinking?

'At first I was terrified he would recognise me and, although there's no way anyone could make me go back to my grandmother or force me into marriage, for a few moments I was a terrified schoolgirl again, hearing her future planned out for her with no say and no way out except to run. When I realised he had no idea who I was, I was curious I suppose, curious how my life might have turned out if I hadn't had the strength to disappear. And—' the heat of her face intensified '—the truth is, when I was a teenager I had a huge crush on him, although he looked at me as if I was nothing more exciting than a cockroach. When it became clear he was attracted to me it went to my head. I felt powerful after all those years of feeling powerless. It was more intoxicating than the champagne. He wanted me not because I was a princess and a means to a throne and a fortune, but me, Amber Blakeley, and that night it seemed like I could see into his soul.'

She stopped, unable to believe the words that had just spilled out of her, unable to believe their truth, but when she finally got the courage to look at Harriet she didn't see surprise or condemnation, but understanding—and confirmation—as if Harriet had suspected how Amber felt all along. But how could she when Amber herself hadn't known?

'I came here because I thought there was a connection,' she said quietly. 'But I was wrong. I didn't see into his soul. I just fancied him, that was all. I made a huge mistake, and now I don't know what to do for the best. Apart from bake.'

Tris paused at the closed kitchen door, unsure whether to open it or not. When he'd received the call telling him that Amber had been in the kitchen for almost an hour he had immediately got dressed and left his apartments to come and find her. It wasn't that he was worried she was hurt but he had noticed a curiously blank look in her eyes when she had left earlier. He had failed her. He was fully aware of that.

Tapping lightly on the door, he waited for an answer and, when none was forthcoming, he carefully turned the handle and pushed the door open just a fraction. His immediate attention was caught by the mass of bowls, cutlery and baking paraphernalia on the worktop opposite, only for the whole scene to fade as he heard Amber speak.

'I just fancied him, that was all. I made a huge mistake, and now I don't know what to do for the best.'

Something brittle, something in the region of his heart, twisted and cracked. She had made a mistake, of course she had. One of the things he respected about Amber was her refreshing honesty when it came to his title and position. The knowledge that she'd chosen him not because of what he was but because of who he was. But she'd chosen him for one night only, not for a lifetime, and now she realised that the night they had shared was a mistake. Carefully, silently he closed the door and took a step back.

He should turn around, go back to his apartments, the soulless, lifeless apartments Amber had been so unimpressed by earlier, go back to bed and forget he had overheard anything. Tomorrow they could resume their slow, stately, courteous courtship and he could rely on Amber's upbringing and sense of fairness to make up for his inability to woo her. To let her in. That was the safest option, the option that gave him the best chance at his desired outcome.

He inhaled slowly.

His desired outcome, the right outcome, was a sensible marriage where both parties knew exactly what they wanted from the union. A marriage giving him the son he needed and a consort willing and capable to put Elsornia first. Even if Amber hadn't been his betrothed, wasn't raised for a situation such as this, she would still be suitable. She was warm, approachable, hard-working with an innate sense of responsibility. And she was carrying his child. What else did he need? He certainly didn't need to remember the night when her smile was full of promise, her eyes full of stars, and she made him feel like a man, not a prince. And that was an outcome best achieved by pretending he had seen and heard nothing.

But the desolate ring in her voice echoed through him. He had let her down tonight, withheld himself, just as he withheld himself from everyone, even his sisters. It was safer that way. A king was always alone; his father had taught him well. But he wasn't King yet, just a prince, and without Amber and the child she carried maybe he never would be.

Without stopping to think, Tris reached for the door handle again and this time made a show of fumbling as he turned it, making plenty of noise as he pushed the door open. Amber turned, surprise mingling with guilt on her face as she closed her tablet. Dressed in pyjama bottoms, a soft cashmere hoodie, with her hair scraped off her face, no make-up and a liberal dusting of flour over her hair, cheeks and front she looked more like the teenager he had first met than the desirable bridesmaid or the elegant companion of the last week. The girl he owed a duty of care to, a girl he had let down.

'Tris! What are you doing here?'

Tris thought quickly. He didn't want Amber to feel that she was under surveillance or that she couldn't wander wherever she wished. 'I wanted a snack.'

'A snack?' One arched eyebrow indicated her disbelief. 'Isn't there an army of night staff ready to bring you whatever you need?'

'A snack and a stroll,' he amended, his urbane smile daring her to question his word. 'I thought it might help me sleep. But the real question is, what are you doing?'

'What do you think I'm doing?' Her words and tone were sassy, but her expression was anxious and still a little guilty. 'I'm baking. Can't you tell?'

Even without the flour and all the ingredients and bowls scattered around, the enticing aroma wafting from the oven would have been a gigantic clue. 'Something gave me that impression, I'm more interested in why. You often bake at midnight?'

'I wouldn't go so far as to say often, but it's not unusual. I bake when I need to think. Like you and astronomy, I suppose.'

With an effort, Tris didn't react to her words. He shouldn't be surprised at her deduction. After all, not only had she seen the telescope on his balcony, but he had used the stars to seduce her. He just hadn't realised that she'd understood that astronomy wasn't just a hobby but a way of centring himself. A way of reminding himself that the universe was bigger than one almost-king and his small, beloved and all-consuming country.

'What are you making?'

'Nothing at all complicated, just a plain sponge and some shortbread. But I was thinking of making pastry or something with dough. My mind is still not settled; I need something more absorbing.'

'A cake seems pretty complicated to me,' Tris said and was rewarded with a genuine if pitying smile.

'It's just mixing things together in the right quantities in the right order, nothing complicated about that. It's no different to making little cakes or tarts as a child.'

'Is that what you did? Is that how you learned to bake?'

Amber looked surprised. 'Of course, didn't you?'

Tris picked up an egg. 'Baking isn't really part of a king's curriculum.'

'No, but you must have at least made little fairy cakes, rubbery and almost inedible but your parents had to eat them anyway?'

Tris tried to imagine his austere, remote father sampling any cooking his children brought him, but his imagination failed him. 'The girls may have, but I doubt it. I don't remember my mother ever setting foot in the

kitchen. Of course they spent most of their time with
her when she moved out of the castle and into the lakeside villa. It's possible they baked then, but not here.
We were never encouraged to hang around the kitchens here.'

'It's never too late to learn.' Amber handed him a
bowl and Tris automatically took it, placing the egg
carefully inside. 'What do you want to bake? I'll show
you.'

'What, now? It's after midnight.'

'Why not? Have you got anything better to do?'

Tris automatically opened his mouth to say of course
he had something better to do, but then he looked over at
Amber, her hair beginning to fall out of its messy bun,
tendrils framing her heart-shaped face, hope in her large
green eyes. He'd been unable to let her in earlier, hadn't
known how to do anything but keep her at arm's length,
but maybe he could—maybe he should—try harder.

'I guess not. Okay, I'm all yours.'

CHAPTER TEN

AMBER STARED AT TRIS, her mouth dry. She hadn't really expected him to agree. The thought of the usually immaculate Tris in an apron, hands covered in flour, was so incongruous her mind couldn't conjure up an image.

'Great.' Incongruous or not, this was an opportunity she couldn't throw away. Wasn't she down here, baking furiously and complaining to Harriet, because Tris was resolutely keeping her at arm's length?

'Great,' Tris repeated. 'What do I do first?'

Amber eyed Tris assessingly. He was still wearing the beautiful grey shirt and well cut tailored trousers he'd been wearing earlier. For a prince the outfit might count as casual but in an already flour-filled kitchen he was dangerously overdressed.

'An apron might be a good start. There're a couple hanging up over there.'

The beep of the timer interrupted her, and Amber busied herself with taking the cakes out of the oven and replacing them with the shortbread before turning to Tris.

'Where shall we start? Cake, cookies, pies, bread—or would you like to go straight for the jugular and have a go at a soufflé?'

'Tempting as a soufflé sounds, I think I'll stick with something simple for now.'

'That sounds like a good plan.' Amber tried to ignore noticing just how close Tris was standing, tried to ignore his distinctly masculine scent, the way his proximity made the hairs on her wrists rise and her pulse beat just a little faster. 'A simple loaf cake. There are some lemons over there; how do you feel about lemon drizzle?'

'I'm not sure I've ever tried lemon drizzle, but I'm willing to give it a go.'

'You've never tried lemon drizzle? How is that even possible? It's a good thing I came along.' She paused. 'But if I'm going to teach you to bake, I need something in return.'

'That seems fair. Name your price.'

'Have you never read a fairy tale? You should never just invite anyone to name their price. What if I asked for your soul, or your firstborn child...?' Her voice trailed off, aware that his firstborn child was indeed in her possession. She rallied. 'Don't worry, I'm not going to ask for anything lasting. But in return for the lesson I'm going to ask you a question and you are going to promise to tell me the truth as best you can.'

Tris didn't respond for a long moment, his smile still in place but his expression the shuttered one she was beginning to know all too well.

'I did tell you to name your price, didn't I? Okay, ask away.'

Amber fumbled for a glass of water, her throat suddenly dry. This was it, this was what she'd been wanting. The opportunity to get to know the real Tris, not the public persona he presented.

'First things first, you need to get your ingredients together. Right, I hope you've got a good memory. You want two hundred and twenty-five grams of butter…' She reeled off a long list of ingredients and first steps. 'Got all that? I'm going to put my favourite recipe on the tablet for you to follow, but yell with any questions. Okay?'

'Yes, chef.' Tris gave a cheeky grin and half salute as he started to gather all the ingredients she'd specified together on the workbench next to hers and she couldn't help but return his smile, warmed by his informality— and the ridiculousness of the starched white apron covering his shirt and trousers.

Humming to herself, Amber started to tidy up and prepare the things she needed to sandwich the cake she'd already made while supervising Tris and thinking about what to ask him. She felt like a princess in a fairy tale with only three chances to get her questions right before he disappeared in a wisp of smoke, leaving her no further forward than she was right now.

'My mother was a doctor.' Amber hadn't meant to say that; she hadn't meant to talk about herself at all. But now she'd started it felt easier than simply interrogating Tris. She needed to learn about him, but maybe he needed to learn about her as well. 'That's how she met my dad. He fell off his bike and she was the surgeon who operated on his knee. I don't think marriage or kids were really on her radar at all. I remember her telling me that as a scientist she absolutely didn't believe in love at first sight, but when she did her rounds to check on Dad after his operation she could barely concentrate on her notes. Of course, ethically, she couldn't do anything about it, but luckily Dad felt the same way and once he was discharged he came back with a thank you card and asked her out. They got married a year later and I showed up a year after that.'

She stared down at her hands, her eyes blurring as she remembered her sweet, slightly eccentric parents. 'Dad was in his forties, Mum almost there. I think it was a shock to both of them, becoming parents. They were both so dedicated to their jobs, but I always felt loved and wanted. That made it easier later, after they died. Anyway, my mum loved to bake. It was how she de-stressed. One of my earliest memories is being given pastry to play with at the table while she made pies. As you can imagine, my grandmother did *not* encourage the habit; baking is very much something that servants did. But her cook used to teach me secretly, as did my favourite doorman's wife on the rare occasions I could sneak away. I'm not sure I could have survived that penthouse if I couldn't bake.'

Amber couldn't believe she had just blurted out so much. But when she looked up at Tris she saw his gaze fastened on hers, empathy warming his grey eyes. 'Your parents sound lovely,' he said softly, and she nodded, her heart and throat too full to speak. 'It must have been really tough for you when they died.'

'It was.' Amber laid the back of her hand onto one of the sponges, relieved that it was cool enough for her to start whipping the cream. She couldn't just stand here blethering on about a past she never really spoke to any-one about. But she also wanted honesty from Tris, and that meant being honest in return. 'I was devastated. Even if my grandparents had been different, I would still have found the whole situation inconceivably difficult. Maybe, in a way, the sheer surrealism of what happened next shielded me from the worst of my grief. My life changed so absolutely that I think I was numb for many, many months. Moving from a small village where I was just Amber Blakeley, normal middle-class girl living a normal middle-class life, to New York, where I was Vasilisa Kireyev, Crown Princess of Belravia and heir to a vast fortune, would have been the most discombobulating thing ever, even if I hadn't been dealing with my parents' deaths.'

Amber swallowed and concentrated on the cream so she didn't have to look at the pity on Tris's face. She'd never really talked about the car accident that had stolen her parents from her. Her grandparents must have grieved in their own way, but Amber had never been encouraged to discuss her feelings or offered counselling. One of the hardest things about opening the Pandora's box that contained her past was realising how much she still had to come to terms with the loss.

'My grandfather died just a few months after I moved to New York and so it was just my grandmother and me. It was hard. She was hard. Leaving the house my parents bought when I was a baby, all my memories, was bad enough, but the sheltered existence she insisted on… I felt like I was imprisoned in that tower. My grandmother would never let me out unaccompanied, wouldn't allow me to select my friends or my hobbies. I used to stand at the window and stare out at Central Park, at the joggers and the dog walkers and the kids and wish that someone would rescue me.'

Amber could feel her cheeks heating; there was no

way she was letting Tris know that the first time she'd seen him she'd cast him in the role of knight in shining armour. She'd spent way too many long, lonely evenings conjuring up tales of rescue, some actually including Tris on a white horse. She busied herself ladling cream into a bowl and fetching the jam. Anything not to look at him.

'Did you know your grandmother well? Before you went to live with her?'

Amber shook her head. 'I'd met her twice, I think. She never came to the house and we never visited her in New York but once or twice she came to London and we met her for dinner in whichever fancy hotel she was gracing with her royal presence. My grandfather never accompanied her. Truth is, my dad barely ever mentioned the whole royal thing. He changed his name when he went to boarding school in his teens as a security measure, but liked being plain Stephen Blakeley so much he just stayed as him; he said he was really proud of his doctor title because he'd earned it with his PhD, but a royal title just meant his ancestor had been more of a thug than the next man.' She managed a smile. 'Anyway, I didn't mean to bore you with the life and times of Amber Blakeley; I was clumsily trying to tell you why baking is important to me. It's not just the creative part of it or the fact that I really, really like cake, but it's tied into the happiest memories of my childhood.'

While Amber spoke, Tris had been busy following the instructions she had brought up for him on her tablet. It was oddly soothing combining the ingredients, seeing all the disparate parts turn into a creamy whole.

Meanwhile, with practised ease, Amber was whipping cream, smoothing jam onto a cake and removing tantalisingly aromatic biscuits from the oven, her every move graceful as if she were in a well-known dance, one whose steps he could barely comprehend. He was glad of something to do with his hands and something to focus on completely as she completely un-self-pityingly laid bare the reality of her childhood. It must have been much harder for her, those long lonely teenage years, after knowing such warmth and happiness, than it had been for him, raised solely for duty and responsibility.

'Okay, let me take a look,' Amber said, coming to stand next to him. She smelt of vanilla and sugar and warmth. How did she have so much light and optimism after so much darkness? 'That's not bad at all. Now, pour it into the tin and smooth out the top and then you can pop it into the oven. A loaf cake takes about forty minutes to bake, so we'll have to think of something else to make while we are waiting. Something quick or we'll be here all night and I want to tidy up and hide all evidence long before the kitchen staff turn up.'

'Or we could eat some of that amazing-looking cake instead,' Tris suggested.

'We could. Of course, for that I need a cup of tea. You can take the girl out of England, but you can't stop her craving her daily cuppa.'

Five minutes later Amber had managed to find a brand of tea she was happy with and made herself a large cup, Tris opting for a glass of wine instead. Two generous slices of the cake she'd made lay on plates before them as they perched on stools side by side. He couldn't remember when he'd last had such an informal meal, even when it was a simple snack. Even the pizza he had painstakingly heated up earlier had been served on a table, already laid with silverware and linen.

Amber took a sip of her tea and then took an audible breath, as if trying to find the courage to speak. 'Thank you for listening just now. I've never actually said any of that to anybody before. Not even to myself really. At the time it was all too much and afterwards I was just so relieved to be away. In a funny way, I should thank you for that as well. I mean I always meant to leave as soon as I'd graduated from high school, but you gave me the impetus to start living my own life the way I wanted to.'

'And was it? The life you wanted?'

Amber forked a portion of cake, looking thoughtful as she did so. 'It wasn't the life I planned,' she said at last. 'I had wanted to study history like my dad. Maybe even become an academic like him. But actually I loved being a concierge, I loved working for Deangelo and setting up the agency was just so exciting and empowering; it felt like I was in the right place at the right time doing the right thing for me.'

Tris laid down his fork. All that had changed thanks to him. Amber was no longer in the right place for her, even if she was exactly where he needed her to be. Victory tasted bitter, no matter how delicious the cake.

But Amber didn't look bitter; instead she leaned back on her stool and pointed her fork at him. 'You know, this whole baking experience was meant to be a chance for me to ask you some questions and instead all I've done is talk about myself. That's partly my fault, but don't think I haven't noticed you encouraging me to carry on. You don't get away with it that easily, Your Royal Highness.'

Tris sipped his wine and tried to look as nonchalant as Amber did. 'I was just showing an interest in everything you said,' he protested. 'Ask away. I've got nothing to hide.'

Her snort was frankly disbelieving. 'In that case, tell me your favourite film.'

Tris took another sip of his wine and another mouthful of cake, barely tasting it. Of course she wasn't going to let that one lie and why should she? He knew she'd noticed his earlier evasion. 'I don't really have a favourite film,' he confessed and watched her eyebrows shoot up in surprise.

'Everybody has a favourite film. Or at least several films they'd find it really hard to decide between; is that what you mean?'

'Not really.' Tris broke off a piece of cake and crumbled it with his fork. 'I just haven't seen a lot of films. I attend premieres on the rare occasion Elsornia hosts them but settling down and watching one isn't something I do for fun.'

'More of a box set guy? We always have a box set or two on the go at the house. Usually some kind of reality guilty pleasure for when we're all exhausted and a dark, twisty detective series for the rare occasions when we are alert.'

'Actually, I don't really watch much TV at all. I don't read fiction either or listen to much music.' He might as well pre-empt the inevitable next questions before Amber asked him to name his favourite song or book.

'Not into culture?' Amber's eagerness had faded,

her body language on high alert as she imperceptibly leaned away from him. 'Not everyone is, I suppose.' But her voice was full of doubt.

'It's not so much that I'm not into it; it's more that I don't really know what I like. Taking time out to read, to listen to music or to watch TV wasn't really encouraged. My father thought activities should be improving. Obviously, a good history documentary or non-fiction book would be tolerated, a visit to the royal box to watch opera or ballet or even live theatre was work and therefore acceptable, but that was it.'

'But your sisters... I was talking to Elisabetta about a show we both liked just yesterday.'

'It was different for my sisters; they lived with my mother, whereas I was brought up here with my father and tutor. My father took my training very seriously; that's why he didn't send me to school and wanted to make sure I used every hour wisely.' Tris deliberately took a large gulp of wine and pushed his plate away. Amber had been so candid with him earlier, had even confessed that she had told him things she'd never told anyone else before, and her trust in him was the greatest gift he'd ever been given. But he didn't know how to return it, didn't know how to put into words how it had been, growing up here on his own with the weight of expectation crushing him, feeling guilty for missing his mother and sisters, guilty for resenting his father and the regime imposed on him.

He started as Amber laid a warm hand on his, her touch shooting through him. 'Tris, you've been an adult for a long time now; your father died a decade ago. Haven't you ever been tempted to do things another way? To veg out and binge on a box set or a really good book?'

'Tempted? Of course, all the time. But my father was right; there's always too much to do to relax. Duty comes first. Besides—' honesty compelled him to continue '—like I said earlier, I don't know where to start. Even if I had the time, I wouldn't know what to choose.' Tris stopped, embarrassed. Not knowing was weakness and weakness was intolerable in a king. He didn't want to look at Amber and see pity in her face.

Amber jumped to her feet and gathered up the plates and her cup. 'I can see I'm going to have my work cut out,' she said. 'Not only am I going to have to teach you to bake, but I'm going to have to teach you to relax as well. I'm going to need to up my rates. My agency is very expensive, you know, and right now you're getting a lot of hours.'

'Oh, I know how to relax,' Tris said, and Amber laughed.

'You're going to have to prove that to me, I'm afraid.' She smiled over at him and their eyes held. Despite, or maybe because of, the lateness of the hour, the confidences shared, Tris could feel his pulse begin to race, the blood rushing around his body heightening every nerve, every sinew, every muscle. He couldn't take his gaze off Amber as her smile wavered and disappeared as she visibly swallowed. He'd desired the elegant bridesmaid in her silk and jewels, but he wanted this tousled, flour-spattered baking goddess so much more. She wasn't an illusion, a dream, a siren ready to seduce and be seduced, but so real she made his heart and body ache, thrilling and terrifying in equal measure.

Slowly, purposefully, Tris got to his feet, the invisible thread connecting their gazes, their bodies, tightening. 'I can absolutely prove it to you. Any time.' He took a step closer and then another as Amber stood still, as if paralysed. There was no champagne to fuel him, no violins serenading them, no stars to witness, just two of them in the dimly lit kitchen, the scent of vanilla and lemon and sugar permeating the air.

All Tris knew was that he had mishandled the situation from the moment he'd set foot in the lawyer's office in Paris. He'd allowed hurt and anger to guide him, keeping Amber at a dignified arm's length, too proud to woo her. He'd blamed her for deceiving him without ever considering her reasons. He shouldn't have had to listen to her starkly told tale of loneliness to trust her. He'd been in the wrong all those years ago and he was in the wrong now. Elisabetta was right; if he wasn't careful, he was going to give Amber every reason to walk away, taking their child with her.

It wasn't just anger and wounded dignity that had made him keep Amber at a distance. The Tris who danced and flirted and seduced wasn't the Tris who worked so tirelessly and endlessly to keep Elsornia healthy and profitable. He barely recognised the man he'd been that night—and that was the man Amber had chosen. Not the workaholic prince who never even took time out to watch a film and couldn't name his favourite song. How could he compete with the fairy tale he'd pretended to be? But how could he not? Not just because he needed Amber to want to stay, but because he needed her. All of her.

Tris pushed away the warning voice reminding him

just how badly this could go, pushed away the memories of his mother's unhappiness as his father put duty before their marriage and her needs time and time again. His father had done his best to make him in his image and mostly he'd succeeded, but couldn't Tris do better here? With Amber staring at him, eyes wide, full mouth parted, sweet, beguiling and so beautiful she took his breath away, he had no choice but to try.

Slowly, slowly he sauntered across the floor towards her. Amber made no move to meet him but neither did she retreat. She simply stood stock-still, luminous green eyes fixed on him, her full mouth half parted, her chest rising and falling. Tris stopped still a pace away and held out his hand. There could be no seduction, no coercion, no expectation. No champagne or stars or beguiling words, but a meeting of equals.

Amber didn't move for several long, long seconds and then finally, just as Tris was beginning to wonder if he had imagined the whole connection between them, she took his hand and half stepped a little closer. Neither spoke, fingers entwined as Tris reached out and drew a finger down her cheek, lingering slightly on her lips before skimming down the long column of her neck, finally resting on her shoulder. She barely moved as he touched her, just an almost imperceptible tremble, her eyes half closing. One more step and she was snug against him, her breasts soft against his chest, long firm legs pressed to his, the warmth of her hair on his cheek.

'I've been thinking about kissing you again ever since I woke up the morning after the wedding,' Tris said hoarsely.

'In that case you should go ahead.' Amber smiled

up at him as she spoke, her shy yet teasing smile full of promise and anticipation. Heat flooded him. She wanted him, physically at least, and that was far more than he deserved. But only a fool would turn down such an invitation. Slowly, savouring every millisecond, Tris ran his hand along her shoulder, cupping the glorious weight of her hair as he reached the tender skin at the nape of her neck before dipping his head to cover her mouth with his.

Last time they had both been too impatient. The moment they'd kissed had been incendiary, sending them both into a dizzying spiral straight into his bed. Despite the insistent demands of his body, Tris had no intention of taking Amber back to his room tonight. Nor, tempting as it was, was he planning to seduce her in the palace kitchens. This kiss wasn't about seduction but about wooing and so he started slow, nibbling her lower lip, holding her gently as if she were made of porcelain. It was almost more than he could bear, the slow, sweet kiss, harder than anything he'd ever done before as he gently but firmly stopped Amber from speeding things up, holding her lightly, not allowing himself to explore her curves even as she pressed against him. He was playing a long game here, not looking for the easy victory, and so he allowed himself to savour every moment of the kiss, to take in every detail, the fresh floral scent of her hair, her sweet vanilla taste, part-cake part-her, the warmth of her touch, the way her fingers entwined in his, caressing and holding, the softness of her mouth, a mouth made for kissing and being kissed. He needed to savour and remember, imprinting every touch and sensation in his memory.

It was a long time since Tris had believed that his future held anything but duty and responsibility. But standing here, the most beautiful and beguiling woman he'd ever met in his arms, he knew that he had a chance at something more. His future was in her hands. As, he suspected, was his heart.

CHAPTER ELEVEN

AMBER COULD TELL that it was late when she woke the next morning, the angle of the sun slanting into her bedroom a tell-tale clue. She stretched, savouring the sweetness that came from a good night's sleep. It had been late, very late, when she'd finally got to bed. She and Tris had done their best to return the kitchen to the spotless state she'd found it in, hiding every trace of their night-time antics. Baking always made her feel better but for once it wasn't the soothing action of creating that had enabled her to fall into the deep sleep she needed, but those minutes, those wonderful, frustrating, unforgettable moments she'd spent in Tris's arms.

What on earth had happened? One moment she'd been telling Harriet that she had made a terrible mistake, allowing a teenage crush and a night's illusion to give her false hope that she might forge a lasting relationship with Tris, the next she'd found herself confiding in him in a way she'd confided in nobody, not even her friends. Not only that, but he had started to let her in, not all the way, but she understood him a lot more than she had this time yesterday.

And then there were the kisses. Just as intoxicating

as she remembered, turning her body limp with desire, her brain to a single-minded entity wanting nothing more than him. She'd yearned for far more than sweet, chaste kisses but this morning she was grateful for Tris's restraint. Their situation was complicated enough without adding sex into it. Of course, some might point out that that particular horse had already bolted but it wasn't the physical consequences of lovemaking that concerned her; it was the emotional ones. Not that she'd been thinking so clearly last night. If the timer hadn't gone off when it had, Amber wasn't sure Tris would have managed to stay so restrained either…

But a proper conversation and a few kisses didn't solve anything. Yes, she felt a little closer to Tris, but whether that closeness would still exist in the morning light she had yet to find out. One thing she knew: she couldn't leave her future in either Tris's or fate's hands; it was time to take some control of her destiny. No more waiting around for Tris to talk to her or let her in; she was ready to start battering down the drawbridge if that was what she had to do.

Reluctantly, Amber pushed back the sheets and swung her feet to the floor. She wasn't going to solve anything or change anything lying in bed, nor was she going to get where she needed to be living in a luxurious apartment two staircases and three corridors away from Tris, surrounded by servants and aides and soldiers.

Pulling on her robe, she padded upstairs to her turret-top terrace, texting Tris as she did so, rewarded five minutes later when he walked in carrying a tray heaped with fresh fruit, coffee and still warm pastries.

'Good morning,' he said and then looked at the sun. 'Or should I say good afternoon?'

Amber was acutely aware that she was still in her pyjamas and robe, her hair barely brushed, her face make-up-free, although she had managed to clean her teeth. But she wanted intimacy and there was nothing as intimate as breakfast. 'Don't tell me you've been up for hours?'

'Since six,' he said and laughed as she pulled a horrified face.

'That's less than four hours sleep; you'd better sit down and have a pastry. As you may have realised last night, I'm a firm believer that food solves everything, even if you don't make it yourself.'

'Yes, last night was very informative.'

Amber felt her cheeks heat at the unexpectedly teasing tone in Tris's voice. 'I'm glad you thought so.' She managed to keep her own tone light. 'I'm planning a repeat as soon as possible. You made a very creditable cake; more lessons are definitely in order.'

'With a teacher like you, how can I fail to improve?'

Amber was fully aware that Tris wasn't really talking about baking. 'I don't know; it seems to me that you weren't quite as inexperienced as I thought.'

This was definite progress, sitting here in the late spring sunshine enjoying brunch together, the conversation easy yet intimate with a subtext only they understood, but there was still a long way to go. Tris hadn't touched her since he'd arrived, let alone kissed her; there was still a distance between them, physically and mentally. Amber's parents had touched all the time, little caresses and pats, careless kisses dropped on cheeks and foreheads, hands reaching for each other automatically. She hadn't realised as a child how rare that casual intimacy was between married couples; it was something she'd always expected to experience herself one day. Now, even though she knew it was rare, she still yearned for a marriage as complete as her parents' had been.

Maybe it was unfair to expect that kind of relationship from a man who had had a very different kind of childhood. But last night there had been glimpses of another Tris, of the man she had danced and laughed and made love with just a few weeks ago.

She sipped her coffee and summoned up her courage. 'I have a request.'

'Anything.'

'I thought we discussed the folly of making unlimited promises last night. What if I asked for half the kingdom or insisted you only served pink food? Although you might find either of those requests a little easier to agree to.'

'Intriguing.' But Tris looked more wary than intrigued.

'I'd like you to take a vacation. A fortnight somewhere here in Elsornia that you really love. Not the castle, not surrounded by servants and guards and bureaucrats and people needing you every second of the day, but somewhere where we can just be ourselves. Somewhere I don't have to sneak into the kitchen to bake if I don't want to be surrounded by sous chefs trying to anticipate my every need.'

Tris put down his coffee, his forehead creased. 'Amber, I understand, I really do, but it's not that easy for me to just take time off.'

She held up her hand to forestall the inevitable reasons why. 'I don't mean today. This time next week I'm flying to London for a couple of days to have my twelve-week scan. I don't expect you to come with me; in fact it's easier if you don't, not until we have a better idea of our future. All it needs is one picture leaked to the press of you and me near a maternity unit and our secret is out.'

'That makes sense,' Tris agreed, but he was wearing the shuttered look that frustrated her so much, hiding his real thoughts and emotions from her.

With a deep breath, Amber continued. 'Normally, if this scan is okay, which, fingers crossed it is, I wouldn't need to have another one until about twenty weeks. But if you want I could book a private scan for sixteen weeks. That's a good time to find out the sex of the baby with some accuracy. I do understand how important having a son is to you. If the baby is a girl…'

'If the baby is a girl I still want to marry you.' Tris's jaw was set, his grey eyes dark with an emotion she couldn't identify. She tightened her hold on her cup, wishing the coffee had the kick of caffeine she needed to help sharpen her mind. Did he mean that? Or was he saying what he thought she wanted to hear? But through the doubt there was a tinge of relief—she would rather wait to find out the sex of the baby. She'd always imagined having a family of her own and, so far, none of this pregnancy had borne any resemblance to those dreams. It would be lovely to keep an element of surprise and anticipation, no matter what happened.

Choosing her words carefully, she looked over at him. 'I appreciate you saying that, I really do, but surely if we know the baby's a girl it would simplify things somewhat? I know co-parenting without marriage will be tricky for you, with the eyes of the world on you the way they are. And I'm fully aware of how difficult life will be for the illegitimate daughter of the King, if her parentage was known. But it would be just as difficult if she was brought up with parents who marry for the wrong reasons. I'm not willing to sacrifice all our happiness for a throne, Tris. I know your parents weren't happy; surely you don't want to repeat that history with your own children?'

'I promise to do all that is in my power to make you happy,' Tris said stiffly and Amber raised her hand and laid it upon his cheek.

'I know, and I also know that I can't rely on you or anyone for my happiness, that I have to take responsibility for myself. But marriage does need two people's focus to make it work, even ones with a much more auspicious start than ours, and my worry is how much of that focus will be actually in your power and how much you will sacrifice to duty. How much *we* will have to sacrifice to duty. So please, when I get back from London, let's spend time alone, just the two of us, and decide if this is something that we can both not just live with, but *want* to live with.'

Tris reached up and covered her hand with his. 'Let me see what I can do; maybe two weeks isn't impossible if I move some things around.'

Amber squeezed his hand in relief. 'Thank you, Tris. I know I'm not the only one trying to work out the right thing to do here. I do appreciate everything you're trying to do, I really do.' She turned her hand and threaded her fingers through his, his clasp warm and strong and comforting.

Amber had no doubt that Tris would try his hardest to be supportive and to make her feel that she belonged in his world. She also suspected that he was beginning to care for her, Amber Blakeley, not just the mother of his unborn baby. But was that enough? Once they were safely married, once the baby was here, would duty dominate his life as it had done in the past, leaving her just a few scraps of his attention? Amber didn't need a man to dance attendance on her all the time, but neither did she want the kind of marriage where she felt she'd be better off alone. She'd seen what was possible in a partnership of equals; could she really settle for less? But sitting here, her hand in Tris's, the sun warm upon her face, she had hope for the first time in months that things might just work out the way she hoped.

Tris stood in the small private courtyard and watched the car containing Amber, and with her all his hopes, disappear out of the discreet side entrance. In less than an hour she would be on a private flight back to London, not returning for a couple of days. If at all. There was nothing compelling her to come back, just her promise.

'You should have gone with her,' Elisabetta said softly, coming to stand beside him. 'That's your baby too. Or she could have had the scan here.' Tris had finally, with Amber's permission, told his sister about the pregnancy the day before, upon the promise of the utmost secrecy. She'd been delighted, if more than a little confused. No wonder when she'd seen the awkwardness between them, the constrained silences as they sought to understand the other better, although the week since his bakery lesson—and the kisses they had shared—had been different. There had been no repeat of the kisses or of the lesson, but there had been an ease which was as welcome as it was new.

'There's no way we could keep the pregnancy private if she had the scan here, you know that. And she wanted to be in London, with her friends. They mean a lot to her, they're her family.' Tris completely understood Amber's reasoning, the common sense part of him agreed with her, but there was another part of him that wished she wanted him there; he couldn't imagine how it would feel to see a glimpse of the baby for the first time, for them to experience that moment together.

Elisabetta shot him a quick glance. 'You're her family too. No matter what happens next, being parents will bind you.'

'Like it bound our parents?' Tris said more bitterly than he meant to, and his sister looped her arm through his.

'No, because you are better than that. Our father failed when he tried to turn you into a carbon copy of him, thank goodness, and Amber has more optimism, more independence than Mama ever did. She'll find her path no matter what—her life so far is proof of that. Leaving New York with less than a thousand dollars in her pocket at just eighteen to start a new life in a new country? That takes a lot of grit, Tris.'

'She should never have had to leave like that. I should never have agreed to our uncle's proposal. But I knew it was what Father would have wanted. Pathetic, isn't it, trying to make a dead man happy? Especially as I never really managed it when he was alive.'

'He was proud of you, Tris, I genuinely believe that; he just had no idea how to show it. You were a good son, just like you are a good brother and I know you will be a wonderful father.'

Tris didn't answer, his eyes still fixed on the spot where the car had disappeared. *A father.* It was strange, but he hadn't really thought about what that meant before. Oh, he had thought about the throne and cementing his position as King, thought about marriage to the woman who had eluded him for so long, but not about the reality of what being a father meant. Not about an actual baby who would need to be cared for, held and rocked and changed and fed. A small child who would need to be played with and taught right from wrong. An older child with opinions and likes different to his own. A combination of Amber and him, maybe with her hair and his eyes, her smile and exuberant sweetness or his diffidence and reserve. Excitement and panic filled him in equal measure. There was so much at stake, so much scope to get things wrong. How did anyone feel fit to embark on parenthood, with all its mishaps and pitfalls?

'How do you know that?' He turned to face his sister. 'What if I get it wrong? I'm too strict? Always too busy? Expect too much? Show my disappointment?'

What if he or she doesn't love me?

He couldn't say the last words but Elisabetta must have sensed them because she wrapped her arms around him in a brief hug before stepping back with a warm smile.

'The very fact you are asking these questions shows

what a wonderful father you'll be. I bet our father never once doubted himself, never once wondered if he was making a mistake. Keep wondering, Tris, keep questioning, keep listening—and, most importantly, keep loving and you will do just fine.'

Keep loving.

It sounded so easy, but Tris knew how hard that could be—and knew how dark the consequences of a loveless childhood could be. Things would be different, he vowed. Whatever Amber decided, he would love their baby, make sure it knew how much it was wanted, how special it was. No matter what.

CHAPTER TWELVE

TRIS'S HANDS TIGHTENED on the steering wheel as he navigated his car around a tight bend. On one side a sheer wall of rock rose dizzyingly into the heights above them, on the other an even more sheer drop fell straight into the valley below. This drive was not for the faint-hearted, but Amber didn't seem afraid; she'd wound the window down and the wind ruffled her hair as she looked out at the countryside spread before her.

This was the wilder, more remote side of Elsornia, an area where few foreign tourists ventured, where villages were few and far between and sheep and goats outnumbered people. Down in the valley the forests spread as far as the eye could see, although Tris knew that another bend in the road would reveal the lake that was their destination.

It was years since he'd last driven along this road, years since he'd been to the villa his mother had retreated to as her marriage broke down, to raise his sisters. He knew the price of that separation was leaving him behind; knowing he'd have chosen to stay didn't make the pain of that choice any easier to forget.

His grip tightened further. Not for the first time, he

questioned his decision to bring Amber to the place which provoked such conflicting feelings in him. But he'd prevaricated enough. Amber needed to know more of him, and the villa by the lake was the only place he had ever allowed himself to feel free. As soon as she'd asked him to take her somewhere special, he'd known this was the only possible destination.

Tris glanced quickly at Amber as she leaned into the breeze, her gaze still fixed on the distant horizon. 'You're sure you're not queasy?'

Despite his attempt to remain nonchalant, a thrill ran through him as he awaited her answer. She looked exactly the same, not an ounce heavier yet, but everything had changed nonetheless. She'd barely greeted him at the private airfield before she handed him a small, fuzzy black and white photo of something that looked like a cross between an alien and a tadpole. Their baby. Staring down at the indistinct image, Tris had experienced emotion like he'd never felt before, pure, overwhelming and all-encompassing, a knowledge that he'd do anything, sacrifice everything to keep this tiny, vulnerable hope and the woman who bore it safe.

'I'm fine,' Amber said, leaning back in her seat. 'I'm officially past the first three months now so hopefully I've avoided all queasiness. Apparently this is when I get lots of energy.'

Tris couldn't stop the wry smile curling his mouth. 'So the last few weeks you've been lacking in energy? Was that when you insisted on learning that country dance at the school, or was it when you walked up to the glacier and refused the lift back down? You *did* look weary when we finally finished washing up after your mammoth baking session, but you are the one who thought eleven p.m. was a good time to start making cakes.'

'Any time is a good time for baking,' Amber said with dignity. 'Have I taught you nothing?'

Tris didn't reply, the next hairpin bend needing all his concentration, but despite the difficult roads he was aware that for the first time in a really long time he was actually relaxed. More than that, he was happy. Waiting at the airfield, he'd been fully prepared for the news that Amber had changed her mind, that she'd decided to stay in London and continue her pregnancy there. But it hadn't just been relief he'd felt when he saw her disembark from the plane; it had been joy. Not because of the child she carried, but because she'd returned. Returned to give him a second chance. He couldn't— mustn't—blow it.

He'd missed her while she'd been away. Missed the way she hummed as she busied herself, her bright, cheery conversation. Missed the way she drew him out, until he found himself opening up, surprising himself. Somehow, over the last two weeks, she'd got under his skin. Tris had no idea what that meant for their future, but he knew he had to do his utmost to make sure the next two weeks were everything she needed to make a decision to stay.

'Do you mind if I put some music on?' Without waiting for his assent, Amber pulled out her phone and connected it to the car's Bluetooth. 'I'd ask you what you wanted, but after the other night I realised that you need a little bit of educating. A lot of educating if I want to be brutally honest rather than diplomatic. Baking obviously, films absolutely, books without a doubt and, most importantly of all, music. Music is good for the soul whether it's classical, pop, reggae or R&B, so I put together a playlist. It's a little eclectic, but I wanted to cover as many bases as possible. Okay, your education starts here…'

The sound of a piano filled the car, soon joined by a soaring soprano voice, followed by a thumping dance track and then an upbeat musical number. Amber hadn't been kidding when she said her playlist was eclectic, but Tris didn't care what the music was. He was just absurdly touched that in the short time she'd been away she'd spent thought and effort putting together a playlist just for him.

In no time at all they started the descent down the mountain to the huge lake which made this part of Elsornia a popular holiday destination. One or two villages turned into fashionable resorts during the summer months, with swimming areas and plentiful berths for boats along the shoreline, but most of it remained unspoilt.

When Tris was small, the lake had been the royal family's favourite summer vacation spot, but after his mother moved permanently to their holiday home his father stayed away, allowing Tris just a month there every summer. He'd worked hard not to envy his sisters growing up in the relative freedom of the countryside, away from castle politics and the prying eyes of the media, spending their term times at boarding school and the holidays with their mother, but there had been times when the contrast between their carefree childhood and his own was too stark and he hadn't returned here since his mother had left, ten years before.

'This is absolutely gorgeous.' Amber stared out of the window like a child looking for the sea. 'The lake is so blue. I don't think I've ever seen water that colour before.'

'Legend says it's so blue because when Hera found out about Zeus's affair with Europa she flew off in anger until she reached this valley. The trees sheltered her from the other gods' view and so she allowed her tears of humiliation and rage and sadness to flow. Of course, Zeus was known for his affairs and there were a lot of tears when she started to shed them. So many that she flooded half the valley with her melancholy.'

'I can't decide if that's a beautiful tale or just a really sad one,' Amber said. 'I suppose creating a lake was a better thing to do than torturing some poor girl who had no choice once Zeus had decided to turn into a ball or a swan or shower of gold, whatever shenanigans he decided upon that time. I always thought it really unfair that the goddesses went around punishing the poor women when it was the gods who did the preying.'

'You know your mythology.'

'I can thank my dad for that; he loved Greek myths. He used to read them to me every night. The children's version at first, then his favourite translations of Ovid, the *Iliad*, the *Odyssey*. We were about to move on to the *Aeneid* when he died. I've still never read it; I didn't have the heart somehow. Maybe one day I'll read it to our baby.' Her voice was wistful, and she blinked a couple of times before turning back to look out of the window.

Tris wanted to say something comforting, something

wise, but couldn't find the words so he drove instead,
after a while humming along a little to the music until
Amber laughed at his attempts to follow the tune. In
no time at all they were on the lakeside road leading
to the villa. It was all so achingly familiar. Trees lined
the road on one side, the lake glinted in the late spring
sun on the other. A few boats bobbed up and down on
the water, birds circling overhead, occasionally diving
into the blue depths and emerging triumphantly, something silver glittering in their beaks.

Amber was transfixed. 'Can you swim in the lake?'

'You can, but it's fed from the mountains so only
the hardiest souls venture in before the summer. And
it's never exactly warm even then, but the outside temperature can get so hot that no one cares.'

'I love to wild swim,' Amber said dreamily. 'Sometimes in London I go to the pond on Hampstead Heath
or the Serpentine Lido but it's not the same as really wild
swimming. I'd like to come back here when it's warm
enough.' Her words warmed him. In spite of the memories the lake held, maybe because of them, Tris had
known it was the right place to bring her. The right place
to see if the liking and understanding so slowly growing
between them could become something more permanent.

They drove on through several villages, the first two
full of second homes owned by wealthy Elsornian families, filled with fashionable restaurants and bistros and
plenty of expensive shops. The next village along was
less well-to-do but a great deal more charming with its
neighbourhood cafés and small *tavernas*. Amber exclaimed in delight as they passed through it, proclaiming
her intention to return and sample cakes from the bakery

on the high street. As they drove out, the road began to snake away from the lakeside, skirting round a tall metal fence. A few hundred yards later Tris turned in at a pair of huge iron gates which swung open at his approach.

'I know you asked for us to spend time alone,' he said as he eased the car along the driveway. 'I can't quite give you that, but I can promise you no officials or secretaries or aides. We employ several local people here—gardeners, maids, people to look after the villa—but they live out. There will always be a handful of bodyguards around, I couldn't lose those if I tried, but they're trained to be discreet. You shouldn't even notice they are here.'

'Thank you,' Amber said. She touched his arm, the ease of the gesture warming him through. 'I really appreciate all the effort you've gone to.'

Just a few moments later they were inside the pretty white villa. It was a complete contrast to the thick-walled stone medieval castle where Tris had been brought up and now lived. Built on graceful Italianate lines, the rooms were light-filled and airy, tiled floors and high ceilings offering respite from the hot summers, whilst large stoves in every room ensured warmth in the brief but cold winter months. Elegantly furnished in shades of blue, it was an inviting space, enhanced by breathtaking views from the floor-to-ceiling windows which ran along the whole back wall of the house, looking out onto the lake.

'Privacy glass and bullet-proof,' Tris informed Amber as she exclaimed in delight. 'The royal guard had a fit when we first started coming here; they said that anyone could just zoom in from the lake.'

'They have a point, I suppose.' Amber stared out at the lake. 'Is it likely?'

'I doubt it. A large area of the lake is a no-go zone and anyone who enters it is immediately accosted. Guards are stationed at checkpoints whenever the family is resident and there's a panic room in the basement, so don't worry. The truth is Elsornia has always been fairly stable; even at the end of the nineteenth century when most small kingdoms were hotbeds of revolutionaries, we only had a few half-hearted attempts. From what I can tell, our firebrands were more interested in cryptic passwords and hosting meetings than actually overthrowing the government. We managed to ride out the period between the Wars and post-war turbulence with nothing more than some fiery speeches and the odd badly attended parade.'

'I don't know much about when my family left Belravia,' Amber said, turning away from the window and walking over to look at a landscape on the wall, 'but it must have been terrifying. My grandfather was only a tiny baby and he had to be smuggled out—they would have shot him if they'd found him. I've never understood why he was so keen to go back after that experience.'

'If he hadn't left then he would have had to go when the Soviets moved in. All that area became part of the Soviet Union. I think your father was very sensible, moving on the way he did.'

'Wise and more than a little relieved. He hated bureaucracy and meetings. I think he'd have been a terrible king, found it all too tedious.' She looked at him curiously. 'Are you ever bored?'

The obvious automatic reply was a quick negative.

Of course he wasn't bored. How could he be? After all, it was a huge privilege to serve his country; his father had impressed that on him every day. But sometimes, sitting in yet another long meeting or budget discussion or on yet another formal visit, Tris had been aware that something was missing. Over the last few weeks he had started to realise just what that something might be: companionship, laughter, maybe even love. 'It's not something I let myself think about,' he said honestly.

'Everyone should be bored sometimes; Dad always said that learning to cope with it builds character. But I promise there will be no character-building in that way this holiday; I have too much educating to do. I hope you got the shopping list I sent you?'

'Kitchen fully stocked, ma'am.' He saluted her and his heart lifted as Amber let out a peal of laughter. It couldn't be this easy, this simple, spending time together. Could it?

'Come on then, show me around,' she said, taking his arm. 'I want every detail of every scrape you got into when you were young. No matter how embarrassing.'

'I'll do my best but, I warn you, my childhood was about as exciting as my adult life so don't expect too much.'

Amber raised her eyebrows. 'I don't know; you managed to get a stranger pregnant from a one-night stand and then found out you were engaged to her all along. That doesn't sound boring to me.'

'No,' he agreed. 'Things have definitely livened up recently.'

Amber kept her hand tucked into his arm as Tris showed her around the villa. Imposing as it was, it was still a family home, not a political seat like the castle, and the tour didn't take too long, even with Amber stopping to admire the view from every single room.

'I've put you in what used to be my mother's room,' Tris said, opening the door into a charming suite of rooms overlooking the lake, a balcony leading from the dressing room.

Amber stopped and looked at him anxiously. 'Won't she mind?'

'Oh, no. She lives in Switzerland now, with her second husband; she never comes back here.'

'That seems so sad when she lived here for such a long time. Why doesn't she come back?'

Tris stepped over to the window. How many times had his mother looked out at the lake and the mountains beyond, feeling trapped and helpless? 'She feels that she was exiled here.'

'Oh?'

Tris had known that visiting the villa again meant laying some ghosts, even if not all the spirits were dead. He tried to keep his voice neutral. 'What do you know about my parents?'

Amber glanced at him quickly. 'Not much. I mean I know your father died when you were about twenty, but I don't think my grandmother ever really mentioned your mother. Nor have you. There're no pictures of her anywhere.'

'No, my father gradually removed them all. He was an unforgiving man and she hurt his pride, if not his heart.'

'I'm sorry, I didn't mean to pry. You don't have to tell me anything else if you don't want to.'

Amber might have meant every word, but Tris knew

that this holiday was crucial in her decision whether to stay in Elsornia with him or return home, and that his inability to open up was weighing against him. 'Do you want some air?' he asked and, without waiting for an answer, unlocked the door to the balcony and stepped outside. How many times had he found his mother out here, a forbidden cigarette in one hand, a black coffee in the other as she stared bleakly at the mountains which cut her off from the parties and company she craved. Only in the summer, when the villages were filled with visitors, did she come alive. He knew without looking that Amber had joined him, leaning on the wooden balcony by his side.

'My mother, like you, came from a dispossessed royal house, which is why my father considered her a suitable bride. Also, like you, a life full of pomp and duty wasn't really what she wanted. Oh, she tried, but my father was a very austere and conscientious man. Elsornia always came first and she really struggled with that, with him. When I was ten, she and my sisters moved here. They told everyone it was temporary, for her health, but the reality was she left my father, and she left me with him.'

'Oh, Tris, that must have been so hard for you.'

His throat dried; the sympathy in her voice was almost more than he could bear.

'My father refused to grant her a divorce. Instead he gave her an ultimatum: live here with her daughters, stay at the castle with us all or leave alone. She chose the girls. She left the villa the week after my father's funeral; less than a year later she remarried.'

'Did you see much of her? Of your sisters?'

'A few weeks in the summer, that was all. My father didn't have much time for my sisters. Girls were no use to him; they couldn't inherit and marrying them off wasn't really an option in the twenty-first century. His loss. My sisters are lovely, warm women and they are also scarily brilliant. As you know, Elisabetta works with me, she speaks four languages fluently and has a PhD in International Relations. Giuliana is a trained pilot and is a shining light in the Air Force and Talia is still at university, doing something with physics I quite frankly don't understand.'

'They sound most formidable; if I didn't already know Elisabetta I'd be terrified of them.' Amber moved closer, placing a soft hand on his shoulder. 'It sounds like your mother had to make some very difficult choices. I'm sure she loves you.'

'It was a long time ago. I don't really think about it any more.' The lie hung there as he turned away and the pressure increased on his shoulder, her other arm sliding around his waist as she pressed herself against his back, all softness and warmth and understanding. It was almost more than he could bear.

'You don't have to pretend with me, Tris. You never have to pretend with me.'

Tris wanted to tell her that he wasn't pretending, that he'd been fine then and he was definitely fine now. That his father had been right, Tris had needed to grow up and start being responsible, not spend his days larking around on the lake and wasting his time playing with his sisters and cousins. But the words wouldn't come. Instead he turned, gathering her into his arms, burying his head into her hair, holding her close.

Her understanding, her comfort was dangerous, but he couldn't step away. He didn't want to need her; he didn't want to need anyone. Need led to betrayal and disappointment; he'd learned that lesson young and never forgotten it. The formal agreement he'd signed with Amber's grandmother, the formal arrangement he'd assumed they'd come to in the lawyer's office in Paris had suited him fine: a wife, an heir, his life neatly tied up with no emotional mess. How could he have believed that future possible when he knew how she felt, how she tasted, how her warmth enveloped him until the chill deep in his bones disappeared? There was nothing neat or tidy about Amber and the way she made him feel. And that made him so, so vulnerable.

Right now Tris couldn't help but accept the comfort she offered, tilting her chin, searching her gaze with his for consent before taking her mouth in a deep claiming kiss that branded her on his heart. This was no seduction, no tease, no sweet playfulness but deep and raw and almost painful.

Amber didn't pull back. Instead she pressed closer, entwining her arms around him, kissing him back fiercely as if trying to prove that he was worth something after all. How he wished he could believe it, could believe in himself as much as he believed in her.

Amber stretched out on the sofa and waved her book at Tris. 'Look what Harriet gave me. Us,' she corrected herself.

'What is it?'

'Baby names. You don't have one of those lists that royal children have to be named from, do you? As someone saddled with Vasilisa as my middle name, I have strong feelings about names.'

'No, no lists.' Tris perched on the arm next to her and Amber leaned her head against his leg, enjoying the intimacy. They'd been at the villa for a couple of days now and every moment felt easier and easier, as if they were together by choice, not circumstance. Tris seemed younger, lighter, away from the castle and the all-consuming summons of his phones and aides, and in return Amber felt herself drawn more and more to him.

Theirs was a slow courtship, a contrast to the way they'd met, when they'd rushed into intimacy with such life-changing consequences. Instead they held hands as Tris showed her his favourite lakeside walk and indulged in long, sweet, slow kissing sessions that left Amber breathless with desire. If this was being wooed then she liked it, this anticipation of touch, this easy communication. It was everything she had always hoped for in a relationship. She couldn't believe this was Tris, the uptight, upright, closed-off prince, jeans-clad and relaxed beside her.

'In that case, do you have any favourites?' Amber was aware she held all the cards in this pregnancy; it was her decision whether they married, whether she stayed in Elsornia, whether Tris was a full-time father or an occasional parent. She wanted the name to mean something to him. As long as he didn't saddle the baby with something as hard to live with as Vasilisa, that was.

Tris took the book from her and leafed through the pages. 'You've been busy underlining,' he said, one hand resting casually on her hair. 'Artemis, Athene, Hector? I sense a theme.'

'My dad really wanted to call me Athene, but my mother said no way—but if the baby has your eyes then it would be fitting, don't you think? Grey-eyed Athene?'

'I don't know; naming a baby after a goddess seems to give it an awful lot to live up to. What was your mother's name?'

'Rosemary. My dad was Svetoslav, but he changed it to Stephen when he moved to the UK.'

'Okay then, Rosa or Stefano. How does that sound?'

Amber sat up, turning to Tris in surprise. 'Really?'

'If it would make you happy.'

She blinked, her throat tight. 'If it would make me happy? I can't think of anything that would make me happier. I've been missing them so much recently. I don't know if it's talking about them with you, or realising I'm going to have this baby without my mother to help me.' She tried to summon a smile but could feel it wobbling. 'I know it's silly, I've had to do so much without her, but I really wish she was here. She would have been such a great grandmother.'

'She'll be with you,' Tris said, cupping her cheek softly. 'Every time you bake with our daughter or son your mother will be there, every myth you read our child your dad will be reading along with you.'

For a moment all she could do was stare wordlessly at him as his words sunk in, each one warming her soul. 'You're right. As long as I keep our traditions alive, as long as they're in my heart they're here. Thank you, Tris.' She leaned in and kissed him, a brief, sweet caress. 'And thank you for the names. It's the most beautiful gesture; I'll never forget it. Never forget that you brought me here to this beautiful place…'

'Amber. It's the least I can do. You're not just giving me a baby; you're giving me a chance to prove myself to you. I know what it's cost you. I just want you to know that I appreciate it.'

'Right now, you're making it very easy…' She didn't know who kissed who this time, the kiss lengthening as she lost herself in him, Tris shifting until Amber was pressed close, her arms entwined around his neck, his hand on her back, warming her through as her body trembled with want, needing him closer, not wanting any barriers between them.

'Tris?' She pulled back, looking him full in the face, letting him see her desire and need, letting everything she felt show in her eyes, in her parted mouth, her ragged breath. 'I want you, all of you. Make love to me, Tris, please.'

He was almost preternaturally still, only his eyes alive, scorching as he stared at her, his gaze moving slowly to her mouth, to the exposed skin at her neck where her pulse beat frantically, to her chest. Slowly, oh, so slowly, he moved it back up to meet her gaze. 'Are you sure?'

'I've never been surer of anything in my life.' And she hadn't. This wasn't the combined magic of moonlight, champagne and a long dormant crush; this was the knowledge that the man beside her would never intentionally hurt her, was beginning to know her heart, and that was far more intoxicating than any romantic evening. 'I want you, Tris.'

Finally, his mouth curved into a wolfish smile and she shivered at the heat in his eyes. 'In that case, my lady, how can I refuse?'

CHAPTER THIRTEEN

'WHAT DO YOU want to do today?' Amber leaned back against the pillows and watched Tris dress with unashamed appreciation. He had far too good a body for a prince who claimed to spend most of his time in meetings; those lean muscles didn't come from a gym but from a man who loved the outdoors and knew how to handle himself in it. She wriggled with contentment as she shifted. It wasn't the only thing he knew how to handle…

They'd been at the villa for nearly two weeks now and Tris had spent every night, since the afternoon they'd started to pick baby names and ended up making love, in her bed. She loved waking up with his arm wrapped around her waist, the warmth and heaviness of him next to her. He made her feel safe. Wanted. Needed—and not just because of the baby she carried. And it wasn't all one-sided. She valued his opinions, his thoughtfulness and good sense, just as she enjoyed watching him relax more and more each day. Amber wasn't entirely sure what she'd expected from their holiday, but it certainly wasn't this contented ease and intimacy.

Sliding her hand down to caress the slight curve of

her belly, she sat up a little more, all the better to watch him dress. 'We made good progress on the films yesterday, although how you fell asleep during my favourite dance movie I do not know. Definitely several marks lost there.'

'No films today.' Tris pulled a T-shirt over his head.

Amber approved of this more casual Tris. His hair was a little messy and he had even allowed a hint of stubble to appear, giving him an edgy sexiness. She especially liked knowing that this relaxed part of him was kept secret from nearly everybody, that it was hers alone.

'Not even one film?'

They'd quickly fallen into a pattern. If the weather was good they went out for a walk or a sail on the lake, coming back mid-afternoon to either watch one of the films from the list Amber had put together or to read in companionable silence. Whilst in London she'd bought an e-reader and filled it with a selection of her favourite books for him.

'You have to start at the beginning,' she'd explained to Tris, so she'd included some of her own coming-of-age favourites and if they weren't exactly Tris's preferred reading he hadn't said so. Like the playlists of songs and the list of movies, she'd tried to put together a real mix to allow him to discover his own preferences—although if that preference didn't include *Dirty Dancing* she had a lot more educating to do.

On cooler or wet days they either explored the charming villages and towns along the lakeside or carried on with baking lessons. The quiet, tranquil days suited her perfectly. The pregnancy and its ramifications had rocked her more than she'd realised; it wasn't until she had her scan that she really understood just how much her life was going to change. She also knew she really didn't want to raise a baby alone if she didn't have to, that she was going to do everything in her power to make a relationship with Tris work.

She just hadn't expected spending time with him to be so easy, to make the thought of extending her stay, even making a life here actually enticing not just bearable. Gone was the austere, closed-off Prince from the castle; instead Tris was proving to be a really entertaining companion. An entertaining companion and a good lover. More, she was beginning to see beneath the surface, beginning to understand how his father's demands and his mother's desertion had shaped him. Every time he let her in she felt herself fall a little more.

If only this holiday could go on for ever, but all too soon they would return to real life and then she'd discover if this was just a holiday romance and all the steps they'd made would be wiped away by the tide of reality.

It was scary how much she hoped for the former, even as she prepared herself for the latter.

Tris crossed the room and sat down beside her, taking her hand in his, his grip firm and tender. 'I hope you don't mind, but when my sisters heard we were here they went on a big nostalgia trip. To be fair, it was their home for a decade; Talia was only four when she moved here. Somehow they seem to have invited themselves for the weekend. I only realised they actually meant it and are on their way this morning when I checked the family group chat. I know you wanted to be alone...'

'I did, but your sisters are different. Of course I'd like

to spend some more time with Elisabetta and meet your other sisters. What do they know about me? About us?'

'Elisabetta knows everything, of course, but the other two know nothing more than when you came: that we met at the wedding and I somehow persuaded you to spend some time here before making up your mind whether to cancel the betrothal agreement or not. I have to warn you that Talia thinks it's all very romantic. In her head the betrothal and your disappearance has made you into some kind of fairy tale heroine. Giuliana, on the other hand, thinks you did exactly the right thing to run away and can't understand what on earth made you come back.'

Interesting—that was pretty much how she'd felt, torn between knowing that life wasn't so easy and neat, that a happy-ever-after was more of a dream than a reality, and the romantic fantasies of her lonely teens. Fantasies that felt more and more real with Tris next to her, lean and strong and still absurdly handsome. But now there was a third way, not so all or nothing, a way of compromise and learning and understanding and, yes, affection and liking at the very least. Maybe even more one day, if the happiness of the last couple of weeks didn't evaporate when they returned to the castle. And guests, even welcome ones, signalled the start of that reality seeping into their idyll.

'Your other sisters don't know about the baby?'

'No. I didn't want to tell them until I knew what your decision was. Although, Amber, even if you decide not to stay, they have a right to know…'

'Of course they do!' Amber interrupted him. 'Both my parents were only children and I'm an only child too. I can give this baby the best three honorary aunts in the world, but how amazing for it to have three actual aunts as well.'

She pushed back the covers, optimism filling her. Staying in Elsornia and marrying Tris wouldn't be easy, she knew that. She'd have to give up her job, live far away from her friends and her life would be under the kind of scrutiny she'd always avoided. But hadn't she been bemoaning the fact that the agency was changing? Weren't her friends moving on to start lives of their own away from the Chelsea townhouse? And although she would have to endure some media scrutiny, Elsornia was a small country with little international influence. Her position would be very similar to Emilia's, and so far she and Laurent seemed to be avoiding too much press speculation. Maybe this would, could, work out after all.

She smiled over at Tris. 'What time are they getting here?'

'About lunchtime. I thought we might pop into the village to stock up. Talia loves the little cakes from the bakery there and Giuliana has been emailing me demanding a specific kind of bread she claims only they make. What do you think about barbecuing tonight? The evenings have been so warm, and I think the girls would enjoy it.'

The optimism deepened. A life with Tris wouldn't be all pomp and circumstance; their child's life needn't be too unconventional. There was still space to live like this, with no servants, to discuss casually popping into the village to buy food for weekend visitors.

'After lunch?' Amber sauntered over to him and entwined her arms around his neck. 'In that case, there's no need to rush. Why don't you come back to bed for a while…?'

Several hours later, she was a little more nervous. After they'd eventually got up, they'd wandered along the lakeside path into the village to stock up on enough food for an entire week of guests, not just a twenty-four-hour visit. Amber loved how little notice the villagers took of Tris and her. They were treated just like any other citizens, with a disinterested friendliness that disarmed her. Afterwards she'd rushed around tidying the villa and making sure that Tris's sisters' bedrooms, still decorated for the teenagers they had been when they'd left, were aired and made up. Tris had suggested asking one of the live out maids who cleaned the villa to come and help, but Amber had wanted to hold on to the sweet normality a little longer. There was something endearing about Tris's complete lack of household skill and he was more of a hindrance than a help as she made up the beds and arranged the flowers she'd bought in the village in each of the rooms. She was aware that this was their home not hers and it was a fine line between making their rooms welcoming and stamping her mark on their childhood home.

'Don't worry, they're going to love you,' Tris reassured her, and Amber leaned into him gratefully.

'I always wanted sisters,' she told him wistfully. 'Maybe it's the books I read. *Little Women, Ballet Shoes*—all those school stories my mother passed on to me, but it always seemed that even when you weren't getting on, sisters were a team. Maybe that's the rose-coloured view of an only child, but I do want to make a good impression on yours.'

She was still patting the last cushion into place when the buzzer indicated that a car was approaching the gate. The invisible guards responded and by the time Tris had opened the front door Amber could see two cars proceeding down the driveway.

'That's odd,' Tris said. 'I wonder why they brought two cars.'

'Maybe they want to leave at different times?' Amber suggested, taking a step closer to Tris, relieved as he clasped her hand in his.

'Maybe. But both Elisabetta and Talia hate the mountain roads; Giuliana is designated driver.' His grip tightened and apprehension crept over her as a cloud covered the warm spring sun. The first car drew up by the side of the house, the second parking next to it and within ten seconds Amber was enveloped in hugs and kisses as Elisabetta and her sisters swooped upon her.

'It's so lovely to see you again—you look really well; the lake air suits you.'

'At last! I've been so excited to meet you. I hope Tris is looking after you properly; he is not half as stuffy as he seems, you know.'

'I can't believe my brother has actually persuaded you to give him a chance; you'll have to tell me how he did it. Tris has many redeeming qualities, but charm is not one of them!'

It was almost overwhelming, but the friendly greetings were a balm to Amber's soul. To be able to give her baby a warm, loving family like this was more than she had ever hoped for, but alongside the relief her heart ached for Tris, raised so differently to his sisters. How different would he have been if his mother had been able to raise him too? But she knew it wasn't too late for him; the last weeks had shown that.

Amber looked around for him, hoping that he'd see how happy this visit was making her, only to realise that he stood stock-still, staring at the occupants of the second car. A tall man, holding the hand of a little girl aged around three, stood next to it, making no move to join their group.

'Nikolai? I didn't know we were going to have the pleasure of your company as well.' It was as if they were back in Paris, Tris's voice was so cold and emotionless.

'Tris.' Nikolai nodded in greeting. 'I bumped into Giuliana yesterday and when she said she was coming here I invited myself along. I hope you don't mind, but I was intrigued to meet your mystery guest.'

'Of course, we are delighted to have you. Amber, this is my cousin Nikolai, and his daughter Isabella. Nikolai, I would like to introduce you to Her Royal Highness Princess Vasilisa of Belravia.'

A chill stole over her, just as much at the formality in his voice as the use of her hated name and title. Somehow Amber summoned up a welcoming smile and held out a hand to Tris's cousin as he sauntered slowly over to them, his daughter still holding his hand tightly. 'It's a pleasure to meet you, and I'm very excited to meet you, Isabella. I know for a fact that we have some delicious cakes in the house; would you like to come and see?'

At the small girl's delighted acceptance, Amber took the proffered hand and, along with Tris's sisters, took Isabella into the house, leaving the two men standing staring at each other. It was no secret that Nikolai's position as next in line to the throne was behind Tris's need to marry and consolidate his role as not just Crown Prince but King, and as far as she knew the antipathy Tris so clearly felt for his cousin was reciprocated, but she had no idea why Nikolai had decided to visit them today.

But what she did know was that their idyllic escape was over and real life had resumed once again. Was the new, fragile tenderness she and Tris had discovered here at the villa strong enough to weather a return to real life or had it all been an illusion? And what did she want? A life here or to return to London? She still had no idea, but she did know that time was running out. She had to make a decision, and soon.

CHAPTER FOURTEEN

'WHY ARE YOU HERE?' With Nikolai's daughter out of earshot, Tris no longer needed to be civil.

His cousin raised an eyebrow. 'Marcel has a cold and my wife has been kept busy caring for him. My poor Isabella is bored with being confined indoors; I thought she might enjoy a trip to the lake.'

'Quit playing games, Nikolai.' Why did it always have to be this way? It would have been easier in the olden days when a duel was a respectable way to solve conflict.

'What do you think I'm going to do, Tris? Break into the villa and kidnap your beautiful Princess? You think I'm that desperate for the throne?'

Tris's jaw tightened. 'This is how it's going to be: go into the villa, make your excuses, collect your daughter and leave. There are plenty of places you can entertain her, places where I am not.'

For a moment Tris saw something flicker across Nikolai's face, something that looked a little like hurt, before the expression was wiped away as if it had never been.

'I came here because I have something to say to you,

and it's in your best interest to listen. Take a boat out with me, Tris? Like old times?'

The request struck a chord. He and Nikolai had been at odds for so long, it was easy to forget the time when they had been close friends, boy adventurers escaping from the castle through the tunnels whenever they could. When did that change? When had his childhood companion become his enemy?

'Half an hour,' he said curtly.

Neither spoke as they made their way to the small dinghy moored on the villa's jetty. Nikolai started the engine as Tris cast off and his cousin expertly steered the boat away from the shore, just like they had all those years ago, both falling back into half remembered roles. Nostalgia and something like regret bit hard as Nikolai coiled the rope: regret for the closeness and companionship he had lost and never replaced.

After they'd travelled a few hundred metres Nikolai slowed down, killing the engine as he turned to face his cousin. 'Remember that time we went fishing at midnight? Your father was furious when they caught us. But then it didn't take much to make him furious, did it?'

'That's what you came here for? To talk about our childhood?'

'I was just wondering where it all went wrong.' Nikolai looked out over the lake. 'It used to be you and me, remember? Betta tagging along, Giuliana furious when we said she was too young, Maria and the other castle kids following our lead. Days and days outside, escaping the confines of our castle, your tutor, our uncle and his lectures. Your mother aiding us with picnics and hidden treasure. It was idyllic, especially when your father was away and the Duke was too busy to worry about us. Idyllic, until one day you stopped playing and suddenly I was the enemy. I admit I hated you for it, partly because I lost my best friend and partly because you were so damn smug all the time. It was amusing shocking you, shocking my uncles, gaining and living up to a reputation. But when I spoke to Giuliana, I realised it was time to put a stop to all this.'

'Put a stop to what?' Tris could hardly believe what his cousin was saying. Was that how he saw it, their growing apart, growing up into such different men? One a playboy prince, partying in every continent, always in the tabloids and the gossip websites, the other dedicating himself to their country. He could hear their uncle, the Duke, reading out yet another headline in the cutting tone he reserved for Nikolai, impressing on Tris his duty to keep his cousin from the throne no matter what. And Tris had agreed. Nikolai was a womaniser, a spendthrift and a drunk and he had started early, embroiled in scandal long before he became an adult.

He looked over at his cousin, ready with a retort, but the words disappeared unsaid. Nikolai had been married for five years now and Tris had heard no hint of infidelity. He was clearly a loving father and even if he hadn't settled to a job or role within the castle, he was no longer living in nightclubs and casinos.

Their uncle was convinced that Nikolai's marriage was a ploy simply to father a son and strengthen his own claim to the throne. Seeing the way he had held his daughter, Tris doubted it. Besides, Nikolai hadn't simply married; he had disappeared from the headlines. If his marriage was merely part of his game-playing, then wouldn't he have continued as before? Their laws demanded a wife and son but not fidelity. There was barely a king in their ancestral line who hadn't had a string of lovers throughout their reign.

Nikolai trailed a hand in the water; he suddenly looked very young and tired. 'I should have said something a long time ago but, I have to admit, it was too amusing being cast in the role of ne'er-do-well villain. But the truth is, Tris, I don't want to be the heir. I certainly don't want to be King.'

There was nothing but sincerity in his cousin's face. Tris folded his arms. 'Why now? What game are you playing, Nikolai?'

'Come on, Tris. I have the perfect life. I love my wife and my children, I have money, can travel anywhere I wish, have all the benefits of being a Ragrazzi and none of the negatives. Why would I want to change that to spend my life wrestling with Parliament and dealing with politics? Why would I want to have to put the country before my own desires? And, more importantly, having seen what being the heir did to you, why would I want to inflict that on my own son?'

They were all good points but, more importantly, sincerity rang in every word.

Nikolai straightened. 'I'd have told you this years ago, but you and the Duke were so convinced I was dying to step into your shoes, I thought I'd string you along for a little longer. But the truth is I am very happy to help you break the covenant. Make women equal in the line of succession, get rid of the ridiculous married-with-a-son-by-thirty-five rule, bring this beautiful and ridiculous country of ours up-to-date. We can ensure that me and mine move far away from the line of succession—let Elisabetta be your heir; she is probably the most qualified out of all of us.'

Tris stared out at the mountains across the lake, barely able to focus on the snow-topped peaks. Nikolai was offering him all he had ever wanted: an update to the succession laws, respite from a hasty marriage. But the freedom weighed heavily upon him.

'Why now?'

Nikolai didn't answer straight away, starting the engine up again and sending the boat flying through the lake. Looking back, Tris could see the villa receding, the guards' towers, hidden from the villa's view, clearly visible from here. They would have binoculars trained on them, their every move tracked. His freedom was, as ever, merely illusory.

Finally, Nikolai slowed the boat down again, running a hand through his hair, his expression thoughtful, his grey eyes sadder than Tris had ever seen them. 'I don't know why my father turned out so differently to his brothers,' Nikolai said. 'The Duke is as joyless and obsessed with tradition as your father was. If only my father had still been alive to be joint guardian after your father died, maybe he could have tempered the Duke's influence. But maybe it was already too late.' Nikolai's father had died in a plane crash when his son had been just fourteen. The tragedy should have brought the cousins closer together, but instead they had been pushed further apart. It was around that time that Nikolai had started to drink and party. Older and wiser now, Tris could see that grief had played its part in his cousin's rebellion. Back then he had merely censured him. No wonder Nikolai had called him smug. He deserved a far more stinging reproof than that.

'I couldn't believe it when I heard that he'd arranged a marriage for you, and that you simply went along with it,' Nikolai continued. 'When the rumours of your intended's disappearance started, I have to admit I was pleased. Not because that left you in an awkward situation, but because it gave you a chance of avoiding your father's mistake, marrying for prestige and position not for love. Marriage is a gift, Tris. My wife makes me a better man every day; you may not believe that but it's true. To marry because of a contract, to marry because of a ridiculous law put in place hundreds of years ago is wrong. If I really hated you, if I really was envious of you, maybe I'd let you carry on. But we were good friends once, practically brothers, and I can't help hoping that a good marriage, to someone who truly loves you, might help you remember the boy you used to be, not the man your father forced you to be.'

Nikolai stopped abruptly, red colouring his haughty high cheekbones. 'I can't believe I just said all that; blame my wife. She believes in talking about feelings. And she wanted me to come here today to tell you this. To set you free. Maybe it's too late for us to be friends again, Tristano, but we are family. It would be good to remember that more often.'

Tris didn't, couldn't, speak as Nikolai picked up speed once again, steering the boat round in a wide arc before heading back towards the jetty. Nikolai was going to help him change the inheritance laws, update them so his sister could be his heir, so that he could become King without a wife and a son beside him. Everything he had planned was now possible—without Amber. He didn't need her, not any more.

The thought echoed around and around in his mind. He no longer needed her, nor did he need the baby she carried. She was free. She could carry on with the life she had built for herself, the life she loved, surrounded by people who cared for her. She had chosen her own path, walked away from her title, fortune and royal destiny without so much as a backward glance. Now she could resume that path guilt-free. It was within his gift to give it to her.

His heart clenched, the pain so fierce, so all-encompassing he almost gasped aloud. It might be within his gift but he didn't *want* to set her free. He didn't want to wake up alone, didn't want to spend the rest of his life in his soulless, impersonal apartments, no time to work out who he was and what he wanted. He liked the way she teased him, enjoyed watching the way she put so much energy into educating him and the pleasure she got when he reported back that he liked a book or a film or a song she had chosen, how she tried to argue with him when he didn't.

He liked the way she was so wholehearted in everything she did, whether that was baking enough food for an entire children's party, filling an e-reader with a library's worth of books or explaining to him in vivid detail just why the original movie was the only one worth watching. Everything she did she did in luminous colour, such a contrast to his own grey life, and she lit up his soul.

His thoughts continued to whirl relentlessly on, examining his feelings in painful forensic detail. He liked the way she drew him out, was interested not just in what he was but in who he was, his title the least meaningful thing about him. The way she embraced everything they did, no matter how dull, how interested she was to meet new people, to discover new things. How she'd sat next to him on the balcony last night as once again he'd named the stars and she'd related the myth behind every constellation, making them laugh as she attempted to make sense of the shapes each constellation was meant to represent. She had an insatiable appetite for life and all it offered, those lonely years in her grandmother's penthouse watching rather than doing making nothing too small to interest her.

There were lots of things he liked about her. Most of all he liked how real he felt with her, but marriage was a two-way deal. What did he have to bring to the table except a title she didn't want and to be a hands-on father for her child? Their child.

Tris knew all too well that Amber's own sense of responsibility and a longing for family weighed heavily in his favour. But was that enough? He loved her, appreciated her efforts to make the relationship work, but he wasn't kidding himself. Amber was working hard because that was what she did. She made the best out of every situation.

Hang on…he *what*? His mind skidded back. He *loved* her?

Tris almost laughed aloud with the inevitability of the discovery. Of course he did. He'd been drawn to her the moment he first saw her, the dazzling bridesmaid with a glorious mane of hair and the wide smile. But he'd fallen in love with the gallant, open-hearted girl who still believed in love and kindness and hope even after her sad and difficult teenage years. Amber might admit to dreaming of rescue, but she'd buckled up and rescued herself. She had a courage and spirit that made her beautiful within as well as without. But he wasn't kidding himself; she was trying to forge a relationship with him because that was what she did, but she didn't love him. And she dreamed of love; she'd been frank about that from the beginning.

With a start, Tris realised the boat had slowed and they were back at the jetty, Nikolai looking at him quizzically, waiting for him to throw the rope around the mooring pole. Hurriedly, Tris gathered it in his hands and with practised ease looped it around the pole. He pulled the rope until the boat was tight against the jetty and the two men clambered out.

With a deep breath, Tris turned to his cousin. 'Thank you.' It was all he could manage, his head filled with too many thoughts and scenarios and feelings.

'I'm sorry things got to this stage,' Nikolai said. 'I'm fully aware how much I'm to blame, that I never reached out even after your father died. I hope it isn't too late.'

'Me too.' With a jolt of surprise, Tris realised he meant the words. 'It couldn't have been easy coming here today.'

'It wasn't. I had to bring my small daughter to give me courage; there was no way she'd allow me to turn back, not when I'd promised her that she'd see her cousins and she could paddle in the lake. But I had to come. My father used to say how vivid and alive your mother was when he first met her, but after several years married to your father she became just a shadow of herself.

That all the expectation and your father's autocratic ways nearly crushed her. How he wished he had said or done something earlier. I didn't want to stand by and see history repeat itself. Maybe I'm wrong, maybe you and the Princess are meant to be, but either way I want you to go into marriage for the right reasons.'

'Come to the villa, Nikolai. Stay for dinner, you and Isabella. My sisters would like that, I'd like that.'

'Thank you.' Nikolai smiled, looking so like the carefree youth Tris remembered it was impossible not to smile back, despite the tumult of emotions tumbling around his brain. 'That would be good.'

The two men walked back to the villa side by side in a surprisingly companionable silence as Tris came to a resolution, as painful as it was necessary. Tonight he would play the host and enjoy the evening with his family and the woman he loved.

Tomorrow he would set her free.

CHAPTER FIFTEEN

'IT'S BEEN SO lovely to see you again.' Amber embraced Elisabetta with a warm hug. 'And absolutely gorgeous to meet you both.' She hugged first Talia and then Giuliana before stepping back, oddly bereft as the girls headed towards the car.

How ridiculous! Talk about an overreaction. She barely knew them for a start, and it wasn't as if they were going far. Elisabetta was returning to the castle, where she both lived and worked, Talia to the University of Elsornia which was based in the country's charming capital city just a few miles from the castle, whilst Giuliana needed to report back at the airbase just outside the city. She and Tris would be returning themselves in just a couple of days; she could renew her acquaintance with his sisters at any time. So why did this feel more like a *goodbye* than a *see you soon*?

As Tris walked his sisters back to their car, Amber tried to shake off the foreboding that had plagued her ever since Nikolai's unexpected arrival. She knew she was just being silly yet somehow her usual pep talks weren't helping and every hour her feeling that things weren't right deepened. She couldn't put her finger on why exactly. After all, Nikolai and Tris had returned from their boat trip if not the best of friends, cordial and with an understanding that evidently astonished Tris's sisters. Nikolai had even stayed until late the previous evening, before scooping up his adorable small daughter to drive her home, laughing that they would both be in trouble with his wife for staying out so late.

Sure, Tris had slept in his own room last night but that had been to allay any suspicions his sisters might have had about their relationship while it was still so fragile and undecided. But Amber had still half expected him to tiptoe down the corridors to her room after she had gone to bed and lain awake far too late waiting for him. She knew he was probably just being careful and had decided not to risk sneaking in, but it had been hard to sleep with his absence somehow filling the bed far more than his actual presence did.

She had also expected him to make an announcement about the baby, or maybe mention it casually while they were out walking, but nothing had been said. Elisabetta was obviously expecting him to say something too, judging by the quizzical glances she had sent Tris's way throughout the evening and today. Amber wanted to believe that Tris had decided to give her more time to decide, to ensure she wasn't ambushed by his excited sisters, but the explanation didn't quite ring true. His distance seemed emotional as well as physical, all the closeness and intimacy gone, as if he were now acting her suitor instead of becoming her lover.

Amber watched him as he closed the car door, standing back as Giuliana reversed the car and he waved his sisters goodbye. There was no discernible difference in him that she could articulate; he was still lighter and warmer than he had been back at the castle, but she *felt* a difference. The lightness seemed forced, his good humour put on, and she would look up to find him gazing at her with such a deep sadness in his eyes that her stomach twisted and her chest ached to see it.

She waved to the Princesses until the car disappeared behind the closing gates before turning to Tris as he made his way slowly towards her. They were alone once more. She should be looking forward to another comfortable evening together, enjoying the still so new intimacy whilst anticipating the night after their separation the night before; instead the silence was weighted with expectation and an air of something momentous left unsaid.

'Should we go inside?' Amber asked with as breezy a smile as she could manage Other words trembled on the tip of her tongue: what had Nikolai said? What was wrong? But the words stayed unsaid; she wasn't sure she wanted to hear the answer. Folding her hands into fists, she tried again but still couldn't speak. She wasn't usually a coward, preferring to make the most out of any situation, no matter how bleak it might seem. Her Pollyanna attitude had got her through tighter spots than this, and yet her usual courage ebbed away. Looking at Tris's set face, it was hard to feel anything but apprehensive.

'Go in? Yes, that seems best. Amber, there is something I need to say to you. Could you spare me five minutes?'

'Of course.' Her apprehension heightened, the cool civility in his voice chilling her. The politeness of his request was so at odds with the companionship they'd shared. Something had happened, something linked to Nikolai's unexpected arrival and their long trip out on the lake. Amber swallowed. She had thought she was used to being alone but not since her teens had she felt as isolated and friendless as she did right now.

Following Tris into the sitting room, Amber perched on a sofa, folding her hands neatly, feeling a little like she had as a teenager sitting in her grandmother's formal, overstuffed room, waiting to be told how to live her life. Sometimes she thought she'd never get rid of her grandmother's critical voice in her head, telling her she was too loud, too exuberant, too impulsive, too untidy. Not regal enough, not poised enough, not good enough.

Elisabetta had warned her that news of her reappearance was beginning to leak out. Amber knew that she couldn't avoid facing her past any longer; she needed to visit her grandmother, not to berate her or blame her but to lay all her ghosts to rest before the baby came.

The irony didn't escape her; if she took Tris with her she would merely be confirming to her grandmother that the harsh treatment and isolation had been right and had led to the desired outcome. Conversely, turning up as a single mother would probably have the same effect, proving that she couldn't be trusted to behave in an appropriate fashion on her own. But she no longer yearned for her grandmother's approval, no longer considered her family. Her opinion didn't matter. Any future relationship would be on Amber's terms, if they had one at all.

She also needed to take control of her own fortune and look at how she could redistribute it, right the wrongs of her great-grandfather when he'd extracted the money from their small country. Tris was right; the best way would be through some kind of charitable foundation. It was that kind of forward thinking that made him such a good king. A good king and a good man.

She pushed the thoughts from her head and tried instead to concentrate on the scene unfolding before her, feeling more like a spectator than a participant. Tris hadn't joined her on the sofa; he stood in front of the window, his expression becoming bleaker and bleaker as he seemed to search for the right thing to say.

The silence stretched on until she could take it no longer. 'Tris, what's happened? Something's changed between yesterday and today; is it to do with Nikolai?'

Tris inhaled. 'Nikolai came here to tell me that he will support my bid to change the constitution.'

Okay. But that was good news, wasn't it? 'In what way? To make it possible for you to be King now, without a son? That's brilliant! It must be such a relief for you.' Numbness crept over her as she saw Tris wince at her hearty tone. But hiding behind good humour and positivity had been her defence for far too long; she couldn't drop it now.

'Exactly that. More, we have decided to legislate to ensure that the current generation will benefit from the change in the law. This means that the oldest child will inherit whenever the existing monarch dies or abdicates, regardless of age, marital status or offspring. By doing so, he has effectively removed himself from the succession as all three of my sisters now come before him. If Parliament ratifies these changes, and there is no reason for them not to with the current existing heirs both sponsoring the bill, I can be officially crowned within the year, with Elisabetta taking on the role as the formal heir to the throne. She will be eminently suited to the role.'

'Oh, yes, Elisabetta will be perfect,' Amber agreed, her hand creeping to her stomach. Surely Elisabetta would only be heir for a short while? If she and Tris were to marry then, no matter whether she was expecting a boy or girl, their baby would inherit the throne one day. Wasn't that what these changes meant?

Only…if Tris didn't have to get married, didn't have to have a son, then their marriage was no longer such a burning issue. In fact, it wasn't even necessary. Her chest tightened, the air closing in around her. No wonder he had withdrawn from her; she was no longer of any use to him.

Here was proof; the intimacy of the last week or so was merely an illusion. He'd tried hard, she had to give him that, but it had all been an act. Numbness began to steal over her as she tried to digest the implications. Had her instincts been so wrong? Was she so desperate after all for a happy-ever-after that she had fallen for a façade?

It had seemed so real. 'I see.'

Tris tried to smile, but there was no happiness or warmth in it. 'The good news for you is that there is no longer any need for you to make a life here. You can go back to your normal life, your agency and your friends. I know how much you hate the idea of living in a castle, being a queen, living the life I must lead. Now you don't have to.'

'No. I suppose I don't.'

'I've ordered you a car; it will be here shortly to take you to the airport. You can go home, Amber. Your kindness in coming in the first place will never be forgotten. I can't tell you how much I appreciate it. But there's no need for you to sacrifice your happiness any longer. You're free.'

Amber tried to find the right words, but for once she, who could usually chatter on to anyone about anything, was lost. What was wrong with her? She should be happy. Tris was right; this was exactly what she wanted made easy and guilt-free.

She had done the right thing in giving both him and Elsornia a chance but they both knew that living in the confined box of royalty wasn't what she really wanted. Yes, she was pregnant, and he was the father, but this was the twenty-first century; she had a home, a job she loved and friends who, even if they were far apart, would always support her. She could and would love and raise their baby alone. Far better to do so than to raise it in a loveless marriage where hope and willingness to try would be bound to end in disappointment and bitterness.

She lifted her head and met his gaze. 'That sounds very sensible. I'll go and pack now. Tris, I'm glad that everything has worked out for you. But I hope you know that I still would like you to be part of our baby's life. Every child needs a father if at all possible, and I think you are going to make a pretty remarkable one. I know your position makes it a little more complicated and I would rather not be the subject of any kind of media circus, but I'm sure if we're careful we can find a way for you to be as hands-on as possible. If that's what you want.'

Tris blinked and for a second Amber could have sworn she saw sorrow and disappointment cross his face. 'Thank you. I would very much like to be involved. I don't intend to marry, not now I don't have to. I'm not sure it would be fair on any woman to always be second best to my role. But I would like to be a father, to be involved.'

Somehow, Amber managed a smile, even though her chest was ever tighter and her heart pulsing with a pain she couldn't identify. 'You're only thirty, Tris. And you have such a huge capacity for love; don't close yourself off from all that, please. I'd better go and pack. I am happy for you, really I am. You've got what you wanted; that must be amazing.'

She got up from the sofa, walked over to him and kissed his cool cheek, feeling him tremble under her touch. For one wild moment she wanted him to seize her, to hold her, to pull her to him and kiss her properly and tell her he couldn't live without her. But instead he stood stock-still as she walked from the room, blinking hot, heavy tears from her eyes.

An hour later, Amber stood outside the villa, the car and driver waiting for her and her small amount of baggage, Tris next to her, still so remote and unreachable. This was what he wanted; surely he should be happy? Surely *she* should be happy instead of feeling utterly bereft. Sick with disbelief and unexpected loss.

'Text when you're safely home,' Tris said, his words so ordinary they seemed utterly incongruous in the charged, unhappy atmosphere.

'Of course.' Amber took a step towards the car then stopped. 'I'll let you know the date of the next scan.

Maybe there's a way you can come, if you have time? I'll have been home for almost two months by then so no one will be watching us; we might make it work. I'll send you the date.' She couldn't help thinking that if he wasn't involved now, then he would just get more and more remote until he was barely part of their lives at all. The thought of a future without him in it was too bleak to contemplate.

'If you'd like me to be there then of course I will be. I don't intend to just abandon you, Amber. I hope you know that.'

'I do.' But her words were more hope than an affirmation. Tris didn't know what unconditional love, what family was, didn't know he could be integral to someone's happiness. He was so likely to assume that she and the baby would be better off without him, to think he offered nothing of substance. By leaving, was she just proving that assumption true?

But he wanted her to leave. Had ordered the car before he had even told her of the change in his fortunes.

The driver put her few bags in the car and Amber didn't move, still not quite ready to say goodbye. Tris stood framed by the villa, the white paint gleaming gold and pink thanks to the setting sun. Her eyes burned. The time she'd spent here had been the happiest of her adult life. Somehow, the villa felt like home.

'Okay then.' Tris leaned forward and dropped a single chaste kiss on her cheek. 'Thank you again. For everything.'

'Read the books, okay? And finish the playlist and watch the films; let me know what you think. And keep baking! You're not too terrible.' She took a reluctant step towards the car, still hoping, but she didn't know for what. This was what she wanted. Why on earth did she feel as if she was being wrenched from all she held dear?

'I will.' He stepped away, face shuttered, mouth set firm.

'Goodbye, Tris. Look after yourself.' Amber took another few steps to the waiting car, where the driver held a door open for her. Suddenly, impulsively, she turned around. 'Tris? Why did you agree to marry me all those years ago?'

She didn't know why, but somehow the question had been niggling away for weeks now, and suddenly it felt imperative to have an answer. Amber knew she was a fool but the teenager staring out of the turret window at the park below, hoping for someone to rescue her, who had spent far too many bored hours weaving elaborate daydreams about the man standing opposite her, still yearned to hear him say that she was worth something. That she had been more than a title and a convenience.

Tris looked away, but not before she saw the bleakness in his eyes. 'You looked lonely,' he said. 'And I understood loneliness. I guess I thought that together we could forge some kind of companionship. That what I could offer you here was better than what you had there. But that was then; you're not that girl any more. You have a career you love, friends who are more like a family, you're confident and beautiful and you bring sunshine everywhere you go. You are going to be an amazing mother. And you deserve more than what I can give you. So go, shine, raise our baby to see life the way you do. I'll take care of you both financially, I hope you know that, but you're free, Amber. Enjoy that freedom for both of us.'

She held his gaze and saw his grey eyes darken and for one long breathless moment Amber thought he might change his mind. Even though she missed her life and the dreams she'd had before Emilia's wedding, she had new dreams now, dreams she had barely known before today and certainly never articulated, but dreams centred around the man in front of her.

'Tris?' The hope swelling in her chest was almost unbearable as their gazes locked and she allowed all the emotion inside her to show in her expression, in her eyes, in the hand she held out towards him. But all he did was lean over to place one light kiss on her cheek before walking away. He didn't look back once.

CHAPTER SIXTEEN

'*SIGNORINA?*' THE DRIVER indicated the open door with a smile. 'I am ready to go if you are?'

Amber stood, torn, her old life beckoning, the life she'd been contemplating receding into the distance. All she had to do was get into the car, let the driver take her to the airport and she could be home, tucked up in her own bed before midnight. Things would never be exactly the same; she knew that even with the money Tris could give her, a secure home in Chelsea and the agency ensuring she would always have a job, raising a child mostly alone would be difficult, but she never shied away from hard work and a family of her own was all she'd ever dreamed of. This wasn't the picture book two point four children and big golden dog and house in the country of her dreams, but it was real and it was hers. All she had to do was get in the car...

And yet she stood, anchored to the spot, replaying Tris's every word in her mind. He'd never said that he *didn't* want her, but he had said more than once that he was setting her free. Obviously, he thought he was doing the right thing. Hadn't she told him herself how much she loved her life, how little she wanted to change it?

So why was she still standing here, unable to get in the car and return to it, guilt-free?

Amber looked around, at the villa, warmed by the setting sun, the lake tranquil behind, the mountains purple in the distance. Did she really want to leave this land of mountains and lakes and valleys? Did she really want to throw away the chance of calling Tris's sisters her family? And, most importantly of all, did she really want a life without Tris in it? She closed her eyes and saw him, gazing up at the stars, expression intent as he explained the constellations to her. Saw him poised, camera in hand, finding beauty in a commonplace scene and helping her to see the beauty as well. She saw him covered in flour, doing his best to follow her instructions, making her laugh as he did so. She saw him sprawled on the sofa with a careless grace, watching a film for the first time, showing every emotion like a small child rather than a jaded adult. She saw him that first night, the way he moved, the way he watched her, the way he touched her... And she remembered the nights here in the villa, sensual and tender and, yes, loving.

Amber swallowed, every nerve reacting to the memory of his sweet, skilled lovemaking. Sure, at times he could be closed off, but she of all people understood the reasons for that. Underneath the dignity he wore like armour, there was a man capable of more love and passion than she'd ever believed possible, eliciting love and passion in response.

Love. The word slammed into her and she gasped at the impact. Of course she loved him, this proud man who bore his responsibilities with dignity, this seductive man who had whirled her away in a dance and changed her life, this thoughtful man who listened to her and made her want to be a better person. She'd expected to recognise love straight away, to be floored by it, but she'd confused love with desire. If love was easy to recognise then there would be no need to kiss frogs…this bone-deep need and certainty was nothing she'd ever felt or even comprehended before.

Was she really going to get in the car and drive away from the one man she had ever loved? He wasn't the Prince she'd daydreamed about in her lonely teens, no perfect knight in shining armour riding to her rescue. That was okay; she didn't need to be rescued.

But maybe he did.

Tris strode towards the lake, needing something physical and hard and exhausting to do. Chopping down a tree maybe, or sawing logs. Anything to stop him thinking, to stop him turning back to the house to beg Amber not to go. He was doing the right thing, the noble thing, so where was the comforting sense of righteousness, of peace? Instead the pain inside was almost overwhelming as he kept replaying the confused expression in Amber's eyes, kept hearing her call his name.

Hang on, that wasn't his imagination. Tris stopped and looked back, incredulous, as he saw Amber making her way towards him, hair tumbling around her face as she hurried along the path.

'Is something wrong?' Panic warred with hope.

She stopped and folded her arms. 'Yes, there is something wrong.'

Panic won out. 'Amber? Do you feel ill? The baby?'

'Not physically, but with this whole situation. You don't get to decide for me, Tris.'

'Amber...'

'When I was twelve my grandmother took me away from everything I knew and told me my entire life was flawed. She told me she knew how I should dress, what I should eat. Who I should be friends with, what I should do with my own time, and she was wrong. The only thing she might have been right about was who I should marry, but not for the right reasons.'

The air stilled around him, as if time had stopped and only the two of them existed. 'It's okay, Amber, there's no need for you to be here. Honestly.' No need but his own almost overwhelming need to hold her. Tris stood very still, watching her as she threw her hands up in frustration.

'You told me you are setting me free as if I'm some kind of bird you caged, but I'm not. I have my own mind, Tris, and I get to make it up. I am *always* free, no matter where I am, no matter what's happening because I don't let anybody cage me, not any more. If I decide to marry you it's because that's what I want, not because I've been coerced into some kind of sacrifice in order to do the right thing. Do you understand that?'

'I... What are you saying, Amber?'

'I'm saying you don't get to push me away before I get to tell you that I love you. You don't get to decide on your own that I don't need you. Because I do. I need you and I want you and I love you, Tris. I don't want you to hop in and out of this baby's life, but to be there all the time.'

Was this a dream? Was he hallucinating here on the

lake shore while Amber was really on her way to the airport? She looked and sounded real, but the things she was saying made no sense. She couldn't really love him; this had to be her sacrificing herself, just the way he was trying to sacrifice his own happiness for her. It was almost funny in a twisted kind of way.

'I appreciate what you're saying, Amber, but…'

'You're not listening to me, Tris. I'm not making some kind of grand gesture, not being some kind of selfless martyr. I am, in fact, being very selfish indeed and claiming exactly what I want. I don't want to have to live without you, Tris, I don't want to go back to Chelsea alone. I want to stay here, marry you and raise a child together. Only…if that's what you want too. If you don't then please just say…' Her voice petered out and the fire in her eyes dimmed. Dimmed because of him, because he was just standing there like an utter fool.

'You really want to stay? With me?' He still couldn't believe it, even though sincerity rang true in every word, in every line of her body.

She smiled then, her whole face lit from within. 'You were my first crush, Tris, even though I pretty much made up your personality. To be honest, I wasn't really sure what I wanted, and my imaginings were a little dull. Lots of holding car doors open for me, bowing over my hand and staring in awe as I descended grand staircases in gorgeous ball gowns.'

'All the above could be arranged; just give me the word. We have plenty of grand staircases at the castle,' he promised, and she laughed.

'Maybe sometimes for old times' sake. Back then I fell in love with an ideal, a face I saw occasionally, and it was that ideal I wanted to sleep with at the wedding. A way of finally putting the past behind me. But you're not that fantasy figure; you're so much better than that. So much more. I know you hide it, even from yourself, but you've shown yourself to me and what I see is pretty damn special. I see a man who is kind and considerate and clever, who can describe the stars to me and makes me want to listen all night. A man who is far too sexy for his own good, a man who will do anything for the people he loves. A man I trust with my heart because I know he'll always look after it. Tris, you are right, this isn't the life I wanted, but if it's a life I share with you, then it's the life I choose. If you will have me.' Doubt crept into her voice and tore at Tris's heart.

He tilted her chin and smiled into her eyes. 'If I'll have you? Amber Blakeley, there is nothing I want more. I can't claim to have fallen in love with you back in New York; you were just a child. But I did see you then, I noticed you and I wanted to help you. I didn't fall in love with the bridesmaid either, although I thought she was one of the most special, most beautiful people I'd ever met. I fell in love with you, the you right here with all your enthusiasms and optimism and dreams. I want your light in my life.'

'Always,' she whispered, her green eyes filled with tears and he wiped them away tenderly.

'I love you, Amber, not because you carry our child and not because I need a queen, but because of everything that you are. Will you marry me, despite all that comes with me? I know we haven't known each other that long, and if things were different then I would have loved to have courted you properly...'

Amber reached up to lay a hand on his cheek. 'But things are the way they are. Fun as courting sounds, I know it's easier if we marry before the baby is born, but there's no reason you can't court me after we're married.'

'Every day,' he vowed, and she smiled softly into his eyes.

'I want to marry you sooner rather than later and embrace all that comes with you, because that's what makes you who you are. I love you, Tris, and I can't wait for the baby to be here and for us to be a family, just like I always dreamed. Here, in the castle or anywhere as long as we are together that's all that matters. Life has taught me that.'

'I love you too, and I promise to do everything in my power to make you happy every day,' Tris vowed as he finally kissed her the way he'd always wanted to, with all the love and hope and passion bursting within him, her own kiss warm and sweet and passionate. As he held her, Tris promised himself that she would never be lonely again; like all the best fairy tales he might have rescued her, but she'd turned around and rescued him right back. And that was how all the best happy-ever-afters were supposed to be.

EPILOGUE

'OH, EMILIA, HE is *gorgeous*.' Harriet picked up the three-week-old heir to the Armarian throne and cradled him tenderly. 'You clever, clever girl.' She looked over at Amber and grinned. 'Wouldn't it be amazing if your Rosa and Emilia's Max made a match of it?'

'No royal matchmaking betrothals in our households, thank you very much,' Amber retorted as she adjusted the frills on Rosa's christening gown—Tris had made several inroads in updating some of Elsornia's more antiquated laws over the last year, but even he couldn't save their daughter from being baptised in the traditional Elsornian royal christening gown, a delicate Victorian confection comprising of several long layers of silk and lace and more buttons than any baby should have to endure. 'Just because mine worked out in the end doesn't mean we're reviving that particular custom. But if I was a matchmaking mama, then obviously I would choose Max to be my son-in-law. Em, he is beautiful. And you look amazing, Thank you for coming so soon after the birth.'

'I wouldn't miss my goddaughter's christening for the world.' Emilia reached out to stroke three-month-old Rosa's cheek. 'I'm so excited to celebrate with you, little one.'

'How are you feeling, Amber?' Alex asked from the sofa she was sharing with her two soon-to-be nieces, a beautiful vintage diamond ring glinting on her left hand. 'It was so brave of you to invite your grandmother. Brave and very forgiving. I'm not sure I could have been so generous.'

Amber looked round at her friends, her heart so full of love and happiness she could hardly believe it. Although they still owned the Happy Ever After Agency, both Emilia and she had had to take a step back, thanks to their royal duties, and since her marriage Harriet spent more and more time in Brazil with Deangelo. The Chelsea house was still the agency's headquarters, but paid staff occupied the vintage desks, the bedrooms turned into more offices for the increasing number of employees whilst Alex ran the agency from the countryside home she shared with Finn and his nieces. Amber spoke to at least one of her friends every day, but they hadn't all been in the same room since Harriet's wedding eight months before. To have the four of them here, in her charming sitting room overlooking the palace gardens, celebrating her daughter's birth, was very special indeed. Even her grandmother's presence in the castle couldn't disrupt her happiness.

Gently shifting her sleeping daughter to her other arm, Amber smiled at Alex, who was as elegant as ever in a green silk shift dress. 'When I visited my grandmother in New York she wasn't the fierce autocrat I remembered; she was just a lonely woman. All she had were her dreams of a throne in a country that doesn't exist any more, acquaintances instead of real friends, no hobbies, no one or anything to love. It made me feel so sorry for her. I have so much and she so little—inviting her to the wedding and the christening was the least I can do. We'll never have the kind of relationship I used to yearn for, but that's okay. I have Tris, Rosa and his sisters, and I have you three, my sisters in every way that counts.'

'You'll always have us,' Emilia said softly, her words echoed by Harriet and Alex.

'And you me. Our lives have changed so much in the last two years, but we're still the same girls who dreamed of our own business and made it happen, the same girls who met one Christmas Eve and realised we weren't alone. Marriage and babies don't change that; it just enhances it, makes our family even bigger. Rosa is so lucky to have you three as her godmothers and aunts, just as I am lucky to have you as friends and sisters.'

She blinked, emotional tears threatening to spill down her cheeks, relieved when the door opened to reveal Tris, smart in his dress uniform, flanked by Deangelo, Finn and Laurent, who immediately made a beeline for his son, pride etched on his features.

'The cars are here,' Tris said, carefully lifting Rosa off Amber's knee and then extending a hand to help her rise. Amber curled her fingers around his, grateful for his strength and solicitude. 'Ready to get this young lady christened?'

'Absolutely.' Amber watched her friends file from the room: Deangelo and Harriet, hand in hand, Finn and Alex, shepherding his nieces in front of them, sharing an intimate smile as they did so, Laurent and Emilia, his arm around her as she carried their newborn son. She turned to press a kiss on Tris's cheek. 'I love you,' she whispered. 'Thank you for making me so very happy.'

'I should be the one thanking you,' Tris said, his eyes soft as he smiled down at their daughter. 'For everything you do and everything you are.' He squeezed her hand. 'Come on, let's celebrate our daughter with our friends and family. She's done the impossible; my mother is considering getting a house in the city so she can see Rosa regularly and your grandmother is both here and behaving. She's a miracle child.'

'She is.' Amber allowed Tris to escort them from the room, knowing she would be able to face the pomp and ceremony of a royal christening with him by her side, flanked by her friends. They'd named the agency well all those months ago. Life was bound to have bumps in the road, its trials and tribulations, but as long as they kept loving each other then she knew they would live happily ever after, just as she'd always dreamed.

* * * * *

A FAMILY
FOR A WEEK

MELISSA SENATE

For my sister.

Chapter One

Holding her twenty-seven-month-old son against one hip, single mom Sadie Winston—and thirty-eight of her relatives—walked around the outdoor petting zoo at the Dawson Family Guest Ranch. Little Danny stared wide-eyed at the goats jumping on and off a short log in the hay-strewn pen. One with bristly black fur came over to sniff Danny's sneaker. "'Oat, 'oat!" her son shouted with a giggle.

The whole clan had arrived a few minutes ago for their annual family reunion, the barn their first stop after check-in. As Danny laughed and pointed at the goats, Sadie looked in every direction—ever so casually, she hoped—for a certain tall, black-haired, blue-eyed man named Axel Dawson. He and his siblings owned the guest ranch, and she'd heard he lived on the property now. She didn't see him anywhere, and Axel Dawson would be impossible to miss.

"'Oat, Mama!" Danny said again, pointing at a white goat chewing on a piece of hay. Sadie set Danny down, smiling as the goat came over to nudge his hand for a pat or a treat. "'Oat, 'oat!"

She kneeled behind Danny and wrapped her arms around him, breathing in the baby-shampoo scent of his blond hair. She closed her eyes for a second, grateful. She'd almost lost him once. She *had* lost him—for over two hours. That she had him back was the whole reason her mother and aunt—reunion organizers for decades—had chosen to hold the event at the Dawson ranch. As a very expensive but priceless thank-you.

Three months ago, on a beautiful May afternoon, Danny had gone missing during a family outing on a small mountain in Badger Tree National Park. One minute, he'd been right there, toddling between her aunt and mother as they all ambled and chatted their way up the easy incline to a wide expanse of forest where they'd planned to stop for a picnic.

Sadie had been deep in conversation with Daphne, her pregnant cousin who was full of questions about impending motherhood, when she'd heard her mom say, "Where's Danny?" A second later, "Danny? Where are you, sweetie?" The four women had looked at each other, each expecting Danny to appear, but he was nowhere to be found.

Panic. They'd rushed in every direction, looking, calling his name. Nothing. Silence. The breeze through the treetops the only sound when they'd forced themselves to stop and listen.

Her mother was on the phone with 911 when Sadie emerged from behind a tree, shaking her head, tears streaming down her face. "Danny!" she'd called out as loud as she could, trying to keep the fear out of her voice so as not to scare him *if* he could hear her. Silence.

At footsteps, they'd all turned expectantly and rushed over, but it was a young couple with hiking poles. No, they hadn't seen a little boy with blond hair and orange light-up sneakers. Sorry. They'd help look, though, they'd said.

Converse County search and rescue, park rangers and local police were there within minutes. A tall, dark-haired man, his orange shirt emblazoned front and back with *Badger Tree National Park Search and Rescue, Axel Dawson* embroidered on the right chest, appeared with a dog, a yellow Lab, and asked for something with Danny's scent. Sadie pulled Danny's hoodie from her backpack, and Axel held it under the dog's nose, then stared at the photos of Danny on Sadie's phone. He'd had her text a few to him, and then he'd rushed into the woods near the last spot the women were sure they'd seen him. Two hours later, Danny was still lost, radios crackling, areas checked rattled off. Axel Dawson had reappeared to speak to Sadie, asking for special words Danny liked, songs he knew, and she'd been so out of her mind she'd barely remembered his favorite word was *nana*— for banana, not grandmother—and he liked the "Itsy Bitsy Spider" song.

Axel had put warm, strong hands on her shoulders, looked her right in the eyes with his startling blue ones and said, as the sun went down behind him, that he'd find her son. He'd said it with such conviction in his voice, in his expression, that she'd believed him more than she'd ever believed anything.

Twenty minutes later, the radios of the park ranger and police officer who'd stayed with the family had blared to life, and the ranger screamed, "Danny has been found! He's alive and well, and they're heading here!" Cheers went up among the group, including the EMTs at the ready. Sadie dropped to her knees with relief. Her mom, aunt and cousin were crying and staring in every direction, waiting. And then out of the tree line came Axel Dawson, his right cheek bleeding from a long scrape, holding Danny tight in his arms as the boy sang "Itsy Bitsy Spider" and made the spider hand gesture up to Axel's chin, the yellow Lab following them.

Sadie had gone flying over, sobbing *thank you* over and over as she'd reached out for Danny. She'd held her son close, covering him with kisses, and then the EMTs had led her over to the ambulance. Danny seemed okay but had his share of scratches. He'd been chasing a woodland critter and had ended up crawling through brush and vines into a well-hidden badger's den and fallen asleep. Dude, Axel's search and rescue K-9 partner, had sniffed him out and stayed put until Axel got in and got the boy out.

Sadie had heard this all secondhand from the police and EMTs, who'd heard it from Axel via radio when he'd been rushing the boy out of the woods. She'd looked for him to thank him again, but he appeared to be getting a serious dressing-down from another man in a park search and rescue shirt, and then she and her family had gone to the hospital to have Danny checked out, and she hadn't seen Axel Dawson again. She'd returned the next day, bringing a pie from her mother, a strudel from her aunt and a hundred-dollar gift card from her cousin to a local restaurant, but she'd heard he'd left town for a while.

Apparently, he'd broken a few rules to find Danny and had been sent home on enforced "rest and relaxation" for two weeks. Sadie had felt terrible about that. A couple of days later, when she'd gotten Axel's address and gone to his cabin nestled at the base of the mountain to thank him in person and apologize for whatever had happened, a fellow ranger had said that Axel had gone to his family's guest ranch out in Bear Ridge for a while. Sadie's mom had immediately tried to book their annual family reunion at the Dawson ranch, but there were no openings till winter—and the family needed all six cabins. A few days later, though, Sadie's mom had gotten a call from the Dawson ranch that a corporate retreat had canceled for the last week of August, and voilà: thirty-eight of Sadie's relatives had descended on the rural Wyoming property.

"Remember, he's single," her mother whispered into Sadie's ear.

Ugh. How did Viv Winston always know what she was doing? How could her mom possibly know that Sadie was thinking about Axel Dawson? Though technically, Sadie was thinking about what happened three months ago. The man was a huge part of that, though.

"Not *that* single," Sadie whispered. "I told you what the park ranger said."

Three of the rangers, two female and one male, had come to the hospital to visit Danny and bring him stuffed toys, which had been incredibly kind, and as they were leaving, Sadie had heard one say, "Is McGorgeous here?"

The other had said, "Give it up, already. I told you I heard Axel Dawson doesn't do commitment."

"I know, but I like to look at him," the other said, and they chuckled.

Sadie had filed that tidbit away. Axel *was* nice to look at, *and* he'd found her son and brought him to her. The combination was potent. The past few months, she'd had a passing thought or two or a hundred about getting to know him better while at the reunion on his ranch. But better to think of him as a superhero like her family did instead of a man she could actually get to know better. Sadie Winston did not, repeat, *did not* want anything to do with a man who didn't "do commitment."

"Oh flibberty-poop," Viv said with a wave of her arm, her ash-blond bob swinging by her chin. She smiled at two of the children who were following a chicken, then sidled closer to Sadie. "Everyone wants love."

Sadie sure did. A nutritionist specializing in geriatric patients for the Converse County General Hospital in Prairie City, which was a town over from Bear Ridge, Sadie had a rewarding job, a nice small house in the center of town, friends, a big family, but she was sick to death of showing up alone to weddings and family parties. She was fine on her own, sure. But she wanted her life's partner, dammit. Someone who'd care if she was running late. Someone to be there. Someone to wake up with, share her day with. Someone to share *life* with. Someone who'd love Danny the way she did. She'd married Danny's father after a whirlwind courtship, despite his telling her he'd never thought he'd be the settling-down kind. She'd believed he loved her so much that he'd change. But when she told him she was pregnant, he'd disappeared with the rodeo—faster than she could even fill out paperwork to change her last name. Ever since, Sadie's motto was *when someone tells you who they are, believe them.* Axel had made it clear to everyone he wasn't the settling-down sort either. She should believe it.

"Zul!" Danny shouted, pointing.

Sadie's heart sped up, and she glanced around. *Zul* was Danny's attempt at saying Axel. Thanks to her family referring to the man as the family hero for the past three months, Danny had turned one of his stuffed animals, a floppy yellow lion with a shaggy brown mane, into "Zul." Sadie's grandmother Vanessa had made a little red cape for the lion, and the hero worship was complete. It was Danny's lovey, and he took it everywhere. Sadie knew her aunt was holding it right now so that Danny could pet the animals. "When Zul?" Danny had asked every day as he flew the lion around.

Finally, Sadie had a real answer for him. Because as the little boy took off running past the goats toward the open barn door, Sadie watched a tall, dark-haired, ocean-eyed man in a Stetson stop dead in his tracks as her son sprinted straight for him.

Axel Dawson.

A toddler—two years old at most—in a straw cowboy hat was running full speed right at Axel. *Whoa there, little guy.* In about a minute, the tyke would collide with Axel's knees. And since Axel had almost done his left knee in this morning from rescuing Hermione, the ranch's famed runaway goat, from a narrow cliff up Clover Mountain just behind the ranch, he didn't think it could take twenty-five pounds of flying energy.

The hat flew off the boy's head, his mop of blond hair flopping as he sped toward Axel, who stood about twenty feet away near the barn door. Two women in their fifties hurried after the bolter.

Axel squinted in the bright sunshine. Holy molasses. Was that little Danny Winston barreling his way? And his great-aunt and grandmother behind him? The grandmother's name was Viv, if he remembered right, but he couldn't recall the great-aunt's name.

Axel's throat went dry, and he swallowed, the late August afternoon suddenly hotter than it was five seconds ago. *Let me be seeing things*, he thought. Correction: prayed.

"Danny, slow down!" one of the women called.

Prayer denied. That little boy in the dinosaur-covered T-shirt, blue shorts and orange light-up sneakers was definitely Danny Winston.

Axel's sister, the ranch's guest relations manager, had told him a family reunion was being held on the property, every bed in the six cabins filled, including cots brought in for the smaller kids. The clan was arriving today—and clearly had, given the crowd in the petting zoo. Had he asked their name? Probably not. Axel's job at the ranch revolved around guest safety and leading wilderness tours through the forest and up Clover Mountain. Knowing names and stocking the cabins with welcome baskets that catered to allergies and favorites was his sister's thing. Axel was more interested in sizing up guests' likelihood of getting lost and needing rescue; he kept watch over those types. There were lots of those. City slickers and country-bred alike.

"Zul!" Danny shouted as he came flying at Axel, twenty-five pounds of energy. The boy wrapped his arms around Axel's leg and squeezed.

Aw. Danny remembered his name. Well, half of it. "Hey there, partner," Axel said, scooping the tot up in his arms, the solid weight of him a reminder of three months ago.

"Hi, Zul!"

"Hey, Danny. Nice to see you again."

The boy beamed up at him with his bright white baby-teeth smile and those huge hazel-brown eyes. He was surprised Danny recognized him after three months, but maybe one of his relatives had pointed him out. *There's that nice man who rescued you from the mountain*, he could imagine one of the Winstons saying.

"Our hero!" called a woman's voice.

Axel glanced at Danny's grandmother as she approached. Her sister, Danny's great-aunt, was right behind her and holding a stuffed lion with what looked like a red cape.

"We hoped you'd be here!" the grandmother said. The Winstons had a strong family resemblance. Many were blond. The grandmother was tall and strong, her own ash-blond hair cut to her chin with a sweep of bangs. She extended her hand, and Axel shifted Danny so he could shake it. "I'm Viv, Sadie's mother. We decided to hold our family reunion on the Dawson Family Guest Ranch in your honor as a thank-you for finding our Danny."

The great-aunt stepped closer and extended her hand. "I'm Tabby Winston, Viv's sister."

As Axel shook her hand and smiled, he noticed Viv send her a scowl. He could feel the tension between the two women all around them. He wondered what that was about.

"I live here now," Axel explained. "Home was a cabin at the base of the Badger Mountain where I used to work, as you know, but I decided to move home—here—a few months ago. My brother, the foreman, and my sister, the guest relations manager, like having a search and rescue specialist on the property twenty-four/seven, and turns out I miss the cowboy life, so here I am."

That wasn't quite the whole story of why Axel had returned to the ranch he'd vowed to steer far clear of for the rest of his days. But then his brother Noah had become a dad—of twins—and his sister had a baby, too, and family tended to bring family around, didn't it? That wasn't the reason he was here either, but he liked the less messy versions of the truth. Poking around in his gut had never appealed to Axel. On mountains, in dangerous situations, when clocks were ticking, there wasn't much time for that kind of thing. Ranch life was a lot safer, and unfortunately, Axel had had a little too much time to think about a lot of things. Including his inability to stop thinking about Danny Winston's mother, Sadie. He glanced around the throngs of her relatives gathered around the barns, pointing at the alpacas and hoisting children to laugh at the goats' antics. He didn't see her.

"Zul!" Danny said, leaning toward his great-aunt and reaching out his hand.

"Here you go, sweets," the woman said, handing him the lion.

"Are we both named Zul?" Axel asked, unable to contain a grin.

"He turned his lion into Axel the Super Lion. Takes it everywhere," Viv said.

Danny flew the lion high and low. "Soup Zul!"

Axel felt a soft one-two punch land in his stomach, the effect that pure sweetness sometimes had on him when he didn't quite know how to digest it. "Well," he said, awkwardly leaning Danny toward his grandmother so he could transfer him to her.

Viv took him. "He's been saying your name ever since we told him we'd be going to the ranch where the hero who rescued him lives."

Hero. Axel hardly thought of himself as that. For a bunch of reasons.

A beautiful woman with long, light blond hair and pale brown eyes he'd never forgotten suddenly burst through a group of preteens. Sadie Winston.

"There you are, Danny!" Sadie said, taking a deep breath. "My little sprinter likes to take off and make his mother a nervous wreck. He'll keep you on your toes this week," she added to Axel, those eyes finally landing on him.

"Nice to see you again," he said. Quite the understatement. Seeing her again wasn't exactly nice.

The sight of her engendered all kinds of insane feelings he wasn't particularly interested in delving into. Her pretty hair caught the sun and held his attention for a second. She wore a white T-shirt, olive-colored pants and gray sneakers.

Out of the corner of his eye, he noticed her mother, Danny in her arms, moving over to where a bunch of chickens were pecking the ground. The great-aunt went to join another group by the alpacas' pen.

Just the two of them now. He had a sudden flash of putting his hands on Sadie's shaking shoulders, telling her he'd find her son. The look on her beautiful face, the absolute fear in her eyes. He wasn't returning to base a second time without the boy, and he hadn't.

He cleared his throat. "It was nice of your family to book the reunion here. Unnecessary, but nice."

"You're all my family has talked about the past three months. So trust me, it was necessary." Her smile lit up her face. "I hope saving Danny didn't put your job at risk," she added.

"It wasn't saving Danny that put my job at risk—it was me and 'my stubborn inability to follow protocol,' according to my boss. But it was for the best. It brought me home after a long absence and—" He stopped talking, realizing he was going off on tangents he had no interest talking about. *So why did you bring it up?* he wondered.

He'd broken some rules to find Danny, mostly concerning Axel's own safety because the sun had just set. His punishment was two weeks enforced R&R, which had been fine with him. He'd surprised himself by returning to the family guest ranch that he and his siblings had inherited when their father died almost a year ago. And he'd never left. He liked his job here, patrolling the vast property on horseback to make sure all was as it should be, guest-wise, ranch-wise. And boy, were there always a lot of kids at the ranch. His niece and nephews—three babies, two his brother Noah's and one his sister Daisy's, and then countless kids of all ages as guests. At first, Axel had been overwhelmed by all the kids, but then he'd settled into the sight of them, charged with their safety on hikes in the forest and the minimountain just a mile behind the ranch. He'd thought being responsible for them would do him in, but instead, it filled him up, gave him back a tiny piece of himself every time he stopped a kid from careening off a cliff.

"Oh, my!" a voice yelped above the fray.

Axel turned; a very elderly woman in a wheelchair was on the path in the main petting zoo, a white chicken on her lap. Fluffernutter. She liked human laps and loved being picked up and snuggled by kids. Most of the chickens accepted their hugs for the extra grain they knew would be coming their way. Any chickens that nipped a two-year-old's hand for daring to come too close were kept in a separate coop with a kid-free run.

"Declan," a younger woman shouted, "take the chicken off your great-great-auntie's lap this instant!"

"Sorry, Great-Great-Auntie," a boy with light brown hair said, scooping up the chicken and setting it down.

"Don't be sorry, Decky!" the elderly woman told him. "I asked him to put the chicken on my lap," she called out. "I miss having my own chickens."

The younger woman nodded at the boy, who put the chicken back on his great-great-aunt's lap. The smile on the elderly woman's face managed to warm Axel's heart.

"That's my great-grandmother, Izzy," Sadie said, her gaze on her relative. She turned to Axel. "She's ninety-nine years old. It was Izzy who started the tradition of annual family reunions. She used to hold them at her small ranch, but she lives with one of her daughters in town now, and no one has a property big enough to hold us all and keep the kids entertained."

"She looks happy to be here," Axel observed, the joy in Izzy's eyes clear from where he stood.

Sadie's mother returned with Danny, the boy still flying his superhero lion. "Axel, we'd like to invite you for a toast tonight at a bonfire by the river. Around eight o'clock? The young ones will need to get to bed soon after, so it'll be quick. Please say you'll come."

He glanced at Sadie, whose eyes had widened as though she'd had no idea such a thing would be happening. The knowledge he'd see her tonight was both very welcome and a problem he didn't want to think about too deeply. Something about her had gotten inside him in a way nothing had for three years. He'd recognized it right away— pure attraction, an inexplicable chemistry out of nowhere, an emotional pull. He'd tried to chalk it up to the situation on the mountain, the frayed nerves, the promise he'd made and would have died to keep. Anyway, Axel Dawson wasn't going back to that time three years ago when a single mother had torn his heart in two.

"Zul and Zul!" Danny gleefully shouted as he flew his lion around and then pointed to Axel.

Oh, man.

"Please come," Great-Aunt Tabby said, approaching them. Her sister, Sadie's mom, lifted her chin and turned away, the tension between the two women so thick Axel could bite it. "We owe you everything."

He was about to say he was just doing his job,

but finding lost people wasn't a "job." It never had been and never would be. Search and rescue was who he was, the call in his blood and veins. That simple and uncomplicated.

He looked at Sadie, who seemed to be biting her lip, her cheeks slightly pink. "Of course I'll come," he said, and the women beamed.

Well, except for Sadie. Something was up there, but again, he wasn't about to think about it.

The way he saw it, after one simple toast tonight, the hero stuff would be over. He'd stay fifteen minutes, shake some hands, smile at some kids and then he'd be free. The name of the game.

Chapter Two

"How ridiculous is this?" Sadie's sister, Evie, younger by three years, complained as she flopped on the twin-size bed in their cabin's bedroom. "Mom and Aunt Tabby haven't spoken, except to yell at each other, in *three* months!"

"Very," Sadie agreed, glancing at Danny, who was fast asleep in his porta-crib at the end of her own twin bed. She should be unpacking her and Danny's clothes and toiletries, but she just wanted to sit her butt down and think. And *not* think at the same time. That was how things had been lately.

For example, she both wanted to think and not

think about Axel Dawson. Everyone had been saying for three months that he was her hero, and damn right he was. But she had to keep her thoughts from running wayward, such as fantasizing about things that would never happen. One of her great-gram's favorite expressions was *You never know.* But Sadie did know because she'd overheard those rangers. She'd be completely delusional to hope that Axel would magically fall for her. Her family hadn't gotten the memo, though, despite her resending it countless times.

On the way from the petting zoo to the cabin, Sadie pushed her great-gram's wheelchair and looked for escape routes while her mom and grandmother pressed for details on what Sadie and Axel had been talking about in front of the barn. Had he asked for her number? Had he asked her out? Would they be riding horses into the sunset this afternoon? Three sets of Winston eyes had been full of hope.

Save me, she'd sent heavenward, but her nosy relatives kept at it.

"My, is he handsome," Great-Gram had said.

"That's some physique!" her grandmother had put in. "You know, he reminds me of—who's that handsome actor, Irish, I think? With the dark hair and blue eyes?"

Pierce Brosnan. And yes, Sadie totally saw it. Pierce back in the 007 days. Gorgeous. Like Axel.

"Look," Sadie had said. "I know you all want me married off, but Axel is not the guy for me. He's not interested in commitment. Do you want me falling for a guy who'll never propose?"

"Like your poor sister," Sadie's mother had whispered, turning and looking to make sure Evie wasn't in the vicinity. She was a few minutes behind them, walking with cousins, it had turned out. Sadie had wished her sister had walked to the cabin with them—she desperately needed her to change the conversation, and that would be easily accomplished, unfortunately, because of Evie's broken heart. Her relatives were all over that—the big breakup two nights ago on Evie's twenty-ninth birthday with the man she'd expected to propose. Sometimes the family was too much, like with Sadie, and sometimes they were heaven-sent, like when you were hurting so bad you couldn't stand up straight. The Winstons had rallied around Evie, keeping constant vigil, bringing her pints of Ben & Jerry's and boxes of Puffs tissues with aloe vera. The reunion would be good for Evie—a week of family support and long walks in the fields and petting alpacas.

Sadie hoped the week would have a similar good effect on her mother and aunt—who were not on speaking terms. They refused to talk about why, so no one could help the situation—and now the two were in separate cabins. Every year prior,

Sadie, her sister, mom, aunt, gram and great-gram all shared living quarters for the annual family reunion. Sadie's dad and grandfather were in cabin number three with Sadie's uncles and male cousins. Everyone was seriously relishing being among their "own species," as they called it, for an entire week.

One of the worst parts of the cold war between her mom and Aunt Tabby? That Sadie felt like it was her fault. The feud had started on the mountain when Danny had gone missing. Ugh. If only Sadie had been watching Danny more closely, she would have noticed he'd run off, and if he hadn't gotten lost, her mom and her aunt wouldn't be blaming themselves and each other—or at least, that was what she figured was at the heart of the fight. Things had been hunky-dory between them until that night.

"It feels so wrong that Aunt Tabby isn't staying with us," Evie said, pulling her shoulder-length blond hair into a low ponytail with a tiny velvet scrunchie from her toiletry bag.

It really did. There were two bedrooms in the roomy cabin, which could sleep six, enough for them all. Three in the larger bedroom, two—well, plus a porta-crib—in the smaller one and, if necessary, one person on the couch in the living room. Sadie's mom, gram and great-gram were sharing one room, Sadie, Danny and her sister in the other. This cabin was only one story, so both bedrooms were on the first floor, key for a ninety-nine-year-old great-gram, and for a mom needing to lug a stroller.

"I know," Sadie said. "I would gladly sleep on the couch and give my bed to Aunt Tabby, but she was adamant about sharing a cabin with her cousins and their families this year."

"Yeah, because she doesn't want to share a room with her sister," Evie said, popping up to unpack her suitcase into the closet and dresser. "What do you think happened between her and Mom? They got into an argument on the mountain when Danny was lost, right? I wish I'd been there so I'd know more. But nothing else makes sense. That's when it started."

Ugh. The elder Winston sisters had always been so close, thick as ole thieves, and now: narrowed eyes, scowls and sarcastic comments under the breath. "I think so, but neither will talk about it. And you know how getting either of them to change their minds about anything is." Both women were equally stubborn and always thought they were right. Sadie loved both women fiercely, but come on—get over it, already! This was the annual family reunion, and they should be celebrating being Winstons—not carrying on some grudge.

"Well, every time Mom asks me if I'm okay about the breakup," Evie said, practically strangling the gray yoga pants in her hands, "I'm going to ask her about her breakup with her sister. Maybe she'll stop asking!" Evie mashed the yoga pants into a ball and dunked them into the dresser drawer, then sighed and folded them nicely.

Sadie eyed her sister as Evie reached into her suitcase for her favorite hoodie, long, pale pink and fleece lined. Evie's face looked like it might crumple into crying any second, and Sadie's heart constricted.

Evie had given her boyfriend of three years an ultimatum two nights ago on, yes, her twenty-ninth birthday, and instead of getting down on one knee in the fancy restaurant he'd taken her to, which was what Sadie had expected all during dinner, he'd tearfully said he just wasn't ready. Evie had left the lovely peridot birthstone earrings he'd given her in their velvet box on the table, gulped the rest of her wine and left, sobbing all the way home. Sadie knew this because Evie had called her two minutes into her walk home, and Sadie had rushed over in her car to pick her up and bring her to her house, where her sister had cried in her arms for hours.

Evie had done similarly for Sadie almost three years ago when her then-husband had told a newly pregnant Sadie he wasn't cut out for fatherhood, sorry, and that he was leaving with the rodeo. They'd been married two months at that point, and according to her ex, marriage made him feel like he was stuck in quicksand. *Ouch* didn't begin to cover how bad that had hurt. She'd loved her husband, even if she knew they'd had some big problems that hadn't quite reared their ugly heads during the three months they'd dated prior to the backyard wedding at her grandparents' house. The divorce, taking all her dreams of a family with it, had devastated Sadie, and Danny's father had never come back, even to meet his son. These days, she was trying, at least, accepting fix-ups and blind dates and saying yes to coffee or dinner with the okay-seeming men she met while at work or around town. So far, she'd give her dating experience a D minus. Maybe even an F.

The Winston sisters both needed a heart boost— not their beloved mother and aunt in a big fight during what should be a soothing, if not fun week away with the whole family.

"Marshall hasn't texted!" Evie muttered, glancing at her silent phone on the dresser top. "Two days and nothing. Doesn't he even miss me? Three years and nothing?" She burst into tears and dropped on the bed, letting herself fall backward.

"Aw, I'm sure he misses you like crazy," Sadie said, going over to lie beside her sister. She took Evie's hand, both their gazes on the ceiling, which was a lovely post and beam, something she hadn't paid attention to when they'd arrived. The cabin was really nice—rustic yet spa-like at the same time. Sadie and Evie were both appreciators of spa-like.

"I want to marry him, Sadie. I want to have four children with him. I want to adopt an adorable shaggy dog from the Prairie City animal shelter. I want to start my future with the man I love more than anything on earth, except you guys. Instead, it's all over." Evie broke down in fresh sobs. "Why did I give him an ultimatum?" she croaked through her tears. "Why couldn't I just be okay with how things were? And things *were* fine. Even if we weren't planning our future."

"You asked for what you wanted and needed," Sadie pointed out gently. "That's the most important thing you can do. You were honest with yourself and him."

Evie swiped under her eyes and squeezed Sadie's hand. "Fat lot of good that did me. Honest and miserable. Thanks so much, universe."

Sadie couldn't help laughing, and suddenly Evie was laughing, too, then she sobered up and let out a sad sigh. A little noise and minigrunt came from the porta-crib, which meant Danny had woken from his nap. "Perfect timing, Evie. Let's go raid the cafeteria. I hear the cook makes incredible gooey desserts. There has to be something out now for hungry new arrivals." It was two thirty, and the cafeteria wouldn't open for full service until four thirty for dinner. However, Daisy, the nice guest relations manager, and Sara, the ranch forewoman, had greeted the family at check-in and said there were always goodies and refreshments on the tables near the door in the cafeteria and in the lodge beyond it.

"Good idea," Evie said, getting up.

If Sadie were being honest, she'd admit that she wouldn't mind clapping eyes on Axel Dawson again. She'd see him tonight, but there were hours to go. *Do not build some fantasy around him*, she warned herself. *He doesn't do commitment. You are looking for commitment. Do. Not. Go. There.*

There was falling ridiculously in love-lust with the man who'd changed her entire life, made happiness possible, made her future possible by finding her son when he'd been missing for hours. She owed Axel and his partner, that heroic Lab who would not leave that certain spot on the mountain, despite it seeming to lead to nowhere a toddler could get into, *everything*. Dude, the dog, knew his job, and Axel, the handler, knew his dog. Because of that, Danny had been found. They were *heroes*. No other word for it.

Which meant Sadie's inability to stop thinking about Axel was hero worship. *That's all it is. Toast the guy tonight and then emotionally move on.*

So easy to say. Doing so would be another story. Which was why she would not give her sister any dumb platitudes about broken hearts and time or changed minds or even her dear great-gram's *you never know*, though that one was true. Sadie would just listen and be there. But gooey desserts always helped, as did Danny's adorable ways, so Sadie got up, scooped her son out of the crib and let his huge hazel-brown eyes work their magic on Auntie Evie, who played five rounds of giggling peekaboo before they headed out of the room.

"The Winstons asked permission to make a bonfire by the river tonight," Axel heard his sister say, "so if you see big plumes of smoke in that direction, the cabins aren't burning down."

Axel looked up from where he sat at his kitchen table. Daisy Dawson, the ranch's guest relations manager, was outside on his porch, bent over with her face close to the screen. "Actually, I was invited to the bonfire," he said. "I'm practically the guest of honor."

She made an *ooh* face—Daisy loved being in the know—and seconds later she was in the kitchen, pouring herself a mug of coffee and joining him at the table. He was already on his second mug since returning from the petting zoo. He'd been going over notes he'd taken at the staff meeting this morning about the ages of the guests, safety issues, special requests—one woman used a wheelchair, one teenager had a broken wrist and another kid was deathly afraid of snakes and would scream at the top of his lungs if he saw one, garter or not, and go running blind, potentially off a cliff. Otherwise, the group members were in good general health, enjoyed light hikes and were used to the setting. Most weren't riders, so he'd have to be vigilant when they were on horseback. He and several of the ranch hands would constantly patrol the trails.

"Remember when I was sent home on enforced R&R after rescuing a kid on Badger Mountain back in May?" Axel asked.

Daisy sipped her coffee and nodded. "Of course I remember. It's what brought you home finally. I owe that rescue everything."

Axel smiled inwardly with a matching head shake. His sister had been trying to get her brothers to come home to the ranch they'd grown up on. The youngest Dawson sibling, Noah, had rebuilt the guest ranch their grandparents had started over fifty years ago, and he ran the entire operation, his wife the forewoman. Daisy had come back in the spring because Noah had needed help with a baby left on his doorstep, a crazy story that had turned into their brother becoming the proud married father of *twin* babies. Daisy had been pregnant then, and when her baby's father left her at the altar— literally—she'd ended up marrying the man who'd delivered her baby on the side of the road. That was also a crazy story.

Two Dawsons were married with children, happily settled into family life, and though Axel had made his sister's day by moving home permanently and building a cabin at the far edge of the property for himself and his trusty partner, Dude, the greatest dog there ever was, marriage was not in his plans. Daisy kept trying to fix him up, and he kept disappointing her. At least there were three other Dawson brothers out there she could work on. Rex, Zeke and Ford were scattered across Wyoming.

"Well, the family here for the reunion this week is *that* family," he explained. "Turns out they booked the ranch as some kind of thank-you."

Daisy gasped. "You're kidding! I wish they'd let me know. I would have put extra goodies in their welcome baskets or something."

Axel finished his coffee. "They keep calling me a hero. I'm only going to the bonfire tonight because they want to toast me. Then I'll leave."

Daisy grinned. "You are a hero, Axel. Accept it."

He wasn't. Heroes didn't let people down, and Axel had let people down plenty in his day, particularly the women who'd come and gone in his life over the past few years. But no one more than his own father a week before he'd died last December. Axel had found or rescued a lot of people in his days—years—on the search and rescue team. But he'd been a clueless idiot about his own father, who'd basically drank himself to death.

Daisy's phone pinged. "Duty calls," she said, popping up. "I'm meeting Sara at the river to set up the bonfire. Two of the hands will be on duty, too, so we should have a lot of eyes on the littles, especially."

He nodded. "I'll come help." He'd keep on his staff shirt, which would put some distance between him and the Winstons. He wasn't a guest who could hang out and chat; he was an employee of the ranch.

Dude came padding over, and Axel gave his buddy a vigorous pat and a kiss on his furry head.

"You stay here and take a nice nap, partner," Axel said to the dog. "Back in a couple of hours."

"Does he know what you're saying?" Daisy asked, looking from Dude to Axel.

Axel laughed. "Nope. He has a great vocabulary, natural to his former job as a search and rescue K-9, but not a string of chatty nonsense like that. He knows from the tone of my voice that it's all good."

"Maybe I can talk Harrison into adopting a dog. I want two pugs, one black, one fawn."

Axel raised an eyebrow. "Pugs? With the smushed-in faces?"

Daisy gave him a punch in the arm. "They're adorable!"

"I like big dogs, but yeah, I guess they are pretty

cute. Think Harrison will agree? He doesn't strike me as the dog type."

Daisy's husband was a businessman who'd originally come into their lives with some diabolical plan to steal the ranch out from under them. Ten years ago, long before their brother Noah had rebuilt the guest ranch, their dad had drunkenly signed over ownership to Harrison's father after losing a poker game. In the end, Harrison had let it all go and ended up with the real prize: Daisy. His sister might drive Axel nuts with her matchmaking and texts with attachments of articles about how married life improves heart health, but she and Noah were his best friends, and he was damned lucky to have gotten so close to the two of them and their spouses, for that matter.

He and Daisy left the kitchen through the arched burnished wood doorway that led to the living room with the vaulted wood ceiling and the stone fireplace, which right now had a huge basket of dried flowers in it, a housewarming gift from the ranch hands, which had touched him. He'd been living here for only six weeks, the house taking record-fast time to build, thanks to the team he'd hired to work beside him. He had to say, he loved this place. The cabin reminded him of the small one he'd left behind at Badger Mountain, but he'd added luxe, modern touches. Even Daisy, who wasn't a log cabin type, said she could hap-

pily live in his house. For a guy who'd planned to
visit the guest ranch only when he absolutely had
to, Axel Dawson had truly come home. His way,
on his terms, which made it feel not just okay, but
right. He felt like he belonged here.

But as he walked out with Daisy, he was well
aware he had some unfinished business to take
care of regarding being back: a letter he was avoiding and had since last December. His father had
left each of his kids a letter with their name on
it inside a folder marked My Will on his kitchen
table. Axel's letter remained unopened under his
socks in his dresser drawer. Eight months and
counting. When Axel got low on socks, and the
envelope appeared through them, he'd get an acidy
pang in his chest and shut the drawer fast, reminding himself to do laundry.

Heroes weren't afraid of letters, and Axel would
be the first to admit he was scared to know what
was inside the one beneath his socks.

Daisy headed to the buggy she'd driven over
in. It was a golf cart that Noah had rigged up to
be ranch employee transportation across the vast
property. They all had one, though Daisy's had
yellow leaves painted on the sides. "You'd better take your own buggy," she said, "or you'll be
trapped without a ride home since I'll be staying
till the bonfire is over."

"Good idea," he said. His cabin was only five

miles from the area where the guest cabins were, and he could run that in twenty minutes, but would he want to after a long day and fifteen minutes of being thanked by Winstons? Probably not.

"See you there," he said, waving as he got in his own buggy.

As he drove, he was well aware that he couldn't get there fast enough. Because he wanted to be looking at Sadie Winston. He wanted to see Danny running around in his light-up sneakers. Maybe tonight would be a way to get them out of his head, out of his system.

Did that *ever* work, though?

Chapter Three

All thirty-eight Winstons had gathered on a rise near the river, mesmerized by the bonfire protected by a circle of rocks that the staff had set up. The children, and there were several, had been ordered under penalty of long time-outs or leaving early not to step past the rocks to get closer to the fire. Each kid had to agree, and only then had Daisy and Sara lit the bonfire.

From where the group sat on blankets, sipping soda or wine and snacking on various treats from little cream-filled chocolates to cheese and crackers to grapes, Sadie watched Axel Dawson walking the perimeter of the fire. He was just as mesmerizing as the flames. Could he *be* more attractive? Tall, over six feet, and leanly muscular with thick dark hair and features that were both refined and masculine at the same time. He wore the forest green Dawson Family Guest Ranch polo shirt and sexy jeans.

Sadie's attention was pulled from him by the clinking of a glass. She looked toward the sound to find her grandmother Vanessa two blankets over, tapping a fork against her wineglass. Her petite grandmother stood, her wavy gray-blond bob blowing in the breeze.

"Welcome, Winstons, to this year's family reunion!" Gram announced. Clapping, cheers and finger whistles followed. "We're here to have a wonderful time and relax and enjoy the guest ranch, but also to thank a very special person— Axel Dawson, the search and rescue specialist who found our Danny-boy when he was lost a few months ago during a family hike. Axel's family owns this ranch, and he now works here. I'd like to raise a toast to Mr. Dawson, our family hero! Everyone, raise your glass or sippy cup!"

Everyone leaped to their feet, the cheering and clapping deafening. Danny slept through all the hoopla.

Sadie looked over at Axel and could swear the

family hero was blushing, which made him more appealing, dammit.

"I had no idea he was so hot," Evie, sharing Sadie's blanket, whispered. "I mean, he's no Marshall Ackerman, but wow."

Sadie smiled and squeezed her sister's hand. Marshall Ackerman was the one who hadn't given in to the ultimatum. Sadie would describe him as attractive enough—he was a very smart tax accountant and a little buttoned-up, but Evie, who'd met him at her previous job—she'd recently become a CPA with a big firm—found him and his sweater-vests incredibly sexy.

"I know," Sadie whispered back. "It's distracting. But I refuse to let his hotness affect me—the man doesn't do commitment."

"That's going around," Evie said with a scowl. Then she raised her glass to toast. "Men—who needs 'em?"

"I'll clink to that," Sadie said on a grin, clinking her sister's wineglass.

As the family settled on the blankets and raised their glasses and cups and sippy cups to Axel, who looked like he might flee at any moment from the attention, Sadie held her own glass up, her gaze locking with his. He nodded at her, and she nodded back.

During the next ten minutes, Axel shook hands and hugged relatives and repeated the story of finding Danny. He gave credit to Dude, the ace yellow Lab with his excellent tracking skills, and held her family rapt. Sadie was now in a circle of relatives, including her sister and four of their cousins, near the fire, Danny still asleep in his stroller beside her. She listened to her cousin Wendy tell a funny story about the parent-teacher conference she went to last June, Sadie's attention more on watching Axel move from group to group. She hoped he wouldn't take off before they got a chance to talk again.

There you go again, she thought. *Wanting to get up close and personal with the anti-commitment one.*

"Excuse me," Daisy Dawson said as she approached their group. Sadie could see the Dawson family resemblance between Daisy and Axel—particularly the blue eyes. "I'm looking for Evie Winston."

"That's me," Evie said, turning from where she'd been chatting with two of their cousins.

"You have a visitor at the welcome gate," Daisy said. "A Marshall Ackerman? Shall I let him in?"

Evie gasped. "Marshall is here?" She turned to Sadie. "Marshall is here!" she repeated. "He's come to his senses!"

Sadie hoped so. The man wouldn't drive a half hour from Prairie City to return a jacket Evie had left at his place or her toothbrush, especially during a Winston family reunion.

"The gate is a quarter mile from here," Daisy said. "I'll walk you over and escort you both back."

"Thanks," Evie said. She turned and opened her eyes wide at Sadie, her expression so hopeful that Sadie sent up a little prayer that Marshall Ackerman had a diamond ring in his pocket. As Evie and Daisy disappeared around a curve, Sadie kneeled beside the stroller and gave her boy a kiss on the head. He was still fast asleep.

"Everything okay?" Axel asked, coming over, gesturing at the path toward the gate. "I saw my sister walking one of your relatives away."

"Everything's fine. That was my sister—Evie," Sadie explained, straightening. "Her ex-boyfriend turned up at the gate. Evie gave him an ultimatum at her birthday dinner—they'd been together three years—and instead of proposing, he said sorry. That was two days ago, but now he's here."

"To propose?" Axel asked.

"She hopes so," Sadie said. "And trust me, so does everyone else. My family is very marriage-minded."

He mock-shivered. "I'm not."

Yeah, she'd heard. But hearing it straight from him stung her anyway. "Why?" she asked. "If I can be so personal. I'm curious about what makes you know you don't want to get married."

He glanced away for a moment, then at her. "The very thought squeezes the air out of my lungs."

That sting she'd felt a second ago? Now a swarm of bees attacked as a memory of her ex-husband flashed into her mind. *I feel like I'm in quicksand, Sadie. Sorry, but that's how I feel. I thought I could do this, but I can't...*

"So marriage is like death?" she asked—coldly, she realized, but she couldn't help it. "A slow, suffocating death?"

He eyed her. "I wouldn't go that far. It's just not for me. I'm a lone wolf."

When someone tells you who they are, believe them...

She lifted her chin. "Well, I'm excited about the idea of finding my Mr. Right," she said, not that he asked. She took a second sip of her wine. She'd chug the entire glass if she were with her sister. "Love, partnership, sharing a life together. That's what it's all about."

He nodded. "I have a great dog."

She couldn't help laughing—not that that was funny. He seemed both serious about that dog comment and not. *You don't know because you don't know him. Keep it that way, missy—or you'll pay!*

Sadie had that funny feeling as if someone was watching her and turned to find her mother, grandmother and great-grandmother, plus her grandfather, two uncles and three cousins watching her talk to Axel. Her mom winked. Her grandmother raised a glass. Her great-grandmother was smiling and giving a little clap.

Oh, brother. If she had a bullhorn, she'd let them know what he'd said about marriage. *A slow, suffocating death, people!* She was paraphrasing, but she was right on the money.

Her grandmother pushed her own mother's wheelchair toward Sadie. The two looked so much alike, but Vanessa was twenty-six years younger. Ninety-nine-year-old Izzy's hair was a beautiful pure white that she always wore in a wispy bun, but she and her daughter both had colorful eyeglasses perched on their noses and hanging off beaded chains, purple for Vanessa and royal blue for Izzy. They both had the same warm, open faces and had never met a stranger. Sadie adored them both. "Izzy and I are pooped," Vanessa Winston said. "See y'all tomorrow for breakfast. I hear the cook makes the best chocolate chip pancakes in Wyoming."

Axel grinned and nodded. "It's true. The best everything. But Cowboy Joe's pancakes are divine. The other day, I had six, and we're not talking silver dollars."

Vanessa and Izzy chuckled, and from the absolute delight in their eyes, Sadie knew they were bursting with approval that she and Axel had been chatting away in their own little duo near the fire, Danny between them in the stroller.

"Night night, you two," Izzy said with a grin, adjusting her small square glasses. "Don't stay out too late."

Oh, brother. "We won't, Great-Gram," Sadie said. "Good night."

"I'd be happy to push the wheelchair and escort you to your cabin," Axel said, stepping over.

Both women beamed. "Oh no, dear," Vanessa said. "You stay and have a lovely evening with our Sadie. Did you know she won a blue ribbon at the county fair for her cinnamon strudel? She's quite the baker. And the loveliest gal inside and out."

Earth, please open and swallow me. Thanks.

"I do love cinnamon baked goods," Axel said with a nod—and a twinkle in his eye. Oh, God. So he had a good sense of humor. Or was he just kind to grandmothers and great-grandmothers? Sadie sighed inwardly.

"Hear that, Sadie-girl?" Vanessa said with a wink. Right there out in the open. No subtlety at all with this crew!

"Night, now," Izzy said as Vanessa waved and headed up the path.

"Good night," Axel called, watching them until they disappeared from view. He chuckled.

"Izzy, my great-grandmother, is ninety-nine."

Sadie wanted to head off anything about that last discussion. "Isn't that something?"

He smiled and nodded. "You're lucky. My grandparents and great-grandparents are all gone. As is my dad. My mother lives in Florida where it's always warm—she has a small orange grove."

Sadie had visited Florida once in the dead of winter and had never been more grateful for a state. "That sounds wonderful. Fresh-squeezed orange juice every morning." She bit her lip, suddenly feeling…shy-ish. "You've got lots of siblings, right? That must be nice."

"It is. There are six of us. Three of us live and work on the ranch. The other three are scattered across the state. They come home for occasions. Like the grand reopening of the ranch last Memorial Day weekend. And for Daisy's wedding— which didn't work out the first time around but she ended up giving birth that same day, so we were all here to welcome little Tony."

"So you have a baby nephew?" Sadie said. "How great for him to have two uncles right here."

He nodded. "I have another baby nephew and niece—twins. My brother Noah's kids. He runs the place, and his wife, Sara, is the forewoman. Turns out I'm better at babysitting than I thought. Chase and Annabel—Noah's twins—love me for some reason. Either that or I bore them to death with my stories about search and rescue, and they fall right asleep."

Sadie laughed. "So you like babies, but you're not planning on becoming a father yourself?" She immediately felt her cheeks burn. Why had she blurted that out? Ugh.

He glanced away again, something he did, she noticed, when he seemed uncomfortable.

He got lucky not having to answer because just then, Sadie could see Daisy Dawson, Evie and Marshall Ackerman heading toward them, and her attention went straight to her sister. Evie and Marshall were holding hands!

And as they got closer, Sadie could see a diamond ring glinting in the glow of the fire and the moonlight on Evie's formerly empty left hand. *Oh, Evie,* she thought, her heart overflowing with happiness for her sister.

Daisy headed over to where the ranch hands were keeping watch on the bonfire, and Evie and Marshall joined Sadie and Axel.

"I see congratulations are in order," Sadie gushed, blinking back tears as she took her sister's hand to see the ring. "It's so beautiful! I'm so happy for you two."

Evie wrapped Sadie in a hug. "I always love a good surprise. And this was the topper!"

Marshall smiled at his fiancée. "I was a fool— no, a complete idiot," he said, his dark brown eyes shining on Evie. "But two days on my own made me realize I can't live without this amazing person. Evie, you're the woman of my dreams. I'm sorry I made the last few days so painful."

"You are so forgiven," Evie said, grinning, reaching up to kiss him. "Oh! Marshall, this is Axel Dawson. He's the search and rescue specialist who found Danny when he went missing. This bonfire gathering is actually about a toast to him. And Axel, this is my brand-spankin'-new fiancé, Marshall Ackerman." She was positively beaming. "My fiancé. That will not get old."

Axel extended his hand and Marshall shook it. "Congrats."

Marshall smiled. "Thanks for saving my soon-to-be nephew. I'm crazy about this little tyke," he added, looking at Danny.

"Well, we've got to go share the big news," Evie said. "Mom is going to flip!"

Sadie watched her sister and Marshall tell her mom, who almost exploded with sheer joy. Hoots and hollers and cheers went out as word spread.

"Well," Axel said, "congrats on gaining a brother-in-law."

"Marshall's a great guy. I'm glad he realized what he'd be throwing away."

Axel stared at her for a second, and Sadie hoped he didn't think she was speaking code for herself! That was how much trouble she was actually in already with this man. Reading into absolutely nothing. Worrying about crazy nonsense. She had to get a hold of herself. Which meant heading to the cabin and getting away from those piercing blue eyes and incredible body—which was very close to her.

"Well," she said brightly, "time to transfer the big guy to bed." She smiled at the sleeping Danny. "To the porta-crib, anyway."

"I was about to head out, so I'll walk you then come back for my golf cart," he said.

Sigh.

"I'll push the stroller," he offered.

"Chivalrous. Your dad raised you right." She smiled, but the look on his face had her biting her lip. She stepped aside and he took the handles and they began walking up the path toward the cabins.

"Actually, my father destroyed everything he touched," Axel said, staring straight ahead. "He was a selfish alcoholic."

She stopped walking and so did he. "I'm sorry. That had to have been hard. Growing up that way."

He nodded and resumed walking. "My mother wised up to his cheating and finally left. We lived in town for years, and she thought it was important that we keep in close contact with our dad, so she'd drive his three boys over every other weekend. That's how I got so close to Daisy and Noah.

They have a different mother but were living here full-time in those days."

"So their mom—your stepmother—looked out for you and your brothers when you visited?" she asked.

"Yup. She was a kind woman, and she died way too young. After that, Rex and Zeke and I didn't come around too often since our mom didn't trust Bo Dawson with our lives even for a weekend. Our oldest brother, Ford, also has a different mother, and he refused to visit at all once he got old enough to protest."

"Did your dad have any redeeming qualities?" Sadie asked, hoping so.

"I suppose everyone does. He was a charmer. Always had nice girlfriends who deserved a lot better. He cared about us in his own way, I guess. Sometimes he shocked me with the undeniable truth that he loved us. But he was a wrecking ball of a man. He destroyed the guest ranch his parents built. He destroyed his marriages. He disappointed his kids constantly. He hurt everyone he came into contact with."

"Is it hard being here, then?" she asked. "You've only been living here a couple months, right?"

He nodded. "It was hard at first. But there's a lot else here. My grandparents' legacy—even if the ranch is a lot different now than the one they began. Family history. Memories—bad but good, too. My dad had absolutely nothing when he died—cirrhosis of the liver from years of drinking—but he left us all this ranch, which at the time was abandoned and a wreck. And letters. We each got a personal letter."

"Did yours help?"

He shrugged. "I still haven't opened it."

She gaped at him. "Really? Aren't you curious?"

"Yes. Very. Always have been since I got it last December. But I can't bring myself to open it."

Huh.

"Well, here you are," he said quickly as though suddenly aware he'd said too much or at least much more than he'd intended on a two-minute walk.

Sadie glanced up at the cute dark wood cabin with its white trim and barn-red door. There were blooming flower boxes in the windows and two white padded rocking chairs on the covered porch. Sadie's grandmother was sitting in one of the rockers, a glass of iced tea and cookies beside her. Izzy's wheelchair was parked beside the little ramp on the side of the porch. Izzy could get around fine on her own, particularly with her cane, but she always used the wheelchair for crowded areas or distances. "How nice of you to walk Sadie home," Vanessa said with a big smile.

Sadie pursed her lips. "Gram, guess what? Evie

got engaged! Marshall came tonight and proposed. They're still at the bonfire sharing the big news."

"What?" Gram flew down the steps and wrapped Sadie in a big hug, her floral perfume, her trademark that Sadie had always loved, enveloping her. "That's wonderful!"

"What's so wonderful?" Izzy asked, coming out on the porch in her flowered ankle-length bathrobe, using her bright red wooden cane with its copper handle.

"They're engaged! Oh, I'm beside myself!" Vanessa said, completely overcome. "I'm going to make a few happy calls to let people know— back in a bit!"

Gram had been one of Evie's biggest ralliers when Marshall had broken her heart, buying her an as-seen-on-TV zip-up blanket with pockets that she'd stuffed with packets of tissues and packs of M&M's and gummy bears, Evie's favorites. Sadie had no doubt Vanessa would go through the list of her besties—her bridge club, knitting circle and ethnic cooking class.

As Gram hurried inside, Izzy settled on one of the rockers, stealing a cookie. "Engaged! Oh, happy day!" Her eyes misted, and she patted her chest. "Well, come up and let me congratulate you two! Oh, how wonderful indeed. My Sadie, engaged!"

Sadie glanced at Axel. Izzy couldn't possibly

think she and Axel were the engaged ones. "Uh, no, Great-Gram, it's—"

"I'll tell you, Sadie-girl," Izzy interrupted. "When that louse of a husband up and left you pregnant and alone, I cried myself to sleep for weeks. All I've wanted in this world is for you to be happy. And now that I'm nearing the end of my days, I'll know my girl has found everlasting love with a real hero. You two have made an old woman so happy," she said, looking from her to Axel. Tears ran down Izzy's wrinkled cheeks.

Oh no. No, no, no. "Great-Gram, I—"

Axel leaned closer. "You can correct her in the morning—or Vanessa will when Izzy heads inside to bed. She's probably tired right now and extraemotional."

Sadie nodded. Extraemotional was an understatement.

"Well, come now, give your great-gram a hug," Izzy said, holding her arms out wide.

Sadie went up the steps and bent to hug Izzy.

"I haven't been this happy since your great-granddaddy was still with us," Izzy whispered, wrapping both hands around Sadie's face. "I love you so much, Sadie. You deserve this happiness. And you," she said with utter reverence, turning to Axel, "our family hero. That precious little boy in that stroller will finally have a daddy, and a wonderful one at that." Tears shone in her hazel eyes.

"Come hug your great-gram. You can call me that or Izzy, whatever you like."

Axel smiled tightly, leaned over and gave his new great-gram a hug.

"If I go into that good night, and I just might, I'll go happy now," Izzy said, a hand to her heart again.

Sadie felt her eyes widen to the point they ached. She glanced at Axel, who looked equally shell-shocked.

"Well, um, good night, Izzy," Axel said, clearly forcing a smile.

"Didn't I tell you to call me Great-Gram? We're family now!"

Sadie bit her lip. Izzy could get a bit addled now and again. This would be easy to correct in the morning when Izzy had had a good night's sleep.

"See you tomorrow, Great-Gram," Axel croaked out. He glanced at Sadie, then at Danny, and then ran for the hills.

Sadie's heart was beating a mile a minute. Oh, God. This was a mess.

Gram would help straighten things out in the morning. Vanessa would simply tell Izzy that *They're engaged!* referred to Evie and Marshall, which made complete sense, and not Sadie and Axel.

"I'm zonked," Izzy said, slowly getting up with the help of her cane.

"Let me go put Danny in his crib, and then I'll be right back." She parked the stroller by Izzy's wheelchair, then rushed inside with Danny in her arms, hoping to catch Vanessa between calls, but when she poked her head in her gram's room, Vanessa was chatting away on the phone about hoping to find the grandmother-of-the-bride dress of her dreams.

Sadie hurried into her room and settled Danny in the porta-crib with barely a stir out of him, then went outside. She helped Izzy into the cabin and to the bedroom she was sharing with her daughter and granddaughter. Vanessa was still on her cell phone, talking excitedly. She lowered her voice when Sadie got Izzy into bed, Great-Gram closing her eyes and snoring within seconds. Today had been a big day for everyone—arriving at the ranch, the orientation and walk around the property, the bonfire and the big news, which was not news at all—but especially for the ninety-nine-year-old.

As Vanessa sat on her bed, telling whomever she was talking to that no, she had no idea if Evie would take Marshall's last name or keep her own, Sadie knew her gram would be on the phone for at least an hour more. She managed a smile at Vanessa and waved, then slipped into her own room.

For tonight, until morning, Sadie was engaged to Axel Dawson. And that was fine with her.

Chapter Four

Axel yawned early the next morning as he towel-dried his hair and ran his hands through it, then pulled on his Dawson Family Guest Ranch staff shirt and a pair of jeans. He'd slept like crud, waking up constantly as though he'd forgotten something important. And then he'd remember: he was fake-engaged for the night. To Sadie Winston. Even being faux-engaged had unsettled him to the point he couldn't sleep. All that talk of a hero for a husband and a wonderful father for Danny.

Eh, it would all be taken care of by now. Izzy's daughter or granddaughter or great-granddaughter had probably set her straight at some point last night. Marshall Ackerman was the only groom-to-be in the vicinity.

It was barely 6:00 a.m., and the sun was dawning a hazy pink over the horizon, but there was a lot to prepare for today—wilderness hikes and trail rides and river swimming, plus some general cowboy duties to help out his sister-in-law, Sara, the forewoman. Axel went to grab a pair of socks from his dresser drawer, and there it was. The letter.

He really should move it somewhere he wouldn't notice it so often. Through the low jumble of rolled-up socks he could see the *Ax* of his father's scrawl on the front of the white letter-sized envelope. Knowledge of his illness had prompted his father to write the letters, but not to talk to his children. What was in there? *Sorry for being a terrible father 98 percent of the time?* That was what Axel figured. Noah and Daisy and Ford had all shared their letters. Noah's had been full of apologies and asked him to think about rebuilding the ranch that Bo had let rot. Noah had surprised all the siblings by stepping up and meeting the challenge, and they'd all invested in the Dawson Family Guest Ranch 2.0. Daisy's letter had also apologized for letting down his only daughter time and again but he'd left her her mother's wedding rings, which Daisy had asked for since she was eleven, when their mother had died. A broke drunk with a gambling problem, Bo could have sold the rings for a decent amount, but he'd held on to them, knowing how much they meant to his daughter. Axel had always thought Bo had hung on to the rings instead of giving them to Daisy so that he'd have something over her, something she wanted from him, to keep her from completely turning her back, which she wouldn't have done anyway.

Axel had. And then his father had died a week later.

He shook that away and thought about Ford, the oldest of the siblings, who'd tried the hardest of all of them to get through to their dad. Even Ford, a cop who'd seen just about everything, had finally had enough. Ford's letter from Bo hadn't been a letter at all but a map, a hand-drawn rendering of where he'd buried Ford's mother's diary, which Bo Dawson had found one day, apparently not appreciated and hidden somewhere on the property in a drunken stupor. Apparently, Bo figured Ford might want to know his mother's secrets, and so he'd left him the map, just a map, no note, nothing. Ford had tried to find it a couple of times since he had known the general area, but hadn't been able to.

As for Zeke and Rex, neither would say a word about their letters. Rex was private, always had been, to the point that no one knew what he did for a living. Axel was pretty sure he worked for the government, either local or federal, in some secret-spy sense. For all Axel knew, though, Rex could be a lobsterman out on a boat all day. The man just would not say. Zeke was a successful businessman a few hours away and had done a lot, remotely, to help Noah in getting the ranch up and going operationally. But on the rare occasions the six siblings were together, every time Daisy brought up the letters their father had left them, Zeke changed the subject or suddenly had to make a call.

Axel grabbed the letter and held it up to the light as he'd done a thousand times. He wouldn't mind making out a few words or a sentence to get the general gist. He could make out the dark scrawl of his dad's handwriting but not individual words. He put the letter in the drawer. He wanted to know what it said—and didn't. The story of his life.

He sure had been chatty last night on the way back from the bonfire about his father, though. What was that about? Why had he said so much? All those deeply personal details about Bo Dawson's issues. Maybe Sadie was easy to talk to. They'd shared a very intense…something on Badger Mountain when Danny had been lost, when he'd promised her he'd find her son. There was a connection there. That was all. So he'd opened up. Not something he ever did, though, so the fact that he had meant something. He just didn't know what.

He grabbed socks and shut the drawer, then

headed downstairs with Dude for much-needed coffee. He'd let the dog out in the yard and had barely had a sip before he heard his sister's sing-song voice out on the porch.

"So I hear congratulations are in order and that I must be so overjoyed to be gaining a sister-in-law," Daisy said.

Axel glanced through the kitchen window. Daisy, her face full of what Axel could call only about-to-burst-out-laughing merriment, peered at him through the screen.

What she'd said hadn't quite registered. Congratulations? A sister-in-law? What?

"Now, I know you, Axel, and there's no way you're engaged, so what the peacock is going on?"

Wait. If Daisy was being congratulated about the "engagement," that meant it had gotten around. But how was that possible?

"A great-gram, that's what," Axel said on a long sigh. He'd been sure the whole thing would have blown over by now, that someone would have explained to Izzy that he and Sadie weren't the engaged ones. If not last night, then this morning.

Daisy, dressed as he was in the Dawson Family Guest Ranch green polo but with khaki shorts, her long light brown hair in a braid, was in his kitchen like a shot, pouring herself a mug of coffee and taking a slice of banana bread while she was at it. "Okay, spill it."

He explained.

"Ooh, boy," she said. "Well, at least ten Winstons congratulated me this morning on becoming part of the family, Axel, and it wasn't even six a.m. You can thank sunrise yoga for so many guests being out and about that early."

He stared at her, horror building in his gut. "I don't get it. Sadie was going to tell her grandmother that Izzy had misunderstood her and they'd tell the great-grandmother—she's ninety-nine, by the way—together."

"Well, it doesn't look like anyone spoke up. So you're engaged." Daisy let out a hearty chuckle. "In fact, a Winston kid who couldn't be older than six came up to me and said she heard that my brother was marrying her big cousin Sadie and now we're all going to be one big family."

Axel gulped.

Daisy laughed. "I'm happy for you, Axel. It's almost like a dream come true, if it were real."

Axel groaned and slugged the rest of his coffee. "Keyword if, and it's not. We'll get it straightened out this morning." He stole a piece of banana bread.

"Speak of the bride," Daisy said, tipping her chin toward the window.

Axel looked out. A ranch hand was driving a golf cart toward his cabin, Sadie in the passenger seat.

"My cue to scram," Daisy said. "I'll do a lot of

smiling and nodding and hasty retreating around the Winstons until you say otherwise."

He groaned. "What a mess."

"An interesting mess, though," Daisy said with a grin, then left.

Axel let Dude in, then stood on the porch, watching Sadie hop out of the buggy and thank the ranch hand, who turned and drove off, following Daisy toward the ranch.

Sadie held up a hand in something of a wave, and he did, too. She looked kind of…stressed. Damn, she was pretty. Her long blond hair was loose and swaying a bit as she walked, catching the early sun. She wore a pale yellow tank top, white shorts and sneakers. A delicate gold necklace with a tiny letter *D* dangling glinted on her breastbone. *D* for Danny, he figured.

"I hear we're still engaged," he said as she approached the steps. "Little relatives of yours are congratulating my sister."

She closed her eyes and buried her face in her hands for a moment, then shook her head and looked at him. "I have made one heck of a mess of this."

"Come on in for coffee. I have bagels, or I could make you scrambled eggs."

Her face brightened—likely because he wasn't furious and screeching his head off about the whole thing. He had a feeling that was what she expected. Normally the idea of anyone thinking he was engaged would bring about that feeling he'd described to her last night: a lack of air in his lungs. But he was oddly calm about it. Maybe because he'd been there when the misunderstanding had occurred.

"I'd love a bagel," she said. "And about ten cups of coffee."

Yeah, me, too, he thought, offering her a smile. "Follow me. Dude's hungry, too."

He led the way into the cabin and she stopped to pet the appreciative yellow Lab and look around, slowly swiveling. "This is some cabin. Not what I expected," she added.

"What did you expect? More rustic?"

"Yes. This place is gorgeous. Such craftsmanship. And so cozy."

He felt a bit of pride as she slowly turned and took it all in, the woodwork and moldings, the furnishings. "I knew I needed to make this place my sanctuary to be really comfortable here. So I did."

She glanced at him, then settled her gaze on a watercolor of abstract sheep. "Makes sense, based on what you said last night. About your dad."

He swallowed. Yup, he'd said all that. He sighed inwardly and headed to the kitchen, so aware of her behind him. Dude followed for his own breakfast.

He fed his dog, then poured Sadie a cup of coffee and gestured for her to sit at the table. "Cream, sugar right here," he added, pointing. "So for bagels I have plain, sesame, cinnamon raisin and everything."

"Sesame with cream cheese would be great."

"I'd almost prefer to keep talking about anything other than the fact that your entire family thinks we're engaged," he said, cutting two sesame bagels and putting the halves in the toaster oven.

"Me, too," she said.

He smiled and sat, drinking the rest of his coffee. "Okay, I'm a bit more fortified now. Fill me in."

She took in a breath and blew it out. "Well, last night, I helped Izzy to bed, and she conked out right away. I'd planned to tell Vanessa what happened, that Izzy thought she'd been referring to us when she'd said, 'They're engaged,' but every time I went to talk to Vanessa, she was still on the phone. I guess I fell asleep because when I woke up at the crack of dawn, everyone was awake and talking about the possibility of a double wedding— my sister, mother, gram and great-gram. My sister was jumping up and down about my sudden whirlwind engagement. My mother was *crying*— seriously, tears streaming down her cheeks to the point she couldn't even speak. My grandmother was on the phone to let everyone know *both* her granddaughters had gotten engaged last night, and I was in total shock. Meanwhile, Danny started screaming his head off, so I took care of him, and when I came back, everyone was knee-deep in making lists of caterers and bridal boutiques and possible venues."

Axel smiled and shook his head. "Having met all these people, I can easily see how that all unfolded."

"I appreciate that. My family can definitely be overwhelming." She took a long sip of her coffee. "And then, I was about to tell them it was all a big misunderstanding when my aunt Tabby burst in and wrapped me in big hug, then my sister, and said she was overjoyed and that for the sake of the two brides-to-be, she hoped she and my mother could put aside their differences for the time being at least. My mother agreed to the truce, and I was so flabbergasted that I still didn't pipe up. It's been three months since their big fight, and two engaged nieces are simply bigger than their fight. I watched them talk—smiling and happy—for the first time since that day on the mountain, Axel. About wedding stuff, not themselves or actually making up, but talking."

He nodded and got up to take the bagels from the toaster oven and slather them with cream cheese. "Well, hopefully, they'll return to being sisters and put whatever happened between them behind them." She looked so eager that he realized her mother and aunt's cold war had been really tough on her, especially because he knew she thought it had something to do with Danny going missing that day. He added a small bunch of grapes to the plates, then brought breakfast over to the table and sat across from her.

She smiled and popped a grape into her mouth. "Thank you," she said, then bit into the bagel, sitting back and relaxing. He felt like jumping up and massaging the tension out of her shoulders. The urge to touch her was way too strong. "So then the lot of them were all excitedly talking again," Sadie went on, "and relatives burst in the cabin to congratulate me and Evie as they heard the news, and now I'm expected to go preliminary gown shopping this afternoon." She dropped her head into her palm, then looked up at him.

"They must have asked where your diamond ring is?" he said, eyeing her empty left hand.

"They sure did. I told them I decided I didn't want a ring this time around, that what mattered to me was our marriage and the wedding ring."

He nodded, not wanting to delve into that. "So where did you tell them you were going this morning?" he asked.

"To see my fiancé before his work starts," she said sheepishly, her cheeks bright red.

He smiled, but then the word *fiancé* reverberated in his head and that airless feeling started in his chest. "They're watching Danny?"

She nodded. "I'm so sorry about all this, Axel. Look, I'll text my sister right now and explain what happened, and she'll set everyone straight. It's embarrassing as heck, but by the time I get back to the cabin, they'll have forgotten it. There's still an engaged Winston sister. My mom and aunt can still find joy and common ground in that, and it'll help bring them together."

He was about to nod until he noticed how sad her eyes looked, how stressed she seemed.

He heard ninety-nine-year-old Izzy's voice from last night. *When that louse of a husband up and left you pregnant and alone...*

He'd always known Sadie was a single mother; he'd known that up on Badger Mountain when the team had questioned her and her family about the possibility of an unhappy ex snatching Danny when no one was looking. She'd said her ex-husband hadn't showed a lick of interest in the fact that he had a child, and she highly doubted he'd been following them and hiding behind trees, waiting for a moment to suddenly kidnap Danny and raise a son on his own. The louse had left her when she'd been seven weeks pregnant and hadn't been heard from since. She'd sent the divorce papers to his parents, and they'd sent the signed set back. Her ex had apparently said Danny wasn't his, and they believed him. A single mother completely on her own—that couldn't be easy, big family around her or not.

"I'll text Evie right now," she added, pulling her phone out of her pocket. "She announced that she and Marshall decided to have the wedding right here at the ranch at the lodge on the last night of the reunion, so everyone will be all excited about that. Evie also said she thought each of us should have her own big day, so that stopped the double-wedding talk." Her eyes misted, and she looked away, clearly embarrassed.

She *wanted* to be engaged, he realized, both superficially and deep down. Even faux-engaged—he understood that with sudden crystal clarity. All that happy attention, all that affirmation, her relatives stopping with the "poor Sadie, all alone" crud. His scruffy, scuffed-up heart went out to her.

Axel put his hand on hers to stop her from texting her sister. "I have an idea."

She peered up at him with those beautiful pale brown eyes.

He slugged his coffee, then looked at her. "I totally get what happened, Sadie. I've been in the middle of that kind of family melee where you're so overwhelmed by everyone's voices that you're speechless even if they're talking about you."

She stared at him with what seemed like utter relief that he understood. "But now we're engaged. What are we going to do? We have to tell them the truth. I mean, it's not like I can let them think I'm getting married when I'm not."

He took another bite of his bagel. "Here's the idea part… Your sister is getting married the last night of the reunion. Let's get through that, everyone focused on Evie and on her wedding, and once you're all home, you can tell them it didn't work out and you didn't want to say anything because you didn't want to take away from Evie's special day."

She stared at him again, her mouth slightly open. "You're serious."

He shrugged. "Why not? That way, a ninety-nine-year-old remains happy. Your mother and aunt will mend their issues."

"Wait. You're willing to be fake-engaged for a week for the greater good?" She gaped at him, head tilted.

And because something is telling me you need this, Sadie. Something is poking and pushing at me deep down, making that very clear. A flash of her face on Badger Mountain, when she'd been terrified, over an hour into her then twenty-four-month-old son missing settled in his mind. In his chest. In his gut. All the questions the police had subjected her and her family to. Was she a good mother? Was she neglectful? Did Danny often run off unattended? There were questions that had to be asked in that kind of situation, a complete picture drawn. But hell, she'd been terrified about her son. Now, she was on vacation with thirty-eight of her relatives, which couldn't be all sunshine and roses even in the closest of families. Yeah, he'd cut her a big break. Why not?

"I'm speechless, Axel Dawson. Well, actually, no, I'm not. You really are a hero."

He smiled. "Wait till you get to know your fiancé," he said. "You'll see I'm not."

She tilted her head again, her expression shifting, and he could have slugged himself. Why did he blurt things out with this woman? Why did he say what was in his head? Why couldn't he stay hard to talk to the way he usually was? Hadn't that been the complaint of 75 percent of the women he'd dated the past few years?

"All I know is that you've saved my life twice now," Sadie said. "And made me breakfast." Her smile lit up her face, and the sun glinted on her *D* necklace.

There was that urge to touch her again, to run his hand along her bare shoulders, to feel her silky blond ponytail. A realization slammed into him. He most certainly could not touch her. Not when they were fake-engaged. Because there was one thing Axel knew always got him into trouble, and that was a blurred line.

Chapter Five

This was nuts. Sadie had gotten through breakfast
(Cowboy Joe's chocolate chip pancakes really were
something spectacular) and a family walk on the
wooded trails by the river, but now she, her sister,
mom and aunt were about to leave for Your Special
Day, a bridal boutique in Prairie City, which was a
half hour away. Gram would be watching Danny
and taking him to the petting zoo and then to the
lodge for the "kid fun zone," where an indoor ob-
stacle course, games and arts-and-crafts station,
broken into age groups and run by the ranch staff
would let tired grown-ups take a breather for a
couple of hours.

Sadie sat on her bed in the cabin, her stomach churning. Her sister was standing before the dresser mirror, putting her hair in a ponytail and dabbing on lip balm that smelled like vanilla. Sadie stared at Evie, her best friend, someone she'd always been able to talk to about anything. Suddenly Sadie was lying to her about something so vital? No—Sadie wouldn't do this. She had to come clean. The sooner, the better. The longer she kept up this lie, the harder it would be to explain.

"I wasn't going to say this," Evie said, turning to face Sadie. "Because it sounds kind of 'poor Sadie,' which I know you hate. Which *I* hate. But one of the reasons why I waited so long to tell Marshall to fish or cut bait was because I hated the idea of getting engaged while you were…still single."

Sadie felt her cheeks flame, and she coughed. Oh, God. This was awful.

Evie sat beside her. "I love you to death, Sadie. You've been my best friend since the day I was born. I have no idea what I'd do without you— for advice, for sharing my every thought and secret, for analyzing Mom and Dad over the years… everything. But when that jerk left when you were pregnant… For the past two years, you've gone from my amazing older sister to more—you're *my* hero, Sadie. You've handled single motherhood like an absolute champ. You're so strong, so independent and such a great mom. But I know how badly that rat bastard hurt you. And there was no way I wanted to get engaged and celebrate all things love and forever when my favorite person in the world was on her own with a baby. Am I making sense?"

Tears streamed down Sadie's face. She had no idea if part of her was crying for the mess she'd made of this lie or all her sister had just said, how moved Sadie was by how much Evie cared about her.

Evie's eyes filled with tears, too. "Something in me came to a head with Marshall on my birthday, though. I realized that his not proposing after three years when we had something so special and good and right was like a slap in the face. Like, my sister didn't go through everything she went through so that you, Marshall Jay Ackerman, could be so lackadaisical about making a real commitment to me."

"I think I know what you mean," Sadie said, swiping a hand under her eyes. "You wanted him to put up or shut up because commitment matters, and you saw how little it meant to Danny's father even when a pregnancy came into the picture."

"That's it, exactly. And now, I'm engaged, and so are you! I can't tell you what that means to me. That you're happy, that you found your guy—and such a great guy—and that we get to do this together. All the fun bridal stuff."

Sadie wrapped her sister in a hug. So much for setting the record straight. *Oh, um, er, Evie? It turns out I'm not engaged and this was all a misunderstanding. Great-Gram mistook me for the bride-to-be and it snowballed and now you poured out your heart and soul to me, but oopsies—I'm still "Single Sadie" and my supposed fiancé and I haven't so much as held hands, let alone kissed.*

Yes, dammit. Just tell her the truth! It'll be mortifying for an hour or two and you'll both be embarrassed but you have to come clean! Of course, things will feel weird and Evie will feel awful that she'd said all that, and you'll create problems between you two when Mom and Aunt Tabby are mending their fences, and today's shopping trip will be ruined for Evie.

Oh flipperty-flubs. If Sadie didn't blurt out the truth right now, there would be no turning back and she'd have to go with Axel's generous idea to keep up the ruse for the week and let Evie have her week of happy engagement without anything mucking it up. As the truth would.

Speak now or forever hold your—

"Ready, girls?" their mom called from the living room.

Evie's smile was so big, so happy, that Sadie sucked in a fast breath and called out, "Yes, we're ready."

Well.

* * *

The moment Aunt Tabby parked her SUV in the public lot in the middle of Prairie City's two-mile-long downtown, Sadie wished she were at the Dawson Family Guest Ranch in Bear Ridge. Sadie had spent her whole life in Prairie City and the big town had a lot to offer, from the vibrant village with shops and restaurants to open spaces. The lot abutted the town green, which had a gazebo and a playground and picnic tables, and it was on a bench beside a bronze sculpture of Hazel Montvale, the town's intrepid female founder, that Sadie had told her then-husband, Kyle Harlow, that they were going to be parents.

She'd chosen the bench for two reasons—one, she loved that statue of Hazel and often, when she couldn't figure something out, she'd think: What would Hazel Montvale do? And Sadie would do the smart thing instead of the dumb thing. Two, the bench was right behind a low fence that surrounded the playground, and she liked the idea of talking about starting their family in the midst of toddlers and little kids on the slides and structures.

Her husband of two months had changed after the wedding. She'd asked her family to be honest about that—had it been Sadie who'd fallen for a scoundrel and dismissed all the bright red flags or had he truly changed? Her mother, honest to a fault, had said that Kyle had changed, that the gold band and the piece of paper had some triggering effect on him, though neither knew from what. He'd gone quiet, then stopped coming home after work, then stopped coming home before midnight and then some nights, didn't come home at all. Pleading for conversation, the truth, answers got her nowhere. And then she'd discovered she was seven weeks pregnant.

When she'd asked him to meet her at the bench on the green, she wasn't sure he'd show up, but he had because it turned out he had news, too. He'd made a mistake, he was sorry, he wasn't cut out for marriage, he loved her, but he couldn't stop wanting to sleep with other women, too. While he'd been talking, her head and her heart had been so numb she almost didn't bother telling him her news. But he should know, so she did and his response was not unexpected. *Sorry. Leaving with the rodeo. Tell the baby he or she is better off without me, that y'all can do way better.*

He'd left her sitting there, and if it were not for the statue of Hazel Montvale to the right of her, she would have fallen to a heap on the ground, unable to sit upright. Sadie had called her sister, who'd rushed over, and Evie had called Sadie in sick to work for the next three days with a bad case of strep throat. Sadie had cried her eyes out—for the lost dreams, for her baby who'd grow up without his father, for being thirty and pregnant and alone with a wedding band that now symbolized nothing.

That he'd gone from warm and funny and soulful to miserable, cheating and gone had done a number on her for a long time. Her ability to trust her own judgment had been destroyed. A few months after Danny was born, Sadie started agreeing to fix-ups and blind dates since her relatives were full of "he'd be perfect for you" lists, but no one was. No one had come close. A few times someone had seemed like a possible second date, but then he'd say something that would indicate he had no interest in becoming anyone's stepdaddy, let alone a loving father.

"Now, Sadie," her mom said, slipping her arm through her daughter's as they walked toward the bridal boutique with Aunt Tabby and Evie right behind them, "just because you had the big white dress and fancy reception the first time doesn't mean you can't have a bigger, splashier wedding this time around. With the *right* groom."

Sadie had always appreciated her mother's *go big or go home* mentality. But she swallowed. "I think the second time around, small and private sound perfect."

Viv Winston gasped. "Sadie Anne Winston, don't you dare think of eloping!"

"Ooh, you're thinking of eloping?" Evie called from behind them.

Sadie turned back. "Just thinking aloud. I don't know what I want yet."

"How about Axel?" Aunt Tabby asked. "He has a big family and probably wants the big wedding."

Sadie couldn't help but notice her mother stiffen beside her when Tabby spoke, Viv's expression tightening, too. Hmm. They might have declared a truce for the sake of Sadie and Evie being engaged, but they were clearly still in the same old fight.

"We haven't talked about that at all," Sadie said fast. "Things happened really quickly."

"I'll say," her mother added, tucking a swatch of her shoulder-length blond hair behind her ear. "I can't believe you two were dating right under our noses the past three months!"

Sadie *wished* they'd been dating. "I, uh, didn't want to jinx it. Whenever I talk too much about what's going on in my relationship, it's always doomed."

"Well, then don't say another word!" Aunt Tabby called out. "We love Axel!"

Her mother lifted her chin. "Even a broken clock is right twice a day," she whispered.

Sadie gasped. "Mom!" Good Godfrey, things between Viv and Tabby were way worse than she realized, given that they were both here.

Her mother gave an embittered shrug and hurried along. Your Special Day was two stores up.

"Mom," she whispered. "Please tell me what's going on between you two. What happened?"

Viv and Tabby—Tabby was four years younger—had always been so close. Aunt Tabby was more than just a beloved aunt—she'd never married and Tabby's house had always felt like an extension of Sadie's own or like a sanctuary to run to when she was angry at her parents or arguing with Evie about something dumb. Aunt Tabby had never wanted children, and often over the years, Sadie had heard overly personal conversations about the subject, sometimes including Tabby and sometimes not. None of the family, except Great-Gram Izzy, seemed to be able to comprehend a woman not wanting to have a baby and raise a family.

Oh, please! Izzy had said. *First of all, some kids turn their parents' hair gray by the time they're five years old. Who needs to spend their lives in a hair salon to turn back time when it's marching forward? And motherhood is not the be-all and end-all of a woman's life. There's her work and volunteering and friendships and bridge partners.*

Everyone had started in about Izzy having a zillion people to care for her in her old age because she had had children, but Izzy had harrumphed and said, *Oh, please, that was what great-granddaughters and grandnieces were for.* It was no surprise that Aunt Tabby worshipped her grandmother. Sadie had always hoped she'd inherited even just a little of Izzy's wisdom.

"Between who two?" her mother now asked.

Sadie made a face. "C'mon. You and Aunt Tabby."

"Everything's fine," she lied way too smoothly. "Oh, look, we're here!"

Sadie glanced at the beautiful window display of Your Special Day. A dress straight out of her dreams was in the window. She shook her head at herself. Why was she letting a wedding gown, which she would never wear because she was *not* engaged, distract her from her mother?

"Mom, please talk to me straight," Sadie whispered as her sister and aunt caught up.

"Ooh, look at those shoes!" Viv gushed, pointing.

"I love them," Evie said, coming up beside Sadie. "Peep-toe 1940s glam. I'm trying them on!"

Sadie glanced at her aunt, who was looking anywhere but at her own sister. She knew she wouldn't get any answers out of these two right now.

Sadie headed into the shop, the mannequins with their gowns and busts of headpieces and veils and jewelry reminding her of the first time she'd come here with these three women. Her grandmother had also joined them. "Let's make this week all about Evie's wedding," she said. *Please all agree that's a great idea and lay off me!*

"Well, take pics of anything that catches your eye for yourself," Aunt Tabby said. "I can help you make a mood board for your wedding."

"I found my dress!" Evie said, her eyes wide on a mannequin by the shoe display.

They all turned to look in the direction Evie's misty eyes were staring.

"Oh, Evie, that is so you," their mom agreed.

"Love it," Aunt Tabby said.

Sadie smiled at the strapless, white satin gown with delicate beading at the waist. It was like the peep-toe shoes her sister had admired: 1940s movie star elegance. As the saleswoman came over, Sadie found her gaze drawn to another dress, one that almost took her breath. She'd worn the traditional big white gown for her first wedding, but this one, tea length and ivory, had a vintage look to it. There was something a little "second wedding" about it, in a good way. Sadie imagined herself wearing that dress, Axel beside her in a bolo tie and Stetson and dark suit, a horse or the pair of alpacas behind them.

Snap out of it! she yelled at herself like she was Olympia Dukakis in *Moonstruck. Axel is never going to be your groom, and from the way your dating life has been going, you're going to be single a long time.*

Thing was, she really didn't want to be. Sadie wanted her life's mate, her love, her future, her family. And the more she looked at the dress and pretty veils, the more heart-pokingly clear it was how much she wanted all this for real. Not the *stuff*—but the love. The partnership. The life sharing. A father for Danny.

Axel Dawson was not that man. Hero or not, Sadie barely knew the guy, even if she felt like she'd known him forever. He'd told her straight out how he felt about marriage. So really, she should put her fantasies aside this week, not that she figured that would be easy or even possible.

Once the reunion was over and Evie was off on her honeymoon, Sadie would focus on what she really wanted and maybe join an online dating site where she could pick her own possibilities and weed out the no-ways and get to know a few guys via email and the phone prior to meeting. According to Aunt Tabby, who lived by her mood boards, you had to create the life you wanted. And if Sadie wanted love and commitment, she'd need to go find it.

Yes, Axel would be hard to live up to; the man was a real-life hero and intensely good-looking with incredible shoulders and narrow hips and—

"Ooh, my treat, Sadie-girl," her mother said, wiggling her eyebrows as she beelined for a display of sexy bras and matching undies, lace and satin and plunging. "Axel won't know what hit him."

Sadie was long used to her mom being right out there with her and Evie's sex lives in addition to everything else. She eyed the lingerie, wondering what kissing Axel would be like. Hot, very hot, no doubt. Wasn't she supposed to be shelving her fantasies about him?

"The black set is so sexy!" her mother gushed.

It certainly was. But when would Axel Dawson ever see her in the scraps of black lace and satin?

"I'll take two sets of these," her mother said, putting the bras and matching undies on the counter. "Evie will love them, too."

Before Sadie could make some excuse to put one set back, a gasp from Aunt Tabby had them turning around, and there was Evie, in her dress and veil and peep-toe shoes. The three of them were speechless, a rare occasion.

"Oh, Evie," Sadie whispered, hand on her heart. "That is definitely the dress."

Tears ran down her sister's face. She was definitely overwhelmed.

Her mother and her aunt Tabby hugged. Actually hugged each other! They seemed to realize they were caught up in an emotional moment and stepped back, each retreating with the expressions they reserved for each other these days, but they'd hugged. A good start. This week of wedding prep, the four of them spending time together over such a happy occasion, would do wonders for the elder pair of sisters.

"I'm saying yes to the dress," Evie said, her eyes misty and her face full of wonder. "And the shoes. And the veil." She bit her lip. "I'm tingling from head to toe."

Sadie eyed the lingerie on the counter and wanted more than ever to hang her set right back up. Evie's face, those tears, that dress—this was how it was supposed to be. Breathtakingly *real*. Faking this engagement, despite the reasons, felt so wrong again.

Her phone pinged with a text and she fished her phone from her purse. Axel Dawson.

Hope you're surviving this afternoon, he'd texted, adding a smiley face emoji wearing a cowboy hat.

Oh, God. The man was thinking about her. Caring about what she was going through. And let her know.

What hit her heart at that moment was very, very real indeed.

Ping! Another text from Axel.

Saw your grandmother with Danny at the petting zoo. Danny was flying his superhero lion over the chickens and promising Zul would save them from a "scawy monster." He's too cute.

Against all reason, Sadie Winston fell headlong in love.

* * *

Yes, a grown man was hiding. Axel Dawson was suffering from an acute case of being asked too many questions and getting too many hugs from strangers who were related to Sadie in some way. He glanced out the round window at the far end of the big barn away from where the horse stables started—yup, there were stray Winstons out there, looking over the horses from their half-open stalls. At least the equipment area of the big barn was shielded from view.

He was so focused on catching his breath from being too much the center of attention for even a minute that he hadn't heard his brother Noah come in until he heard him returning a rake to a supply closet. Tall, dark-haired and blue-eyed like himself, his youngest sibling looked a lot Axel, though they had different mothers.

"Ah, Axel, just the man I was looking for," Noah said. "Any reason why the guests are congratulating me on becoming an honorary Winston?" He pulled something out of the small messenger bag across his torso and held up a T-shirt that read Team Winston. "Your *fiancée's* grandmother gave it to me."

Axel grimaced as Noah smirked at him, holding the navy T-shirt with orange letters up to his chest. "I was hoping Daisy would have explained so I wouldn't have to. It's crazy enough to know it without having to say it all over again."

"Wait. You're actually engaged?" He eyed Axel. "Nah, there's no way."

"Of course I'm not," he said, touched at how well his brother knew him. Noah was the one who'd rebuilt the Dawson Family Guest Ranch from absolutely nothing. This barn had been a falling-down mess, one wall caved in from where their father had crashed into it with his truck last fall. Luckily, the buggy Bo had often driven around the property hadn't done too much damage when he'd ended up smashed into ranch outbuildings. How the man had survived all that was beyond Axel.

Only to be gotten by excessive drinking. Liver damage. He shivered despite the warm eighty-degree temperature.

Axel whispered the explanation—just in case big Winston ears were listening on the other side of the window. "So it's just for the week," he added. "A ninety-nine-year-old is happy. A formerly dueling mother and aunt are now on a bridal boutique shopping trip. Sadie's been through enough—I can do this for her."

Noah nodded slowly. "I knew there was a heart in there," he said, slapping a hand against Axel's chest.

"Let me ask you a question *and* change the subject," Axel said. "Did you open your letter from Dad right away?" Bo Dawson had died last December. It was now late August and Axel's unopened letter was still burning a hole in his sock drawer. Almost nine months had to be some record for ignoring a bequeathal.

Why was this on his mind so much now? Ever since he'd blurted out his life story to Sadie on the walk to her cabin last night, he couldn't stop thinking about the letter.

"Are you kidding?" Noah said. "I was afraid to touch it. Forget opening it. I kept expecting it to burst into flames or something."

Phew. So Axel wasn't crazy.

"But you did open it," Axel said. "Clearly. Because in the letter, Dad wrote that he thought you should rebuild the ranch, and you did that."

"Took me three days to open the envelope. Probably would have taken months otherwise, but curiosity got me. And Daisy kept calling me and asking if I'd read it yet. Like every half hour. I had no choice, man."

Axel laughed. "Yeah, our sister has a way of making things happen."

Three days for Noah, who was the curious type, was the equivalent of almost nine months for Axel, who'd always been more apt to *ignore* than act.

That idiotic trait and bad habit was pretty much the reason Axel was fake-engaged to a woman he'd spent about ten or so total minutes with three months ago. He'd thought he could avoid and deflect the Winstons this week by hiding in barns and behind buildings, but the family had been after him all morning, peppering him with questions about himself and his own family, their kind, open faces truly showing deep interest in him as a person—and future member of their clan. If only he'd insisted that Sadie come clean, rip off the ole Band-Aid in one painful tear. The truth would have put everything back to normal.

Maybe. Or maybe the truth would make everyone uncomfortable during a family reunion. He could practically hear them coming at Sadie, disapproval tingeing their voices: *Why didn't you correct Izzy in the moment? Why didn't you say something first thing the next morning? Why'd you pretend to be engaged during the bridal shopping trip?* Then faces would register understanding, and it would be *Poor Sadie. She probably wanted to be engaged like her younger sister so bad she didn't want to explain the misunderstanding.*

The one thing Axel did know for sure in this world was that when he opened that letter from his father, he'd have to deal with whatever was in it. Just like he was having to deal with being hugged and congratulated and told not to elope to Vegas, that just because it was a second wedding for Sadie didn't mean the whole family didn't want to watch her walk down the aisle to a real hero.

Actually, we're not really engaged, he'd wanted to scream about five times today. *Ninety-nine-year-old Izzy misunderstood and no one corrected her or anyone when word spread like wildfire.*

In fact, he was the one who'd told Sadie to let it go, to *not* correct, to let the "engagement" stand for this and that reason. Yeah, yeah, he was doing Sadie a favor and keeping the peace in her family, but was that all that had been about? Axel felt like there was something else poking at part of him deep down, demanding his attention.

Ugh. Like he wanted to analyze himself? That was his sister's job and she was annoyingly good at it. Maybe he'd go visit his baby nephew Tony and see what Daisy had to say about the why and what of his brain.

"Yoo-hoo!" called out a woman's voice. "Axel? You around here somewhere?"

Axel's eyes widened and he stared at his brother in horror. "Save me," he whispered.

Noah laughed. "He's in the big barn," the traitor called. "We'll be right out, ma'am."

"Well, aren't you a dear," whoever it was called back.

Noah smiled. "Your in-laws are calling. Shall we?"

"I'll get you," Axel said, shaking his head at his brother.

Outside, Noah lifted his hat at Sadie's grand-mother and great-grandmother and headed to-ward the petting zoo, which had a good crowd. The Winston clan sure loved those animals. They spent more time petting the goats and marveling at the alpacas and miniature pigs than they did at any other activity, such as riding or hiking.

"Oh, good, we found you," Vanessa said. "Someone said they thought they saw you head into the red barn. Axel, with all of us right here at the ranch, I can see you and Sadie aren't getting any time to yourselves, so Izzy and I thought the two of you would like to go into Bear Ridge for dinner and a movie. Just get away for a bit. You tell Sadie we'll watch our precious grandbaby."

Dinner and a movie?

"You go ahead and let her know right now," Izzy said with a nod. "Oh, she'll be so glad to have a night out on the town. Our Sadie-girl works so hard and then takes care of that little one on her own, then is always seeing to what we need. She deserves a night out away from all the hoopla."

Both women, with eyes so much like Sadie's, stared at him. And stared some more.

Axel pulled out his phone. "I'll, uh, text her."

Your gram and great-gram think you deserve a night out away from "all the hoopla." Dinner?—A

"What's he doing?" Izzy asked Vanessa.

"Texting," Vanessa told her mother. "Remember, it's like a letter over the phone."

"Like email?" Izzy asked.

"But faster," Vanessa said.

"So fast she already responded," Axel said, swallowing. "Her answer was Yes, please."

The women beamed. "Have a wonderful time, Axel."

As he watched Vanessa push Izzy's wheelchair, two girls with blond braids coming flying at them and talking excitedly about the miniature pigs, he wondered just what had happened to his life.

Chapter Six

Almost like a real date but not, Sadie thought as she eyed herself in the mirror above the bureau in her cabin's bedroom. Based on Axel's text, he'd obviously been ambushed by Vanessa and Izzy. He'd probably felt cornered into texting her about the date right then and there. But Sadie *could* use a night away from her family—despite the fact that the reunion had barely gotten underway. Plus, she and Axel could figure out how exactly they were going to pass as engaged when they'd never spent any time together. Though, of course, her gram and great-gram had fixed that tonight.

"You're not wearing that, are you?" her mother asked from the doorway, her arms crossed over her chest with a tsk-tsk expression. "You're going out on the town with your husband-to-be! Doll up a little!"

Inward sigh.

"I think your yellow sundress would be perfect for tonight," Viv added with a firm nod.

Sadie glanced at her pink T-shirt and her favorite jeans, soft and worn. "Bear Ridge is a casual town, Mom." She *was* planning to change, not into a dress, though.

Sadie had brought two dresses for just-in-case situations while at the dude ranch, but even the more casual sundress was too much for tonight. "I'm going with the white jeans and the floaty blue-and-white peasant top Evie gave me for Christmas last year. I love that blouse."

"Fine," her mother conceded. "But with those cute metallic wedge sandals—not sneakers!" Viv added. "A little makeup would be nice, too."

Viv Winston would definitely win any Pushy Mother of the Year award. But maybe Sadie could glam up a little. At the ranch, she just put on sunscreen and lip balm, but she *was* going out to dinner. Even if her grandmother and great-grandmother had commandeered her "fiancé" into it. Sadie really did want to get out of Dodge—for a few hours.

"Don't forget a light dab of perfume," her mom said as she stood and headed for the bureau. "I'll take the tags off the new bra and undies—"

Okay, there was a line and her mother had crossed it. Sadie's cheeks were hot—either from embarrassment or disappointment that no, she would not be wearing the sexy bra and underwear tonight. Even if she wanted to lead her "fiancé" to bed, this was *way* too soon. Sadie had left her things on the shelf at Your Special Day, but apparently her mother had bought it along with Evie's.

"I'll save those for the honeymoon," Sadie said, about to tell Viv to leave her be before Sadie lost her mind.

Thankfully, her mother's phone pinged with a text and Viv skedaddled to meet four of her cousins for smoothies and sunset yoga at the lodge.

Sadie put on some makeup, gave herself a once-over and had to admit she did look like she was going on a date. *Oh, what the hey*, she thought and dabbed her favorite perfume on her wrist and behind her ear.

She headed through the quiet cabin onto the porch to await Axel. Vanessa and Izzy, babysitting Danny, were with a big group of relatives on a sunset river walk, and her sister was actually in Prairie City for the night since she was having dinner with the Ackermans and staying over at their house tonight. Sadie breathed in the quiet, random voices and laughter and crickets in the background. She could hear a car coming, and her heart sped up.

A navy SUV pulled up beside the cabin and there was Axel in dark gray pants and a button-down shirt, rolled at the forearms. Seemed he got the memo about tonight, too.

He opened the passenger door, which got the evening off to a very date-like start. When he got in, she was too aware of him so close to her. He smelled delicious.

"Have a craving for any type of food in particular?" he asked.

"Hmm, I could go for Mexican. Enchiladas or sizzling fajitas, maybe. And a margarita. I really need one of those."

"Me, too," he said with a smile. "Mexican it is. There's a place right in town that I've always heard was good or we could go to Prairie City—I think there are two Mexican restaurants there."

"I'd love to try the Bear Ridge one since I've never been. But you haven't either?"

"It was one of my dad's hangouts so I tend to avoid it, but he always raved about the food. Let's give it a try."

"If you're sure," she said, trying to give him an out. Based on what he'd told her about his father, she wasn't sure he'd want to be reminded of the man. But as she sneaked a glance at him, his expression was tension free as he started the car and drove off. "So, my grandmother and great-gram cornered you, did they?"

He laughed. "Izzy is very persuasive."

"That she is. I think the generations got even pushier. Well, except for my generation. Evie and I are pretty mellow."

"Glad to hear that, fiancée," he said, shooting her a grin. His face lit up and so did her heart. "I figured a night to ourselves would give us a chance to talk through how we're supposed to act around your family."

"So your brother and sister know the truth?" she asked. "I figured they did—just want to double-check. Your siblings haven't welcomed me to the family."

"Yup, they know the whole story. They'll nod and smile and be vague, particularly Daisy, whose entire job is dealing with guests."

The moment Axel drove past the open gates of the Dawson Family Guest Ranch, waving at a young woman in the forest green "Welcome" shed, Sadie felt herself relax. They were headed into a Winston-free zone, no talk of weddings and wedding night lingerie. Sadie could catch her breath.

Fifteen minutes later, they'd arrived in the center of Bear Ridge, a small town with a teeny village center. There was an old-timey general store that also served as the post office, plus a library, town hall, various businesses like a law office and nursing home, and a few restaurants. Manuela's Mexican Café was colorful and illuminated with many hanging lanterns. There were tables out front, separated from the street by a row of planters full of flowers.

"Inside or out?" Axel asked as they approached the restaurant.

"I think in," she said. "I'd like to be in the midst of all that fun ambience."

He smiled and opened the door. The restaurant was low lit and more romantic than Sadie realized it would be, the lanterns casting soft glows all around. Paintings and Mexican artifacts covered the walls, and a huge cactus was by the hostess's station.

"Evening," the hostess said. She wore a sleeveless red velvet dress, a ton of necklaces and bracelets and killer black patent heels. Her long silver hair was the only giveaway that she was in her sixties. "Table for two?"

"Yes, please," Axel said.

The woman peered more closely at him and gasped. "Now, I know that Bo Dawson, God rest his soul, passed on last year, but my goodness, you're his spitting image. One of his kids?"

Axel gaped at the woman. "Axel Dawson," he said, extending his hand.

The hostess clasped his with both of hers. "Manuela Gomez," she said with a smile. "Owner, hostess and keeper of history. And yup, I knew it! Bo Dawson was a regular here for years—thirty years from the week we opened. I'll never forget the first time he came in because he fell madly in love with his waitress and came in twice a day every day during her shifts until she agreed to go out with him. Her name was Diana."

Surprise lit his eyes. "Diana is my mother's name," he said, and Sadie got the feeling he wanted the woman to keep talking *and* to go away. "Could it be her? I didn't know she worked here."

"Definitely her because she married him a few months later and they went on to have three children, all boys, and you are one of three, no? I think he was divorced with a young son at the time."

Ford, Axel's eldest brother, Sadie realized. Axel didn't respond to that, which made Sadie wonder if Bo Dawson *had* been divorced at the time. Then again, if he'd married Diana after just a few months of meeting, he likely had been.

"Diana was putting herself through college when they met," Manuela said. "Her old clunker of a car always broke down and so he gave her his truck so she could safely get to work and school. He would walk the five miles from his ranch here to sit in her station and have tacos just to see her because she was so busy. And he never showed up without either flowers or candy. Your mom was a jelly bean addict."

From the look on his face, Axel definitely didn't know about any of that either. "Still is," he said.

Manuela smiled. "I guess it didn't work out between them in the long run since I know he remarried after some years and had two more kids, but while your parents were dating, I remember thinking, now that is a man in love."

Axel smiled tightly.

"Well, here I am rehashing old times and you two are probably starving!" Manuela said, grabbing two menus. "Come, let me give you one of my favorite tables." She led them to a roomy square table for two by the ornate fireplace that was festooned with tall glowing white candles inside the hearth. She looked up and snapped her fingers, and a waiter immediately appeared. "You take good care of these two," she told the young man.

After they ordered—margaritas, frozen, no salt for Sadie and straight up for Axel, steak fajitas for her and enchiladas *suizas* for him—the waiter quickly returned with their drinks and a basket of homemade tortilla chips and three kinds of salsa.

"First," Sadie said, raising her glass, "a toast to escaping the craziness."

"I'll definitely drink to that," he said, clinking his glass with hers.

"So was all that Manuela had to say a surprise to you?"

He set his drink on the table and swiped a tortilla chip through the salsa *verde*. "I knew that my mother put herself through school as a waitress but not that she worked here. I definitely didn't know any of the other stuff Manuela mentioned."

"Sounds like your father was madly in love with your mom."

"In the beginning, sure. He probably swept her off her feet with his grand gestures of giving up his truck and walking five miles to see her with jelly beans. And then time ticks on and they're married with three little boys, and is he home? No. He's probably here, drinking at the bar and falling in love with another waitress and bringing her Kit Kats."

Yikes. "It doesn't help to know he had a compassionate, loving side, despite all his faults?"

Axel took another sip of his margarita. "Help? Not at all. In fact, it makes it harder. If Bo Dawson had been more of a complete one hundred percent jerk, I would know what to do with my—" He stopped talking and grabbed a chip.

"Your...feelings about him?" Sadie attempted.

He glanced at her, his blue eyes a mix of emotions. "Yeah. Sometimes it's easier for things to be more black-and-white. You can close a door that way. Yes, he was a serial cheater and alcoholic who left my mom with three kids under six and unsteady child support *and* a man who'd walked ten miles there and back to see her because he'd given her his truck so she'd have reliable transportation to work and school."

"I like that part," Sadie said.

"Me, too. But Bo was also famous in the family for passing out drunk on the porch, needing his young boys and their visiting older brother to help pull him in the house. Sometimes we couldn't budge him and just had to cover him with comforters. Toward the end, he was crashing into the barns in the buggy or his truck. He wouldn't listen to anyone." For a moment he seemed to be lost in a memory.

"Oh, Axel, that sounds rough," Sadie said, her heart constricting for the kid he was.

He sipped his margarita and glanced out the window, then back at her. "Then there's a memory that always comes to me when I'm thinking about my dad at his worst. A good memory."

Sadie wasn't surprised there was one and probably many.

"When I was a kid and my grandparents were still alive," he said, "we had this Dawson Family Guest Ranch tradition that every time they brought home a new animal, one of us kids got to name it. The day it was my turn, my grandparents brought home a black goat with gray horns and I named it Flash. I was crazy about him. At the time, I considered him my best friend."

"Aw," Sadie said, biting a chip. She could see him sharing his troubles and hopes with Flash the goat.

"One day, Flash took off at night and got lost up on Clover Mountain. I was so upset, trying not to cry and failing. So many wild animals lived up there and I thought for sure Flash would be eaten within hours. Well, my dad took me out to look for Flash, and when we found him trapped on a ledge but had no way to call for help—this was before cell phones and my dad had lost his radio—we hunkered down because he knew I couldn't bear to leave Flash there. Finally, well after midnight, a search party came and Flash lived a good long life."

"It's clear he did care about you, Axel," Sadie said.

The waiter arrived with a tray of their food, and Axel seemed relieved for a reprieve from the highly personal conversation.

"Your family seems close," he said, cutting into his enchiladas.

She smiled, heaping steak and vegetables onto the flour tortillas. The food smelled so good she could barely wait to take a bite. "We are. Sometimes they drive me nuts, but I know how lucky I am. My mom is super pushy, but I'll tell ya, when you need your mama, there's no one you'd want more than Viv Winston at your side. Sometimes I think all that fierce family love ruined me for relationships."

"Wait, what?" he asked, his fork paused midair.

"Maybe I expect too much. Want too much. Think the man I'm seeing will treat me the way my family does and then be disappointed when a guy forgets something important I mentioned during the last date or doesn't consider my feelings."

"Sadie. There's no such thing as expecting too much. The man in your life *should* love you fiercely."

"That's what I want," she managed to say but the conversation was all too much. She'd said too much. "For me and Danny."

He looked up then, his blue eyes locking with hers, then got busy eating.

They clearly both needed a break from how personal this had gotten.

"So things are better between your mom and your aunt?" he asked.

"Not really. They're doing things together for the sake of me and Evie, but I hear the under-the-breath snipes and see the looks."

"What do you think started it? You said it had to do with something on the mountain the day Danny went missing?"

"I think they both blamed each other. Danny was walking with them, behind me and my cousin Daphne, and then he was gone. But they won't say why they blame each other. I can't see how they can. They were both walking with him and watching after him as he toddled along. He was only twenty-four months then."

"Think this week will help repair the relationship?" he asked.

"I hope so. When I see them like this, it makes me realize this could happen between me and Evie—and she's my best friend. Just like Mom and Tabby were best friends. I hate to think of anything coming between *us* for months."

When the waiter appeared to clear their plates, Sadie hadn't realized they'd finished practically every bite. Moments later, he appeared with two desserts on the house, thanks to Manuela. Sadie was stuffed but she couldn't resist a sopaipilla with its cinnamon sugar and a bite or three of the cheesecake flan.

Conversation during dessert and two cups of coffee each had turned to their favorite desserts and then favorites in general. Sadie discovered that Axel was a french fry addict and could eat turkey and provolone sandwiches on French bread every day for lunch and pretty much did. He loved Marvel and DC movies and Westerns. He liked the color orange. His favorite season was summer, same as Sadie's.

I want to kiss you, she thought as he reminisced about Flash the goat, his favorite childhood pet.

After goodbyes and hugs to Manuela, they were back in his SUV. Sadie was again so aware of him so close beside her that she started rambling. "So who's your favorite superhero?" she asked. "Let me guess. Iron Man. No, Captain America."

"Neither," he said with a smile, turning toward her. "My favorite superhero is Zul, the flying lion."

Before she could stop herself, she reached a hand to his face, too touched to speak, and he leaned over just slightly and kissed her gently on her lips. Mmm. She kissed him back and suddenly their hands were everywhere, hers on his rock-hard chest, wishing she could undo some buttons and feel his bare skin, his hands on her neck, in her hair. He was definitely her favorite kisser. That was for sure.

Even the thought of marriage makes me feel like the air is squeezing out of me.

Oh foo. This kiss had to end. Now. She couldn't get carried away with Axel "Marriage Is Suffocation" Dawson.

She pulled back. "As much as I want to keep doing that, you heard me say tonight that I'm looking for someone to love me and my son fiercely. You're not that guy."

He stared at her but didn't say anything. She'd rather have a firm *You're right, I'm not* than his silence. She'd actually prefer a *You're so wrong, I'm already crazy about you so let's forget the past and start anew with how we feel right now.*

But he didn't say that either, of course. He just

covered her hand with his for a second to say he understood and then nodded and started the SUV.

Axel liked how forthright Sadie was. He'd liked kissing her even more. They'd gone out tonight to escape her family's closing in on them, and instead, he walked right into *his* family's closing in on him. Between Manuela's stories and everything he'd said at dinner, Axel had felt off-kilter as they'd gotten into the SUV to head to the ranch.

And he was including that lighthearted dessert conversation of their favorites. He'd been charmed and amused and touched by Sadie and the stories about her favorites. Butter pecan was her favorite flavor of ice cream because she'd tried it for the first time the day before her great-grandpa had passed away and it always reminded her of how sweet and loving he'd been. She loved romantic comedies and tearjerkers, and had seen the movie *9 to 5* with her favorite singer, Dolly Parton, at least twenty-five times and credited it for making her laugh through her divorce.

She loved Pink Lady apples and the color teal and being near bodies of water, whether the ocean or a pond. And her favorite person, her very favorite of all favorite people, was her son, Danny.

His head and chest and every part of him had been so full of Sadie Winston by the time they'd gotten from the restaurant into his car that he'd been dying to kiss her. When she'd touched him, put her hand to his face, he couldn't resist the overwhelming urge, and as he leaned toward her, she leaned toward him, and whammo. A kiss that had exploded in his head.

Then it ended all too soon. But Sadie was right. She was looking for something real. And he was Status Quo Axel and liking it that way. Needing it that way. His head was in a good place right now and he wasn't about to muck that up when it had taken so long to get here.

Sadie's phone pinged, and she fished it out of her purse.

He caught her expression change as she read it. "Everything okay?"

"Actually, no. My mom says that Vanessa and Izzy are both sneezing and coughing up a storm. She thinks we should get Danny and stay at your house for a couple of days till they're not contagious. She'll take care of them, she says."

Wait. Sadie and Danny—in his house? Staying with him? For a couple of days?

"I'm sure we can stay in the lodge, right?" Sadie asked. "I'll text Daisy."

"There aren't guest rooms in the lodge. Just the couches in the main room. Of course you two will stay with me. We have extra buggies, so I'll borrow one for you so you can get back and forth to the action as you want."

She bit her lip and stared at her phone screen. Then she looked out the window. "I don't know, Axel. Things got kinda hot and heavy before. How are we going to share your house for an hour, let alone a day or two?"

"I won't let my lips get anywhere near yours," he said. He held up two fingers. "Scout's honor. And you know I was an Eagle Scout."

She tilted her head. "Your dad helped with that accomplishment?"

"Actually, a time or two when he was around and alert. My oldest brother helped the most. I'd call Ford and he'd ask his mom to drive him over for a couple of hours."

"That's really nice," she said. She bit her lip again. "Well, if you're sure you don't mind having us at your home. Danny wakes up early. And sometimes he still wakes up during the night."

"No problem," he said.

Or was it?

Chapter Seven

They'd stopped at Sadie's cabin to pick up her and Danny's suitcases—which her mother had already packed so that Sadie and Axel wouldn't have to come in and risk the flu or whatever virus had befallen poor Izzy and Vanessa. Both women had bad colds, and Axel's sister had already dropped off two get-well baskets of OTC medicine, throat lozenges, boxes of tissues, fuzzy socks and crossword magazines. Daisy had even instructed a ranch hand to drop off three trays of dinner earlier, and the cabin was already equipped with an electric kettle, mugs and tea.

Axel had surprised Sadie and her mom on the porch of the cabin when he told them there was no need to take the porta-crib because he not only had a crib upstairs in the guest room for his visiting baby niece and nephews but also a playpen downstairs in the living room along with various other baby stuff, like a foam play mat and kiddie area in one corner with toys that were probably too young for Danny but that he'd love nonetheless.

"Well," Vanessa had said with a huge smile. "Danny will fit right in over there."

Axel had barely flinched at that, aware of many sets of eyes on him.

Danny was thrilled by the idea of going to Axel's house. And he was practically jumping in his seat when Axel mentioned that Danny could pet his sweet, friendly dog named Dude if he wanted but only if a grown-up was there.

Fifteen minutes later, settled in the cabin, Danny petted Dude over and over and told him a few stories in toddler speak that Axel couldn't make heads or tails out of, but Sadie seemed to understand every word. Then Danny moved over to the play mat in the corner by the window, where there were stuffed toys and cardboard building blocks. Sadie explained that Danny was building a castle for his superhero lion.

"How high are you going to make it?" Axel

asked, sitting cross-legged on the big foam mat. "As tall as you are?"

"Tall you!" Danny said, then doubled over in laughter. Toddler humor.

Danny's laughter was infectious, and both Axel and Sadie were laughing, too. Axel was aware of Sadie watching them from the big brown leather couch that faced the stone fireplace. She was sitting in his favorite spot, the left-hand corner. He suddenly wanted to be sitting right next to her. No, he wanted her on his lap, straddling him, kissing him the way she had in his car, her hands in his hair.

She'd nixed any chance of that—wisely—so keep this G-rated, he reminded himself. *Focus on the kid, not the mother.*

"You're gonna make the castle as tall as I am?" Axel asked Danny. "That *is* tall."

"Zul help?" Danny asked, tilting his head, his hazel-brown eyes wide.

The expression on the adorable little boy's face almost did Axel in with his sweet earnestness. "Of course I'll help."

"Hear-wo," Danny said, smiling. "Right, Mama?"

Oh, God. Now he *was* done in. He wanted to scoop up this kid and give him a big hug. He couldn't look at Danny Winston without remembering the relief he'd felt when he'd followed Dude and spotted the orange sneaker through that thicket of branches. Danny was soothing to be around, even if his occasional high-pitched shrieks could crack double-pane glass.

"Right, Danny," Sadie said with a nod.

Axel kept his gaze on the growing tower of blocks.

Danny yawned and rubbed his eyes, then added another block to the tower.

"It's almost eight o'clock," Sadie said. "His bedtime is seven thirty, but my mom said he took an extralong nap this afternoon. I'd better get him to sleep."

"Time for bed, buddy," Axel said, giving Danny's blond hair a ruffle.

Danny yawned again. "Zul story?" he asked, looking between his mom and Axel.

He looked at Sadie. "He wants me to read him a story?" he asked.

Sadie nodded. "My mom said she packed a few of his favorites. He likes the same ones over and over."

"Sure, I'll read you a story," Axel said.

Danny held out his arms to Axel, and he swallowed. He wasn't expecting that.

"I'll take you up to bed," Sadie said fast, bolting up. "You're going to sleep in Axel's special nursery."

"Zul, Zul!" Danny said, hoisting his arms up toward Axel.

"I don't mind," he whispered to Sadie and then scooped the boy up. "Okay, let's head to bed."

"Zul, too?" Danny asked, looking around. He pointed by the blocks.

His superhero lion lay on the mat beside his castle. Sadie got it and handed it to her son.

"Zul and Zul!" Danny said with glee, flying the lion in his red cape as far as his little arm would allow.

Axel smiled and started up the stairs, Sadie following. He set the boy on the changing table and let his mom get him ready for bed in his spaceship pajamas, then Sadie brought him to the bathroom they'd share for brushing teeth. A few minutes later, Danny came running in with Zul and lifted his arms to Axel. He picked up the boy and sat in the padded rocking chair by the window, and Sadie handed him a picture book.

"Let's see," Axel said. "This book is called *Snowy the Owl*. I love owls, too."

Danny shook his head and waved Zul at Axel. "Story Zul."

Axel was beginning to speak toddler. "Ah, you want a story about Zul the superhero lion?"

Danny nodded and settled in, his head in the crook of Axel's arm, the baby-shampoo scent of him rising up. A pang gripped him in the chest, and he had a flash of the woman he'd loved three years ago sitting in a rocker and reading a story to her baby. Axel had been so attracted to Lizzie, a single mother of an eleven-month-old baby girl, maybe mistaking that for love, and when she'd left him for a bull rider, he'd been out of sorts for months, missing her, missing the baby he'd gotten close to. That was when he'd stopped dating single mothers. It was when he'd stopped dating with an eye toward a future, period. The way he'd felt about Lizzie and her daughter had superseded all the usual reasons he'd never gotten seriously involved with a woman—his upbringing, his cynicism, his lack of faith in people. And then wham, all those walls had built back up even stronger.

Now here he was, sitting on a rocker with a little baby-shampoo-scented kid on his lap, about to make up a story about a superhero lion named after him. This had gotten out of hand.

Whoa, he told himself. *Dial back the intensity. It's a story. You're doing Sadie a favor so she and her son don't get sick. You and Sadie already agreed there would be no more kissing. Don't make this into more than it is.*

Talking-to over, he cleared his throat.

But it already was more because he recognized that what he felt for Sadie Winston was a lot more than lust.

He cleared his throat again and glanced up at Sadie, leaning against the doorway. Waiting.

"Once upon a time, there was a superhero lion named Zul," Axel began.

Danny's eyes were wide on his. So far, so good.

"Zul flew all over the place looking for animals and kids who needed help. One day, Zul saw a little owl who couldn't get back in his nest."

"Oh no!" Danny yelped.

"Don't worry," Axel assured him. "Because Zul was there!"

"Yay, Zul!" Danny said, flying Zul around until a yawn had his arm drooping with his eyes.

"Zul said, 'Hey little owl, hang on to my cape and I'll land you right in your nest.' And Zul did. The little owl was very happy to be home. Zul flew away, his red cape zipping behind, looking to be helpful. The end."

Danny's eyes drooped again, then opened, then drooped hard. A moment later, he managed to get them half-opened, then they closed.

"Good night, little buddy," Axel whispered. There. He'd gotten through this unscathed. He'd told the boy a story and Axel's world hadn't imploded. Mother and child didn't have to affect him if he didn't *let* them.

A few years ago, not long after he'd gotten his heart handed to him by Lizzie, he'd run into Mack, a widowed, grizzled mountain man who'd lived alone for decades in a small cabin he'd built himself. Out of nowhere, the man had said to Axel, finger waving, "I'll tell ya the secret of life, buddy boy. It's ruling your emotions instead of letting them rule you. Be the boss of yourself." Axel had thought that was excellent life advice, not that the mountain man seemed too emotionally healthy and the rangers checked in on him a few times a week. A grown son had been trying to get him to agree to go into assisted living and Mack had put up a fuss, but Axel had heard he'd finally agreed.

He glanced at Sadie, who seemed *very* affected. She was staring at him, and he could swear she might cry.

He carefully stood and walked over to the crib and lowered Danny in, putting Zul under his arm. "Success," he whispered to Sadie. Her eyes were misty. "You okay?"

"You're the first man besides his grandpa to tell Danny a story," she said. "It's very sweet to watch someone tell your baby a story—especially off the cuff. Guess I got a little emotional."

Ah, okay. It was a mother thing and not a *him* thing. Phew. Sadie turned out the light and they left the room, leaving the door ajar.

"Well, I think I'm ready for bed myself," she said, yawning what had to be the fakest yawn he'd ever seen.

She needed some space from him and this—he got it. He did, too.

But he could barely drag his eyes off her, let

alone make his body move farther from hers. If he was honest with himself, he'd admit to wanting to sit with her and talk or watch a movie and eat popcorn. And yes, he wanted to kiss her. More than kiss her.

"If you need anything, just knock," he said, knowing that distance from her was exactly what he needed.

She gave him something of a smile. "Good night," she said. "Thanks for dinner. And for letting us stay here. And for the story."

"My pleasure," he said, holding her gaze. "Pleasant dreams," he added like his grandparents always used to when he was young.

Watching her walk away was so damned hard.

An hour later, Axel lay on his bed, hands folded behind his head, staring at the beamed ceiling. His thoughts were a jumble of everything that had happened that night. The Mexican restaurant. Manuela. The text from Sadie's mom about her and Danny needing to stay at his cabin. Playing with Danny and reading to him. Being so attracted to Sadie that he could barely think of anything without her popping into his mind every five seconds. Her face, her long light blond hair, her pale brown eyes. Her pink lips.

He could not start something with Sadie that wouldn't end with what she wanted; he wouldn't do that to her. She wanted her Mr. Right. He wanted nothing to do with emotional involvement. He was done with love and commitment and caring too much. Yeah, yeah, it had been three years since he had his heart torn out of his chest, but he felt nowhere close to wanting a relationship. Maybe one day the feeling would go away. He had no idea. He knew the idea of getting seriously involved with someone, particularly someone with a child, gave him that airless feeling in his chest.

He wanted the best for Sadie and therefore, he'd keep his hands and lips to himself. Not that she'd invited him to kiss her a second time. She'd made herself crystal clear. She knew what she wanted just as he knew what he didn't want.

He would walk the five miles from his ranch here to sit in her station and have tacos just to see her because she was so busy, he heard Manuela say in his head. *And he never showed up without either flowers or candy. Your mom was a jelly bean addict.*

When Axel and his brothers were young, the three would pool their money on Mother's Day and their mom's birthday and buy Diana Dawson two pounds of jelly beans from the loose candy bins at the general store, trying to avoid the black licorice ones that she hated. They'd each take turns filling the bag and then the lady at the counter would always add a red ribbon and make a bow, and they were always so proud to hand their mom her gift. She always shared, too.

While your parents were dating, I remember thinking, now that is a man in love...

Oh hell, he thought, getting up and going over to his dresser. He sucked in a breath and opened the sock drawer and pulled out the letter from his father.

He sat on his bed and opened it. Finally. After almost nine months.

He pulled out one sheet of plain white paper. Four addresses were scrawled on it in Bo Dawson's handwriting. Just addresses—all local to Bear Ridge. None he recognized as remotely familiar. The first was on Main Street. He grabbed his phone and did a search for the address—Manuela's Mexican Café.

Huh. The universe had a funny way of getting someone's attention. He'd never stepped foot in Manuela's until tonight for the very reason it was listed on the paper—it had been his father's hangout. But he'd gone because Sadie had wanted Mexican, and he'd thought he was being ridiculous for avoiding a place just because his late father frequented it.

And he'd ended up learning quite a bit about his parents.

Then had been propelled to finally open the letter from his dad.

He stared at the addresses. So what was this? Bo sending him on some kind of tour of his life? Seemed like it, given what he'd discovered about the first address on the list.

The other three addresses were scattered across the town.

I don't know that I want any more information, he thought.

A memory started to form in his head and he tried to push it away, getting up and dropping the letter on the bed and heading for the window. He looked out over the vast field and trees as it hit him, the night he'd tried so hard not to think about. The universe *had* sent him to Manuela's tonight. The universe *had* gotten him to open up the letter. Maybe he was *supposed* to be thinking of the last time he saw his dad. Even if it crushed him. Talk about stealing the air from his lungs.

One cold December late afternoon, Axel had stopped by the ranch on the way back from training the newbies from the S&R team on easy Clover Mountain. He planned to talk to his dad about rehab. He'd tried a few times before and had gotten nowhere, but Axel had heard from Daisy that she'd been talking to Bo on the phone and he'd been slurring his words, then started snoring. *Nice talking to you, Dad.*

Axel had been researching local rehab facilities and found one that could take Bo that weekend. As he'd pulled up in the drive to the main house, Bo was zigzagging to his truck, which had one caved-in bumper and a lot of new dents. His father was clearly drunk, and Axel had grabbed Bo's keys and refused to hand them over. His father had cursed up a storm, then taken a swing at Axel and fallen flat on his face, passed out cold.

Axel had carried him into the house, no easy feat, got him on the couch, took off his boots and covered him with a blanket. Then Axel had burst into tears.

The crying had helped actually, releasing all that pent-up frustration and anguish and power-lessness. He had no doubt that in the morning, Bo would be up to the same old tricks. Axel had called Noah, who lived second closest to the dilapidated ranch at the time, and told him what happened, and Noah said he'd stop by in the morning and try to talk some sense into Bo. Axel had left and vowed never to return; enough was enough.

That was six days before Bo Dawson died.

Pain clenched at his gut, and he gripped the windowsill, trying to put it all out of his mind, but he couldn't. Noah had reported that their dad had given a repeat performance the next afternoon, down to the punch and passing out, this time in a snowbank in the yard. They'd even gotten their police officer brother involved, Ford coming all the way from Casper in uniform since their father respected any kind of service, whether military or law enforcement or janitorial. Bo hadn't been drunk enough to dare punch a police officer, even his own son, but he'd ordered Ford off his property if he "was going to be a damned killjoy." Ford had let Axel and Noah know the man just wouldn't listen to reason and they couldn't force him into rehab.

The thing that got Axel most? That Bo had obviously known he was dying—the letters he'd left to all six kids made that clear. He'd wanted to go out his way, Axel supposed. And he had.

"Mama? Mama?" a little voice called out.

Axel practically jumped in his dark room. Danny. He went into the hallway, saw no sign of Sadie, so he poked his head into the nursery. Danny was standing up in the crib, holding Zul. The little guy stared at Axel in the dim lighting from the night-light, then popped his arms in the air like he had earlier.

"Can't sleep, huh, buddy?" Axel asked, walking over. "Me neither. Not that I've tried."

Well, he needed a distraction and this was one hell of a distraction.

"How about another story about your superhero lion?" Axel asked, putting Danny on his lap. The boy immediately settled against his chest, his eyes heavy. He'd be out in about half a minute. "Once upon a time there was a lion named Zul. One day,

Zul woke up in the middle of the night, unable to sleep. He wanted someone to tell him a story, but everyone else was sleeping. So he decided to tell *himself* a story. He crawled into his bed, pulled the covers to his chin and told himself about the time he saved a little duckling named George from a fast-moving current in the creek. Before he knew it—"

Axel felt Danny's head press more heavily against the crook of his arm, and he looked down. Bingo: fast asleep. Fourteen seconds. That had to be a record.

"Thanks," he heard Sadie whisper.

He looked up and there she was in the doorway with a sweet smile on her beautiful face. She was barefoot and wore pink sweatpants and a white tank top and looked unbelievably sexy.

"I'll take him to his crib," he said, standing up.

"You're a natural, Axel Dawson. Shame about you not wanting kids of your own." Her eyes widened. "Oh, God, who am I—my mother? I'm really sorry. I had no business saying something like that. People have a right to their feelings without anyone else butting in with their one cent."

"Oh, I wouldn't shortchange yourself," he said and then shut up before he elaborated about how she had this ability to get him talking and thinking and doing things he wouldn't have otherwise.

He'd thought it was the universe's mysterious ways getting him to open the letter.

No. It was the talk he and Sadie had had in the restaurant.

"I'm good with little kids because I had practice," he said, wondering why he was going there. But then he blurted out, "I was seriously involved with a single mother with a baby girl who I was very attached to, and when it was over, I doubled down on my old ways of looking for only casual relationships. So between helping take care of that baby and helping out with my niece and nephews, I've got a ton of experience with the diaper crowd."

"Sorry about the heartache. I know how that goes. And thanks to my great-gram, I know you know I do."

He smiled. "They're a great family. You're lucky."

"Well, I've only met two of your five siblings, but I'd say you're darn lucky yourself."

"That is true," he agreed. "I lucked out in that department, at least."

He moved closer to her—to leave the room so that Danny could sleep in peace, but she was right there, in the doorway, and suddenly they were kissing again. She'd made the first move and he'd made the second and now they were in the hallway against the wall about to knock over the watercolor of rushing rapids. Now he knew where that part of the Zul story had come from.

"Why can't I keep my hands off you?" she whispered against his lips, pressed up tantalizingly against him.

"Feel free not to," he said, then regretted it. Even if he was attracted to her on a bunch of levels—okay, all—he wasn't getting emotionally attached.

She seemed to sense his withdrawal despite his not moving a muscle. "Maybe we should save the making out for when my family is around," she said, and he heard the element of disappointment in her voice. He was getting to know her a little too well. "You know, to make the engagement seem real. We were supposed to talk about that and never did. But now I'm zonked," she said, fake-yawning again and backing toward her room. "So, see you in the morning."

She hurried down the hall, and her door closed a second later.

He could knock and they could talk, really talk. But his feet were suddenly weighted to the floor, and Sadie had fled for a reason. He should let her be.

Wasn't getting emotionally attached. Even he knew when he was full of it.

Chapter Eight

When Sadie woke up the next morning and eyed the time on her phone, she was surprised it was past seven. Danny's middle-of-the-night story must have had him sleep in. She went into the nursery but the crib was empty, which meant only one thing—

"We're making pancakes," called Axel's voice. "Morning, sleepyhead."

Toddler laughter. "Mama sleephead. Hahaha-hahaha."

She smiled, that sound her favorite of every sound in the world.

"I've got him, so feel free to take your time,"

Axel called up. "I'm not expected at work until nine for a wilderness tour."

"'K, thanks," she called out.

"Mama, sleephead!" Danny shouted with glee.

"Well, she's awake now!" Axel said and it was apparently very funny because Danny started laughing again.

"Should we put blueberries in our pancakes?" Axel asked. "Or have them on the side? So many questions!"

"In, in!" Danny said.

Sadie stood at the base of the stairs, smiling and wanting to cry at the same time. This was what life would be like if Danny had a daddy—the right daddy. One who'd get up early with him. Make him a good breakfast. Make him laugh.

This is what I want for my son, she knew more than she knew anything else. And the man being the "right daddy" this morning wasn't available for the permanent position. He was a temp. This week only.

As Sadie passed the watercolor of the rushing rapids on her way to the guest room, she remembered her shoulder tipping it askew, Axel's tall, strong, warm body against hers on the wall, his hands on her shoulders, her neck as he kissed her. She'd practically flung herself at him—not even practically. She had. Seeing him in the rocker, taking care of Danny in the middle of the night, telling him that story. She'd been overcome, and added to how attracted she was to him, she'd let impulse win.

You've got to stop that, she told herself as she went into the bathroom with the toiletry bag her mother had packed for her and took a shower, grateful for the excellent water pressure on her tense muscles. Axel had everything in here a guest could need, including a hair dryer. Once in her room, she got dressed in a T-shirt and shorts, then texted her mom to see how Gram and Great-Gram were doing. Her mother ruled against visiting so she wouldn't get Danny or Axel sick and thought they'd be much better by tomorrow.

Downstairs, she found Danny in a high chair near the table. Axel had made smiley face blueberry pancakes. The mouth was strawberry slices.

"Hi, sleephead!" Danny said and laughed again.

"Hi, precious," Sadie responded, kissing Danny on the head. "Mmm, your breakfast looks delicious."

"And here is yours, milady," Axel said, putting a plate on the table. Three pancakes. A side of blueberries and strawberries. Syrup, butter, orange juice and cream and sugar were in the center, and then he set down a steaming mug of coffee.

Everyone needed an Axel. The man really was a superhero.

"Noah texted," he said. "Turns out Daisy needs

help with something at her house, so I'll see you two later." He gave Danny's hair a ruffle.

"Bye, Zul!" Danny said, waving his pancake-laden fork in the air.

Axel smiled. "See you later, buddy." He turned toward Sadie. "I don't know what time I'll be back, but make yourself at home, come and go as you please."

Her heart pinged. "Thanks for everything, Axel."

He nodded and then was gone.

"I like Zul," Danny said, picking up his sippy cup.

"Me, too," she said. "Me, too."

Turned out a bird had somehow gotten into Daisy's house over an hour ago and she needed help shooing it out. Her husband, Harrison, was on a business trip for the next few days, and though Noah and Sara lived just down the path in the foreman's cabin, they were already out dealing with feed deliveries, so Axel was now bird shooer.

"Where's Tony?" Axel asked, glancing around for his three-month-old nephew.

"He's napping upstairs in his crib. Good timing, too, because I can just imagine the bird pooping on his head. It's been that kind of day and it's not even eight a.m."

Whoosh!

There the little bird went, flying not too far

overhead. It was brown, gray and white and flying around Daisy's living room. She'd opened the
sliding glass doors and all the windows but birdie
seemed to prefer flying against the walls instead
of into freedom.

"I summon all the powers of Zul to mind-trick
this bird out the side door!" Axel said in his best
Darth Vader voice.

"Um, who?" Daisy asked, staring at him as if
he'd grown another head.

"Zul. Danny's superhero lion," he said.

Daisy's mouth dropped open. "Oh, my God.
You're falling for Sadie and you adore that kid!"

"What? I'm trying to get the bird out of your
house."

Daisy raised an eyebrow. "Yes, by calling on
the imaginary powers of a two-year-old's stuffed
lovey. Oh, Axel. You're a goner."

He frowned at his sister, who he'd never told
about Lizzie, and followed the bird with his gaze.
Now it was flying along the ceiling. "We're talking about *me*, remember? Or have you forgotten
I'm the guy who actually caused his blind date to
go running out of your dinner party."

He felt bad about that one. A few months ago,
Daisy had slyly set him up with the woman who
used to lead wilderness tours for the ranch, and
he'd been wound so tight in those days that he'd
gotten into an argument with Daisy's husband—

who'd been the family's enemy back then—and the date had fled. She'd also quit not long after, taking a job with his old S&R team. That had worked out well, since he'd taken over as wilderness tour leader and safety director for the ranch.

Whoosh! Whoosh-whoosh!

Ah—birdie flew out the sliding glass door.

"Phew," Daisy said, hurrying to close the windows and the doors. She turned toward him. "Axel Dawson, you can say whatever you want. Actions speak louder."

She had him there. "Maybe I shouldn't tell you that Sadie and Danny are staying with me for a couple of days. Her grandmother and great-grandmother have bad colds, so Sadie's mom is taking care of them at their cabin and sent her daughters to their fiancés."

Daisy grinned. "Oh, what a tangled web—wonderfully tangled!"

"I don't know how wonderful it is, Daize. First off, it *is* deception. Second, yeah, I do have feelings for Sadie, and, of course, I feel close to her son—Dude and I found him when he was missing. But I'm not looking for a relationship. I don't *want* a relationship."

"Why do you think you can control that?" she asked, shaking her head.

Be the boss of yourself, he heard the mountain

man say. *Rule your emotions instead of letting them rule you.*

Now that he thought about it, though, Axel realized he was hardly the boss of his emotions. "I'm not pronouncing it out of nowhere—it's just how I *feel*, Daisy."

"Exactly. Because the heart is mightier than the head. Just accept it."

Okay, now he was confused. "What I'll accept is a cup of coffee," he said. "The chocolaty-hazelnut kind you gave me the other day, if you still have some."

She narrowed her blue eyes on him. "Changing the subject, I see. And yes, I always have chocolate-hazelnut."

He followed her to the big country kitchen, and Axel leaned against the counter. "I opened my letter from Dad."

Daisy gasped and turned to him. "Um, Axel, you could have led with that. What did it say?"

"It actually didn't say anything. Just a piece of paper with four Bear Ridge addresses. That's it. No explanations, no annotations."

She added the coffee grounds into the filter and hit Brew. "Really? Recognize any of them?"

"Turns out, completely by coincidence, I went to one last night." He explained about the grandmother and great-grandmother ambushing him into taking his fiancée out to dinner. "I walked in the door of Manuela's Mexican Café, and the owner took one look at me and knew I had to be Bo Dawson's son. She told me that's where he met my mom—when she was a waitress there."

"Wow," Daisy said. She poured his coffee, added cream and two teaspoons of sugar and handed the mug to him.

"Thanks," he said, lifting the mug. He took a long sip. "Apparently, Dad was so in love with her that when her car broke down, he gave her his truck so she could get to school and work, and he'd walk five miles from the ranch to see her. Then back. He brought her candy and flowers."

"Bo had a good side, Axel. We know that. My mom was madly in love with him despite his flaws."

Daisy and Noah's mother had come along not long after Axel's had had enough of Bo's hard-living ways—drinking, gambling, staying out late, flirting and no doubt cheating. Axel and his brothers had adored their stepmother, Leah, who was kind and compassionate and treated them like they were special. He'd never forget that. He'd been devastated when she'd died. Axel had been thirteen, Daisy eleven, Noah nine. Axel's mother hadn't been comfortable letting him and his brothers visit their father longer than a day with just Bo supervising. As teenagers, they'd barely seen him at all except for occasions, and he never failed to let them down in big and small ways that had stung.

Now he had a list of four addresses.

"So you think the other addresses will tell a story, too?" she asked.

"I have a feeling, yes. Not sure I want to hear it, though."

"You don't, but you do. That's always the way it is with complicated stuff, Axel."

Didn't he know it.

For the next couple of hours, Sadie and Danny explored the grounds around Axel's gorgeous log cabin. They'd found a hammock in the side yard, and she and Danny had stretched out for a while, soaking up the beautiful September sunshine before Danny got bored and wanted to run around, flying Zul. Then they'd met up with family for an early lunch at the cafeteria, Danny gobbling up the chili and corn bread. As always, there were multiple kid zones in the lodge, for the under-five, under-twelve and the teen set, and so she'd watched Danny have a blast in the toddler playground. The kid rooms were supervised, which was nice because there was also a refreshment table offering coffee, and Sadie needed some.

Ping.

A text from her sister: I hear you're staying at Axel's for a couple of days till Gram and Great-

Gram are better. How about if Marshall and I bring dinner over tonight? We can pick up from the caf or bring in Thai or Italian—whatever you guys want. I've been craving pasta like crazy lately.

Sadie swallowed. She loved the idea of texting back, Sure, and get pasta carbonara for me, penne in butter and cheese for Danny and baked ziti for Axel. Oh, and garlic bread.

She knew Axel loved baked ziti and garlic bread because they'd talked about their favorites last night. *I could eat five servings of even meh baked ziti myself,* he'd said.

She sucked in a breath and texted: My sister has invited herself and her fiancé over to your house for dinner tonight, but they're bringing the food. Italian? Baked ziti for you and tiramisu for dessert?

She hit Send and looked to see what Danny was doing. He was sitting at a little table with a staff member, coloring a picture. She eyed her phone. Nothing.

A full minute later, still nothing.

He's busy, for God's sake. He's on a wilderness tour and is responsible for the safety of several of your relatives. Except the trek was at nine and it was now past two.

She imagined him reading her text and thinking: *She's going too far. She and Danny were foisted on me and now she's arranging dinner get-*

*togethers at my house with her family? It's getting
to be much too much.*

Her stomach hurt.

Ping.

Sounds good. Don't forget the garlic bread.—A

He'd added the smiley face emoji in the cowboy hat again.

Her heart did five backflips.

She texted Evie to let her know they were in and
their orders. As she finally pocketed her phone, her
cousin Daphne, who'd been on the hiking trip on
Badger Mountain that fateful day Danny had gone
missing, came up to the table and poured herself
a coffee. She'd been pregnant then and now had a
baby girl named Bea.

"Daph, has my mom or Tabby ever talked to
you about what happened between them that day
on the mountain?"

Daphne pushed her long red hair behind her
shoulders, then added cream to the cup. "They're
still in a fight? Jeez. I remember them arguing
while the search crew was looking for Danny but
I didn't hear what they were saying since I was so
focused on the search. I sure hope they make up
this week. I mean, how can they not?"

"That's my hope, too. I'm about to go see my

mom—she's taking care of Gram and Great-Gram, who have colds."

"Hey, my sister and I are about to take her kids over to the petting zoo. I'm happy to take Danny along if you want a break."

Sadie smiled. "I'll bet he'd love to go with you guys. Text me when you're ready to leave the zoo and I'll come pick him up." She walked over to where Danny was admiring his drawing of Zul.

"Look, Mommy!"

She kneeled and smiled at the drawing. "It's Zul, saving the day. I love it. Hey, I'm going to see your grandma right now. Want me to give it to her as a present from you?"

Danny beamed. "Yes!"

"And while I do that, do you want to go to the petting zoo and see the animals with cousins Daphne and Lauren and their kids?"

"Yay, petting zoo!" Danny scrambled off the chair and ran straight to Daphne, where the group was waiting.

"Have fun!" Sadie called, blowing a kiss. She waved at Daphne and watched the group leave, finished her coffee and then headed out for her cabin. She hoped to run into her "fiancé" while she was walking but she didn't see him anywhere. She saw his brother Noah and his wife, Sara, the forewoman, and gave them a wave, but no Axel. What she would give to drink in the sight of him…

She made her way the quarter mile down the path to her cabin. The guest quarters managed to be secluded and not at the same time. Each cabin was spaced far enough apart that you couldn't see the others, trees giving privacy. Sadie loved the woodsy setting and breathed in the fresh scent of pine and flowers and earth.

As she rounded the cabin to the front, she saw her aunt Tabby stomping angrily away, her shoulder-length auburn hair bouncing behind her. Uh-oh.

"Tabby?" Sadie called out. "You okay?"

Her aunt turned and marched over, tears and anger in her eyes. "No, I most certainly am not! Vanessa and Izzy are my mom and grandmother, too, not that your mother seems to remember that!" She stalked off before Sadie could say another word, then ran back and kissed Sadie on the cheek. "I don't mean to take out my frustration on you, Sades. Love you! Toodles!" Then she stalked away again, and Sadie could see her swiping under her eyes.

Oh, dear.

Sadie shook her head as she walked up the cabin steps and knocked since her mother had texted five times she should do so instead of coming to "cold central."

"Coming!" she heard her mother call.

Viv opened the door and frowned. "Honey, this

is sick bay. You can't be here! You'll get sick, then Danny will, then Axel will!"

She held up the drawing. "I'm dropping this off. Danny drew it and wanted you to have it."

Her mother smiled. "Love that boy. And so talented. I'll put it on the minifridge for now. Shoo now, before the germs get you."

"You have those germs all over you, Mom," Sadie pointed out. "And you don't seem to have caught their colds."

"I just don't want a cold getting in the way of you spending this quality time with Axel or you and Evie making plans for the weddings. Nothing is worse than feeling rotten with a cold, honey."

"Ain't that the truth," Vanessa called out in a congested voice. Sadie heard her blow her nose— loudly.

"Aw, poor Gram and Great-Gram." She lowered her voice. "Look, Mom, I truly appreciate that you care about me. But, I ran into Tabby leaving and *I'm* not leaving this porch until you tell me what is going on between you two. What happened, Mom? You have to tell me because it's my fault."

Viv frowned and then looked sad. "How is it your fault?"

"You know why. You and Tabby stopped talking the day Danny went missing."

"That's not your fault. It's Tabby's—" She clamped her mouth shut.

"Aha!" Sadie said. "So you blame her for Danny going missing?"

"I hear Izzy calling for me," Viv lied. "You can't keep an ill ninety-nine-year-old waiting when she wants her chicken soup."

"Mom, c'mon. This is our family reunion. Were you trying to shut Tabby out of helping nurse her own mother and grandmother? She's their daughter, too."

"So *everyone* should get sick?" Viv asked. "Tabby's the one who wanted to stay with our cousins instead of bunking with us like she always does at the reunions. So tough noogies."

"Mom, seriously."

"I'm being serious as a you-know-what." Viv stepped aside. "Toodles, hon. Say hi to Axel and kiss my darling grandbaby for your ole ma, will you?"

The door closed.

Could her mother *be* more frustrating? How could two grown women who used phrases like "Toodles" be so stubborn?

Some family reunion. Her mother and aunt weren't speaking. Her grandmother and great-grandmother were sick with colds, and Sadie couldn't visit with them if she wanted to keep the peace with her mom. And Sadie's whole world had turned upside down with one little white lie.

At least Sadie knew she had pasta carbonara in her future. And garlic bread. And Axel.

Chapter Nine

As was the case these days, Axel both liked and didn't like that Sadie was sitting on the living room carpet with Danny next to the tower of blocks when he got home. Like they lived there. Like they were his family. His wife, his child.

He got that discomfort in his chest, as though air was squeezing out. But at the same time, good goose bumps traveled up his spine at the sight of beautiful Sadie and her sweet toddler, whom he had to admit he adored. When he'd worked at Badger Mountain, he was used to coming home to an empty house with Dude, his partner on his missions, and then it would be just the two of them unless he went out with some of his colleagues on the search and rescue team. He'd tended to save that for only events—birthdays and welcomes and retirements. So it was always just him and Dude in his cabin, first the small one and now here at the ranch.

Then again, these past weeks, being right on the property, he found himself spending a lot of time with his brother and sister and their families— and liking it. For the longest time, the thought of the Dawson Family Guest Ranch had reminded him of his father, of bad times. But now, the place made him think of his baby niece and nephews, of dinners with his siblings and their spouses, commiserating on tough days when there were guest injuries or issues, laughing at Daisy's funny stories, feeling grateful when Noah would talk about those months he and a team had spent rebuilding the family ranch into something new but that still paid homage to their grandparents.

Axel had been changing without even realizing it, he now knew.

"Zul!" Danny said as Axel came inside, leaping up and careening straight for him. The little boy wrapped his arms around Danny's legs, and Axel scooped him up, hoisting him high.

"Building Zul's tower, I see," Axel said. "Looks

great." He put Danny on the ground and the boy ran to his blocks, toddler-telling him all about it.

Sadie smiled up at him. "Evie and Marshall will be here at seven with Italian from Figorella's. I love that place."

"Not in Bear Ridge, right? I haven't heard of it."

"Prairie City. My parents go every Friday night."

The small talk made him aware of how strange this was. This woman and child in his house, staying with him till at least tomorrow. Her family coming over as their guests.

It's just till tomorrow. They'll head for the cabin. At the end of the week, they'll return to Prairie City. This will all be over.

And you'll be on your own again.

The idea of them leaving didn't sit right either, though.

For the next hour there was tower building and then Sadie gave Danny his bath, and then it was Zul story time, so once again, he settled Danny on his lap, the baby-shampoo scent of him reminding him of another time, another child, and again, the air seeped.

Another single mother in the doorway, watching, seemingly happy.

Seemingly. Interesting. Was he expecting Sadie to pull a fast one on him? They weren't even in a real relationship. He was losing his mind, clearly.

Maybe it had just been a long day.

With Danny tuckered out and in his crib, fast asleep within minutes, they tiptoed out of the nursery and went downstairs. Her sister and her real fiancé would be here any minute. Danny had eaten earlier and Sadie had mentioned she'd put his penne in the fridge for tomorrow's lunch.

Axel was starving. And looking forward to the baked ziti and garlic bread and tiramisu.

"You two are such a great couple," Evie whispered after dinner as Axel got up from the table to collect the empty tiramisu dishes. Marshall hopped to it as well, and the men brought the dishes and silverware into the kitchen.

"He's a good guy," Sadie whispered in turn, not surprised she and Axel had come across as a real couple during dinner.

They talked so easily, were truly interested in what the other had to say, and Axel had cute stories to tell about putting Danny to bed and building towers. He really did seem like Sadie's fiancé and Danny's dad-to-be. To the point that at times during dinner, Sadie had almost forgotten he *wasn't*. And he was warm and friendly to her sister and Marshall, sharing memories about growing up on a dude ranch and about his work as a search and rescue specialist. Evie was in love with Dude and couldn't stop petting him. The Lab had spent the meal under her feet for that reason.

"It's so obvious how much you two care about each other," Evie added, then took a sip of her coffee. "The way he looks at you—warms my heart. With such love and respect."

Well, he did seem to respect her but he certainly didn't love her.

Evie's diamond ring twinkled on her finger as she covered Sadie's hand with her own. "I'm so happy for you and Danny, Sadie. You truly found a real hero."

Okay, a crummy weight lodged in Sadie's heart. She wanted this to be real. She wanted Axel to be her and Danny's hero, and for her and Danny to be *his* heroes. She needed a little rescuing in some ways and so did Axel. And she was up for the job.

If only, if only, if only.

As the guys came back, Sadie thanked them for being on table-clearing duty, and they went into the living room and plopped down on the comfortable sofa with their coffees.

"So I brought this fun game," Evie said, getting up and walking over to the foyer where she brought in a paper bag. She sat and pulled out a bright red box. The Love Game: So You Think You Know Your Significant Other?

Uh-oh. Party games could be fun but this one was going to be a disaster. *Please don't let there be embarrassing questions about sex*, she thought, bracing herself for the worst and most mortifying.

"Okay," Evie said, taking the lid off the box and pulling out stacks of cards. "We each get three cards with a letter on it—A, B and C." She handed those out. "These are our answer cards for the multiple-choice questions. We keep those hidden from one another. Then, we take turns picking a face-down question card from the stack. Each card has a multiple-choice question for you to answer about your partner. After you read the question aloud, your partner chooses from the three possible answer cards—A, B or C—and places his answer card facedown in front of him. Then *you* answer. If you two are in sync, you get ten points. If not, you lose ten points. The losing couple treats the winning couple to dinner next time!"

Sadie glanced at Axel. He didn't look miserable or like he wanted to crush the cards in his hand into dust. That was good.

"Who wants to go first?" Evie asked.

Sadie swallowed. *Not me.* Axel didn't shoot his hand in the air either.

No one seemed eager, not even Marshall, who presumably knew his fiancée well after three years.

"Guess I'll go first!" Evie said, taking a sip of her coffee, then picking up the top card from the face-down stack. "'Your partner forgot your birthday. Will your partner, A, Say, oh, sorry, happy birthday, by the way. B, Rush out and buy you a card and gift. C, As if my partner would forget my birthday—puhleeeze!' Okay, so Marshall, now you choose either an A, B or C card as your answer and put that card facedown. Then I'll answer."

Marshall eyed his cards and swished his mouth around. "Hmm," he said. "Okay, got it." He put a card face down on his knee.

"The only possible answer is C," Evie said. "As if I'd let you forget! Am I right, Marsh?"

Marshall grinned and triumphantly held up the C card.

"Well done," Axel said to him.

Evie beamed. "Okay, we'll go clockwise, so it's your turn, Sadie."

Sadie glanced at Axel, then picked up a card. "'Your partner comes home with an adorable puppy in a cardboard box. You're a cat person. You, A, Instruct your partner to find another home for it ASAP. B, Bring it to the animal shelter. C, Name your new puppy and welcome him to the family.'" All eyes turned to Axel. He quickly chose his answer card and put it on his knee. "I'm going with C," Sadie said.

Axel didn't know her well enough to know what a sappy soft heart she was, right? As if she could not immediately fall in love with a little or even big puppy with its sweet puppy eyes. Axel was probably the same. Or maybe he knew her better than she thought.

Her faux fiancé smiled and held up the C card. "Dude turned Sadie into a dog person."

"I happen to love both dogs *and* cats," Sadie said, a little too happy that she and Axel had earned their ten points.

Marshall picked a card and turned to his fiancée. "'I'll be away on a transcontinental business trip for two months. We'll keep the love alive by, A, Cheating to remind us that we prefer each other by the time I return. B, Lots of video calls, phone convos, texts with heart emojis and as many visits as we can. C, As if I'd ever leave you behind.'"

Evie chose her answer card, keeping the letter hidden against her chest.

"Is that your final answer?" Marshall asked.

"It's my final answer," Evie said, patting Dude, who'd curled up beside her.

"First of all," Marshall began, "I would never, ever, ever cheat on Evie. I'm lucky enough to have her. Second, if a business trip does call me away for two months, which will feel like forever, I would FaceTime every night, call, text and hope Evie would visit as often as she could. Not being able to leave each other's side doesn't sound so healthy."

Evie grinned and held up her B card.

"Yes!" Marshall said, high-fiving his fiancée.

"Your turn, Axel," Evie said.

He took a long sip of his coffee, then picked up a card. Was it her imagination or did he flinch slightly as he read it to himself?

Uh-oh. That meant the question was either embarrassing or too personal.

Axel cleared his throat. "'Your partner wants five kids. You're not sure you want kids at all. You, A, Assure your partner that compromise is the name of the game. B, Tell your partner it's over. C, Get them upstairs to the bedroom pronto.'" Axel didn't look at Sadie. He kept his gaze somewhere between his lap and his coffee mug.

"Oooh, hard one," Evie commented. "I mean, if one partner doesn't want kids and the other wants five… Even compromising on two could be impossible. One wants a big family and the other doesn't want kids at all."

"That's a toughie," Marshall agreed. "Evie and I both want at least three, so phew," he added.

Sadie bit her lip. She wanted the answer to be A. She needed the answer to be A. But only because Axel didn't want *any* kids. Compromise *was* the name of the game—most of the time. But some things were deal breakers for good reason in relationships. Not wanting kids could be one of those.

Then again, Axel didn't want to get *married*.

"I'm not sure," Sadie said, picking up her coffee cup and taking a long sip.

"Well, pick your answer based on what you think Axel's answer is," Evie suggested. "That should make it easier."

Yeah, it did. But he wouldn't choose B—*tell your partner it's over*. Not during a "love" game with her sister and her fiancé when she and Axel were supposed to be a madly-in-love engaged couple themselves.

She looked up at Axel—and felt instantly better. He was sitting there, all handsome and agreeable and kind, his piercing blue eyes grazing over her before he plucked a chocolate chip cookie off the plate on the table. She *did* know him, she realized. He wasn't going to pick A, the one about compromising. He'd pick C, the lighthearted answer about making whoopee to make babies. It was the "right" answer for the game, for the situation, for the present company. Even if he didn't mean it. Just like he didn't mean that they were engaged. It was all pretend.

Pretend, pretend, pretend.

"My answer is C," Sadie said, suddenly not having much fun.

"Is that your final answer?" Marshall asked with a grin.

"Yes," Sadie said, trying to inject some levity into her voice.

"Okay, Axel, is my sister right?" Evie asked.

"Of course she is," he said, turning the card over and showing everyone the C.

Sadie wanted to cry. Because it meant she'd been right about knowing him, understanding him. And because he was lying through his very nice teeth.

And she *did* want five kids. Okay, three, like her sister and brother-in-law-to-be. Two for sure. But Axel had made it crystal clear he wanted *no* kids. No wife. No forever.

The game moved on, the questions a little easier on Sadie's heart and mind when it wasn't her turn. They played for another forty minutes or so, but then Evie started yawning and Danny let out a "Mama?" from the nursery, and they were hugging Evie and Marshall goodbye.

"Next time, our place to finish the game!" Evie said, waving as she and Marshall headed down the porch steps.

Suddenly it was just the two of them. Now Sadie wished her sister and Marshall were here as buffers. Because she had no right to be upset. The man was not her fiancé!

Danny had quieted for a minute there, and either he'd fallen back to sleep or was waiting for her to come. "Mama?" he called again. "Zul?"

Sadie's heart clenched. He was also calling for Axel. Her son adored the man. It went beyond naming a superhero lion after the man who saved him on the mountain.

Oh, boy. What had she done? After this week, when Axel disappeared from Danny's life, how did she think the little boy was going to react to that? Why had she put her own son in a position to be hurt by his hero?

She closed her eyes for a second and then dashed upstairs, willing herself not to cry. Putting her own heart in jeopardy was one thing—Danny's was off-limits to that.

"Sadie? You okay?" Axel asked from behind her.

She didn't respond.

"Sadie," he said again, putting a hand on her shoulder at the landing.

She whirled around. "Many nights my son calls for me when he wakes up and can't soothe himself back to sleep. But tonight he also called for *you*."

He froze for a second. "Because he knows he's in my house. That's all. He knows I'm here."

"He's two years old. All he knows is that 'Zul' is in his life, intensely suddenly. He doesn't understand context. And when we leave, not just your house, Axel, but the ranch and your life, he's going to be very confused." Tears stung her eyes.

"Zul?" Danny called.

Now tears slipped down her cheeks. "Let's go in. We can talk after."

He gently reached up a hand as if to wipe away the tears, but she turned away and headed into the nursery.

"Zul," Danny said, shooting his arms up toward Axel. Sadie could tell that Danny was tired and probably had had a strange dream that had woken him up. A little soothing and he'd be asleep in no time.

Axel glanced at her—for permission, she realized—and she let out a breath and nodded, her heart splintering.

As Axel picked up Danny and cuddled him close, rubbing his back, Danny said, "Dada," and then his eyes closed.

Sadie gasped under her breath.

Dada.

Axel had gone stock-still.

Danny had fallen asleep, and Axel walked him around the nursery a couple of times, then paced in front of the crib before gently lowering him. Danny stirred and pulled Zul under his arm, then his little chest was rising up and down, up and down.

Sadie hurried out of the nursery and Axel followed, keeping the door slightly ajar. She rushed down the stairs and stood in the middle of the hall, her arms crossed over her chest. Axel came down slowly, staring at her, his hands shoved in the pockets of his jeans.

"We'll leave in the morning," she said. "Enough is enough. I'll explain the misunderstanding about the engagement to my family and they'll have to get over it. Danny comes first here. He called you Dada. *Dada*," she repeated. "That's a big problem, as you know. A big confusing problem for Danny. And it's my job to protect him from things like that." She shook her head, tears stinging.

He didn't say anything. Just nodded—miserably.

"Well," she said, lifting her chin. "I'll go clean up. I need to do something with all this…angst, so don't try to be nice and stop me."

"Okay," he said. "Can I at least help?"

She burst into tears.

Axel stepped forward and pulled her into his arms and though part of her knew she should run into the kitchen and start scrubbing, she let herself have this. She sagged against him, wrapping her arms around him. The hug, warm, tight, was so comforting. "Whatever you need, Sadie. What Danny needs. That's all I've ever cared about."

That was only partially true. They *needed* to complete their very small family—a loving, committed life partner for Sadie, a dad for Danny. Axel had taken himself out of the running for that.

"No matter what, Sadie, everything is going to be okay. Know why?"

She looked up at him. "Why?"

"Because you're a great mom."

She swiped under her eyes and felt herself calming. "I'm trying to be. But I messed up here. I should never have let this lie go on. And tonight? Full-out lying in my sister's face?" She shook her head. "Evie is my best friend. What am I doing?"

"You got caught in a crazy moment and you went with each subsequent moment and the moments snowballed. You're doing this for Evie. Remember that. You would have come clean, but then she said all that stuff about not wanting to get engaged until you found your Mr. Right."

"I know, but…" But what? She was going to march over to the cabin in the morning and announce she let them all believe a lie? That she'd gone to a bridal boutique and played a game meant for couples when she was really as single-Sadie as ever?

Yes, dammit. Because her son was calling her fake fiancé *Dada*. And that was the deal breaker.

Your toddler calls your faux fiancé Dada. Do you, A, Let your precious son believe that when nothing could be further from the truth. B, Tell everyone you're a big fat liar. C, There is no good answer.

She was going with B. She had to tell the truth.

Evie's wedding was at the end of the week. The truth would make her sister feel like dog doo and she'd be furious at Sadie for perpetuating the lie, for not telling at least *her* the truth when they were so close. Her mother would cry. Vanessa would have to call everyone she knew and would never get off the phone for the rest of the family reunion. Izzy, beloved Great-Gram, would be confused. Her mom and Aunt Tabby would go back to not even trying to be civil around each other for the sake of the engaged Winston sisters.

And Danny would ask where Zul was. When he'd see him.

What a mess. She could clean up the one in the kitchen by putting the dishes in the dishwasher and tossing the take-out containers in the trash.

"How can I not tell everyone the truth?" she asked him.

"This is one time I wish I was a superhero. That I could turn back time to the second Izzy thought we were the engaged ones, and neither of us said otherwise. But—"

"But you can't and neither can I."

"Actually, I was going to say, but then I—" He stopped again and stared at the floor, then at the window in the hall, then at Dude, who was staring at them.

"Then you what?" she asked, holding still. Then he *what*?

"Then I wouldn't have gotten to know you, Sadie. And I like what I know. I wouldn't have gone to Manuela's Mexican Café. I wouldn't have opened the letter from my dad after almost nine months of being scared to death of it."

She almost gasped. She hadn't expected him to say anything like that.

"You opened the letter?" she repeated. "Did it work the same magic that Daisy's and Noah's did for them?"

"I don't know yet. It's a list of four addresses. Nothing else. Just addresses. Manuela's was one of them."

"He's sending you on an explanation of his life," she said slowly. "Oh, Axel. I think that's what you need to make peace with all that happened between you two."

"I was thinking that maybe I'd check out another of the addresses tomorrow. But—"

She waited.

"I accidentally went to one of the addresses with you the other night and it helped, having you there to talk to about everything. Given that I don't know what the next place will be or what it will call up in me, I'd appreciate having you there. Again. I mean, if you want."

"Of course I want."

He pulled her into his arms again and hugged her. "Thank you," he whispered. He turned to Dude. "Time for a long walk, partner." He looked at Sadie again. "You okay about being here alone for about half an hour?"

She nodded. "I could use the alone time right now. For about that long."

"Me, too," he said.

Then he and Dude were out the front door, taking her heart with them.

Chapter Ten

Axel woke up with the roosters the next morning, not that the ranch had roosters because they would wake up the guests at 4:30 a.m. He wanted to be out before Sadie and Danny left, and he didn't want Sadie to feel that she had to say goodbye, which would be weird and confusing for Danny. He'd make a point of running into them on the ranch later and he'd give Danny closure. He wasn't sure what, but he'd think of something. Something to assure him that even though the tyke wouldn't be seeing Axel much, Axel would always be thinking of him.

Damn. That part was true. He would always be thinking of Danny. The little kid had gotten inside him. And so had his mother.

Last night had almost done him in. The after-dinner game. The question about kids—and he'd answered as he'd known Sadie would have liked, but it had cost him. That lie hadn't been a momentary blip that he could forget about. It served to remind him that Sadie did want a bigger family than she had right now, one that included a husband and siblings for Danny.

And then Danny had called for him. And squeezed the air from Axel's lungs even harder by calling him *Dada*.

Dada. Axel.

He'd returned from a walk with Dude, who could roam loose around the property near his cabin. This was all Dawson land, and guests never ventured this far out even when lost. The walk hadn't done him any good. His shoulders were just as bunched up as when he'd left. He'd been hoping and not hoping—his life story—that Sadie would still be in the kitchen or maybe reading or watching TV in the living room so that they'd be forced to deal with each other, to talk. But the cabin had been quiet and Sadie's door was closed. He'd peeked in on Danny and found Sadie asleep in the yellow glider on the moon-and-stars rug in the nursery, a throw half covering her.

He'd stood there staring at her for a good minute, his heart moving in his chest, the air seeping in and out of his lungs, whatever *that* meant, and he knew he wouldn't be walking away from Sadie Winston so easily. He had…feelings for her. And he adored her son. He'd have to deal with that.

But she was going to tell her family the truth today. Unless he could save her from the fallout by magically proposing to her for real. But he couldn't do that. He wasn't up for a real relationship with real expectations and real emotions. At least in this faux engagement he could pretend—and pretending was easy.

He stopped at the ranch cafeteria for breakfast before the daily staff meeting at seven and poked his head in. Yes. The place had just opened and not a Winston was here yet. If any had been here and saw him sitting alone, they'd insist he join them and that would create more weirdness later, once word spread that they weren't engaged.

How was she going to tell her family the truth? So damn awkward. And he knew she'd be mortified for a good long time. Dang it.

He went up to the counter, where a long, polished wood bar separated the dining area from the kitchen. He waved at Cowboy Joe and the two cooks working on bacon and sausage. Fran, in her hunter green polo, sat in her tall-backed chair at the counter, ready to tap his order into her computer tablet. She was seventy and a whiz at her job, keeping the line moving. Axel had a smile for Fran, despite not feeling it. He went with the famed blueberry pancakes and a side of bacon. Coffee and orange juice were on a self-serve station to the side, and he planned to refill at least three times.

He took his order ticket and got himself coffee and juice, then sat at a table by a window, heart weighed down with at least five bricks. Was Sadie texting her mom right now? I have something to tell you.

He hated the idea of her dealing with all this on her own. The telling, the confused stares, the *Oh, Sadie, how could you?*

He sure did seem to care about her.

Axel pulled out his phone and texted her: You could always tell them that we decided to call off the engagement, that we want to give the relationship more time. You don't have to say we never were a couple, let alone never engaged.

He set aside his phone, sipped his coffee and waited for a ping. He had no doubt she was awake, probably getting Danny ready for the day in his favorite dinosaur T-shirt and orange sneakers.

His phone stayed silent.

He drank more coffee and stared at the stupid phone. *Ping already, dammit.*

Nothing. He went up to the counter for the first refill of caffeine—and heard the ping from there.

He would have rushed back to the table but he didn't want hot coffee sloshing all over his hand.

I care about this woman a little too much, he realized.

He sat and picked up his phone and read her text.

My mom let me know Gram and Great-Gram are back on their feet, so I texted my mom and crew to meet me and Danny for breakfast at the caf in fifteen minutes. I'm going to tell them the truth.

You can make me the heavy, he texted. Tell them I ended the engagement.

Nah. My sister will feel awful about getting married this coming weekend in that case. What's that wise saying? The truth shall set me free? Everyone will be mad for one second, then forget it and focus on the real bride—Evie. That's my hope anyway.

Mad for one second? That crew? Ha. Her mother and aunt had been mad at each other for months.

I'll be thinking of you, he texted.

She didn't respond to that one.

He sure hoped his breakfast would be ready soon. He needed to be out of here before Sadie and her family arrived. Luckily, a minute later, Fran called out his ticket number in her booming voice, always good when there was a crowd here, and he got his tray. Mmm, the pancakes and bacon looked and smelled amazing.

He sat and drizzled maple syrup on the pancakes, but after taking all of three bites, Sadie, Danny and family came in—sister, mother, aunt, grandmother and great-grandmother. Everyone was chatting and happy so she clearly hadn't told them yet. He got it—she didn't want to ruin their appetites.

Sixty-year-old Cowboy Joe, who never took off his Stetson, came out from the kitchen making peekaboo faces at Danny. "Peekaboo, I see you!" Joe said, covering and uncovering his face.

"Dada!" Danny said, reaching for Cowboy Joe with a big smile.

Axel's mouth dropped open. He glanced over at Sadie and hers had done the same.

Cowboy Joe grinned and took Danny, hoisting him high in the air. Danny gave his grizzled brown-gray beard a yank.

Vanessa laughed. "He's been calling every man with dark hair Dada since we got here. Couple of days ago he called out to a ranch hand who couldn't be more than twenty, and the guy almost fainted."

Sadie's face brightened. She looked at Axel, who gave her a "phew" smile and she smiled back.

It was a phase. A toddler phase. Calling men *Dada*. Danny had a mama and applied that to only Sadie but he didn't have a dada so all men were that.

You're not special to him, after all, Axel told himself, but suddenly his pancakes were turning into cement in his stomach. What the hell was this? Wasn't he supposed to be elated that he wasn't special? That he wasn't anyone's dada?

False alarm, he texted Sadie. He could hear her phone ping. He watched her reach for her phone and read the text. She glanced at him.

I should still tell, she texted back.

Let Evie be. Let Izzy have this time. Let your mother be overjoyed. You'll fix it when you get home. You'll tell them I ended the engagement, that I couldn't commit after all, and everything will be fine—no one will be mad at you that way.

Except she didn't *look* fine as she read the words.

And he didn't *feel* fine.

Sigh. He really didn't know what the heck was going on with him. Or her. Or them.

"Why is your handsome groom-to-be sitting all by his lonesome?" Izzy asked after placing her

order for scrambled eggs and toast. She didn't wait
for an answer as she made her way slowly to his
table with her red cane.

Sadie watched as Axel stood and took her great-
grandmother's arm. Izzy leaned forward to offer
her cheek for a kiss, and Axel obliged with a warm
smile, then helped her into a chair. Sadie's heart
physically moved in her chest, and she put her hand
over the spot. My word, did she love this man.

Oh, God. She really did love him.

Once the whole group was seated and awaiting their tickets to be called, Axel stood behind
Sadie and put his hands on her shoulders. How
could someone so anti-marriage be so good at this
faux engagement? He was ridiculously believable
as her fiancé.

"Pick you up at four to head into town, Sadie?"
he asked.

For a second she had no idea what he was talking about. Until she'd walked here and Danny had
called Cowboy Joe *Dada*, she'd thought she was
going to come clean to her family during breakfast,
just blurt it out, rip off the Band-Aid. That and her
time with Axel at an end had made her miserable
last night, and she'd thought of little else. But now
that she felt better about the Dada thing—clearly
a phase—she didn't feel so panicked. What he'd
texted made sense to her, and yeah, gave her a
huge out, and she thought he was right. Let her

family have this week instead of making everyone upset and uncomfortable—especially Evie after all her sister had opened up about. Viv had three wedding-related meetings set up for Evie this morning. Evie, Sadie, Viv and Tabby were all going. That was another thing Sadie didn't want to mess up—if Tabby was coming, that meant the two elder sisters had at least talked to declare another temporary truce for the week.

The afternoon meeting was about the letter from his father, she realized—the list of addresses. Sadie was so curious. One coincidental visit to Manuela's and he'd learned so much about his parents—particularly his father. Some very nice things. Things that had actually gotten him thinking. Let him open that letter after almost nine months.

She liked his hands on her shoulders. The warm weight of them was comforting—and a nice touch.

"Danny and I will be there," Sadie said. She'd be spending the day with her family and could feel the relief radiating that she wouldn't have to tell them the truth about her and Axel just yet.

Not that she was happy about it. Saying Axel had dumped her once they got home would be adding another lie to the mix. But then again, it would finally be over, just like *they'd* be over, and she would be heartbroken and could use the familial support and boxes of Puffs tissues and Ben & Jerry's. That heartache would not be fake.

"Danny, too?" her mom asked. "Why don't you let me and Great-Gram and Great-Great-Gram take our precious boy today. We barely got to see him the last two days, didn't we," she said, giving her grandson, beside her in a high chair, a soft tap on the nose.

Danny giggled. "Gram. Gray-Gram. More Gray-Gram!" He couldn't say "great-gram" and referred to Vanessa as "gray-gram" and Izzy as "more gray-gram." The family cracked up every time he said it. Only Izzy actually had gray hair since his gray-gram Vanessa kept hers an ash blond.

"And Gray-Aunt Tabby," Sadie's aunt put in, staring down Viv.

Good for you, Tab, Sadie thought. She narrowed her eyes at her mother. Tabby was fierce in staking her claim on spending time with her family, whether wedding-related or enjoying the ranch. *Don't you dare tell her no when you already agreed she was joining,* Sadie yelled in her head.

Viv lifted her chin but didn't say anything, which meant a huffy *fine*. Luckily, their order tickets were called and everyone stopped talking.

"Allow me," Axel said, bringing over two trays at a time until everyone was served.

Could the man be more gallant? She had chosen her faux fiancé well.

"Any*hoo*," Viv said, cutting into her cheese omelet, "Sadie and Axel, you two go off and wedding plan or whatever you're doing in Bear Ridge at four o'clock. We're happy to have our darling boy for as long as you need."

Sadie sipped her coffee. "Thanks, all of you. He sure is getting lots of great family time this week."

She'd miss her son—and she always felt like something wasn't quite right in the world when she was away from Danny—but she knew it was good for her relatives and for Danny to spend a lot of time together. Back home, during the week, Danny went to the excellent day care at work for hospital employees, and she got to stop in several times a day to see him. She always had lunch with him. Her mom would be retiring from her own job as a librarian later this year and she said she wanted to watch Danny full-time until he started preschool. Sadie liked that he was getting this early exposure to different kids and adults, but it would be nice for his grandmother and great-grandmother and great-great-grandmother to spend time with him.

"Well, see you later, then, Sadie. Bye, all," Axel said. He smiled and waved and then was gone.

"Such a handsome one!" Izzy said with a twinkle in her eyes.

"And such a gentleman!" Vanessa said. "Like my daddy was."

Aw, Sadie wished her great-grandfather could be here with them but he'd passed away four years ago. The male relatives, including Sadie's dad and grandpa, were spending a lot of time fishing and riding horses, neither of which Sadie's crew was interested in. Viv and Vanessa always thought of the family reunions as "girl time" since they got "quite enough" of their husbands at home.

Izzy gave a firm nod. "Got that right."

That got breakfast off to a good start, so they turned their attention to eating and complimenting their entrées and the coffee. When everyone was done, Sadie dropped Danny off with her cousin, Vanessa and Izzy went to wilderness yoga for seniors, and Sadie and her sister, mom and aunt got in Evie's car for a trip to Prairie City, where Viv had made appointments at a florist, a caterer and a party store that had everything from Halloween costumes to elegant candlesticks.

Evie wanted a rustic-elegant simple wedding for her and Marshall's eighty-two guests. According to her long chat the other day with Daisy Dawson, who'd organized a few weddings at the ranch so far, thirteen centerpieces were all they'd need to doll up the ballroom on the second floor of the ranch's lodge. The grand white building, which had been recently built, had been made to look antique.

There were arched floor-to-ceiling windows across one entire wall, a gorgeous chandelier, a polished wood dance floor and a large deck that would be festooned with white lights. Evie explained how the room would be arranged for the reception. The ceremony itself would be held outside behind the lodge, and the ranch would provide the arbor, red carpet to create the aisle and chairs. The weather for Saturday evening was supposed to be low seventies and not a drop of rain in the forecast. The reception would be in the lovely ballroom and spill onto the stone deck.

"That all sounds absolutely perfect," Aunt Tabby said as Evie drove down the service road that led to the freeway. "I never got married, of course, but if I had, I would have wanted the wedding you're planning."

"Did you just never fall in love?" Evie asked— daringly since their mom had always told her daughters that Tabby Winston viewed her single-hood as a failure that she didn't like to talk about.

Tabby didn't respond right away. "Actually, I did fall in love. With a wonderful guy and he proposed." She glanced out the window as though it was still painful for her. Sadie's heart went out to her aunt. She'd never heard this story before.

"Oh no," Evie said. "Please don't tell me he left you at the altar."

"Worse," Tabby said, tucking her auburn hair behind her ears.

"What could be worse?" Sadie asked, thinking of how she'd overheard that the father of Daisy Dawson's baby had left her at the altar when she was nine months pregnant. A guest had happened by and helped deliver little Tony right on the side of the road—and now they were married.

"I left *him* at the altar," Tabby said, shaking her head. "What an idiot I was."

"Don't beat yourself up," Viv told her, turning slightly to look at her sister in the back seat. "You did what felt right at the time. That's all you can do." Clearly, Viv knew all about this, and that made sense, since the sisters had always been so close.

Sadie looked at her mom in the passenger seat. That had been kind of Viv to say. Maybe there was hope here after all.

"I guess," Tabby said. And it was clear that Viv and Tabby had talked a lot about the subject over the years.

Evie pulled over onto the shoulder of the road and put the car in Park. "Wait a minute." She turned around to face her aunt. "You called off the wedding at the last minute? What happened?"

Tabby sighed. "Some other guy turned my head around and made me think *he* was the real one, the real Mr. Right. He swept me off my feet, and suddenly I thought I'd found the man I was truly meant to spend my life with. And ooh boy, was your gram mad at me. She thought I was nuts to throw away a good man for a whirlwind romance. I was so in love, though, and no one could tell me anything. But—"

Uh-oh.

"He dumped me after three weeks," Tabby continued. "I realized what a horrible fool I'd been, but my fiancé wouldn't take me back. I don't blame him. He married someone else six months later. Kudos to your gram for not once saying I told you so. You, too, Vivvy."

Viv leaned over and put a hand on her sister's arm. That was nice to hear, that Viv had been there for Tabby—and that Tabby remembered and brought it up. That was the kind of thing that cemented a relationship, that had to matter more than a silly argument.

Sadie gave her aunt's hand a squeeze. "I'm so sorry, Aunt Tabby."

"Didn't you start dating eventually, though?" Evie asked, pulling onto the road since their appointment was in fifteen minutes with the caterer.

"I did, but I never fell for anyone again. I liked some of the guys very much, tried to love some over the years, but I couldn't imagine marrying any of them. And I must have gone on a thousand dates since then. Here I am, still single."

"Eh, not everyone has to get married or have kids," Viv said. "You've had a fun and interesting life. You have a career, you have a big family you help out with, you travel, you volunteer. Girls, did you know your aunt Tabby volunteers at the NICU twice a week? The sickest babies, too."

Sadie knew Tabby volunteered at the hospital because she'd run into her there a few times, but she didn't know about the NICU. Her aunt had always said she was on a rotation of departments.

"Well, I missed out on the chance to have a baby of my own, so I figured I'd help out with those sweet infants," Tabby said. "And besides, I hope I've been more than just Aunt Tabby to you two girls. You know you're like daughters to me."

"We know, Tabs," Evie said, reaching her right arm out to rub Tabby's shoulder.

"We certainly do," Sadie added. Tabby had always been like a second mom to her and Evie. The older she got, the more Sadie realized how careful Tabby had been not to overstep on their mother's ways and style when it came to her nieces, even when Tabby thought Viv was dead wrong about something. They were lucky to have her.

If Aunt Tabby wanted a boyfriend or a husband she could certainly get out there and find herself one. She was lovely and vibrant.

"Do you all want to know a secret I've been keeping?" Tabby asked with a shy smile. Tabby was never shy about anything. So what was *this* about?

Viv turned around. "Now you're keeping secrets, too?" she snapped.

"What's that supposed to mean?" Tabby asked.

Viv glared at her sister. "We said we'd try to put aside our issues for the sake of the reunion. But now you have a secret from me?"

Oh, Mom, Sadie thought. *Why are you so dramatic?* Viv was the older sister and could be a lot less mature than Tabby.

"Well, we haven't exactly been talking," Tabby pointed out, her hazel eyes flashing.

"Your fault as well as mine," Viv insisted, crossing her arms over her chest, her signature move. "But a secret warrants talking!"

"Fine," Tabby said. "I'll tell you now. I have a date tonight."

Viv's mouth dropped open, and the energy in the air instantly changed from tense to pure curiosity. "A date with who?"

"Cowboy Joe," Viv said. "That handsome devil who runs the ranch kitchen in the caf. He's a widower and asked me out, and I said yes."

Sadie burst into a grin. Cowboy Joe was around sixty, she thought, tall and rangy with a full head of gray-black hair, a grizzled beard and squinting brown eyes. He reminded her of the actor Sam Elliott. Apparently, he'd been the chef at the ranch when Axel's grandparents had owned it, but he'd had to leave when Axel's dad ran the place into the ground. Noah Dawson had rehired him once he rebuilt, and Cowboy Joe had said he loved being "back home."

Sadie couldn't stop smiling. "That's great! He's quite handsome. Looks like a real cowboy."

"And he's so charming and nice," Evie said. "Did you see the way Danny ran right to him in the cafeteria and Joe picked him up and played peekaboo with him? He's a doll."

"You could have told me you were looking to date," Viv said. "I would have set you up with my endodontist—he's divorced and looking."

"He's my endodontist, too, and has bad breath," Tabby pointed out.

"Ew," Evie said, shaking her head and grimacing in the rearview mirror.

Sadie laughed. "Where are you guys going on the date?"

"Joe is taking me into Bear Ridge to a steakhouse that has a dance floor. You know how I love to dance."

"Well," Viv said, "do you want my opinion, not that you asked?"

Sadie rolled her eyes. Her mother was too much sometimes.

"Sure," Tabby said, clearly bracing herself for judgy Vivian.

Viv lifted her chin. "I think Cowboy Joe is a real catch and that your date sounds wonderful."

And sometimes Sadie's mother was just right. *Go, Mom.*

Tabby grinned. "I wonder if he'll try to kiss me. I hope so. He's been widowed for three years. He said he hasn't done much dating but there was something about me." She was beaming.

Sadie was so happy for her aunt. If only Axel Dawson would feel that way about Sadie—that there was something about *her* and fall madly in love…

"We're here!" Evie said, pulling into the little parking lot behind Calista's Catering.

Now Sadie would spend hours helping her sister plan a wedding she wished were her own—with a groom who never would be. At least Sadie was still faux-engaged, she thought, not that it really helped.

Chapter Eleven

"So what happens when the Winstons leave on Sunday?" Noah asked in the big barn after the staff meeting.

Axel kept his focus on straightening out the tack area, despite its being perfectly tidy and the ranch hands' job. "What do you mean?"

"He *means*," Daisy said as she tightened her long ponytail, "are you and Sadie going to keep up the pretend engagement, or are you going to break up?"

Actually, Axel knew what Noah had meant but was procrastinating answering. The sun caught on both his siblings' wedding rings, and Axel found himself staring at the gold bands. Even Noah, who'd been a wild child, had settled down and had never been happier. That had caught Axel by surprise. But Axel had never been a wild type, except for the lone wolf part. He did like sitting out on mountain ledges and taking in the panoramic views of such natural beauty and quiet and perfection. Lately, though, when he felt he needed one of those ledge sits, he kept envisioning Sadie beside him. A little conversation, a little silence. Just having her there, next to him.

"Sadie will tell her family that I ended the engagement, that I couldn't commit after all," Axel explained. "Everyone stays happy this week and once home, Sadie can save face."

"Oh, propose to her for real already," Daisy said. "Then you'll be happy, too."

Axel's eyes almost popped. "Excuse me? *What?*"

"I see how you look at Sadie," Daisy explained. "How you treat Danny. That's not pretend, Axel."

Noah looked at his sister, then at Axel. "You know, last night Sara asked me if you and Sadie were the real thing now, Ax. She said the two of you seemed truly in love."

Axel frowned. "It's called *acting.*"

"You were never in a school play for a reason," Daisy pointed out. "And you're the worst liar."

"Then how do I have y'all fooled?" he asked, wanting this conversation over.

Daisy chuckled—dryly. "Maybe you don't. Maybe you really have fallen for Sadie Winston."

Axel shook his head. "I'm not looking for a real relationship, Daize. I know you want me settled down with a family, but that's not me. I'm on my own and fine that way."

He knew Daisy's master plan when he'd first come back to the ranch three months ago had been to get him settled here. She'd been trying to fix him up so he'd fall in love and stay put, build a cabin on the property. Well, she'd gotten part of her grand plan—he'd built the home on the ranch— but he hadn't fallen in love. He wouldn't let himself. Because he knew what happened the last time he'd let his heart be the boss. He'd gotten run over by a tractor, twice. Once for the woman who'd left him. Once for her baby girl whom he'd never seen again. *You don't love, you don't lose.* It was that simple and really, someone should embroider that on a pillow.

"Gotta take him at his word," Noah said, shrugging at Daisy. But Axel caught the little smile passed between the two. Harrumph.

"Anyhoo," he said, using his faux mother-in-law-to-be's favorite way to change subjects. "Guess where I'm headed this afternoon."

"Did you just say anyhoo?" Noah asked, peering at him. He put his hand to Axel's forehead as if to feel for fever.

Daisy laughed. "Fine. We can change the subject, Avoider Axel. Where ya headed?"

Axel took the folded letter from his pocket. "This is the letter Dad left for me." He handed the piece of paper with the four addresses to Noah. He'd already spoken to Daisy about the list.

"What's the one on Main Street?" Noah asked, narrowing his eyes as if trying to place it around his favorite places in town—the coffee shop, a fish and chips place he and Sara frequented.

"Manuela's Mexican Café," he said. "Turns out that's where Dad met my mom."

Noah nodded. "He's definitely trying to tell you a story with these addresses. I wonder what the other places are. You recognize any, Daisy?"

She looked over his shoulder. "Hey, 22 Colby Way—I know what that is. It's Gram and Gramps's old house. Before they bought this land and built the ranch. Dad grew up there till he was five or six, I think."

"Yeah?" Axel asked, eyeing the address. "Maybe I'll check that out first."

Noah looked at the list again. "I don't recognize the others. Hurley Lane is a private road with one big ranch on it. An older couple lives there, I think. Not sure what Dad's connection to the Hurleys was."

Well, that was helpful, actually. Axel didn't like the unknown, and now three of the four addresses were accounted for and one could be crossed off—Manuela's. He reclaimed the list and returned it to the envelope and his pocket.

"Why would he send me to Gram and Gramps's old house?" Axel asked. "They moved out of there over fifty years ago."

"He must have had a good reason," Daisy said. "Want company there?"

Axel swallowed. He was going to get it for this. "I appreciate that, but, uh, Sadie's coming with me. We're leaving at four. I think I'll start with the old Dawson place and see what I can find out."

"Interesting," Daisy said, a twinkle in her blue eyes. "Sadie, your fake fiancée, is going with you on this personal mission. Away from the ranch and her relatives, the ones you need to play house for."

"We're…" Axel began, then clamped his mouth shut. They were what? Friends? He supposed he'd been about to say that but he and Sadie were more than friends. Friends didn't kiss the way they had—two times. Friends didn't have the intensity of attraction that they had.

"Let us know what you find out, will you?" Noah asked. "I'm curious why he's sending you to these places. Must be some things he wants you to find out."

Axel nodded. "Will do."

Noah and Daisy finally left, again giving each other a knowing look that had him inwardly groaning.

Axel stared at the hay bales, trying to get his brain back on the ranch, on his day. He had a busy one, leading two wilderness tours, patrolling a beginner's horseback riding program and helping the hands mend a section of fence. Then at four, he'd meet Sadie and go into the great unknown, where he kind of felt he was already.

"So what's your dream wedding?" Evie asked as she and Sadie both flopped on their beds in the cabin. Today had been a long but fun day of tastings, choosing flowers and buying centerpieces. Evie had already booked friends of Marshall's as the band: the Hell Yeahs. They were alternative country-rock who did amazing covers of all of Evie's and Marshall's favorite songs. "Ugh, that was a dumb question, sorry," she added with a grimace, turning on her side to face Sadie. "You probably made your dream wedding when you got married the first time."

Sadie smiled. "Are you kidding? That was more *Mom's* dream wedding."

Evie laughed. "Yeah, I do remember her saying to you, 'You want a poufy princess dress, *right*? You want filet mignon in béarnaise sauce, *right*?

Your bridesmaids are all wearing the same dress, *right*?'"

"I wasn't into wedding planning and Mom was, so I just said 'right' to everything unless it was truly awful. À la, 'You will aim your bouquet only for Evie or Tabby, who I will strategically place together. Strongest catcher wins, right?'"

"Ugh, thanks for saving me from that." Evie giggled. "I'll never forget Izzy catching the bouquet on her lap in her wheelchair and saying, 'Well, I *am* single.'" Evie cracked up.

Sadie laughed. "If I'd been into planning, I would have created a wedding like yours. Elegant yet simple. Pink and white flowers. White lights. A great band and great food."

"Simple works especially when you've got the highlight in the groom," Evie said. "I can't wait to say I do and kiss my husband and be a team. A whole new life is awaiting me—that's how it feels. I'd love to get pregnant right away. I hope I do."

Sadie smiled and turned on her side. "You're so lucky," she said and the wistfulness in her voice made her remember she was supposedly just as lucky.

"Maybe you and Axel can get married in the lodge, too," Evie said.

Sadie was lucky, too, because just then, their mom poked her head in their room and this stab-in-the-heart conversation was cut short. Danny was in her arms, a piece of what looked like a cider doughnut, his favorite, in his hand. The big smile on his face said Mommy was right about that. "Guess what Tabby's date for tonight had a ranch hand send over to our cabin?" Viv asked. "Oh, just a big box of two dozen freshly baked doughnuts of every kind imaginable. Come and get 'em before I eat all the cream-filled ones. You know you love those, Sadie. Hurry before Axey gets here. It's almost four."

Axey. Now he had a nickname? Sadie sighed and pulled herself up by the bedpost.

"Tell Izzy to leave me a powdered jelly!" Evie said.

"Oops!" Izzy called out. "How about half of one?" Sadie could hear Izzy chuckling from the living room.

She smiled. Saved by doughnuts. And Aunt Tabby's new romance. She was glad some people were having real affairs of the heart even if hers was fakety-fake.

Their destination, 22 Colby Way, was a tiny yellow house down a dirt road. A white farmhouse was about a quarter mile beyond and Axel figured the yellow house had been the hands' quarters at one time.

"I guess this was their starter home when my grandmother and grandfather were newlyweds,"

Axel said. "Doesn't look like it could fit more than two people."

Sadie stared up at the lemon yellow house with white trim. "It looks sweet and cozy. So what's the plan? Knock?"

"I guess."

They got out and walked up the two steps to the stoop. He'd been right to invite Sadie to join him. He wouldn't want to be here alone. Axel pressed the doorbell and a young woman came to the door.

"Hi," Axel said. "I recently found out that my grandparents used to own this house and I thought I'd come take a look if that's all right. I understand if it's intrusive."

The woman peered at him. "Are you a Dawson?"

Axel nodded. "How'd you know?" Maybe she'd known his father.

"Well, my grandparents owned this house for like the last fifty years. They retired and sold it to my husband and me. I know they bought it from the Dawsons, who ran the dude ranch before it went south."

Axel smiled. "It's north again. It's completely rebuilt and reopened."

"Oh, that's good to know. Well, come in. I'll show you around. The house is tiny so there's not much to see."

There was a little kitchen with barely room for

a two-person round table. Square living room. A very small dining room. A bathroom. The woman led them upstairs. "Two bedrooms up here. And the attic. But that's full of old furniture and my family's keepsakes, like old report cards."

Axel glanced around. Not much to see. He followed the woman downstairs, Sadie trailing. He wondered why his dad had bothered putting this place on the list. Fifty years was a long time. Maybe because Bo Dawson had lived here as a kid and he remembered it?

"Could we look out back?" Axel asked, peering out the window at the long but narrow backyard. There was a line of trees at the edge of the yard and a rickety tree house of sorts.

"Sure," she said. "Take your time. Oh—definitely go up in the tree house. The walls are covered in framed kitschy photos of who knows what. I think some of it might have been there when my grandparents bought the house. They loved the tree house and kept adding to what was already on the walls."

Axel and Sadie went outside and walked to the edge of the yard. Nothing to see here either. He shrugged. "Not much of a story."

"How old was your dad when your grandparents sold the house?" Sadie asked.

"Ten, I think."

"Well, maybe this counted as home to him and he wanted you to see it for yourself."

"I guess. Let's check out the tree house."

There were seven steps up and Axel tested the bottom rung—very sturdy. The tree house was built rock-solid—more like a cabin than the usual kiddie play structure. He wondered if his grandparents had built the tree house or if the other owners had. He climbed up, and since it was sturdy he went to the top and motioned Sadie up. There was a door that swung in, two windows and a braided rug in the middle of the dusty floor. No one had been up here in a while, it seemed. The walls were indeed covered, practically every available spot, with framed pictures of all kinds. One was an old rodeo advertisement from the '50s. Another was a Wyoming Wildcats team photo from the '90s. There were lots of framed local ads of livestock auctions and bull riders.

Axel drew closer to another one, a handwritten list, it looked like, in a gold frame.

My rules for life.

By Bo Dawson, age 10 and a half.

Axel sucked in a breath. "Sadie, come look at this."

She gasped. "They kept this up here for fifty years?"

"Well, the tree house is full of memorabilia, either theirs or my grandparents' or a mix. Like the woman said, I guess her grandparents liked it as it was and kept it."

"Well, now we know why this place was on the list. Because it was home and maybe he knew the tree house was left alone. Maybe he'd stopped by as an adult."

Axel stepped close and read the list his father had made.

My rules for life.
by Bo Dawson, age 10 and a half.

1. Try to do the right thing even if you don't want to. I only want to half the time.

2. Say sorry only if you mean it.

3. Your parents think they know everything but they probably do.

4. I wish we had money.

5. Someday I'm gonna have everything I want. I might even be president.

6. Birthdays are big deals and you should get everything on your list.

7. Everyone should have a dog. It's not fair I don't have one.

8. I'm good at math but not good at spelling or reading fast and I don't care.

9. There's no such thing as ghosts.

10. I wish I had a brother. If I ever have a family, I'm gonna have ten kids.

Axel stood there, speechless, oddly moved by the eclectic list. He loved having a piece of his father as a ten-year-old, so sure of himself.

"Six kids probably felt like ten," Sadie said with a smile.

Axel turned to her. "No doubt." He turned back to the list. "He loved Dude. Any time I'd bring the dog by, my dad would make such a fuss over him, get right on the ground and scratch him all over. One time he told me to wait a second, then came from the house with a chew toy he said he'd bought for the next time he saw Dude."

"Your dad definitely had his good side, Axel."

He nodded. "People are complicated. As I said before, it's so much easier if things are black-and-white. Either-or. Good and bad."

She reached for his hand and held it, and he squeezed it, then let go. This was too…personal, intimate, close, and the air started slowly disappearing from his lungs.

"Do you want to ask if you can have this?" Sadie suggested.

He took out his phone and stood back and snapped a photo of it. "I think it belongs here. Fifty years and counting."

"I'm surprised your grandparents didn't take it to the new house and hang it in his room or something."

He looked at the list again, his dad's handwriting as a ten-year-old not too far off from his adult handwriting. "Maybe they thought it belonged here with this chapter of their life. You know what I mean? Like, this is who Bo was when he lived in this house."

She smiled. "I can see that. And maybe the tree house walls were full of photos when your grandparents bought it and they kept the tradition by adding to it and leaving it. The new owners certainly didn't remove anything in fifty years."

He slowly turned, taking in all the stuff, imagining his dad here as a kid, lying on the rug, staring at the pictures, dreaming of the future. The thought made him smile. "I'm ready to go," he said.

Sadie climbed down first and he followed. The owner of the house happened to be watering flowers in the backyard, so Axel waved and called out thanks as they headed to the street where his car was parked.

He opened Sadie's door for her, then got in himself, his chest seizing on him. His father was once a kid making lists about his rules for life. How had that firecracker of a boy let his life unravel, especially when he had so much? The ranch, wives who loved him, six children who needed him.

"You okay?" Sadie asked once they were buckled up.

"I don't know why hearing about his life hits me so hard," Axel said, staring out the windshield. "He was an addict—to gambling and alcohol—and couldn't help himself. I know that—intellectually. But here—" he slapped a hand on the left side of his chest "—I'm just so…" He let it go. What was the point?

"Angry. Hurt," Sadie finished for him.

He turned to her. "Yeah, those."

"Want to visit another address or was this enough for one day?" she asked.

"This was more than enough." He shook his head. "Done in by a silly list written by my dad as a kid. What the hell is wrong with me?"

"You're human. And it's incredibly painful all you're dealing with, Axel. You once said you felt like his death was your fault."

He sucked in a breath. "I should have dragged him to rehab. They would have done a physical and found that he was dying."

"You didn't know. That doesn't make losing him your fault," she said gently. "How'd you get the news?"

He turned to her, surprised she'd asked. Most people would want to change the heavy subject. Not Sadie. "I was far out on a cliff on a search and rescue job and a chopper picked me up to take me to the hospital. Noah had found him barely conscious on the couch. He realized Bo was truly in trouble and called 911. I made it to his bedside five minutes before he passed away."

"Oh, Axel."

"All six of us got there in time. One of the last things my father said was, *You're all here.* And he said it with tears in his eyes and such surprise on his face. He left this world knowing that no matter what, we cared, we were there for him."

"I'm so glad for that. For him and for all of you."

"Me, too," Axel whispered.

She leaned over and pulled him to her and he wrapped his arms around her, the embrace, the scent of her, the softness of her so comforting.

"Thanks for being here," he said. "I owe you one."

She laughed. "Uh, I owe you a week's worth, so trust me, I still owe *you*." She looked at him and shifted in her seat. "Let's head to the cabin. I'll make you some comfort food."

"Home-cooked meal? Sounds good to me."

The thought of Sadie in his house, sharing a meal with her, just the two of them cocooned, sounded better than good. It sounded *necessary*.

Chapter Twelve

Sadie looked through the cabinets in Axel's kitchen and the fridge, and once decided on her menu, she took out the ingredients. At first, she thought she'd make his favorite, baked ziti, but he'd had that last night *and* he was out of both ziti and penne. But he had pizza dough and marinara sauce and mozzarella cheese, which meant yummy, gooey pizza.

I sure do feel at home here, she thought, spreading the sauce and generously laying on the cheese. She slid the pizza into the oven and set the timer, imagining herself living here, she and Axel taking turns making dinner, Sadie coming home from work at the hospital to a warm, cozy, luxe cabin with spaghetti and meatballs on the burners, garlic bread in the oven, *their* dog, Dude, excited to see her and Danny.

A few steps ahead of yourself, girl, she warned herself, but she loved the pictures in her head and refused to blink them away. *Axel coming down the stairs with just a towel wrapped around his sexy hips, kissing her hello, the towel dropping...*

Okay, now she was truly carried away. Although he had gone upstairs to take a shower, to erase the day, and it *was* possible he'd come down in just a teeny towel tied loosely around his hips, hair dripping onto his naked chest... Unlikely but still possible.

Except she knew Axel and he'd never do that, despite her wishing he would.

Back to reality. Which meant checking in with her mom to see how Danny was.

He's happy as can be, her mom texted back. We're at the petting zoo. Don't rush—we're about to head to dinner in the caf and I'll get Danny to bed on time and give him a kiss from you and Axey.

Again with the Axey.

Just in case she wouldn't be back before Danny's bedtime, she FaceTimed her mother so she could see Danny and tell him she loved him. "'Oats funny!'"

Danny said, and when they disconnected, her sister sent her an adorable shot of Danny feeding hay to a little white goat.

"Something smells amazing," Axel said, coming downstairs with damp tousled hair—almost like in her minifantasy. Ooh la la. He was beyond sexy in his faded jeans, navy T-shirt and bare feet. He smelled like shampoo and soap—even more delicious than the scent of pizza.

"It's a surprise," she said. "But it's definitely comfort food."

"Can't wait. And after dinner, I thought we'd play that So You Think You Know Your Significant Other? game."

She gaped at him. "Really?"

He laughed. "No. I am *completely* joking."

"Thought so," she said with a knowing nod, then peered in the oven. The cheese was bubbling. Five minutes and the pizza would be done.

"Glass of red wine?" he asked. "Daisy gave me a bottle called Dancing Alpacas for doing her a favor last weekend. I can't promise it'll be good. Do you think our alpacas break out into the Macarena when we're all not looking?"

She laughed. "Maybe the chicken dance. And I'd love a glass." Wine, pizza and handsome, sexy Axel. It was almost too much.

The bottle featured an upright brown-and-white

alpaca with his hooves in the air. She smiled as he poured two glasses.

He handed her one, then held up his. "To us getting through a trying week together."

Happy chills raced up her spine. "I will drink to that." What she wanted to say was that she was touched by his toast. The past days had been trying on lots of levels and they *were* going through it together. The faux engagement. The walk through his father's life.

I feel so close to you, she thought wistfully, unable to drag her eyes off him. His still-damp dark hair, the blue eyes, strong jawline and incredible shoulders, broad and strong.

She had to stop staring, so she took a sip of the dry, spicy wine, which sent a warm glowy boost where she needed it. "Not bad at all," she said, holding up the glass. "We can eat in the living room if you'd like, get comfy on the couch. Dinner is that kind."

"Oh good. Movie?"

Again, goose bumps. Dinner and a movie. She thought about her mom telling her not to rush. She and Axel could both use a relaxing night, a little escape into a movie.

He sipped his wine and gave a "not bad" nod, then flicked on the big-screen TV and rolled through the guide. "There it is. No need for anything else if *The Princess Bride* is on."

She grinned. "I totally agree. And I haven't seen it in years." Those happy chills were back, breaking into goose bumps on her arms. This felt like a date.

It is a date. Whether he likes it or not, and who knows, maybe he does like it. Maybe Mr. Marriage Squeezes the Air Out of My Lungs is falling for me as hard as I'm falling for him, and who can stop the progress of true love? Not even Prince Humperdinck.

While Axel set the coffee table, Sadie made a simple salad and tossed it with creamy Italian dressing.

"Be right back," Axel said and went out the kitchen door into the yard, which confused her because he didn't bring Dude, who'd already gone out when they'd returned. When he came in a few minutes later with a bouquet of wildflowers, she went completely still, the air squeezed out of *her* lungs.

This *was* a date.

He smiled at her, and everything inside got the warm fuzzies and not from the wine. She watched him grab a vase off the mantel and fill it with water and then put in the flowers. He set the vase on the big coffee table. "Dude," he said to the dog, who sat on the side of the table, gnawing at a rawhide, "when a woman cooks for you, you bring her flowers, even if they're from the yard."

"Wildflowers are the best kind," she said, the warm fuzzies getting hotter.

Ooh, boy, did she want to kiss him. Run her hands along his broad shoulders, across his back, in his hair. The oven timer dinged, jolting her out of her little dream.

"You sit and enjoy your wine," he said. "I'll get the pizza."

She did as he said, leaning back on the comfortable cushion. When was the last time she had a night like this that didn't involve someone she was related to or a colleague from work during their monthly movie nights in the hospital basement?

Within a half hour, the salad was almost gone, the pizza only crumbs and the bottle of Dancing Alpacas wine consumed. She and Axel were laughing and calling out famous lines from *The Princess Bride* as they watched, both declaring it in their top ten favorites of all time. And then the movie was over and she leaned her head against his shoulder—without thinking, just *feeling*.

He didn't stiffen. Or flinch.

Instead, he turned and lifted his hands to either side of her face. "I want to kiss you more than anything in the world right now."

"But will you still want to kiss me to-mor-rohhh?" she sang, her lips a mere inch from his. That was the issue. She wasn't so sure he *would* want to. He'd made himself so clear on the subject of a romantic relationship. This would not be going anywhere.

"I'll never stop wanting to kiss you, Sadie."

Oh, my. She could let herself have this. Tonight. Maybe she could get him out of her system that way. *Yeah right*, she thought. *Like that will happen. Stop rationalizing. If you let this happen, be prepared to accept what* will *happen—tomorrow morning.* She was going to have her heart handed to her either way.

She leaned forward and touched her lips to his and that was that. He kissed her so passionately her toes truly curled. Then his hands and lips were all over her, her mouth, her neck, her breastbone. He lifted her tank top to trail kisses across her stomach, and she flung the shirt off, watching his gaze move to her lacy pink bra—not the sexy one from the bridal boutique but plenty hot nonetheless. She peeled off his T-shirt, and his chest was everything she'd fantasized about. Muscled and hard. Every part of her body hummed and tingled and she gave completely in to the delicious sensations. She heard the zipper of her flippy yellow skirt being pulled down, and she reached for his zipper, eliciting a groan that sent shock waves through her.

And then they were naked, kissing, touching, feeling. She was kissing his neck when she saw one of his hands reaching for something on the coffee table—his wallet. She gasped inwardly, so ready. Then she heard that telltale tear of a foil packet and she resumed her trail of kisses along his chest.

"Okay?" he whispered in her ear.

"Okay," she whispered back.

And then she lost all ability to process anything but how good making love to Axel felt and how completely in love with him she was.

Sadie woke up in the morning with a big smile on her face, but it faded when she realized she was alone in Axel's king-size bed. The door was closed and she strained to listen for sounds—running water or the clank of silverware; he could be taking a shower or making them breakfast. But there was silence.

And then she saw the folded note with her name on it propped against the lamp on the bedside table.

Yup. Gone. With the wind. The summer breeze. *I told you so, Sadie Winston!*

Had it been worth it? Yes. Every amazing, I-am-a-red-blooded-woman moment of it. It had been a long time since she'd been with a man. Since before her divorce. Her heart might feel a little pushed around but her body felt rejuvenated and alive and relaxed as if she'd gone to a yoga class with her own attentive magic yogi.

But there was one part of her that felt all achy and bruised. In her chest, to the left.

She'd been right to keep her expectations in check—not that that helped.

She grabbed the note and read it. *Morning. My brother needed my help so I had to leave early. Sleep in, relax, hang with Dude, whatever you like. Feel free to take the buggy home—I biked in. Talk to you later, Axel.*

Sigh. Sigh, sigh, sigh.

Feel free to take the buggy home. As in, leave at your leisure, but leave.

Well, come on, she *had* to leave. She was someone's mother, for heaven's sake. And she was at the ranch for her family reunion, not to luxuriate in her fake fiancé's bed all day. Even if she'd been invited to do that, which clearly she hadn't. He needed her gone when he returned and she knew it.

Ain't that romantic, she thought, lying down and pulling the covers up to her chin. He'd been honest from the start, though. He'd told her who he was. She'd let herself get caught up in the fantasy.

But last night had been so real—nothing about their wonderful evening had been fake. Their chemistry during dinner, their fun during the movie, the kiss that had led to much, much more. All very real, very honest emotions on both sides. She'd had an entire talk with herself about how things would likely be in the morning, hadn't she? She'd known this would happen, that Axel would not be beside her when she woke, feeding her red grapes.

Get up and go, she told herself. *Your life is elsewhere.*

A half hour later, showered and dressed, she went downstairs and into the kitchen to find the room spotless, even though they'd left it a complete mess last night. Axel had either gone down in the middle of the night or taken care of the kitchen before leaving this morning. The coffee maker was on and had at least two cups in it. She poured herself one and added cream and sugar, the hot brew helping.

She sighed for the fiftieth time and let Dude out and watched him sniff the grass and roll around in the sunshine. Back inside, she refilled his water bowl, though she was sure Axel had done that, then she gave him a pat before grabbing her purse and the key to the buggy, which he'd left on the counter next to the coffeepot with a big note: *Key to the buggy—leave it in the console. A.*

The man thought of everything—unfortunately. Because it meant he hadn't been there when she'd woken up for a reason. He hadn't wanted to be. Too much? Too intimate? Too much to say without being able to say anything because it was awkward?

She got in the buggy and drove to the big barn, parking on the side where he'd see it easily from any direction. She left the key, then got out and walked around the back of the barn where the horse stables were at the far end. Looking at the beautiful horses would cheer her up, get her ready to face the day and the truth.

"So have things evolved?" Sadie heard Daisy Dawson say from inside the barn.

"Evolved?" came Axel's voice.

Sadie stopped dead in her tracks and held her breath, flattening herself against the outside of the barn.

"With Sadie," Daisy said. "There's no way you're spending so much time together and nothing is happening. I see how you two look at each other!"

"Daisy, I keep telling you, I'm not in the market for anything right now. Can't you torment Rex or Zeke or Ford? They're the brothers you should be focused on—at least I'm *here*."

Torment? This line of questioning was *torment*? Asking about his feelings for her?

"Here but not here!" Daisy said, and Sadie wanted to clap like Meryl Streep and Jennifer Lopez had at the Oscars during Patricia Arquette's feminist acceptance speech.

Silence. Sadie could envision Axel throwing up his hands.

"You're so infuriating!" Daisy said. "Why do

you keep saying you're not ready for a real relationship? What does that even *mean*?"

"It's very clear, Daisy. Not ready. A wife, a child. I'm not ready."

"Not willing is more like it, supposedly older and wiser brother. If this is about coming from a broken home and having a negligent father, keep in mind that both Noah and I took to marriage and parenthood with flying colors and we all had the same dad. *You* determine who you want to be, not your past."

"I have work to do, Daisy," Axel said, his voice tinged with impatience.

Silence, and then, "Well, fine. Let the best thing that ever happened to you get away!"

Aw, that was kind of Daisy. Sadie wanted to rush in and hug her.

"Daize, I appreciate that you care. I really do. But this is my life, okay? Back off."

"You think this kind of love happens all the time, Axel? You should grab it and never let it go."

"Who said anything about love?" Axel said.

Sadie inwardly gasped, her heart clenching, and she staggered backward a bit. The pain in her chest almost knocked her to her knees.

Her "pep" talk in his cabin of you-knew-what-you-were-getting-into had clearly been rationalizing. Because hearing it like this—straight out after they'd slept together—was worse than she could have imagined.

Tears streaming down her cheeks, she ran to the stand of trees at the other side of the barn. She made sure no one was around and then wiped under her eyes and sucked in a breath and started walking.

She was surprised she could move at all with her heart breaking into pieces with each step.

She heard a gasp and turned and standing there staring at her was Daisy Dawson in her green Dawson Family Guest Ranch polo and a straw hat.

Oh no. Daisy walked up to her, peering at her as if trying to tell if Sadie had overheard that little conversation.

The red-rimmed eyes must have given that away.

"Sadie? Were you by any chance just over by the barn?"

Sadie nodded and felt her eyes well up again.

Daisy slung an arm around her shoulder. "I have the best chocolate-hazelnut coffee at my house. Want a cup or three?"

Sadie bit her lip. She turned around, curious if Axel had come out of the barn. Not that he'd necessarily know she'd overheard and that Daisy knew it; he could easily think they'd just happened to cross paths.

But he didn't come out of the barn. He was likely stewing.

Daisy was nice to offer to sit and talk with her, commiserate, tell Sadie her brother was a big fool, but Sadie had a feeling she'd feel worse. "I would love a cup, Daisy, but I'd better get back to the cabin. I miss Danny."

Daisy's blue eyes were sympathetic. "I know just what you mean. If I'm feeling bad, sometimes all I have to do is set eyes on Tony and the world rights itself."

Sadie smiled. "Exactly."

"I'm sorry you overheard that. Axel is…frustrating. But I'll bet he comes around."

Sadie wasn't sure what to say to that. She didn't want to wait and hope a man "came around." She wanted to be worth loving, plain and simple. And if Axel couldn't handle real emotions, real love, well, then he wasn't the man for her, was he?

Tough talk when she felt like she might crumble any second.

Ping.

A text from Axel: Can we talk?

Wow. The It's Not You It's Me conversation about to happen and so fast. Axel wanted to wipe his hands of what had happened last night, get them back on their "friendly" track.

Sadie held up her phone and showed Daisy, who smiled. "See, he's coming around already. I know my brother, Sadie. Don't give up on him." Daisy squeezed her hand and then headed toward the lodge.

I don't want to, Sadie thought. *But I know what I know.* Still, better to get this over with. There wasn't a lot of truth going around this week, so when a big bolt of it popped out, it could really knock someone upside the head.

Sadie texted back: Meet by the creek at the big rock? Now-ish?

See you in five.

She had no doubt what he was going to say. He was so sorry about last night, he shouldn't have let it happen, and in the light of day, he realized that he was still the same Axel he'd been the night of the bonfire, when he'd told her what marriage meant to him.

Sadie walked past her cabin, suddenly needing everyone in it to wrap her up in their support and love. Especially Izzy, who gave the best hugs and smelled like roses. But she kept going, also needing to brace herself for the conversation she was about to have.

And for the end of her and Axel. Maybe not the fake them. But the real them who had never had a chance.

Axel saw Sadie sitting on the big flat rock on the creek's bank, her back to him. The sight of her, even at quite a distance, caused a little stir in his chest. He was always happy to see Sadie. But he wasn't looking forward to this conversation. He wasn't sure what he wanted to say. To apologize for leaving her alone in his cabin this morning after the night they'd had, the most intimate physical experience two people could have.

When he'd woken up, Sadie spooned against him, he'd relished the feel of her so close to him, a new day with the woman who'd turned his life upside down and all around. But the more he lay there, the more that air-seeping feeling started working its way into his lungs, and when he got Noah's text, he'd felt relief. A reason to leave.

This shouldn't be complicated—*he* was making it complicated—but it was.

"Hey," he called out.

She turned around and didn't look too happy. She wore what she'd been wearing last night, and a barrage of memories hit him. Digging into that delicious pizza. Sharing the Dancing Alpacas wine. Watching *The Princess Bride* and shouting out lines of dialogue through most of it. Feeling so light and easy. Feeling so…close to her. So attracted. And the kiss, which had exploded into the best sex he'd ever had. More than just passionate.

Because you feel more for this woman than you want to deal with?

"Look," she said, staying seated but facing him.

"I'm going to be honest. I returned the buggy to the big barn and I happened to overhear your conversation with your sister. So everything you might want to say now? You already said it."

Oh hell. Punch to the gut.

Dammit. A lot of what he'd said came back to him. Echoing in his head.

Particularly: *Who said anything about love?*

He grimaced. "Daisy has a way of making me feel like a cornered wolf when she gets on the topic of my love life."

"You told me your position on serious relationships the first night of the reunion. I guess I was hoping I might have changed your mind, that I was special enough, that I meant enough to you for that to happen." She looked away, and he wanted nothing more than to pull her to him and hold her.

"You *are* special to me, Sadie. You and Danny both. But I have to face up to why I left this morning. Yes, Noah asked for my help with the horses because the trainer needed the morning off. But I was relieved to have an excuse to leave."

She sucked in a breath and glared at him. "I already know that. No need to be *this* honest, Axel."

"I want to be honest because you *do* mean a lot to me. I wasn't planning on falling for a guest this week, Sadie. I wasn't planning on being fake-engaged. I wasn't planning on sleeping with you.

But it all happened. And I was a jerk this morning for leaving. I wanted to say that most of all."

She stood, her pale brown eyes flashing. "If you say you're sorry I will push you in the creek, Axel Dawson."

He knew what she meant. She didn't want to hear sorry or regrets.

But he was sorry that he'd hurt her, that he was hurting her now.

"We have a few more days to get through," she said, arms crossed over her chest. "Let's get through them. I'll explain our lack of togetherness to my family by saying you're very busy. If you wouldn't mind showing up for my sister's wedding Saturday night in the lodge, I would appreciate it. We'll leave Sunday morning and that'll be that." Her voice was so tight, so clogged.

He stared at her, feeling something in his chest shift. "Of course I'm coming to the wedding."

"Great," she said. "We'll get through that and then this whole fake nonsense will be over."

"Sadie. There was nothing fake about last night. Nothing."

She lifted her chin and didn't say anything. "Well, I'd better get back. I miss Danny."

Me, too, he thought out of nowhere, but he did.

Chapter Thirteen

For the next two days, Sadie kept her and Danny booked with ranch activities so that she wouldn't have a spare moment to think about her aching chest and how much she missed the sight of Axel. She had seen him at a distance twice, and both times had hurt. She hadn't texted him and he hadn't texted her. When she wasn't learning how to ride a horse and taking Danny for butterfly-sighting walks along the creek and going to every educational talk about the animals in the petting zoo (she now knew that cows had four stomachs and that goats did not have front teeth on their upper jaws), she was helping Evie with her wedding checklists and making sure all was set for the big night.

Everyone wanted to know "where that handsome fiancé of yours is," including Danny, who kept asking for Zul.

"Mama, Zul tay?" her son asked as they left the cafeteria after lunch, Danny holding his superhero lion.

Toddler speak for *Will I see Axel today?* Sadie scooped Danny up in her arms. "Axel has been working super hard on the ranch but I think we'll see him today."

Danny's smile could turn any grump's frown upside down. He looked *so* happy.

Her heart clenched. On one hand, it wasn't fair to Danny to suddenly pull Axel from his life. On the other, that was how it would be once they were home. But they *weren't* home now, they were at the ranch and she should probably make the most of it for Danny and let him spend time with his hero. She put him on the ground and he flew his lion in the air, running in big circles.

"Zul! Zul!" Danny suddenly shouted and went sprinting toward the alpaca enclosure.

Sadie looked over. Oh, God, there he was. Looking incredibly sexy in dark jeans and the hunter green polo, a brown Stetson on his head.

Just like the first day we arrived, she thought,

*when Danny went running for the man who'd
saved him on Badger Mountain.*

Sadie slowly made her way closer, but not too
close. She watched as Axel scooped up Danny in
his arms and held him up high, giving him a big
smooch on the cheek. Danny wrapped his arms
around Axel's neck.

"Yoo-hoo! Sadie! Axel," Sadie's mom called,
heading over with Aunt Tabby, Vanessa and Izzy
in her wheelchair. Aunt Tabby and Viv had been
somewhere between small talk and real conversation the past couple of days, ever since Tabby
had opened up about having a date with Cowboy
Joe. Tonight, they'd be going on their third date
in three days.

Sadie stepped closer. If she acted like she and
Axel were having problems, which, of course, they
were, her mother would pester her for details.

"Listen, lovebirds, I have a great idea," Viv said.
"You two have barely seen each other the past two
days! Why don't you go into town and spend some
time together? There's a special scavenger hunt in
the kid zone and I'll bet Danny wants to find some
secret treasure."

Danny nodded vigorously and attempted to say
treasure. Viv plucked him right out of Axel's arms.

"Go ahead, we'll take care of our little precious," Viv said, kissing Danny on the head.

Sadie tried to think of a few reasons why she

couldn't go anywhere with Axel but nothing good was coming to her. She could barely think straight with those piercing blue eyes on her.

"I do need to go into town," Axel said, staring at Sadie. "We can run an errand and stop for an early dinner. Maybe that fish and chips place."

What was this? Was he kidding?

He looked dead serious. Oh, wait. He probably was planning to visit another address on the list from his dad and liked the idea of her coming along like the last two times. But Axel Dawson's personal life had nothing to do with her. Not anymore. They were still pretending to be engaged but they were not pretending to be friends.

"I, uh, thought I'd see if Evie needed any help with final wedding details," Sadie said. There— perfect excuse. The wedding was the day after tomorrow. Sadie had been gearing up for having Axel as her date, since that was a given, and talking herself through how on earth she'd deal with that.

"Actually, hon," Viv said, "Evie texted a little while ago. She's with her mother-in-law-to-be and grandmother-in-law-to-be today, picking up her dress and making sure the alterations are exact. Personally, I think *I* should have gone. I would have noticed if anything was even a smidge off!"

No one disagreed with that assessment of her skills.

"Oh," Sadie said.

Axel held out his arm. "Shall we go?"

Uh, he didn't have to go overboard, she thought, shooting him a surreptitious dagger.

She gave Danny a kiss goodbye, waved to her relatives and then off they walked, her hand around his arm. Once they were out of hearing distance, she pulled away. "And what was *that* about?"

"Just trying to keep up appearances, Sadie. Your mother is like a hawk. You heard her—she notices *smidges*."

Well, that was true. "I guess. But still. You didn't need to give me your arm. This isn't Regency England."

He raised an eyebrow. "I'm glad the suggestion was made to spend time together. I've missed you, Sadie. I was hoping we could talk."

"Is there anything to say? I'm looking for a husband and father for my son. One who's madly in love with Danny and with me. If that's not you, then…"

"Like I said the other day, Sadie, I didn't expect to fall for you."

She stopped in her tracks. Those words of his— from when they'd met at the rock at the creek—had swirled around her mind these past two days. She'd been such a walking ball of heartache that she'd almost missed it in the moment.

He'd fallen for her. He'd said it. And now he'd said it again.

She'd sat with it the past couple of days, wanting to give him time and space to maybe figure things out. If he'd fallen for her, he'd have to accept it. He might not have wanted to, but he had, and you couldn't stop a speeding train. And that was what love was. A locomotive.

But then no text, no call, no asking to see her. If Danny hadn't beelined for him just now, would he have asked to spend the afternoon with her in town? No, because he clearly hadn't accepted it.

"I've thought of little else but you and Danny these past two days. So many times I wanted to go see you but—"

She didn't want to do this. A repeat of the last conversation. She *couldn't* do this. But you know what? She was going to do something *else*. Work with what she had. She was in love with Axel Dawson. He was the man for her. He wasn't ready to see that, fine. But he'd given her what she needed to know: he hadn't meant to fall for her. But had.

"Do you have to go into town?" she asked.

He nodded. "I'd like to visit the next address on my dad's list. But I know I don't want to do it alone. And by alone, I mean specifically without you, Sadie. You're really good moral support."

He wanted to be with her. He needed her. And

he had fallen for her. She had the guy right where she wanted him, really. Right?

Because this was the same guy whose overheard conversation with his sister had ripped her heart in two.

Who said anything about love?

No one—which was why she was going to help get him there. The man loved her. She was pretty sure, anyway. Seventy-five percent sure. Axel had been hurt—and by a single mother with a baby—and was protecting himself, maybe without even realizing it. So hell yeah she was going to try.

"Well, when you put it that way," she said, taking his arm again. "Of course I'll go."

He looked into her eyes, and she could see relief cross his face. "Good. And thank you."

"Let's not talk about us, okay? Pinkie swear," she said, holding up her right one.

That would probably be more of a relief to him. And necessary to giving him some breathing room from any heaviosity. She'd just *be* today. And that would be enough.

He held up his left one. "Pinkie swear."

They wrapped pinkies.

A lovely breeze lifted her hair, and she raised her face to the gorgeous sunny weather. She was getting her mojo back where Axel was concerned. She felt more in control of her own destiny instead of allowing him to dictate and decide. She'd do what she could to make him see sense: that she was it for him. And if he didn't? As Mom and Aunt Tabby and Gram and Great-Gram would say: his flipping loss.

Of course, she'd be brokenhearted and sobbing for three days, but she'd know she'd tried, that she'd put herself out there for the future she wanted.

"So guess who the latest ranch romance is," Sadie said. "You will never believe this."

"Your aunt Tabby and Cowboy Joe?" he asked.

She gave him a gentle sock in the arm. "How did you know? It's brand-new. They've been on three dates in three days!"

"That's exactly how I do know. I saw them walking arm in arm by the creek, then feeding each other ice cream during off-hours in the caf yesterday, and a few hours ago, I saw them kissing goodbye behind your cabin."

Sadie grinned. "Whodathunk you could go to a family reunion and fall in love?" She almost choked the moment she realized what she'd said.

"I'm happy for them," he said. "Cowboy Joe is a great person. I've known him a long, long time." He pointed up ahead at his buggy, parked near the petting zoo. "There are the dancing alpacas. I mean, they're standing still but now when I look at them, I imagine them doing the Macarena."

She smiled and looked at them, the two furry

beasts standing so close to each other, their heads over the fence. Did he *have* to reference their night together? The wine that had helped lead to that killer kiss and everything else that had happened?

He must have caught the shift in her expression because he quickly added, "Sorry."

Channel Taylor Swift and shake it off, she told herself. "So," she began as they got into the buggy, "where are we headed?"

"An isolated ranch ten miles or so from here. The Hurley place. I don't know who they are or what connection my dad might have to them. Noah and Daisy didn't either."

They drove in silence, which she appreciated, enjoying the breeze through the half-open windows and the views of farmland. As they turned up the long drive for the Hurley ranch, Sadie could see up ahead that the house was not in great condition. The gray barn was peeling and there didn't seem to be any animals. Maybe it wasn't a working ranch.

As Axel pulled up to the house, a middle-aged man came out. He wore jeans and a cowboy hat.

"Who are you?" the man asked.

"My name is Axel Dawson and—"

A huge grin broke out on the man's face. "Dawson? Why didn't you start with that?" He held out his hand. "You one of Bo's kids? I know he had a lot of 'em."

"Smack in the middle of six." He turned to Sadie. "This is Sadie Winston."

The man nodded at her. "I was real sorry to hear he passed. We were away and missed the funeral. We owe everything to Bo Dawson," he said, gesturing with his chin toward the house. "I'm Matt Hurley. I live here with my wife, Sue. Our two kids are grown and off on their own, thanks to Bo."

Axel did a double take at that. "Thanks to Bo?"

"Up until about a year ago, I used to drink heavily. Bo helped me out a time or two, brought me home, got me in bed. My wife threatened to leave me. Bo got me to quit, gave me a lot of pamphlets to read, took me to meetings. I cleaned up my act because of him."

"Wait. My father? He was drunk himself eighty percent of the time."

"He got worse toward the end, I guess," Matt said. "No one knew he was dying. He kept that a secret. I think he drank more then. But he'd said his kids were mad at him and wanted him to stop and so he tried and said we'd do it together. And he got me to stop. I thought he stopped, too. He said nothing was more important than family. Certainly not a bottle of Jack Daniel's or cheap beer."

Sadie squeezed Axel's hand. Every time she learned more about his dad, she heard something that made him sound like the hero he must have taught Axel to be. Not perfect. Far from it. He'd done his share of damage. But he'd done good, too.

Matt took off his hat and held it to his chest, as if in honor of Bo. "If it weren't for Bo Dawson, my two boys wouldn't be speaking to me right now. My wife would be married to someone else. Your dad saved my hide."

Axel put his hand on the man's shoulder. "Thanks for telling me. It's nice to know."

"Why'd you come by, anyway?" Matt asked.

Axel showed him the list of addresses. "My dad left this for me. No annotations, nothing. Just the addresses. He must have wanted me to know about you and maybe to check in."

"Stop by anytime and bring your girlfriend," Matt said, smiling at her. "Any kid of Bo Dawson is family to me and Sue."

We're actually engaged, Sadie almost said.

Matt hugged them both and headed back inside. For a few moments, she and Axel just stood and looked at the house, at the barn, and Sadie could imagine he was thinking of his dad walking up those steps, helping someone out, doing for Matt what he wouldn't let anyone do for him.

Finally, Axel took her hand as they walked to the SUV. She could hold his hand forever.

"He wanted me to know he was a good person, in case I'd forgotten," Axel said, opening the passenger door for her. "That's what the list of addresses is about."

Sadie nodded. "Looks that way."

"The more I learn about him, the more I don't think I knew my dad at all," he said. "And I thought I did. I thought I had him all figured out."

"People are that way. Even the ones closest to us."

He buckled up and then looked at her. "There's one more address but I've been shocked enough for one day. Why don't we drive into town and go get coffee and walk around?"

"Perfect day for it."

So they did. They got iced coffees from Java Jamboree and walked along Main Street, stopping at the dog park to watch the little dogs yip and sniff each other.

"Suit for Evie's wedding or a tux?" he asked as a tan pug stared at them.

"No doggy treats, sorry," she told the cute little pug, and they resumed walking. "Evie said anything goes for the dress code. No one came here expecting to attend a wedding on the final night, and no one came to a dude ranch with a fancy outfit. Though none of us live all that far away, she doesn't want anyone having to drive home and back. It's come as you are."

"I'll wear a suit since I don't have that excuse. My fancy clothes *are* at the dude ranch."

She could see him all dressed up. At least her final night at the Dawson Family Guest Ranch would be amazing. Her dear sister married. Axel beside her in his suit. The next morning she and Danny would go home, back to real life, and this would all seem a dream. The fake engagement and the one incredible night she'd shared with Axel.

Maybe it was all just a fantasy she had to let go of instead of trying to make Axel see his sister was right—that when you found love like this you grabbed it and never let it go.

Who said anything about love?

Was she flattering herself that he felt about her the way she did about him? She knew he adored Danny. And the way he'd been with her on his couch, in his bed—that hadn't been just sex.

I'm saying something about love, she thought as he stopped in front of Bear Ridge Ice Cream and Candy, so good that she often drove out of her way to come out here.

"I could go for a double scoop of mint chocolate chip and maybe coffee chip or chocolate peanut butter," he said. "In a waffle cone."

"Don't tell Danny we stopped here. He loves this place."

"I wish he were here," he said. "I've missed him terribly the past couple of days."

"He's gotten to you, huh?" she asked even

though she was the one who'd said they shouldn't talk about them. Danny counted as them.

Please say, Yes, I love that kid like he's my own flesh and blood, and in fact, I love you, too.

"He got to me on Badger Mountain. Just like you did."

"And this week?" she asked, practically holding her breath.

"This week has been scary as hell," he said. "I'm engaged, about to become a dad." He smiled.

Oh. He was kidding about the scary as hell. When he'd said that, she thought, *Yup, this man loves me like* crazy. Now she wasn't so sure.

He held her gaze for a moment, everything he was flashing in his blue eyes. She wanted to kiss him, wrap her arms around him, hold him tight and never let him go.

But a group of teens were trying to exit the busy shop and the moment was gone in a snap, ice cream choices their biggest concern.

Ice cream was a lot easier than figuring out how he felt. She knew that was true as she studied the sign announcing the flavors and looked at the big containers in the display case.

"I'm thinking double fudge brownie," she said, eyeing the delicious-looking ice cream. "You set on what you're getting?"

Silence.

She glanced up and Axel was standing ramrod straight, the color blanched from his face.

"Hello," a woman said stiffly, looking at Axel, then at Sadie, then at the door. The woman was in her early thirties, tall and slender, with shoulder-length auburn hair. She held a dish of ice cream in her hand; the cute little girl at her side, maybe three or four years old, licked a scoop on a cone. The woman took the girl's free hand and hurried her out.

Axel still didn't move.

Sadie glanced out the window; the woman and girl were gone. *Oh*, she thought. *Ohhh. I certainly know who they were.* The ex who'd left him and her daughter, whom he'd been so attached to and never seen again.

Till now.

"You okay?" she asked. "We can skip the ice cream if you just saw a ghost."

He glanced at her. "How'd you know?"

"Because I know *you.*"

"I'm fine," he said and glanced up at the teenager behind the counter. "Sadie, what'll it be?"

His forced smile didn't fool her. He wasn't fine. One of the biggest reasons that kept him insisting marriage and a family weren't for him had just walked out of the shop.

Either running into the woman and her daughter would give him some kind of necessary closure that he'd been lacking or he'd brood on it and it would make him retreat further behind that brick wall he'd built around himself.

Which was it?

Please be the former, she thought, suddenly having no appetite for ice cream.

Chapter Fourteen

"Well, I think we should *all* go," Aunt Tabby said, staring at Viv.

"I think *you* should go if you want to," Viv snapped. "Count me out."

The guest cabin wasn't big enough for all these women and their arguments. Aunt Tabby stood in the arched doorway to the living room, glaring at her sister on the window seat. Sadie and Evie were on the sofa, and Vanessa was knitting socks—Sadie was pretty sure they were for Axel, unfortunately—on the rocker near where Danny sat piling his beloved blocks.

Viv and Tabby had been arguing all morning about whether or not the group should go on the wilderness tour up Clover Mountain, an easy mile loop without steep inclines. Izzy would be going on the bird-watching adventure along the creek with another group of relatives since a hike would be too much for her. Today was the last day for a guided hike since tomorrow was Evie's wedding and they'd spend the day preparing for the big event after sunrise yoga.

Sadie certainly wouldn't mind the forced proximity to her fake fiancé, who'd be leading the tour. He'd made himself scarce since they'd returned from Bear Ridge yesterday. On the drive home, he hadn't mentioned the ex and her little girl, and Sadie hadn't either, though she was full of questions. Did you want to marry her? Had you proposed? Had the ex been The One and no one else could compare?

Those kinds of awful questions had kept her up last night. She hadn't heard from Axel since or seen him around the ranch.

"This is our family reunion," Tabby pointed out, her voice nearly breaking. "We should all go on the *family* hike!"

Sadie looked at Evie, who was sitting on the other end of the couch, going over the seating arrangements. Sadie could tell her sister was trying to ignore the bickering.

"Been there, not doing that again," Viv said, crossing her arms over her chest. "End of story." She glanced at Evie. "Honey, remember not to put Grandpa next to Uncle Robby. They always argue about politics. Separate tables."

"Oh, right," Evie said. "If only I could concentrate while my mother and aunt are arguing loudly." She shot each woman a pointed look.

"Your mother is the queen of obstinate!" Tabby said.

"Says the princess without a country!" Viv countered.

"How dare you," Tabby snapped.

"Mom, Tabby, please," Sadie said. "Danny can hear you."

At the sound of his name, Danny glanced up from where he was piling a tower of blocks.

Both women looked chastised but tossed each other a final scowl.

"Besides," Evie said, turning off her iPad and stretching, "as the bride, I decide everything the twenty-four hours before my wedding, right? It's a new Bridezilla tradition. And I say we *all* go on the hike."

"But—" Viv began.

"Mom, listen," Sadie said. "Maybe all of us going on another hike with Danny, seeing him safe, not getting lost, will help you and Aunt Tabby put the past behind you. Until you deal with it, since you won't *talk* about it, you'll never get past it."

Evie nodded. "Exactly. And you have to both go. It's what I want as a wedding gift. I mean that."

Viv eyed her younger daughter. "Oh, fine."

"Fine," Tabby snapped.

It did sound fine to Sadie. She had a feeling Evie was right and that their mom and aunt would work out their issues on Family Hike 2.0.

She also had to admit she liked the idea of knowing she'd see Axel later. Even for an hour and shared with many of her relatives.

This morning, Axel was riding parallel to the pasture trails to make sure not a single Winston fell off their horse. Now that the family reunion was winding down, many in the group wanted to try activities they hadn't earlier in the week. Horseback riding was one.

He was glad to be on horseback himself, his mind on patrol and safety. Last night, seeing his ex and her daughter, now a little girl instead of the baby he knew, had played over and over in his mind like a recording. Lizzie's stiff hello, the girl, whose name was Jolie, enjoying her cone, the hurry out the door. He was grateful for that last one.

Interesting thing was, Axel hadn't felt anything for his ex. He always thought if he ran into her, he'd be brought to his knees, but he'd felt nothing, except for the shock of actually seeing her. Even her daughter hadn't really registered, most likely because she looked nothing like the baby she'd been. There was no connection.

What he did feel was a strange sense of reinforcement, the reshoring up of his complete lack of interest in going through that again.

Sadie wanted him to set himself up for the possibility.

He couldn't. He'd taken the advice of the mountain man who'd told him to be the boss of his emotions and run with it, so far and wide that Axel himself wasn't the boss. Or that was how it felt, anyway. He knew he had serious feelings for Sadie and her son. But something even more powerful was keeping him back.

He could hear Daisy yell up a storm if she got wind of that. *And you're gonna let whatever that is win?* she'd demand.

He turned Goldie around and stayed in line a good hundred yards from three teens on quarter horses, keeping an eagle eye on them. They were talking and laughing and having a good time, but not so focused on the land or their horses. They weren't far from the stables, but Axel would keep his mind on his job and not on Sadie. Hard as it was.

He was leading a wilderness tour later today and he wondered if she'd show up. He wanted to see her so bad he couldn't stop picturing her beautiful face. Then Danny's sweet face and mop of blond hair, Zul waving around high over his head, would pop into his mind.

Axel thought about what Sadie had overheard: *Who said anything about love?* The pain it had caused her, the change between them.

When he thought about the word love and Sadie and Danny Winston, something in him shuttered. Closed up, closed off.

For a guy who was in charge of safety, should he be this damned scared?

Axel sure knew his wild berries and trees and leaves and worms and caterpillars, Sadie thought as the group walked up Clover Mountain, which was just a flat wooded trail with ever-so-slight inclines now and again. He had the entire group hanging on his every word as he pointed out which berries were edible and which would give you the stomachache from hell. They'd been hiking for about forty minutes and would turn around at the hour mark, taking a break for water and cereal bars. Danny sure would sleep well tonight. He'd done a lot of walking. Right now, they were in a clearing surrounded by dense woods, and there were so many birds and butterflies that Danny was constantly entertained.

A western meadowlark with its yellow belly

flew to a low branch were Danny was standing, and Danny shouted, "Yell bird" and went racing after it.

"Danny!" Sadie called after him. "Always wait for the group!"

Danny kept going, but this time, Axel was near and scooped him up.

"Gotcha!" he said. "Wilderness hiking means staying with your group, right, buddy?"

Axel had given a three-minute prehike talk about exactly that and hike safety before they'd started walking. He managed to look incredibly sexy in his staff shirt and khaki cargo shorts. And with Danny in his arm, he looked like a dad.

She wished Axel could see himself the way she saw him.

"But yell bird," Danny said.

"You can see the yellow bird if you look up in the trees. See, there's one!" Axel said, pointing.

Danny flew his superhero lion around in circles where Axel was pointing.

"This is exactly what happened last time," Viv said, hands on hips as she glared at her sister. "I asked you to keep an eye on Danny not thirty seconds ago so I could have my cereal bar early. And what happens? He goes racing off to who knows where!"

Sadie froze. What was going on here? Danny was fine. And this hike was supposed to make things better between her mother and aunt—not worse.

Tabby's eyes misted. "He didn't run off this time. He was right ahead of us and Axel was there."

"He could have run in any direction," Viv said. "Luckily, Axel was up ahead and paying attention."

Tabby burst into tears and dropped on an uncomfortable-looking rock. "I feel awful about what happened on Badger Mountain. I've apologized a million times for not paying closer attention. I can't possibly feel worse, Viv."

Viv's expression remained stony. She crossed her arms over her chest.

"Mom, seriously?" Sadie said.

Evie was shaking her head.

"Danny was lost for two hours!" Viv said. "Just like—" She clamped her mouth shut and turned away. "Just forget it," she added, throwing her hands up in the air.

Evie stepped closer to Viv. "Just like who?"

"Just like Tabby, that's who. When we were kids, she ran off when I was supposed to be watching her. She was missing until close to midnight."

Vanessa gasped. "Oh, Vivvy. You can't possibly blame yourself for that. You were a kid. You were only nine! Tabby was five."

"Wait a minute," Sadie said. "Why don't I know this story?"

"Or me," Evie asked.

"My mother said that Tabby and I could pick flowers," Viv explained. "But there was a butterfly and Tabby chased it and I got tired of running after her so I kept picking flowers. But she never came back." Their grandparents' house abutted woodlands. Sadie and Evie used to love playing in there as kids, annoyed that their mother always insisted on coming with them, keeping them in sight. Now Sadie knew why.

Tabby looked incredulous that Viv remembered this. "Well, I did. Because I'm right here fifty years later."

"It was my fault," Viv said. "I didn't pay attention to where you were, that you weren't close by anymore. It was the most sickening feeling not to know where you were."

"Viv, I don't remember that," Tabby said. "I mean, I remember it coming up a few times, Mom and Dad reminding me to stay close. But I don't remember being lost."

"I do," Viv said, her brown eyes teary. "Mom does."

Vanessa put a hand on Viv's shoulder. "I remember being scared, like any mother would be. Like Sadie was when Danny was lost. But I certainly didn't blame you, honey. I wouldn't have blamed you if it had happened when you were ten or twenty or now. People run off when you're not looking sometimes. Danny getting lost wasn't Tabby's fault. Just like it wasn't your fault when she got lost."

"I guess the whole thing brought all that up in me," Viv said. "Such an old event. But so close to the surface, I guess. That fear, I can still remember it so vividly."

Evie nodded. "So Danny going missing reminded you of it and maybe these past three months, you've really been mad at yourself."

"Sounds like you've never forgiven yourself, Viv," Axel said.

Viv glanced at all of them, then turned to her sister. "I'm sorry, Tabby. I've been awful the past few months."

"You sure have been," Tabby said with a smile. She opened her arms and Viv embraced her, the two sisters hugging tight.

"Oh, you," Viv said, wiping under her eyes.

Sadie smiled. "Well, turns out this hike *was* a good idea."

"Snack?" Danny said and it was the perfect icebreaker to a lighter mood. Everyone laughed and there were hugs all around.

"How about we have our snack right here on this special location forever known as Sister Make Up Point, and then we'll turn back," Axel said.

"Ooh, our own point!" Viv said, her eyes lighting up. "Will that be added to the guidebooks?"

She was serious. Sadie sent Axel a smile.

Axel grinned. "It might be unofficial but important nonetheless."

"Snack?" Danny asked again.

Gram and Gray-Aunt Tabby had his strawberry cereal bar and water bottle, so he ran to them, and they sat on rocks and chatted about the walk. The sight of the three of them, the feud over and done, lifted a big weight off Sadie's chest.

A phone buzzed, and Sadie glanced around. It was Evie's. Her sister smiled at the phone in her hand and walked a few feet away to answer. That smile meant it was Marshall—or Marshy as she liked to call him.

"Oh no, you didn't!" Evie yelped into her phone. Her expression was pure fury.

Uh, what?

"No, you are not inviting your ex-girlfriend to the wedding," Evie said, "and that's final! Do you see me inviting my exes to the wedding? No. Because it's not done." She listened. "Oh, really? Well, I guess the wedding is off, then!" She shoved her phone in her pocket and burst into tears.

Oh no. What the heck was this? Marshall Ackerman, usually supernice and thoughtful, wanted his ex at his wedding? Had he gone *insane*?

Sadie glanced at her mom, aunt and grand-mother; they looked as worried as Sadie felt.

"Evie, I'm sure that with a few minutes to think about it, he'll uninvite her," their mom assured her. "If it's that important to you, that's what matters."

"He says if it's that important to him, it should be important to me!" Evie said. "Just because they were together from middle school through college and she was a big part of his life doesn't mean she gets to be at my wedding."

"Is she married?" Sadie asked.

Evie shook her head. "No! She has a serious boyfriend, apparently, but still. She probably still loves Marshall. She's the old part of his life. I'm the present and future!"

"Evie, just call him and tell him you'd feel un-comfortable," Aunt Tabby said. "I get it. And I rarely take your side when you and Marshall are arguing."

That was true. Tabby didn't play devil's advo-cate so much as be willing to tell Evie when she was overreacting or being too self-centered.

Evie's phone buzzed. She looked at the screen and seemed to be reading texts. "Oh, really!" she bellowed at it. "Well, I guess we're not getting married!" She shoved her phone in her pocket again and stalked off beside a tree.

"Aunt Evie mad," Danny said.

Sadie ruffled Danny's thick blond hair. "Aunt

Evie got into an argument with someone. That means they both want their way about the same thing. But they'll work it out. Family always does."

Danny got bored fast. "Zul?" he held out his arms, and Axel picked him up.

Axel smiled at Danny, then turned to Sadie. "I've got him. You deal with this."

Sadie nodded and went to Evie. "Evie, meet him in person and talk this out. You're getting married tomorrow night!"

"Guess not!" Evie said, sparks shooting from her brown eyes. She was spitting mad.

"Now you listen to me, Evie Winston," Sadie barked. "You are engaged for real, unlike me, when getting married to the man I love is all I want. There is no way you're calling off your—"

Sadie froze, her mistake ringing in her ears. Oh no. Oh, dear.

Please tell me I didn't say that out loud.

Even Evie, in her tizzy, caught the slip. "Unlike you?"

"Yeah," Viv said. "What do you mean, unlike you?"

Everyone was staring at Sadie.

Sadie glanced at Axel, who gave her a sympathetic look.

"Engaged for real, *unlike me*?" Tabby repeated. "So you're not engaged?"

"I don't understand this at all," Vanessa said. "Are Sadie and Axel engaged?"

"Let Sadie explain herself," Viv said. "Pipe down, everyone."

Oh foo. She sucked in a breath. "Axel and I are not engaged. We never were."

"What?" Viv bellowed.

All eyes were on Sadie. She wanted to run down the mountain and hide but she had to get this over with. Maybe it was for the best that the truth had come out. Telling everyone when they got home to Prairie City that Axel had broken their engagement and it was over? A lie too many. That wasn't who Sadie Winston was.

"The night Evie got engaged," she began, "Axel walked me back to the cabin. I told Gram the news about Evie and Marshall, and she said something like 'They're engaged!' and ran in to make her phone calls, and that's when Izzy came out to see what the hoopla was about and mistook me and Axel for the engaged couple. Izzy was so happy for me she cried. She said she could go gentle into that good night knowing her divorced great-granddaughter who'd been through so much heartache had found love with a true hero."

"I guess I can see Izzy saying that," Viv said, arms crossed on her chest, of course.

"I can vouch for it. I was there," Axel put in. He still held Danny, who was not paying a lick of attention to the boring grown-up conversation. He was talking to Zul the lion in a low voice, telling him about his new powers.

A bunch of eyes turned to Axel with glares. He'd gone from can-do-no-wrong Axel to big, fat liar.

"So neither of us corrected Izzy," Sadie continued. "And then she went to sleep. I figured I'd tell Gram what happened, but Gram was on the phone sharing the big news about Evie and Marshall for hours. I didn't get the chance. By the time I woke up, Izzy had spread the word that Axel and I were engaged, and everyone thought both Evie and I had gotten engaged that night."

"You could have said this that morning!" Viv's eyes narrowed.

"I know, Mom, but then you and Tabby were talking for the first time in months because you thought both Winston girls were engaged. And you, Evie, you told me you hadn't wanted to get engaged while I, a single mother, was alone. You said my getting engaged meant everything to you. How could I tell you—"

"Oh, God," Evie said. "I remember that conversation in the cabin. I can understand why you didn't pipe up."

"So it was all a misunderstanding?" Vanessa asked. "You're *not* engaged?"

Sadie shook her head. "No. I'm not."

"And you went along with this?" Viv asked Axel.
He nodded. "I did. And I'd do it again."

"Trust me that being fake-engaged to me wasn't easy for him," Sadie said, trying not to look at him.

"Well, that was kind of you for Sadie's sake," Viv said. "But I'm still mad at both of you. I guess I understand how it happened, though."

Evie nodded. "I totally understand how it happened. I'm sorry, Sadie."

Aw. That meant Evie got it, understood all the muckety-muck that led to her keeping up the ruse.

Sadie hugged Evie, whose eyes were misty.

"I guess I can also see how you felt like you had to keep it up," Viv said. "We do have a habit of dominating conversations and not letting anyone get a word in."

"By *we*, she means me, too," Tabby said. "And Gram."

"Guilty," Vanessa said, holding up her hand. "Sorry, honey. I hope we didn't make you feel like getting engaged is the be-all and end-all. You know that's not how I feel."

"I know," Sadie said. "I got caught up in the hoopla myself. To be honest, I liked being engaged. Even pretend."

Everyone's eyes turned to Axel, who was still holding Danny, waving his superhero lion flying above his head. Viv took out her camera and snapped a photo of the two of them. Axel looked like a deer caught in headlights.

Her mother stared at her for a moment as if she was putting more than two and two together. Sadie had no idea what Viv was thinking.

"Just in case we don't see you after tonight, Axel," Viv said. "I'll text you the photo to remember Danny by."

Sadie swallowed. Viv wanted Axel to have a photo of what he could have because her mother knew that her daughter was madly in love with the guy.

And the look on Axel's face told a different story. A story with an ending that said, *I'm free. I'm finally free.* She felt tears sting her eyes, and she blinked them away.

"I don't think we should tell Izzy till we get home," Vanessa said. "It'll be too confusing. Let's just enjoy Evie's wedding. There *will* be a wedding, right?"

Now all eyes swung to Evie.

"As long as the ex-girlfriend isn't coming, yes," she said. "Marshy will put me first, right? I mean, my feelings have to be more important on this than having his old girlfriend at his wedding."

"Evie, honey," Tabby said. "Why don't you call Marshall and tell him the wedding is definitely on, but his girlfriend ain't coming and that's that."

Evie called. They all waited. "Marshall, the

wedding is on, but your ex is not coming and that's that." She listened, and Sadie's entire body felt like it was on pins and needles.

"I know. No, I know. I know."

What did she know?

"She knows what?" Tabby whispered.

Viv shrugged.

"No, *you're* the best," Evie said. "No, *I'm* sorry. I love you, too. Bye, sweetie." Evie pocketed her phone, now beaming. Phew.

Sadie smiled. Now that was a good ending to a story.

"The wedding is on," Evie said.

There were cheers and claps.

"I'll take my grandson," Viv said, plucking Danny from Axel. "You and Sadie probably have some loose ends to tie up. I hope you're still going to be her date at the wedding. I mean, we did order you a filet mignon and made up the seating arrangements, so it would spoil everything if you bailed on us."

Oh, Mom. I do love you.

"Of course I'll be there," Axel said. "I mean, if Sadie wants me to be."

Evie squeezed Sadie's hand. "C'mon," she said, gesturing for the relatives to start down the trail. "Let's let them talk."

Sadie waited until the group was far enough

ahead not to hear. "I guess you're officially off the hook."

"I would like to attend the wedding, by the way. And not just because my dinner was ordered and I'd mess up the seating arrangements."

"You actually want to spend more time with my family than you have to?" she asked.

"Your family is fantastic, Sadie. They're wonderful. You really are lucky."

"I know. Sometimes they're smothering. But always in a good way."

He smiled. "The wedding will be a really nice ending to a special week."

Really nice. Ending. Special week.

It was over. He was going to say goodbye. After everything they'd been through? Shared together?

Her heart broke. It had been breaking ever since the morning she'd woken up alone in his bed, when she knew she'd gotten herself in over her head, but now it cracked completely in two.

"Evie hired a great band," she said, trying not to cry.

"See you tomorrow night, then."

"See you," she said.

And then they started down the mountain. Together but very much separate.

Chapter Fifteen

In the morning, the entire cabin went to sunrise yoga, including Izzy, who did some moves from her wheelchair. Then they went to the caf for breakfast, where Cowboy Joe had a crepe station in honor of the bride, who lived for crepes of all kinds. The handsome cook would be Tabby's date for Evie's wedding that night.

"Crazy, huh?" her mother whispered as Sadie gave Danny's mouth a dab with a napkin—strawberry and cream crepes were delicious but messy. "We come here to honor Axel, and two of the closest people to us find love. Evie and Marshall not only got back together, but engaged. And Tabby is in love."

"Thank you for not mentioning my fake love," Sadie whispered back.

"You okay?" Viv asked.

"I'll be okay. I have to be. Danny comes first."

"You fell for him, huh?" Viv asked. "Hard."

Sadie nodded. "Head over heels. But he told me not to on day one. I just didn't listen."

"You listened, hon. You just went with your heart. To me, that's the best way. It means you tried, you risked, you put yourself out there."

Unlike Axel.

"Axel's flipping loss," her mom added, shaking her head.

Sadie smiled. She called that one. "So you and Tabby are good now?"

"I feel terrible for how I acted. Blaming her for my precious grandson going missing when it wasn't her fault he ran off in a split second. All because the whole thing triggered a childhood memory— a scary one for me. I didn't even know that episode was still bothering me, but it sure was. All these years."

"I can understand, Mom. You were scared for your little sister."

Plus, she better understood now that some scars ran deep.

Viv leaned close and kissed Sadie's cheek. "I

think Axel will come around. The way he looks at you, Sadie. And it's so clear he loves Danny."

"I don't know. I think I have to face facts. Enough pretending, right? The truth is the truth."

"Well, if you do have to let go of him, I can fix you up with my dentist's nephew. He's quite a catch."

Sadie smiled. "Thank you, Mom."

Viv gave her a one-armed shoulder squeeze and went back to her honey-banana crepe. Sadie poked hers around on her plate. She couldn't imagine ever being ready for more blind dates. How could any guy ever measure up to Axel Dawson?

Cowboy Joe came over with his big smile and trademark brown Stetson to deliver a box of chocolate rugelach to Tabby. "Enough to share with the whole cabin," he said. That got him a kiss from his girlfriend, who was beaming.

Sadie might be leaving her heart here when she left, but she loved that her aunt was so happy. She glanced at Evie, who was assuring Izzy that there was plenty of Frank Sinatra and Etta James in the song rotation. Marshall had come over last night, full of apology about suggesting his old girlfriend attend the wedding. Apparently, the two had run into each other in town earlier that day, and Marshall was so excited about marrying the woman of his dreams that he'd invited the ex—no more to it than that. Evie had felt much better about the whole thing.

Little things, big things—you never knew what would get you and whip you up, Sadie thought. She didn't want to let Axel go, but maybe she had to. He had his little things and big things and right now, they were stronger than his feelings for her. Ugh, she hated even thinking that, but it was true, right?

At the back of the cafeteria, she noticed Axel's sister, Daisy, and sister-in-law, Sara, restocking the grab-and-go bars on either side of the doors. The two women were chatting and, if Sadie wasn't imagining things, looking in her direction. She had a feeling they were discussing the Winston guest Axel had gotten fake-engaged to. Before she left tomorrow morning, Sadie would take Daisy aside and thank her for trying to push her brother when it came to matters of the heart, matters of *his* heart.

But at least she had tonight with him, and there was nothing fake about it. He'd be her date fair and square. She'd have a night to remember, and then she'd try, hard as she could, to move on.

Axel was on his second mug of coffee when his doorbell rang. Good chills ran up his spine at the idea that it was Sadie, whom he hadn't seen since they'd come down Clover Mountain. Even if she was here to tell him off, that he was no hero after all if he was afraid of the three of them—him, her and Danny—he'd be glad to see her face.

And he already knew he wasn't a hero.

That wilderness tour had been unexpectedly eventful but not in the terrible way that would send a search and rescue specialist into overdrive. Sadie's mother and aunt had finally made up. And his and Sadie's phony engagement had come to a sudden stop.

If it were Daisy at the door, asking him if he missed being fake-engaged even just a bit, he'd say no, of course not. But the truth was, he did miss it. He'd liked being paired with Sadie. He'd liked the hugs and warm wishes, and that had surprised him almost more than anything. Being part of something so…special even when it wasn't real had given him something of a spring in his step, as his gramps used to say.

And now he was back to being on his own, just Axel, the way he supposedly liked it. He'd take a day or two to shake off all that had happened, to get used to Sadie and her thirty-eight relatives being gone from the ranch, from his daily world, and his life would go on.

He went to the door and did a double take. "I am not seeing my brother Rex standing on my porch. This has to be a mirage." The sun *was* bright, not a cloud in the sky, but Rex Dawson, the middle of the Zeke, Rex, Axel trio, definitely was standing there. All the Dawson siblings resembled each other. Rex was tall and muscular with dark hair and blue eyes. He wasn't in his usual dark suit and Stetson, which meant he wasn't on the way to the airport or a meeting and had some time to spend. No one in the family knew exactly what Rex did for a living. FBI? Spy? Something secretive.

Rex grinned. "Oh, it's me all right. In the area on business and thought I'd come by and see everyone. First stop had to be your cabin. Daisy had told me it was luxe woodsman, and she didn't do it justice. *I* could live here." Rex lived in hotels since he did so much traveling, but at heart he was a cowboy, just like all the Dawson siblings.

"See, everyone says that when they see it. It tends to remind them of a lodge at a fancy ski resort or dude ranch."

Rex looked around. "Well, the lodge here is nice, but this is spectacular. Kudos to you. I thought you'd never come back here, Axel, but I can see how you can live here."

He hadn't told Rex or Zeke about the contents of the letter Bo had left him or learning about how their mom had met their dad. He had a lot to fill Rex in on.

In minutes, Axel and Rex were on the sofa in the living room, Dude at Axel's feet and coffee and Cowboy Joe's famed doughnuts in front of them. Axel told him the whole story, everything, and didn't bother leaving anything out. He and Rex didn't see each other often, but he'd always felt close to the guy. Same with Zeke and Ford. Axel had gotten almost *too* close with Noah and Daisy the past months. But he wouldn't trade the ability to talk to them about anything *for* anything.

"Sounds like this woman got to you," Rex said, popping a piece of cinnamon-sugar doughnut in his mouth.

"She did. But she wants the whole thing— marriage, a big family."

"And what do you want?" Rex asked. "Really?"

"To see them often." And that was true. He wanted to see them every day.

Zeke laughed. "So you want a relationship with Sadie, just on your terms."

"Yes," Axel said, grimacing. "I hear how it sounds, but yes. Why pretend I can deal with more than that?"

"You pretended exactly that for a week and seemed to like it just fine," Rex pointed out.

"Something's holding me back. I'm not totally sure what it even is. But it's stronger than I am, and you know what I can bench."

"Knocked out by your own punch," Rex said, sipping his coffee. "Now that's dumb."

He supposed it was, if his brother *had* to put it that way.

"Can you stay awhile?" Axel asked. "You're welcome to the guest room."

Rex shook his head. "I'm leaving late this afternoon. Another meeting in Jackson tomorrow."

"Ever gonna tell us exactly what it is you do?"

"One of these days," Rex said.

Axel hoped so, out of pure curiosity. "You ever get tired of all those meetings, all that travel, all those suits? I mean that in both senses."

Rex laughed. "Yes. Trust me." They finished off the doughnuts and had another round of coffee. "So. About Dad's letter. Maybe I could come along on the last address."

Axel raised an eyebrow. Rex had always been quiet about his take on Bo Dawson, keeping his feelings to himself. That he wanted to experience whatever good would come out of that final address was saying something. "You ever gonna tell us what was in the letter Dad left you?"

"I don't really want to talk about my letter," Rex said—and then looked immediately uncomfortable, like his shirt was suddenly squeezing the life out of him.

"I get it. It took me almost nine months to even open mine."

Rex sipped his coffee. "I'm curious what the last address is."

"Me, too. The first three helped—a lot."

"Not enough, though, Ax. Not if this Sadie is about to be the one who got away."

"I thought I was the one who got away."

Rex smiled and shook his head. "Nope. And you'll probably find that out in a week or two."

"Too much chitchat," Axel said, feeling like *his* shirt was getting too tight. "Let's go see what this last address is."

His phone pinged with a text. Daisy.

Hey, can you watch Tony for about an hour from one to two-ish? I want to check over the lodge and make sure everything is set up for the wedding.

You can get two brother babysitters for the price of one, he texted back. Rex is here.

Yay! she texted in reply.

"Looks like a little babysitting, then we'll hit the road," Axel told Rex.

"Good thing the back seat of my Jeep is full of presents for people under a year old," he said. "I might have bought out Baby Town before I drove over."

Axel smiled. Rex had better watch out or he'd be next on Daisy's hit list to get him married and adding a baby cousin to their brood.

Ahhh, if you had to have a broken heart, it helped to be sitting in a massage chair with heat functions at Esme's Day Spa in Prairie City, getting a pedicure. The bridal party would all have the same shade on their toes: Rouge Decadence, which was a sparkly bright red that Sadie loved. They'd already gotten their nails done in Ballet Slipper, a very pale pink, and had rejuvenating facials with potions and creams and cucumber slices over their eyes—that had been heavenly. Next, they'd be off to hair—beachy waves for everyone. Evie might be a serious CPA, but she was a skilled makeup artist who always did the family's faces for events—including her own wedding. Sadie wouldn't mind if this day went on forever.

"So I have an evil idea," Evie whispered. "Involving your date for tonight."

"Uh-oh," Sadie said while the pedicurist slathered a deliciously scented scrub on her legs.

"It's a risk, but might be worth it. And hey, I took a risk by giving Marshall an ultimatum, but it knocked some sense into him. So I say risk is good."

Sadie eyed her sister, intrigued and scared at the same time. "Exactly what did you have in mind?"

"I'm thinking you go see Axel in person. Not a text, not a call. Face-to-face. You tell him you appreciate all he's done for you this week, and that's why you're truly letting him off the hook by accepting another date for the wedding."

"But he already said he wants to go," Sadie pointed out.

"Yes, yes, he did. And do you want to know *why* he wants to go? Because he's in love with you and wants to be with you but isn't there yet. He needs a little push."

"I don't know, Evie. I've played enough games."

"This isn't a game," she said seriously. "Your happiness is important to me, Sadie. I don't care about deposits and plate costs. I care about you. And why the hell should Axel get to sit next to you and be your date at this special event when he's not planning to be your date ever again?"

Well, when she put it that way. Ouch.

"What I mean is," Evie continued, "maybe Axel should know that you're starting fresh—with another date to the wedding. Unless you *really* want him as your date, Evie. I know you're in love with the guy. But isn't tonight going to hurt?"

"It will either way," Sadie said, her stomach twisting.

"Yeah. I know. That's why I think you should give my evil plan a try. It might be the push that Axel Dawson needs."

Maybe? "I'll think about it while I'm getting my hair fussed over," Sadie said.

But she already knew her sister was on to something. Having Axel as her date to such an important event in her life *would* hurt. All night she'd just be wishing it meant something more than…friendship or a final favor of sorts. She'd slow dance with him and— Oh, who was she kidding? She'd never get through one dance in his arms without crying. She'd never be able to listen to Frank Sinatra again.

"Marshall has several interesting, attractive friends who would love to be moved from the singles table to be your plus-one," Evie said. "Just let me know."

"To be honest, Evie, I'd rather have no date than a stand-in. If I uninvited Axel, I mean."

"I understand," she said, leaning over to give Sadie as much a hug as the huge massage chairs would allow. "Whatever you decide, Sadie."

"I'll talk to Axel when we get back. Before the makeup session."

She'd likely cry it all off otherwise. Because she had a feeling this conversation wasn't going to go well.

Two hours later, her beach waves loose around her shoulders, Sadie texted Axel that she'd like to talk to him, that it was important. When she saw him, she'd speak the truth. No games. Just how she felt. She'd know in that moment. Right now, her mind was all over the place.

I'm actually at Daisy's house babysitting my nephew. Come over?

Be there in a few, she texted.

She sucked in a breath and headed up the path to the beautiful white farmhouse on the hill, where Axel had grown up a good portion of his childhood.

She walked up the porch steps, her heart suddenly beating so fast she wanted to just sit. But she knocked.

He came to the door, absolutely gorgeous, holding an adorable baby who couldn't be more than a few months old. He had big blue eyes—the Dawson eyes—and wispy brown curls and big cheeks. "This is Tony. Tony, meet the lovely Sadie Winston."

She managed a smile. "Hi, Tony. You sure are precious."

Another man, who looked a lot like Axel, came up behind him. "Hi, I'm this big lug's brother—Rex Dawson."

"Sadie Winston," she said, shaking his hand. "I'm sorry for barging in. I didn't realize Axel had company or that Daisy did." She shook her head, nothing coming out right. "We can talk later, Axel."

"No, now is fine," Rex said. "Trust me. I was just about to surprise Noah with my presence at the ranch—a rare occurrence. Back in thirty, Axel."

"Nice to meet you," Sadie said.

Rex smiled. "Likewise." He got in a buggy and drove off.

She and Axel made small talk for a minute or so about his brother, who was in town for only a few hours, and Tony and how the weather was terrific for a wedding.

"Speaking of," Sadie said, her heart now twisting.

The more she looked at Axel, particularly *this* Axel, with a baby in his arms, the more she knew she needed to let him go. Being a fake dad-to-be for Danny was fine for him, being a doting uncle was fine for him, but being a real dad wasn't. And Sadie needed a real husband, a real father for her son. She needed real love, big love.

She'd be her own date to the wedding.

"I think I should attend the wedding solo," she said. She stopped short of explanations since she knew none was necessary. He knew why.

"Oh," he said. "I feel bad about ruining the seating arrangements."

She glared at him. That was what he felt bad about?

Suddenly she realized how right her sister had been to tell Axel he was off the hook. That was how he looked at it, she realized. He just wanted to finish out the week because he cared about her and her family and at heart, he was a good guy.

Just not one in love with her.

She cleared her throat and ignored the stinging sensations in her eyes. "Evie has a blind date arranged for me—she's promoting one of Marshall's friends from the singles table to be my plus-one."

"Oh," he said again, staring at her. "So you have another date."

"Well, if I want. And to be honest, I don't want another date. You're a hard guy to top, Axel Dawson."

He stared at her, so many emotions in his eyes she couldn't read what he was thinking. "I'm sorry I can't be what you need," he said very solemnly. "I wish I could."

Dammit. "Oh, really?" she asked. "Because you do know it's up to *you*."

He rocked the baby in his arms. "It's not that simple."

"Then I guess this is goodbye," she said. "I have the wedding tonight and we're leaving after breakfast in the morning. I'll tell Danny you said bye and give him a hug for you."

He winced. "I'd like to do that myself. If that's all right."

"Fine. Because I know Danny would feel bad otherwise. We're leaving at eight sharp."

She looked at sweet Tony, then at the man holding him. And she turned and left before she completely fell apart.

Chapter Sixteen

Axel and Rex easily found 62 Bear Ridge Lane, which was right off Main Street, a three-family house with two balconies on the top stories. A woman in her early sixties was sitting on a chair on the porch, a small dog in her lap. She had a hard edge to her but was attractive with lots of wild auburn curly hair and dark brown eyes. She wore a lot of silver bracelets on both arms and a long sundress. The dog wore a hot-pink collar dotted with rhinestones.

"Cocker spaniel," Rex said to Axel. "Always loved the long, floppy ears."

Axel eyed his brother. "Should we ask if she knew Dad?"

"Excuse me, miss?" Rex called out from the walkway. The guy never waited. He just *did*—his MO. Not a bad trait, in Axel's opinion.

The woman peered at them. She didn't look particularly friendly.

"Did you know Bo Dawson?" Rex asked.

"Who's asking?" The woman grabbed a pair of glasses from the small round table beside her. She put them on, and her entire expression changed. "As I live and breathe. Honey Bear," she said to the little dog, hand to her chest, "do you know who these two men are? I do. Yes, I most certainly do. They've got to be Bo's kids."

"I'm Axel, and this is Rex."

She got up and put the dog down. Honey Bear came over to sniff their legs, then went up to the porch and curled up on a red floor pillow. "I heard all about you. The six of you. Five boys and a girl. Well, adults, of course. But Bo always referred to y'all as the kids."

"Your address was listed in a letter that my dad left me," Axel said. "Just a bunch of addresses, no notes about them. So we were wondering what your relationship was to Bo."

"Huh, interesting. Well, I'll tell you. I was his last girlfriend. My name is Nell. He dumped me out of nowhere, told me it was over, he was sorry but he was moving on, and I was devastated. I loved your dad something fierce. Next thing I know, I get a letter from him from beyond the grave—freaked me out. I knew he'd passed on and I couldn't imagine why I'd get a letter after. He asked the manager of the bar we used to go to to send it to me if anything ever happened to him."

Axel looked at Rex. His dad had been making amends all over town, it seemed.

"The letter was short and sweet. He said he'd been crazy in love with me but he was no good and didn't deserve me, that he'd wrecked everything meaningful in his life and he'd wanted us to part before that happened. He wrote that he knew he was dying and needed me to move on with a good man worthy of a woman like me. Do you believe that? Worthy of a woman like me. No one's ever said anything like that to me before." Tears came to her eyes. "I did eventually start dating again and about three months ago, I found my Mr. Right. We're going on a cruise next month."

"I'm sure Bo would be comforted to know that," Axel said.

"Your father was a lot to handle, but I would have cared for him till the end. If he'd let me. I feel so bad that he died alone, without a loving woman at his side. But I guess he had his kids there."

Rex nodded. "We were all there."

"Good," she said. "I loved him despite his flaws. I loved him as he was."

"I'm glad he had that in his thoughts," Rex said. "I'm sure it was comforting."

Honey Bear got up and started barking at two kids on bicycles.

"Oh, hush now," she told the dog. "I'd better get her inside. Day camp just let out."

Rex smiled at her. "Thanks for talking to us."

"Bye now," she said and scooped up Honey Bear.

Rex seemed mystified. "Wow."

Axel nodded. "What you said."

"He thought he was leaving her for her own good," his brother said as they headed up the sidewalk and turned the corner onto Main Street. Rex shook his head. "The notions we get in our head, right?"

Axel didn't respond to that.

Rex eyed him. "I think Dad's trying to tell you something, and just in time. There's a reason you finally opened his letter to you now."

That reason was Sadie.

He could feel something shift inside his chest, but he couldn't quite figure out what it meant.

"I've got to hit the road. I'll drop you off, then hit the airport. Kiss Tony, Chase and Annabel for me. I already miss my little niece and nephews."

"Will do," Axel said.

"Don't let her get away, Ax. Think long and hard but not too long. Things change fast. Trust me."

Sadie's beautiful face and Danny's adorable one floated into his mind, Zul the superhero lion in his hand, of course.

Again, there came that feeling, that movement in his chest, something happening. *Be the boss of yourself,* he heard the mountain man say, but suddenly, it meant something else. It meant not to let old wounds or bitterness or fear tell him what to do.

He needed to see Sadie. He needed to be with her and maybe he'd understand what the hell was happening inside him. Maybe it was all Nell had said. All the stories he'd heard from the people whose addresses had been on the list. Maybe it was Sadie and Danny themselves. Maybe it was everything.

He glanced at the clock on the dash of Rex's Jeep. It was 5:06 as his brother pulled up to Axel's cabin. The wedding had already started. In fact, Evie Winston and Marshall Ackerman were saying their vows right now.

Maybe that was a sign—that he should stay put at home with Dude.

Or maybe he had a wedding reception to crash.

Sadie had a waiter remove the place setting of her plus-one and scooted over a bit so that she'd have more elbow room. There. See, who said attending a wedding alone didn't have a silver lining? More space. At Sadie's table were her parents, her dad looking quite handsome in his suit, her grandparents, Aunt Tabby and Cowboy Joe, and Izzy. Danny and the other young kids were next door in the kid zone, where three ranch staffers were showing them a grand old time and getting paid time and a half. Izzy said she and Sadie would be each other's dates since that "handsome fiancé of yours obviously had a ranch emergency."

That was when Sadie sucked in a breath and told her great-grandmother, who at ninety-nine deserved not to be pandered to, the entire story. The truth.

Izzy's hazel eyes got misty. "You cared so much for my feelings that you and that tall drink of water pretended to be engaged all week? Why, that's the sweetest thing I ever heard."

A huge weight lifted off Sadie's chest. Izzy was the best. She hugged her great-grandmother, inhaling her trademark scent of roses. "I love you, Great-Gram."

"Love you, too, Sadie-girl," Izzy said.

A slow song started playing, "Fly Me to the Moon," one of Izzy's favorites, so Sadie asked her great-grandmother to dance. It involved pushing her in her wheelchair in little movements, but Izzy had a great time and sang along. Back at the table,

Sadie told her mom and grandmother that she'd come clean to Izzy, and they were glad to hear it.

One of Sadie's favorite songs started playing, a beautiful ballad. She sipped her wine and closed her eyes, wondering what Axel was doing right now. Playing fetch with Dude in the yard. Eating dinner alone. Out riding and not thinking about her at all.

"May I have this dance?"

Sadie gasped. Standing beside her was Axel in the flesh. Well, dressed, but very much there. He wore a gray suit and Stetson and was so gorgeous and sexy she couldn't speak for a second.

"You clean up well," was all she could manage to say.

"And you look absolutely beautiful," he said, taking in her beachy waves, which, of course, he'd seen earlier, and the mauvey-pink maid of honor dress that showed a bit more cleavage than Sadie was used to.

"Make a habit of crashing weddings, do you?" she asked, her heart hoping against hope that he was here because he couldn't live without her.

Maybe he was just passing by. *Yeah, Sadie—in a suit. In the lodge.*

He got down on one knee.

Sadie gasped again. She was aware of the table going silent.

Axel pulled out a black velvet box and opened

it, a stunning round diamond ring twinkling at her, baguettes on the side. "For real this time, Sadie. I love you and Danny with all my heart, and you'd make me very happy if you'll marry me."

Viv let out a small shriek. Vanessa grabbed her husband's arm. Izzy pressed her hand to her heart.

"Yes!" Sadie whispered, out of breath. "Yes, yes, yes." She flew into his arms, and he stood and lifted her, spinning her around and kissing her.

"Hey, what did I miss?" Evie asked, dancing over with her new husband.

"Oh, just this," Sadie said, holding out her hand.

Evie yelped and hugged her and then Axel. "I have the best evil ideas, don't I?" she whispered to Sadie.

Sadie laughed. "You certainly do."

Axel and Sadie danced every slow dance for the rest of the night, then hugged everyone good-bye and went to pick up Danny from the kid zone. The room had long turned into a *sleep* zone, and Axel carried a fast-asleep Danny out to his SUV. Turned out that Sadie and her little boy weren't leaving at eight sharp tomorrow morning, after all.

They were home.

Epilogue

Four months later...

Viv Winston gasped so loud in the doorway of the bathroom that her mother and sister came running, Izzy wheeling herself into the hallway to see what the fuss was.

Sadie, her sister, mother, aunt, grandmother and great-grandmother were over at Evie's house in Prairie City for their weekly Saturday lunch, where they gossiped and ate and laughed and had a grand old time for hours. Danny was there, too, in the play area Evie had long ago set up for visits from her favorite and only nephew.

Sadie and Evie burst into laughter as their mother, so emotional she couldn't speak, grabbed the two home pregnancy test sticks out of both her daughters' hands and held them up.

"I'm going to be a grandmother!" she screamed.

"I'm going to be a great-grandmother!" Vanessa screamed.

"I'm going to be a great-aunt!" Tabby shouted, clapping.

"I'm going to be a gray-gray-grandmother!" Izzy yelled, throwing her hands up in the air and waving them.

They all cracked up at that and Sadie and Evie left the bathroom, hugs and kisses and congratulations all around. They hadn't planned to be pregnant at the same time, but they'd talked about how great it would be if they were, and when Sadie had mentioned that she was late, Evie had said she was, too, and they'd run to the drugstore for matching tests.

Two plus signs.

"Should we have told our husbands before our relatives?" Sadie asked Evie.

"With this crew, are you kidding? You can't keep anything private. Hurry and tell Danny he's going to be a big brother before anyone beats you to it."

Sadie laughed. Viv was on the phone, making reservations at her favorite restaurant for that night—without even asking if anyone was free. Big news like this took precedence over plans anyone else had. And Vanessa was on the phone with her bridge and knitting clubs. Aunt Tabby was texting Cowboy Joe—their romance was still going strong, and Tabby had never seemed happier.

Izzy, meanwhile, called Sadie and Evie over. "Just to make double-decker definitely sure I heard right. You're *both* pregnant. Both."

Sadie chuckled. "Yes. Both. For real."

"I knew it would all work out, didn't I?" Izzy asked.

"You sure did," Sadie said.

After a big hug with Great-Gram and Evie and a wave to Viv and Vanessa, who were both still on the phone calling every person they knew, Sadie picked up Danny from his play area, Zul the superhero lion still his favorite toy. Just when Danny finally learned to say Axel, his hero had become his father and was now Daddy. Zul had stuck for the superhero lion, and Axel loved that.

"Guess what?" she told Danny as she put him in his car seat. "You're going to be a big brother. Mommy and Daddy are going to have a baby."

"Baby bwuther?" Danny asked.

"Or a baby sister."

"Or a baby Zul!" he said, bursting into laughter and flying Zul above his head.

Sadie laughed and backed out of the driveway.

You never knew. That was *her* motto these days. She couldn't wait to get home to the luxe log cabin on the edge of the Dawson Family Guest Ranch where she now lived with her sexy husband and Danny, *their* son. Axel had formally adopted him, the final court appearance just two days ago. And now he'd be a father again.

She couldn't wait to tell Axel the news. She had no doubt he'd be overjoyed. The wedding crasher who'd proposed to her at Evie's reception had become a true family man. The other day, Daisy had said that happiness radiated from him, and Sadie had teared up at that. It was absolutely true.

At their wedding two months ago, his brothers had been amazed at the changes in the former lone wolf. Sadie had finally met Zeke and Ford, more tall, muscular, dark-haired, blue-eyed Dawsons, and between her family and his, plus friends and coworkers, the wedding had been a big, happy affair. Sadie had worn the dress she'd fallen in love with in Your Special Day and her mother's wedding veil, which Evie had also worn for her wedding. For something borrowed, she'd worn Aunt Tabby's pearl earrings. For something blue, her grandmother's delicate sapphire necklace. Izzy had contributed the something old with her beautiful diamond bracelet, which her own mother had given her as a wedding present almost eighty years ago.

She pulled up to the cabin and took Danny out

of his car seat. "Want to tell Daddy the news about your baby brother or sister?"

"Yes!" he said.

Axel came out on the porch, smiling and waving. Danny, as always sprinted ahead, waving Zul the superhero lion.

"Big news!" Danny said.

"Oh yeah?" Axel asked, raising his eyebrow at Sadie.

"I big bruwtha!" Danny said.

Axel's eyes widened. He stared at Sadie, who nodded as tears filled her eyes.

He raced down the porch, his son in his arms, and wrapped his free one around her. "Our family is getting bigger?"

She nodded. "And a new little cousin on my side, too. Evie's also pregnant!"

"How'd I get so lucky?" he asked. "A great little boy and another child on the way."

"Zul sup hero," Danny said, flying him around. "Zul saves day!"

Axel hugged them both close. "Zul is the best. I owe him a lot."

"We have thirty minutes to ourselves before we're expected in town for dinner to celebrate," Sadie said.

"Just enough time to call Daisy and make her day. She'll text my brothers the news."

"I love our big combined family," she said. "And I love you."

He kissed her tenderly on the lips. "I love you, too. Both of you! All three of you," he added, touching a hand to Sadie's belly.

Then they headed inside, a forever family.

* * * * *

MILLS & BOON

Coming next month

A YEAR WITH THE MILLIONAIRE NEXT DOOR
Barbara Wallace

"Stella…" He breathed her name into her mouth like it was a prayer. She felt his fingers sliding along her cheeks until they cradled her face. He combed back her hair and pulled away.

"Stella," he repeated.

He was rejecting her.

"Well, isn't this humiliating," she said, backing away. "I…"

Linus backed away, too. The tenderness she imagined in his gaze had morphed into embarrassment. "I should go," he said.

"Yeah, I think that's a good idea."

She kept her attention glued to the coffee table while Linus got up and limped toward the front door. "I'm sorry," he said when he reached the landing. "But I don't think either of us wants to do something we'll regret."

Not trusting herself to speak, Stella only thanked God for that. She'd rambled on about her failings and made a fool out of herself, but at least she hadn't done something she'd regret.

*

Linus closed his front door and collapsed against it. That might have been one of most difficult things he had ever done. *Give yourself a pat on the back, old boy. You behaved like a gentleman.* Eighteen months ago, if a beautiful woman threw herself in his arms, he would have kissed the daylights out of her. Lips that soft and delicious? How could he resist?

But he did resist. Had to. It was clear his neighbor needed a friend far more than she needed sex.

I need to prove I'm not a disappointment.

How could the woman with whom he'd spent the evening disappoint anyone? It was inconceivable. She was funny. Beautiful. Smart.

His rejection probably hadn't helped her self-esteem issues. Still, he'd done the right thing. Maybe that meant he was evolving into a better person. Because for once he cared more about helping a woman than seducing her.

Now if he could only stop thinking about how amazing Stella's lips tasted, he'd be fine.

Continue reading
A YEAR WITH THE MILLIONAIRE NEXT DOOR
Barbara Wallace

Available next month
www.millsandboon.co.uk

LET'S TALK
Romance

For exclusive extracts, competitions
and special offers, find us online:

f facebook.com/millsandboon

🐦 @MillsandBoon

📷 @MillsandBoonUK

Get in touch on 01413 063232

For all the latest titles coming soon, visit

millsandboon.co.uk/nextmonth

MILLS & BOON

THE HEART OF ROMANCE

A ROMANCE FOR EVERY KIND OF READER

MODERN

Prepare to be swept off your feet by sophisticated, sexy and seductive heroes, in some of the world's most glamorous and romantic locations, where power and passion collide.
8 stories per month.

HISTORICAL

Escape with historical heroes from time gone by. Whether your passion is for wicked Regency Rakes, muscled Vikings or rugged Highlanders, awaken the romance of the past.
6 stories per month.

MEDICAL

Set your pulse racing with dedicated, delectable doctors in the high-pressure world of medicine, where emotions run high and passion, comfort and love are the best medicine.
6 stories per month.

True Love

Celebrate true love with tender stories of heartfelt romance, from the rush of falling in love to the joy a new baby can bring, and a focus on the emotional heart of a relationship.
8 stories per month.

Desire

Indulge in secrets and scandal, intense drama and plenty of sizzl hot action with powerful and passionate heroes who have it all: wealth, status, good looks...everything but the right woman.
6 stories per month.

HEROES

Experience all the excitement of a gripping thriller, with an inte romance at its heart. Resourceful, true-to-life women and strong fearless men face danger and desire - a killer combination!
8 stories per month.

DARE

Sensual love stories featuring smart, sassy heroines you'd want as best friend, and compelling intense heroes who are worthy of the
4 stories per month.

To see which titles are coming soon, please visit

millsandboon.co.uk/nextmonth

JOIN US ON SOCIAL MEDIA!

Stay up to date with our latest releases, author news and gossip, special offers and discounts, and all the behind-the-scenes action from Mills & Boon...

 millsandboon

 millsandboonuk

 millsandboon

It might just be true love...

MILLS & BOON
MEDICAL
Pulse-Racing Passion

Set your pulse racing with dedicated, delectable doctors in the high-pressure world of medicine, where emotions run high and passion, comfort and love are the best medicine.

MILLS & BOON
Desire

Indulge in secrets and scandal, intense drama and plenty of sizzling hot action with powerful and passionate heroes who have it all: wealth, status, good looks… everything but the right woman.

Six Desire stories published every month, find them all at:

millsandboon.co.uk/Desire

MILLS & BOON

HISTORICAL

Awaken the romance of the past

Escape with historical heroes from time gone by. Whether your passion is for wicked Regency Rakes, muscled Viking warriors or rugged Highlanders, indulge your fantasies and awaken the romance of the past.

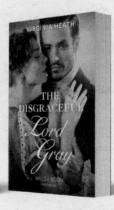